His
REVENGE

REVENGE
COLLECTION

November 2015

December 2015

January 2016

February 2016

March 2016

April 2016

His Delicious
REVENGE

Sara
CRAVEN

Published in Great Britain 2015
by Mills & Boon, an imprint of Harlequin (UK) Limited,
Eton House, 18-24 Paradise Road, Richmond, Surrey, TW9 1SR

HIS DELICIOUS REVENGE © 2015 Harlequin Books S.A.

The Price of Retribution © 2012 Sara Craven
Count Valieri's Prisoner © 2013 Sara Craven
The Highest Stakes of All © 2011 Sara Craven

ISBN: 978-0-263-91788-8

25-0216

Harlequin (UK) Limited's policy is to use papers that are natural, renewable and recyclable products and made from wood grown in sustainable forests. The logging and manufacturing processes conform to the legal environmental regulations of the country of origin.

Printed and bound in Spain
by CPI, Barcelona

THE PRICE OF
RETRIBUTION

Sara Craven was born in South Devon and grew up in a house full of books. She worked as a local journalist, covering everything from flower shows to murders, and started writing for Mills and Boon in 1975. When not writing, she enjoys films, music, theatre, cooking, and eating in good restaurants. She now lives near her family in Warwickshire. Sara has appeared as a contestant on the former Channel Four game show *Fifteen to One*, and in 1997 was a UK television *Mastermind* champion. In 2005 she was a member of the Romantic Novelists' team on *University Challenge – The Professionals*.

PROLOGUE

July

THIS flat was smaller than his previous one, yet now it seemed
strangely vast in its emptiness, an echoing space, rejecting him
as if he was an intruder.

He stood in the doorway of the sitting room, his gaze moving restlessly over the few items of furniture that had been delivered over the past week.

There were the two long, deeply-cushioned sofas in dark
green corded velvet, facing each other over the custom-made,
polished oak coffee table. The bookcase, also in oak, the first
of three ordered from the same craftsman. The thick cream
rug, circular and luxurious that fronted the carved wooden
fireplace.

A fairly minimal selection, yet all things they had chosen
together, planning to add to them—over time.

Only there was no time. Not any more.

His throat muscles tightened to the point of agony, and he
dug his nails into the palms of his clenched hands to dam back
the cry that threatened to burst from his lungs.

And down the hall, behind the closed door of that other
room—the bed. Memories he could not allow himself to think
about.

He wasn't even sure what he was doing here. Why he'd
come back. God knows, it hadn't been his original intention.

Brendan and Grace had pressed him anxiously to go back and stay with them, but he couldn't face the thought of their shocked sympathy, however genuine and well-meant. Couldn't stomach the prospect of being treated as walking wounded. Or feeling the complete fool he undoubtedly was.

His mouth tightened as he remembered the barrage of cameras and shouted questions waiting for him outside the registry office as he walked alone down the steps. He'd been spared nothing, and tomorrow the papers would be full of it. The tabloids would probably feature him front page.

But there were issues that mattered far more than the destruction of what had become his cherished privacy.

Decisions would have to be made, of course. The furniture disposed of. The flat put back on the market. That was the easy part. It could be done at a distance by other people, in the same way that flights and reservations for a suite in an exclusive resort hotel in the Bahamas had already been cancelled. The special orders for flowers and champagne rescinded. The plans to charter a boat in order to visit some of the other islands shelved.

However, retrieving himself from the wreckage of his life would be a very different matter. But there he could at least make a start.

He turned and walked swiftly down the passage, to the room he'd designated as his working space. Not to be confused with the similar room next door, although both had been rudimentarily equipped with a desk and chair, a filing cabinet and a shredder.

He reached into his jacket pocket and extracted the crumpled sheet of paper which he'd carried with him since that morning. He did not attempt to read it again. There was no need. He could have recited its contents from memory—something else that must stop right here and now.

He unfolded the letter, put it down on the desk, smoothed it flat with his fist, then fed it into the shredder, which accepted the offering, reducing it to fragments with its swift high-pitched whine.

It was done. Now all he had to do was erase it from his brain. Not so simple a task. But, somehow, he would manage it. Because he must.

He glanced at his watch. There was nothing more to keep him here. But then, there never had been. Waiting for him now was a different hotel suite, this one bland and anonymous. No intimate dinner for two to be anticipated, no vintage champagne on ice or rose petals on the pillows. And, later no eyes, drowsy with shared fulfilment, smiling into his.

Just a bottle of single malt, one glass, and, hopefully, oblivion.

At least until tomorrow when, somehow, he would begin his life again.

CHAPTER ONE

The previous April...

'BUT you don't understand. I'm meeting someone here.'

As the sound of the girl's voice, husky with desperation, reached him across the room, Caz Brandon turned from the group he was chatting to at the bar, and looked towards the door, his dark brows raised in faint annoyance. Only to find his irritation changing in a flash to interest as he surveyed the newcomer.

In her early to mid-twenties, he judged, medium height, slim, and rather more than attractive, with a mass of auburn hair falling in gleaming waves past her shoulders. Wearing the ubiquitous little black dress, sleeveless and scoop-necked, like many of the other female guests, but setting her own stamp upon it with the slender skirt split almost to mid-thigh, revealing a black velvet garter set with crystals a few inches above her knee.

An intriguing touch, Caz decided with frank appreciation. And one that offered grounds for speculation. Although, admittedly, this was hardly the time or the place to let his thoughts wander, however agreeably, when he was entertaining the European and Southern hemisphere editors who worked for his company, prior to the strategy meetings which would begin in the morning.

'I'm afraid this is a private function, madam, and your name is not on the list.' Jeff Stratton, who was handling security for the reception, spoke quietly but firmly.

'But I was invited.' She took a card from her evening purse. 'By this man—Phil Hanson. Look, he even wrote the place and the time for me to meet him on the back. If you'll just get him, he'll confirm what I say.'

Jeff shook his head. 'Unfortunately there is no Mr Hanson listed among those attending. I'm afraid someone may have been having a joke with you. However, I regret that I must still ask you to leave.'

'But he must be here.' There was real distress in her voice. 'He said he could get me a job with the Brandon Organisation. It's the only reason I agreed to come.'

Caz winced inwardly. The situation seemed to be morphing from a simple security glitch into a public relations problem. If someone had been making free with his company's name in order to play an unpleasant trick on this girl, he could hardly shrug and turn away. It had to be dealt with, and he, rather than Angus, who headed his PR team, was the one on the spot.

He excused himself smilingly to the rest of the group and walked purposefully across the room.

'Good evening,' he said. 'Miss...?' And paused interrogatively.

'Desmond,' she said, with a slight catch of the breath. 'Tarn Desmond.'

Seen at close hand, she was even lovelier than Caz had first thought, her green eyes over-bright as if tears were not too far away, and her creamy skin flushed with embarrassment. While her hair had the sheen of silk.

'And whom did you come here to meet?' he prompted gently. 'A Mr Hanson, you said? Did he claim a connection with the Brandon Organisation?'

She nodded. 'He said he worked for a Rob Wellington in Personnel. That he'd introduce me to him.'

Caz swore under his breath. This was getting worse all

the time. He sent a silent signal to Jeff who melted unobtrusively away.

'I'm afraid we have no employee called Hanson.' He paused. 'How well do you know this man?'

She bit her lip. 'Not very. I met him at a party a few nights ago. We got talking and I mentioned I was looking for a job. He said he might be able to help, and gave me this card.' She added with faint weariness, 'He seemed—nice.'

Caz gave the card a brief glance. It was a cheap mass-produced thing, with the name Philip Hanson printed in ostentatiously flowing letters, but no other information, not even a mobile phone number. But the time and place of this reception was written quite unmistakably in capitals on the back.

The deception was quite deliberate, he thought, if inexplicable. Tarn Desmond had been sent here.

He said easily, 'Well, this is an awkward situation, Miss Desmond, but it doesn't have to become a crisis. I'm sincerely sorry that you should have been misled like this but there's no need for us to add to your disappointment.'

He paused again. 'You must allow me to make amends. May I get you a drink?'

She hesitated, then shook her head. 'Thank you, but it might be better if I did as your Rottweiler asked—and simply left.'

Infinitely better, Caz thought wryly, at the same time aware of his own reluctance to see her go.

'But not totally empty-handed, I hope,' he said. 'If you want to work for the Brandon Organisation, why not contact Rob Wellington through the usual channels and see what's available?' He smiled at her, noting the beguiling fullness of her lower lip, and heard himself add, 'I'll make sure he's expecting to hear from you.'

The look that reached him from beneath the long, darkened lashes was frankly sceptical. Clearly, she didn't want to be made a fool of a second time, and who could blame her?

'Well—thank you again,' she said, and turned away. As

she did so, a breath of the scent she wore reached him—soft, musky and sexy as hell, he decided as his senses stirred. And he was treated to another glimpse of the glittering crystals on that garter as she departed.

If she'd come here to make an impression, it had certainly worked on one level, he thought ruefully as he returned to the bar. But she would need better credentials than that to convince his Head of Personnel that she deserved a place in the company. Rob was in his forties, happily married, and quite impervious to the charms of other women, however young and alluring.

As for himself, thirty-four and conspicuously single, he needed to put the delectable Miss Desmond out of his mind, and get back to the serious business of the evening.

But that, he discovered, was not as easy as he thought. Like her perfume, she seemed to be lingering on the edge of his consciousness long after the reception was over, and he was back in his penthouse apartment, alone, with all the time in the world to think. And remember her.

Tarn walked into the flat, closed the door and leaned against it for a moment, eyes closed as she steadied her breathing, before crossing the hall to the living room.

Della, who owned the flat, was sitting on the floor absorbed in painting her toenails, but she glanced up at Tarn's entry, her expression enquiring and anxious. 'How did it go?'

'Like a breeze.' Tarn kicked off her high-heeled sandals and collapsed into a chair. 'Dell, I couldn't believe my luck. He was right there in the bar. I saw him as soon as I went in.'

She grinned exultantly. 'I didn't even have to get past security and go looking. And he was across almost as soon as I went into my spiel, oozing charm and concern. He swallowed every word, and wanted more. It was almost too easy.'

She took the card from her bag and tore it up. 'Goodbye, Mr Hanson, my imaginary acquaintance. You've been a great help, and well worth the effort of getting this printed.'

She looked back at Della. 'And thanks for the loan of the dress and this pretty thing.' She slipped off the garter and twirled it round her finger. 'It certainly hit the target.'

'Hmm.' Della pulled a face. 'I suppose I should congratulate you, but I still feel more like screaming "Don't do it".' She replaced the cap on her nail polish, and looked gravely up at her friend. 'It's not too late. You could still pull out and no harm done.'

'No harm?' Tarn sat up sharply. 'How can you say that? When Evie's in that dreadful place, with her whole life destroyed—and all because of him.'

'You're being a bit hard on The Refuge,' Della objected mildly. 'It has a tremendous reputation for dealing with all kinds of addictions as well as mental problems, so it's hardly a dreadful place. It's also very expensive,' she went on thoughtfully. 'So I'm surprised Mrs Griffiths can afford to keep her there.'

'Apparently they're obliged to take a quota of National Health patients as well.' Tarn paused. 'And don't look so sceptical. Chameleon may have earned me a lot of money over the past few years, but not nearly enough to fund Evie at a top private clinic. I swear I'm not paying her fees.'

She drew a shuddering breath. 'When I came back and saw her there, realised the state she was in, I swore I'd make him pay for what he's done, and I shall, no matter how long it takes, or what the cost,' she concluded fiercely.

'Well, that's precisely it. You see, I was thinking of a totally different kind of harm,' Della returned, unperturbed. 'The potential cost to you.'

'What are you talking about?' Tarn was instantly defensive.

Della shrugged. 'I mean that when push comes to shove, you may not find it so simple to deliver the death blow and walk away, leaving the dagger in his back. Because you lack the killer instinct, my pet. Unlike, I've always thought, the eternally fragile Evie.'

She allowed that to sink in, then continued, 'For heaven's sake, Tarn, I know you're grateful to the Griffiths family for all they've done for you, but surely you've repaid them over and over again, financially and in every other way. Do you still have to come galloping to the rescue each time there's a problem? Surely there's a moment to say—"Halt, that's enough," and this could be it. For one thing, what about your career? Yes, the kind of work you do requires you to seem invisible. But you shouldn't actually become so in real life. You can't afford it. Have you thought of that?'

'I always take a break between projects,' Tarn returned. 'And by the time negotiations have been completed on the next deal, this will all be over, and I'll be back in harness.'

She looked down at her hands, clasped in her lap. 'Besides, I promised Uncle Frank before he died that I'd look after Aunt Hazel and Evie, just as he always looked after me. As I've told you, they only decided to become foster parents because they thought they couldn't have children of their own. Then, when Evie was born, they could have asked Social Services to take me away.'

She sighed. 'But they didn't, and I'm sure that was his doing rather than Aunt Hazel's. I was never the pretty docile little doll she'd always wanted. That became abundantly clear as I grew up. But I couldn't blame her. Looking back, I probably gave her a very hard time.

'But losing Uncle Frank knocked them both sideways. They were like boats drifting on the tide, and they needed an anchor. I can't ignore them when they need help.'

'Well, if Evie reckoned on Caz Brandon becoming the family anchor in your place, she gravely miscalculated,' Della said with a touch of grimness. 'He isn't a man for serious relationships with women. In fact, he's famous for it, as you'd know if you hadn't been working abroad so much, and only back for flying visits. Evie, on the other hand, has been right here all the time, and should have been well aware that he's not the marrying kind.'

She hesitated. 'I'm playing devil's advocate here, but is it possible she may simply have—misunderstood his intentions?'

There was a silence, then Tarn said huskily, 'If so, it was because he meant her to do so. That's the unforgivable thing. Del—she's really suffering. She trusted that bastard, believed every lie he told her.' She shook her head.

'She may well have been incredibly naïve, but I've seen him in action now, and he's quite a piece of work. The arch-predator of the western world on the look-out for another victim.'

She gave a harsh laugh. 'My God, he even asked me to have a drink with him.'

'Which you naturally declined.'

'Yes, of course. It's much too soon for that.' Tarn's lips tightened. 'He's going to find out just what it's like to be strung along endlessly and then discarded like a piece of trash.'

'Well, for God's sake, be careful.' Della got to her feet. 'Caz Brandon may like to love them and leave them, but he's no fool. Don't forget he inherited a struggling publishing company seven years ago and has turned it into an international success.'

'The bigger they are,' said Tarn, 'the harder they fall. And his business achievements don't necessarily make him a decent human being. He needs to be taught that you can't simply take what you want and walk away. That eventually there's a price to be paid. And I intend to teach him precisely that.' She added tautly, 'For Evie's sake.'

'Then all I can say is—rather you than me,' said Della. 'And now I'm going to make some coffee.'

Left to herself, Tarn sank back against the cushions, trying to relax. She didn't really need coffee, she thought. She was hyped up quite enough as it was, the adrenalin still surging through her. And this was only the first stage of her plan.

The next big hurdle, of course, would be getting a job at the

Brandon Organisation. This evening was a walk in the park compared with that.

But you can do it, she told herself robustly. There's a lot riding on this—the total and very public humiliation of Caz Brandon. In some way.

For a moment, the image of him filled her mind as completely as if he was standing there in front of her. Tall, broad-shouldered and elegant to his fingertips in his dinner jacket and black tie, his dark hair combed back from a lean incisive face. Hazel eyes, long-lashed under straight brows, a firm-lipped mouth, the nose and chin strongly marked.

Oh, yes, she thought savagely. She could see why Evie had fallen for him so far and so fast. With very little effort, he could probably be—irresistible.

And she gave a sudden shiver.

She'd been in New York when Aunt Hazel's call had come, she recalled later that night, when sleep remained curiously elusive.

'Tarn—Tarn—are you there—or is it just that nasty machine?'

She'd known at once from the agitated tone that it meant trouble. In any case, her foster mother rarely rang just for a catch-up chat. And lately there'd been hardly any calls at all, Aunt Hazel, she'd supposed, being totally preoccupied by preparations for Evie's forthcoming and presumably triumphant marriage.

She said briskly, 'Yes, I'm here. What's the matter?'

'It's Evie. Oh, God, Tarn.' The words were tumbling over each other. 'My poor baby. She's taken an overdose of sleeping pills—tried to kill herself.'

Tarn heard her with horrified dismay. Evie might be something of a flake at times, but attempted suicide? That was unbelievable. Awful beyond words.

'Tarn—did you hear what I said?'

'I heard,' Tarn said slowly. 'But why should she do such a thing? In her letters, she always seemed so happy.'

'Well, she's not happy now, not any more.' Aunt Hazel was crying with loud, breathy sobs. 'Perhaps never again. Because he's finished with her—that man—that brute she was going to marry. The engagement's off and she's had a complete nervous collapse as a result. She's been rushed into some kind of rest home, and they won't allow visitors. Not even me.

'Tarn, I'm going frantic. You've got to come home. I can't be alone at a time like this. I may go to pieces myself. You have to find out what's going on at this place—The Refuge. They might talk to you. You're so good at this kind of thing.'

Except, Tarn thought grimly, that would-be suicides and mental breakdowns were well outside her experience zone.

She said gently, 'Don't worry, Aunt Hazel. I'll get the first available flight. But you shouldn't be on your own. Would Mrs Campbell stay with you till I get there?'

'Oh, no,' the older woman said quickly. 'You see I'd have to explain—and I can't. No-one else knew about the wedding, apart from us. It was all going to be a totally hush-hush affair. And if Mrs Campbell ever found out, she'd tell everyone that my poor girl's been jilted, and I couldn't bear that.'

'Hush-hush?' Tarn repeated astonished. 'But why?'

'Because that's the way they both wanted it. No fuss.' Mrs Griffiths was crying again. 'Who could have thought it would end like this?'

Who indeed? Tarn thought grimly as she eventually re-placed the receiver. And why on earth would the head of publishing conglomerate the Brandon Organisation want his forthcoming marriage to be a secret? Unless, of course, there was never going to be any marriage—and that was another se-cret that, this time, he'd carefully kept to himself.

Because St Margaret's Westminster and an all-day party at the Savoy or some other glamorous venue, accompanied by all the razzmatazz at his disposal seemed more the style for a billionaire tycoon.

Not that many of them crossed her path very often, she reminded herself wryly.

She still found it almost impossible to credit what had happened. It was true that her foster mother had always been an emotional woman, and prone to exaggeration yet this time there seemed every excuse for her reaction.

She wandered restlessly round her loft apartment, as she considered what to do.

A flight to Heathrow for the following day was, of course, her main priority. But she had also to deal with the problem of Howard, who would not be pleased to hear that she wouldn't be accompanying him to the Florida Keys to stay with some friends he had there.

Tarn herself had mixed feelings about the cancellation of the trip. She and Howard had been dating for a while now, but she'd been careful to keep their relationship as casual and platonic as all the others she'd embarked on in the past. Not that there'd been that many.

However, she recognised that this state of affairs could probably not be maintained indefinitely. This invitation was clearly intended to move things to a more intimate level, and she'd accepted, mainly because she could think of no good reason to refuse.

Howard Brenton worked as management editor with Van Hilden International, the company which published the celebrity 'biographies' which Tarn now so successfully ghosted under her company name 'Chameleon'. Which was how they'd met.

He was attractive, amusing and available (three starred A's on the Manhattan scene). Tarn liked him, but wasn't sure if love would ever be on the cards. But, she'd eventually decided, perhaps it deserved to be given at least a fighting chance.

After all, what was she waiting for? she'd asked herself with faint cynicism. Prince Charming to gallop up on a white horse, like Evie, who'd been sending her letter after letter rhapsodising over the manifold perfections of Caz Brandon, the man she was going to marry?

But now it seemed that her own warier approach was the right one because Evie's idol had proved to have feet of clay.

She shook her head in angry bewilderment. How could it all have gone so wrong? And, apparently, so fast? Evie's last screed, cataloguing in some detail her future husband's numerous acts of generosity and tenderness had arrived just over a week ago, indicating that her path in life would be strewn with roses. Tarn would have sworn there wasn't a single doubt in her mind.

Yet there must have been something, she thought. Some small clue, some hint she could trace that would signal all wasn't well. And if there was, then she would find it.

She booked her flight, left a message on Howard's voicemail, suggesting they meet for a drink in their favourite bar as soon as he finished work, then went across to her desk.

She opened a drawer and extracted Evie's letters, collected into a bundle, and secured by a rubber band.

There were a lot of them, each envelope containing page after page of ecstatic outpourings from Evie's first meeting with Caz Brandon in a classic secretary/boss situation down to what had probably been the last, she thought biting her lip, and she wasn't altogether sure why she'd kept them.

Unless she'd believed they were some kind of proof that fairy tales can come true. If so, how wrong was it possible to be?

Evie, she thought, had always been a great one for writing things down. As well as the mass bombardment of letters, she'd kept a diary since she was a small child, and later produced reams of poetry to celebrate the girlhood crush of the moment.

She made herself a beaker of tea, settled into her favourite cream leather recliner and began to read.

'I've got the most fantastic job working for the most fantastic man,' Evie had written in her swift, untidy scrawl, the words leaping off the page. 'His regular secretary is away on maternity leave, so, hopefully, I'm in for the duration. And after that—who knows?'

Ironically, Tarn could remember feeling relieved that Evie had finally found work that suited her, and also thinking with amusement that all it had taken was a good-looking boss.

Evie's next letter was a fairly bread and butter affair, but the one after that bubbled with excitement. The boss from heaven had asked her to work through her lunch hour, and had ordered a platter of sandwiches which he'd shared with her.

Well, what was he supposed to do—eat them in front of her? Tarn muttered under her breath.

'He was asking me all sorts of questions about myself—my interests—my ambitions.' Evie had gone on. 'He's just so easy to talk to. And he smiles with his eyes.'

I just bet he does, thought Tarn. She recalled smiling herself over Evie's raptures the first time around. But how could she ever have found them amusing?

Curiosity had led her to look at Caz Brandon on the Internet, and she had to admit he was everything Evie had said and possibly more. But why couldn't I see what he really was? she asked herself as she read on. A cynical womaniser playing with a vulnerable girl's emotions.

Over the next week, Evie's hero stopped being Mr Brandon and became Caz instead.

'Caz took me for a drink after work at this fabulous wine bar,' Evie confided in her next effusion. 'It was simply heaving with celebrities and media people and I was introduced to them all. I didn't know whether I was on my head or my heels.'

After that, the invitation to dinner seemed almost inevitable. Evie gave a description of the restaurant in total detail— the décor, the service, every course they'd eaten and the wine he'd chosen.

Like a child in a toyshop, Tarn thought, sighing.

And the toys kept on coming. There were more dinners for two, plus theatre visits, concerts and even film premieres.

Then, eventually, there was the weekend at a romantic inn in the depths of the countryside.

'Of course I can't go on working for him,' Evie had written. 'Caz has this strict rule about not mixing business with pleasure, and he says I'm all pleasure. So I'm being transferred to another department.

'He's also arranging for me to move into my own flat so that we can be together whenever we wish, but I'll be protected from people gossiping and drawing the wrong conclusions.

'I know now what the marriage service means by "to love and to cherish", because that's how Caz is with me.'

A gap of a few weeks followed, while the loving and cherishing presumably continued apace, then Evie wrote again.

'Tarn, we're engaged. He's bought me the most beautiful ring—a huge diamond cluster. It must have cost an absolute fortune, and shows how much he must love me. I'm only sorry I can't wear it to work, but I realise that would hardly be discreet.

'I can hardly believe he's chosen me. All his other girlfriends have been so glamorous and famous. But, by some miracle, I'm the one he wants to spend the rest of his life with.'

Well, it was feasible, Tarn had told herself, dismissing her instinctive uneasiness about this whirlwind courtship. Evie was pretty enough to catch anyone's eye, and her lack of sophistication might come as a welcome relief to a man accustomed to high-powered women.

'His flat is wonderful,' the letter had continued. 'A big penthouse with views all over London, and an amazing collection of modern art. I don't pretend to understand all of it, but he says he'll teach me when we're married.

'And he has the most incredible bed I've ever seen— Emperor sized at the very least. I tease him that he may lose me in it, but he says there's no danger of that. That however far away I went, he'd find me. Isn't that wonderful?'

Not the word I'd have chosen, thought Tarn, dropping the closely written sheet as if it had burned her fingers. Or not any more. 'Hooked and reeled in' now seemed far more apposite.

The letters that followed were full of wedding plans, the chosen dress, flowers and possible honeymoon destinations, which Tarn had glossed over at the first reading. Now they assumed an almost unbearable poignancy.

And finally, 'Being with Caz is like having all my sweetest dreams come true. How can I be so lucky?'

Only Evie's luck had changed, and she'd suddenly discovered what a short step it was from dream to nightmare. So much so, that the thought of life without him had become impossible, and she'd tried to end it.

Tarn sat staring down at the mass of paper in her lap. She thought of Evie, wisp-slender, with her unruly mass of blonde hair and huge blue eyes, the unexpected late-born child, her flaws excused, her foibles indulged. Adored and cosseted for the whole of her life. Expecting no less from the man who, for reasons of his own, had professed to love her.

How blatantly, unthinkingly cruel was that?

Her throat was tight and she wanted very much to cry, but that would not help Evie. Instead she needed to stay strong and feed the smouldering knot of anger deep within her, bringing it to full flame.

She said aloud, her voice cold and clear, 'You've destroyed her, you bastard. But you're not going to get away with it. Because, somehow, I'm going to do exactly the same to you.'

Several weeks on, the words still echoed in her head. And tonight, thought Tarn as she punched her pillow into shape and curled into the mattress. Tonight she'd taken the first real step on the path to Caz Brandon's ultimate downfall.

CHAPTER TWO

THE REFUGE was a large redbrick house in Georgian style, standing in several acres of landscaped grounds.

As she'd approached it on her first visit, Tarn, seeing the people sitting around the lawns in the sunshine, had thought it resembled an exclusive country house hotel, until she realised just how many of those present were wearing the white tunics and trousers of medical staff.

And, as she got inside, the illusion of peace and comfort was completely destroyed. She'd known that permission for her to see Evie had been given reluctantly, but she'd not expected to be taken into a small room leading off the imposing tiled hall, obliged to hand over her shoulder bag and informed tersely it would be returned to her when she left, or have to submit to a swift search before being taken upstairs to be interviewed by Professor Wainwright, the clinical director.

And her protest about the way she'd been treated cut no ice with the grey-haired bearded man facing her across a large desk.

'Our concern is with the well-being and safety of the men and women in our care, Miss Griffiths, and not your sensitivities,' he told her tersely.

Tarn decided not to argue over her surname and looked him coldly in the eye. 'You cannot imagine for one moment that I would wish to harm my sister.'

He opened the file lying in front of him. 'Your foster sister, I believe.'

'Does it make a difference?'

'It's one of the aspects of her case that have to be considered,' he returned, and paused. 'You understand the conditions of your visit, I trust.'

Tarn bit her lip. 'I am not to question her about what happened or the events leading up to it,' she responded neutrally. *Not that I have to as her own letters have told me all I need to know. But I don't have to tell you that.*

She added quietly, 'Nor am I to apply any pressure on her to confide in me about her treatment here.'

'Correct.' He looked at her over the top of his rimless glasses. 'It is unfortunate that we have had to temporarily exclude her mother from visiting Miss Griffiths, but it was felt that she is an excitable and over-emotional woman and her presence could be less than helpful.'

'Is anyone else allowed to see her?'

'No-one.' He closed the file. 'This may be reviewed if and when she begins to make progress.' He pressed a buzzer. 'Nurse Farlow will take you to her.'

At the door, she paused. 'I brought my sister some of her favourite chocolate truffles. They were in the bag that was taken from me. I'd still like her to have them.'

'I'm afraid she is not allowed presents of food at the moment. In future you should check whether any proposed gifts are permitted.'

It was more like a prison than a clinic, Tarn thought, as a sturdy blonde woman escorted her silently through a maze of corridors. And they seemed to be treating Evie more as a criminal than a patient.

Didn't they understand what had happened here? How Evie had been used by this rich bastard then callously dumped when he'd got all he wanted and become bored? How her attempted suicide was an act of total desperation?

When they eventually halted at a door, the nurse gave Tarn a warning glance. 'This first visit is for fifteen minutes only,' she informed her brusquely. 'At the end of this time, I'll be back to collect you.'

She opened the door, said, 'Someone to see you, dear,' and urged Tarn forward.

Tarn had almost expected a cell with bars on the window. Instead she found herself in a pleasant bedroom with modern furnishings, seascape prints on the neutral walls, and soft blue curtains. Evie was in bed, propped against a pile of pillows with her eyes closed, and Tarn almost recoiled in shock at the sight of her.

Her fair hair was lank, her face was haggard and her body looked almost shrunken under the blue bedspread.

Thank God they've kept Aunt Hazel away, Tarn thought, swallowing, or she'd be having permanent hysterics. I feel like bursting into tears myself.

There were a pair of small armchairs flanking the window and Tarn moved one of them nearer the bed, and sat down.

For several minutes there was silence, then Evie said hoarsely, 'Caz? Oh, Caz, is it you? Are you here at last?'

For a moment, Tarn was unable to speak, shaken by a wave of anger mixed with pity. Then she reached out and took the thin hand, saying quietly, 'No, love. It's only me.'

Evie's eyelids lifted slowly. Her eyes looked strangely pale, as if incessant crying had somehow washed away their normal colour.

She gave a little sigh. 'Tarn—I knew you'd come. You've got to get me out of here. They won't let me leave, even though I keep asking. They say if I want to get better, I have to forget Caz. Forget how much I loved him. Accept that it's all over between us. But I can't—I can't.

'They give me things—to help me relax, they say. To make me sleep, but I dream about him, Tarn. Dream that he's still mine.'

Her fingers closed fiercely round Tarn's. 'I didn't want to go on living without him. Couldn't face another day with nothing left to hope for. You understand that, don't you? You must, because you knew what he meant to me. How I built my future around him.'

Tarn said steadily, 'I suppose so, but ending it all was never the answer, believe me.' She paused. 'Evie, you're a very beautiful girl, and one day you'll meet another man—someone good and decent who'll appreciate you and genuinely want to spend his life with you.'

'But I wanted Caz.' Her grip on Tarn's hand tightened almost unbearably. 'I gave him everything. So how could he reject me like that? Not want me to love him any more?'

'I don't know.' Tarn freed herself gently. 'But we mustn't talk about that now or you'll get agitated and they'll know. Which means I won't be allowed to see you again.'

'And you're all I've got.' Evie sank back against her pillows, her face white and pinched. 'Because Caz is never going to come here, is he? I've been hoping and hoping, but it isn't going to happen. I know that now.'

A slow tear ran down her cheek. 'How could he do this to me? How can he just—walk away as if I didn't matter?'

Tarn felt the anger rising inside her again, and curled her nails into the palms of her hands to regain her control.

'But you do matter,' she said, her voice shaking. 'And one day soon he's going to find out just how much, and be sorrier than he's ever imagined.'

She handed Evie a tissue from the box on the bedside table. 'Now dry your eyes, and try to look as if my visit has done you some good. And next time I come we'll talk seriously about how to deal with Mr Caz Brandon.'

That night over supper, she said, 'So what did you think of Evie's fiancé, Aunt Hazel? Did you ever feel that things weren't quite right between them?'

Her foster mother put down her knife and fork and stared at her. 'But I never met him,' she said. 'I knew only what Evie told me, and, of course, she absolutely worshipped him.'

'Never met him?' Tarn repeated slowly. 'But how can that be? You mean she never brought him home?'

'Well, she'd hardly be likely to,' Mrs Griffiths said with a touch of defensiveness. 'I mean—he lives in the lap of luxury, and this is such an ordinary little house. But they were planning to give an enormous party when their engagement was announced, and I was going to meet him then.'

'I see,' said Tarn, without any truth whatsoever. She hesitated. 'And you were all right with this?'

'As long as my girl was happy, I was too,' said Mrs Griffiths with finality, and the subject was ostensibly dropped.

But it provided Tarn with food for thought during the remainder of the evening.

When Tarn returned to The Refuge a few days later, she was surprised to be accorded a wintry smile by the Professor.

'I think you will find your sister has improved slightly. She is looking forward to seeing you again.' He paused. 'But you will have to remain her only visitor in the immediate future. Have you brought her any messages from anyone else? If so, may I know what they are?'

'Her mother sends her love.' Tarn lifted her chin. 'I hope that's acceptable.'

There was another slight hesitation before he said, 'Perfectly,' and buzzed for Nurse Farlow.

Evie, in a dressing gown, was sitting in the armchair by the window. Her newly washed hair was waving softly round her face, and her face had regained some colour.

'Wow.' Tarn bent and kissed her on the cheek. 'You'll be out of here in no time at this rate.'

'I wish,' Evie said with a sigh. 'But there's no chance. That's been made perfectly clear to me. It's what happens when you do crazy things. And all because of him.' She punched her fist into the palm of her other hand. 'That was the real madness—to believe even one word that he said. To trust him. I ought to have realised he was just using me.'

Her voice cracked. 'Oh, God, he's the one I should have tried to kill for what he's done—not myself. You talked about making him sorry. That's not enough. I want to make him wish he was dead.'

'Well, maybe we can.' Tarn took the chair opposite. 'But stay calm, honey, because there are some things I need to know from you.'

Evie stared at her, biting her lip. 'What kind of things?'

'Stuff you might have told him. About your mother. About me.'

There was a silence, then Evie said, 'I didn't tell him anything. He never wanted to talk about family things.'

'You didn't find that—odd?' Tarn spoke carefully.

'It was the way he was.' Evie shrugged. 'I accepted it. Why do you ask?'

'Because it helps if he doesn't know I exist. When I meet him, he won't be on his guard.'

'You're going to meet him?' Evie was suddenly rigid, her colour fading. 'No, you can't. You mustn't. You—you don't know what he's like.'

'But that's exactly what I'm going to find out,' Tarn told her. 'I need to know everything about him, because, in order to damage him, I have to discover his Achilles' heel—and he will have one. Everyone does.'

She paused. 'You're sure you never mentioned me? Told him my name?'

'No, never.' Evie shook her head slowly. 'Why would I?' She gave a quick shiver. 'All the same, keep away from him, Tarn. It—it's not safe. He has powerful friends.'

'I won't take any unnecessary risks. The fact that he has no idea who I am gives me a head start.' Tarn tried to sound reas-

suring, even if she was bewildered by Evie's warning. Surely
Caz Brandon was powerful enough on his own. 'But if I'm
to cause him the kind of pain he's inflicted on you, I have to
get close to him in some way. Find where the wound will be
deepest.'

'You imagine you can do that?' Evie whispered. 'Then perhaps you're the crazy one. Not me.'

'I can at least try,' Tarn returned. She hesitated. 'I'm not
going to mention any of this to your mother. And you shouldn't
talk about it either, to anyone. It has to be our secret.

'Also, I shall move out of Wilmont Road,' she added. 'Go
to stay with a friend.'

'You mean it, don't you? You're really going to do this.'
Evie shifted restively in her chair, her face taut, almost frightened. 'Oh, I wish I'd never mentioned him.' She added pet-
tishly, 'Now, I'm starting to get a headache. Perhaps it would
be better if you left.'

'Yes, of course.' Tarn got to her feet, eying her with concern.
She said gently, 'Evie—this man has to be taught he can't go
through life trampling on people. What he did to you had almost fatal results, and I cannot forget that. You're in no position to fight back, but I am.'

She tried a coaxing smile. 'And you really don't have to
worry.'

'You don't think so?' Evie hunched a shoulder and turned to
stare blankly at the window. 'That's because you don't know
him.' And she shivered again.

It was her hair that Caz recognised. Even though it was no longer cascading to her shoulders, but decorously confined in a
neat braid, and tied with a navy bow which matched her neat
pantsuit, there was no mistaking that glorious rich auburn.

He had never really expected to see her again, yet here she
was just the same, entering the lift at the fifth floor, glancing

at her Blackberry with a preoccupied frown, and apparently quite oblivious to everything else.

He said, 'It's Miss Desmond, isn't it?'

She looked up with a start. 'Oh,' she said, and bit her lip. 'It's you.' She paused. 'I'm so sorry I didn't realise who you were the other evening, Mr Brandon. I feel seriously embarrassed.'

'Don't worry about it.' Caz paused, his mouth relaxing into amusement. 'But while I have no wish to add to your discomfort, I should perhaps point out this is the directors' private lift, and, if spotted, you could get told off for using it.'

'Oh, Lord.' She pulled a face. 'I think that was mentioned, but I forgot and just took the first one to arrive. I apologise again.'

'Do I take it you're working here now?'

She nodded. 'Since Monday.' Her sidelong glance was part shy, part mischievous. 'I actually took your advice and applied through the proper channels. Mr Wellington was good enough to hire me—temporarily anyway.'

She paused. 'Should I get out at the first floor, or travel to ground level and risk a reprimand?'

'Stay on board,' he said. 'If anyone notices, refer them to me, and I'll tell them we were renewing an old acquaintance.'

'Ah,' she said and pressed a button on the display. 'I think the stairs might be more discreet.' She added, 'Sir.'

As the doors opened, she gave him a last brief smile and vanished.

There should be a law, Caz mused, banning girls with legs as good as hers from wearing trousers in the office. Just as there was almost certainly a law condemning his thoughts as a kind of passive sexual harassment, he thought, his mouth curling in self-derision.

Easy, boy, he told himself. Or you'll break your own golden rule about non-fraternisation. And we can't have that.

If you need female distraction, ring Ginny Fraser, and see if she's free for dinner.

He did, and she was, and that should have been the end of it.

Yet, later over lunch in the executive dining room, he heard himself saying, his tone deliberately casual, 'I bumped into your newest recruit today, Rob.'

'I hardly deserve the credit for that,' his Personnel Chief said drily. 'You did tell me we might receive an application from her. I simply—took the hint.'

Caz stared at him, appalled. 'Oh, God, surely not.'

Rob Wellington grinned. 'No, don't worry. Absolutely not. Laurie interviewed her first, then sent me a note saying she was frantically over-qualified for any of our vacancies, but we'd be mad to pass her up on that account. I had a chat with the lady and agreed. So at the moment, she's working as editorial assistant in features and fiction on All Your Own covering Susan Ellis's maternity leave.'

He poured himself some more coffee. 'Anyway, judging by the reference we got from Hannah Strauss at Uptown Today in New York, Ms Desmond could easily be running the entire magazine single-handed.'

Caz's brows lifted. 'If she was such a success in Manhattan, how come she's back in London, at the bottom of the ladder again and working for comparative peanuts?' he asked sceptically. 'It makes no sense.'

'I asked her about that,' said Rob. 'She said she'd come home because of illness in the family, and decided to stay for a while.' He paused. 'I have to say she seemed extremely eager to work for us. Should we suspect her motives for any reason?'

'Maybe we should simply be flattered.' Caz thought for a moment. 'Do you know anything about a Philip Hanson? Have we ever employed anyone of that name in any capacity, however briefly?'

Rob frowned. 'Off-hand, I'd say no. But I can check our records.'

Caz pushed back his chair and rose. 'Forget it,' he said. 'It's not that important, and you have enough to do.'

And I, he told himself, will also dismiss the whole business from my mind.

And as a positive move in this direction, when he got back to his office, he asked Robyn, his PA, to send Ginny Fraser some flowers.

Tarn switched off her computer and leaned back in her chair, flexing her shoulders wearily. It had been a fraught few hours, but she knew the task she'd been set was a job well done, and would be recognised as such.

How odd, she thought, that I should care.

Yet, in other circumstances, she knew she might have enjoyed her time on All Your Own. Working on her own as she did now, she'd almost forgotten the buzz of office life. Her colleagues were friendly and professional, and she liked the editor, Lisa Hastings, another recent appointment.

In fact she'd been the first to hear Lisa's cry of anguish as she scanned the pages of script that had just been handed to her.

'Oh, God—someone please tell me this is a joke.'

'What's happened?' Tarn had asked Kate who was in charge of the magazine's layout.

Kate cast her eyes to heaven. 'You've heard of Annetta Carmichael, the soap star? Apparently, when they killed her off as the Christmas Day ratings booster, she decided to take up a new career as a writer, and she's been offered megabucks for her first novel, a searing exposé of the secret world of television. A woman's fight to maintain her integrity against a sordid background of tragedy and betrayal.'

She grinned. 'You can practically hear the axe being ground. However, Brigid, Lisa's predecessor, thought it would be a great idea to commission a short story from her for an equally generous payment. I think the finished product has finally arrived, well after its deadline, and well short of the required standard.'

'I'd like to throw it back at her and tell her to start again,' Lisa was saying savagely. 'But she's pushed off to some

Caribbean hideaway with someone else's husband, and is, according to her agent, incommunicado.'

She slammed the pages down on her desk. 'And we need this. It's already been announced—"Annetta—Fiction's Latest Find."' She snorted. 'Fiction's greatest disaster if this is anything to go by.'

'What's wrong with it?' Tarn asked.

'You mean apart from a poor beginning, a boring middle, and a hopeless ending?' Lisa gave a groan. 'It needs an instant re-write, but it's my little boy's birthday today and I swore to my husband that I would be back in plenty of time for the celebrations. I should have known something would crop up and ruin things.'

Tarn hesitated. 'Would you like me to take a look at it?' she asked diffidently. 'I have done stuff like this in the past, and it would give you a chance to get off as planned.'

Lisa stared at her in open surprise. 'Are you serious? Because anything you could do—even if it was just sorting out her spelling and grammar—would be a tremendous help.'

Back at her desk, Tarn gave a silent whistle as she looked through the pages. Everything Lisa had said was perfectly justified, she thought grimly. It was a genuine horror.

But she remembered all the endless reams of frightful autobiography, and the rambling taped reminiscences that she'd transformed into readable—and saleable—prose in the recent past.

This at least had the benefit of being short. And, buried inside, were the actual bones of a story.

I've never ghosted fiction before, she thought. This will be a challenge. But I'll have the new draft done when Lisa arrives tomorrow.

The offices were beginning to empty as she began. By the time she'd completed the story to her own satisfaction, boosted by regular visits to the coffee machine, the building was dark and still, with only the occasional security patrols to disturb her concentration.

She printed off the new version, clipped the sheets together and took them to Lisa's work station.

She returned slowly to her seat, tucking her white blouse neatly back into her grey skirt as she went, then sat down to finish her final cup of coffee.

She was tired and hungry too, having eaten nothing since her mid-day sandwich. But she felt a curious sense of satisfaction all the same.

Just as if I was a bona fide employee, she thought wryly.

But then, she reflected, she'd had little opportunity to be anything else. Since she'd manufactured that meeting in the executive lift two weeks earlier, she hadn't managed to set eyes on Caz Brandon, even in passing.

She'd been aware, without conceit, that he'd again found her attractive, but there'd been no follow-up on his part, and office gossip said that he and TV presenter Ginny Fraser were a serious item.

Besides, she'd also been told, he never played around at the office. Which just showed, she'd thought angrily, how little they knew. But which also demonstrated that he must have wanted Evie very badly. And if he'd betrayed his own dubious principles once, he could surely be induced to do so again.

However, it was all a bit like the old recipe for Jugged Hare, which began 'First catch your hare...'

It was also time to visit Evie again, but she would have preferred to wait until she had something positive to report. And heaven only knows how long that will take, she told herself with a sigh.

She slipped on the black jacket hanging on the back of her chair, picked up her bag, and went to the double glass doors, using her security code to activate them.

As she walked down the corridor to the lifts, a man's familiar voice said, 'Doing overtime, Miss Desmond?'

Tarn whirled with a gasp, her bag crashing to the floor, as startled as if a ghost had suddenly materialised in front of her.

Only moments before, she'd been asking herself quite seriously if she was wasting her time, and should jettison all thoughts of revenge and simply resume her own life. Now here was Caz Brandon appearing out of nowhere in this otherwise deserted building, as if her thoughts had conjured him up out of thin air.

She said huskily, 'You frightened me.'

'I got a hell of a shock too when I came back to pick up my briefcase and saw there were lights on this floor,' he returned tersely. 'What are you doing here at this time of night?'

'As you said—overtime.' Tarn dropped to one knee and began to retrieve the objects that had fallen out of her bag. 'But don't worry. It's the voluntary, unpaid kind. I had a project I was keen to finish.'

'Keen isn't the word,' he said drily. He picked up a lipstick that had rolled to his feet and handed it back to her. 'Aren't there enough hours in the working day for you? And haven't you got better things to do with your evenings than hang around here?'

'Most of the time, yes,' Tarn told him coolly as she rose and fastened her bag. 'This was a one-off.'

She was playing it all wrong, she knew, but his unexpected arrival had flustered her badly.

Also she felt scruffy in the clothes she'd been wearing all day, and wished she'd put on some more lipstick or at least freshened her scent.

He, on the other hand, looked unruffled and elegant in a dark suit and crimson silk tie.

This is my golden opportunity, she thought. Another one may never come my way and I'll have simply wasted the last weeks of my life. I've rehearsed this scenario so many times, yet suddenly, ridiculously, I can't think what to say. What to do.

He said abruptly, 'You look tired. When did you last eat?'

'I had lunch.' That should have been a come-on, but all she sounded was defensive.

'Then I'll take you out for some food, and a drink. There's a little Italian place I use that stays open till all hours.'

'No—please. I'm fine.' Dear God, this was a Rubicon moment but her brain didn't seem to be working properly. She rallied. 'I really can't put you to so much trouble.'

He shrugged. 'You're not.' His tone was laconic. 'If you like, consider it a reward for loyalty above and beyond the call of duty.' He paused. 'So, shall we go?'

And she heard herself say, in a voice she hardly recognised, 'In that case—yes—please.'

CHAPTER THREE

THIS was what she had wanted, had tried so unavailingly to plan for, Tarn realised with a kind of wonderment as she walked beside him down the lamplit street. Yet now it had so unexpectedly fallen into her lap, every instinct she possessed was telling her to run away. Fast.

As they approached the kerb, she stumbled slightly and his hand shot out and took her arm.

'Be careful,' he cautioned as he steadied her, the warmth and firmness of his clasp seeming to penetrate the fabric of her jacket.

She muttered a word of thanks, longing to wrench herself free but not daring to, furious at her own clumsiness and bitterly aware of the harsh inner tensions which had caused it. Conscious too that, in spite of her dislike of him, her skin was tingling at his touch.

Oh, I'll be careful, she thought, the breath catching in her throat. My God, I will!

They crossed a road, then another, before walking the fifty odd yards down a side street to the Trattoria Giuliana.

It was busy, the hum of laughter and conversation quietly relaxed and delectable smells of herbs and garlic pervading the atmosphere. Caz was warmly greeted by the smiling proprietor and they were immediately shown to a corner table, where two glasses of *prosecco* were placed in front of them.

To her shame, Tarn realised her mouth was watering.

Caz raised his glass. *'Salute.'*

She returned the toast haltingly, glad when menus soon followed and she could focus on something other than the man watching her with frank intensity across the table.

Get a grip, she castigated herself, as she scanned the listed dishes. If he finds you attractive, make the most of it. If he was anyone else, you'd be relishing the situation and wondering how soon you could begin to flirt a little.

And all this talk of him avoiding office entanglements is just garbage. Evie wasn't a one-off. He's making that perfectly clear right now.

But if he's to suffer as much as he deserves, then you need him to be more than simply attracted to you. He has to want you so badly that it's like a sickness with him. A sickness for which you will never provide the cure.

And you're used to keeping men at arms' length. You've been doing it since adolescence. You can manage it again for as long as it's necessary.

Besides, he's the boss and you're just a lowly handmaid toiling on one of the Brandon Organisation's many publications, so you have every excuse for maintaining a respectful distance. But, it's also time to move from awkward to friendly.

She sighed lightly and looked at him her eyes smiling under her sweep of lashes. 'I seem to be spoiled for choice. As you eat here regularly, what can you recommend?'

He returned her smile. 'If you don't object to veal, the *Saltimbocca Romagna* is usually excellent.'

'I have no real hang-ups about food,' she said. 'I'll have it, with the *gnocchi* to start.'

'And I'll have the same, but begin with the wild mushroom risotto.'

He gave the order, and they agreed on a bottle of Friulano to go with it.

'So,' he said when the waiter had departed, leaving bowls of olive oil and chunks of bread to dip into them on the table.

'You seem to be enjoying your work on All Your Own. How do you rate it as a magazine?'

Tarn thought for a moment, then nodded. 'I'd say it hits most of its targets.'

'It certainly used to,' he said drily. 'However, the previous editor was keen on attracting a much younger readership.' He drank some *prosecco*. 'The numbers took a dive as a result.'

'Ah,' she said. 'So that's why I've been re-writing Annetta's story. It was intended for the youth market.'

'Re-writing?' His brows lifted. 'Is that within an assistant's remit?'

'Anything would have been an improvement on the original submission,' Tarn said, mentally kicking herself. 'But Lisa will naturally do the final draft.'

'I wasn't being critical. I'm seriously impressed.' He pushed a bowl of herb-flavoured oil closer to her. 'Try this with some bread. You look ready to fade away with hunger.'

His caring side, thought Tarn, fighting down cold fury as she tasted and made appreciative noises. And it was certainly a lovely restaurant, its tables far enough apart for privacy and set with snowy cloths, gleaming silver and crystal. But its air of quiet luxury was enhanced by a good atmosphere, and later arrivals than themselves were being accorded the same friendly welcome.

I wonder if this was where he brought Evie—that first time, she thought. If he also suggested to her what she might order. Asked if she was enjoying her work.

And Evie would have lapped it up. Unused to places like this, she would have gazed around her, getting more excited by the minute. Unable to believe how lucky she was to be in this glamorous restaurant with this equally glamorous man.

Everything about him spoke money—the exquisite tailoring, the expensive shirt, the plain platinum wristwatch. And all this, allied to the aura of power he carried so effortlessly, added up to a lethal combination.

She was like a lamb to the slaughter, Tarn thought bitterly. And he's probably used the same first date script with me as he did with her—learned by heart and used to decide whether the girl rates a follow-up rendezvous.

And I have to make it imperative for him to see me again—and not just by accident next time, but because he can't keep away.

He said reflectively, 'Tarn. That's a very lovely name—and unusual too.'

'Yes,' she said. 'A little too much so, I used to think. There can't be many girls called after a mountain lake, so naturally, when I went to school, I got re-christened "Drippy".'

His brows lifted. 'Anyone less so I've yet to meet. What did you do?'

'Nothing.' Tarn shrugged. 'Just pretended I hadn't heard and didn't care. But the name stuck and followed me from year to year. I hoped they'd get tired of the joke but they didn't.'

He pulled a face. 'Kids can be monsters. Have you ever told your parents what they put you through and extracted a grovelling apology?'

'No,' she said. 'I never did.' And paused. 'Anyway, where did Caz come from?'

He sighed. 'You're not the only sufferer. I was born on January the Sixth and my mother insisted I should be called after one of the three Kings, and fortunately she picked Caspar over Melchior and Balthazar or I should have been in even more trouble.'

He smiled at her. 'So that's the first thing we have in common.'

'And probably the one and only.' She managed to infuse her tone with a note of faint regret.

'Why do you say that?'

'Isn't it obvious?' She shrugged again. 'You own the company. I work for it.'

'And you find that an insuperable obstacle in the way of our better acquaintance?'

'I think it has to be.' She gave him a reflective look. 'And if you're honest, so do you.'

Except honesty isn't really your thing, is it, Mr Mighty Publishing Tycoon?

He spoke slowly, his lean, brown fingers toying with the stem of his glass in a way that dried her throat in some inexplicable manner. 'If you're asking whether or not I usually date my employees, the answer is an emphatic "No."' He added, 'Besides, this isn't really a date.'

She flushed. 'No—no, I understand that.'

'But it will be next time.' It was said casually, almost thrown away, and, with that, the wine arrived, followed almost immediately by their first course choices, and Tarn, biting back an instinctive gasp of surprise, was left floundering, even wondering if she'd heard him correctly.

Because it was all happening too fast. And this was not part of the plan at all. He was not supposed to be in control. She was.

She tried to concentrate her whole attention on the *gnocchi* in its wonderful creamy sauce, but, in spite of herself, found that she was stealing covert glances at him under her lashes. No matter what her secret feelings might be, she could not deny his attraction. Or this slow, almost inexorable build in her physical awareness of him. His mouth—the way his smile lit his eyes, just as Evie had said—his hands…

All of them things she had not allowed for. And what she least wanted to deal with.

But, for now, there was chat. In any other circumstances, an easy, relaxed exchange of views on books, music and the theatre. Perfectly normal and acceptable. But, here and now, feeling more like a journey through a minefield.

Don't be paranoid, she whispered silently. *Where's the harm in his knowing you like Margaret Atwood and John Le Carré? What does it matter if you prefer Bach to Handel and*

Mozart to both of them? Is it a state secret that your favourite Shakespeare play is Much Ado about Nothing?

For heaven's sake, relax. You needed to engage his interest. You've succeeded beyond your wildest dreams. So capitalise on it.

The *saltimbocca* was served, delicate veal escalopes wrapped round *prosciutto* and sage leaves, accompanied by green beans and lightly sautéed potatoes. The white wine, fragrant as a flower, was poured.

Caz raised his glass. 'I should propose a toast,' he said. '"To us" seems slightly presumptuous at this stage, so let's drink to the health of your patient instead, and hope for a complete recovery.'

Her hand jerked, and a few droplets of wine splashed on to her shirt as she stared at him.

She said huskily, 'What do you mean?'

His brows lifted in faint surprise. 'I was told you were back in London because of a family illness. Did Rob Wellington get it wrong?'

'No, he's perfectly correct,' she said. She drew a deep breath. Forced a smile. 'I—I suppose I didn't expect him to pass it on.'

'He feels you'll become a potentially valuable member of the workforce, and is worried we'll lose you.' He paused. 'I imagine you'll be planning to return to the States at some point—when there's no longer any cause for concern.'

'Why, yes,' she said. 'But it probably won't be any time soon. Progress is steady but slow, I'm afraid.'

'Is it a close relative who's sick?'

'My cousin.' She met his gaze calmly. 'She hasn't anyone else.' After all, Aunt Hazel was out of the equation for the foreseeable future, so it was almost the truth and easier to remember than an outright lie.

'I'm sorry,' he said. 'It must be very worrying for you.'

'Well, yes, it was at first,' Tarn said. *And how dare you say*

you're sorry when you don't mean it—utter some meaningless,
clichéd regret when it's all your fault that it ever happened.

She swallowed back the words—the accusations that she
wanted to scream at him. Introduced a bright note into her
voice. 'But I hope she's over the worst of it now.'

That was good, she thought. That suggested an eventual
happy outcome on the horizon. And not a hint of breakdown, or
isolation, or the kind of secrets that would lead to destruction.

At the same time, she didn't want to answer any more questions in case the answers became too revealing, so she decided
to drag the conversation back to less personal topics.

She looked down at her plate. 'You were right about the
veal,' she added lightly. 'It's delicious—absolutely marvellous.'

'So you'd risk having dinner with me again?'

Oh, God, out of the frying pan straight into the fire...

She drank some of her wine, letting it blossom in her mouth,
while she considered what to say.

'I don't think that would be altogether appropriate.' She
permitted herself a rueful shrug.

'Ah,' he said. 'For the reasons already stated?'

'Of course.'

'And not because you find me physically repugnant?'

She leaned back in her chair. 'Now you're laughing at me.'

'Not really,' he said. 'Simply trying to establish quite an
important point. Well?'

She hesitated. Sent him a defensive look. 'You don't make
things easy, do you?'

'Perhaps not,' he said softly. 'Maybe because I prefer to aim
for—ultimately and mutually rewarding.'

The words seemed to shiver along her nerve-endings as if
her senses were suddenly awakening to undreamed-of possibilities. Her skin was warming as though it had been brought
alive by the stroke of a hand. Her nipples were hardening, aching, inside the lace confines of her bra. And while the imme-

diacy of her response might be shocking, it was, to a certain extent, understandable.

Because instinct told her that Caz Brandon was not simply suggesting the likelihood of sensual delight, but offering it to her as a certainty.

An overwhelming prospect for someone of her ludicrously limited experience, she thought, and stopped right there, suppressing a gasp.

Oh, dear God, what was she doing to herself? Was she going completely crazy? Because she knew perfectly well that whatever he might be promising was never going to be fulfilled.

Evie, Evie, she whispered under her breath. *If this is how he came on to you, no wonder you simply fell into his hands. He could make anyone believe anything.*

Yet she was in no real danger, she reminded herself emphatically. Not when she could visualise her foster sister lying in that bed, in that clinical room, her slender body reduced to painful thinness, and her once-pretty face a haggard mask of unhappiness. That was the image that would armour her against succumbing to the wiles of the man confronting her across the candle-lit table.

He said, 'I was always told that silence means consent. But with you I need assurance. Does it?'

She pulled herself together, and met his gaze directly. She said in a low voice, 'How can I possibly answer you? We hardly know each other.'

'How strange that you should think so,' he said. 'Because I felt a kind of instant recognition, and thought you were conscious of it too. As if it was inevitable I would look up some evening and find you standing on the other side of the room.'

He was actually shaking his head. 'It's never happened to me before. If I'm to be candid, I didn't particularly expect it or want it.' His smile was brief almost harsh. 'You're an extra complication, Tarn Desmond, in an already crowded existence.'

'So I believe.' The swift, taut reply was framed before

she could stop herself. Fool, she castigated herself silently. Imbecile. Although his private life was hardly a state secret. That there were pictures of him with various glamorous companions all over the Internet. With one exception…

His slow answering grin mingled amusement with pleasure.

'So you've been checking up on me,' he said. 'That's encouraging.'

'Professional interest,' she told him coolly. 'I like to know the calibre of the people I work for.'

His former words were still ringing in her head. Presumably this was his tried and tested line, she thought, the sheer arrogance of the man catching her by the throat.

It should have made her furious—hardened her resolve, but instead she felt momentarily flurried—almost bewildered.

'And yet you took Philip Hanson at face value,' he said. 'Why was that?'

'A momentary glitch,' she said after a swift, startled silence. She'd almost forgotten that particular fiction. 'He was very convincing.'

'He must have been.' His mouth twisted. 'You'd certainly pulled out the stops when you were dressing that evening, and all for someone you hardly knew. Was that wise?'

'I didn't dress for him,' Tarn defended. 'I wanted to make an impression at the party.'

'Then you certainly succeeded,' Caz told her. He frowned. 'Yet I still wonder why he steered you towards us. I'm not complaining you understand, just—slightly puzzled.' He paused. 'You haven't tried to track him down since?'

She shrugged. 'I wouldn't know where to start. I suppose I really do have to treat it as a stupid, unkind joke.'

'If so, it was one that signally misfired,' Caz returned drily. 'We should both be grateful to him.'

'Both of us?' Her brows lifted. 'I rather think all the gratitude's on my side. Because I must also thank the girl who's having a baby, and created a vacancy for me, however temporary.'

'This is beginning to sound like an Oscars ceremony,' he said. 'In a minute, you'll be blessing your parents for having you.'

Perhaps, she thought. If I'd ever known them. If they hadn't left me alone in the world, dependant on strangers.

Aloud, she said, 'And what's so wrong about that?'

'Nothing,' he said. 'Except it's a task you should really leave to me.'

Tarn looked away. She said, 'If all this is another joke, can we end it here and now, please. I think it's gone quite far enough.'

'This is a beginning,' Caz told her quietly. 'Not a closing. But I can see I'm going to have to work damned hard to prove to you that I'm serious.'

And with that, the waiters appeared to clear their plates, and produce dessert menus, giving Tarn a much-needed breathing space as she contemplated what to say next. How to react.

Tricky, when all she really wanted to do was empty the remains of that expensive wine over his head, call him a treacherous, unfeeling bastard and storm out.

But that would only provide her with a momentary satisfaction. While he could laugh off his brief humiliation as a lovers' tiff, and every man in the restaurant would be on his side.

And what she wanted—required—was for him to experience the kind of pain that he'd inflicted on Evie.

And it will happen, she vowed inwardly. I'll make it happen.

'Tell me something,' he said, when the *panna cotta* with its red berry *coulis* had been ordered for them both. 'Is there someone in New York? Someone you plan to go back to?'

'Why do you ask?' She drank some more wine.

'Because I need to know what I'm up against. If it's just the office hierarchy thing that's making you so elusive, or if there's something or someone else.'

Or maybe I'm just trying to demonstrate that you're not Mr Irresistible, she told him silently. On the other hand, it would

be stupid to let you think I'm totally uninterested and alien-
ate you completely. So it's time to tug on the thread a little.

She met his gaze squarely. 'There's no-one,' she said. 'Not
any more.'

This time it was the whole truth. Howard had reacted badly
to the news that she would not be accompanying him to the
Keys. And her subsequent explanation had left him not merely
unmoved, but getting angrier by the moment.

'Everything you've ever told me about this Evie says she's a
total flake,' he'd finally thrown at her. 'You're crazy to get involved in her problems. I had a lot riding on this trip, Tarn, and
you've just—blown it out of the water. And why?' His voice
had risen and people at adjoining tables had glanced at them
curiously. 'Because your sister's boyfriend's dumped her? Big
deal. What about you—dumping on me? And what the hell do
I say to Jim and Rosemary?'

He'd finished his drink and left, leaving her to pick up the
check. Nor, she thought, could she really blame him.

She'd gauged when he'd be back from the Keys and rung
him. It was almost certainly over between them, such as it had
been, but, all the same, she didn't want to part bad friends.
However, her call had gone straight to voicemail, and not been
returned. So that episode in her life was definitely in the past,
and she only wished she could feel more regret. Especially as
he was probably the closest she'd ever been to commitment.

But there was no point in thinking like that. One day, when
all this was over, she'd find someone. Or maybe they'd find
her. Wasn't that how it was meant to be?

But before that could happen, she had a part to play.
Retribution to exact.

Caz said quite gently, 'I hope the parting wasn't too painful.'

She shrugged. 'Not very—especially when compared with
other people's experiences.' She gave him a half-smile. 'I think
I probably had a lucky escape.'

'Then I'll have to make sure that you'll continue to think so.'

There was a note in his voice which was almost a caress, and Tarn felt her skin shiver again in unwelcome response.

'And what about you? How have you managed to avoid serious involvement?' She spoke lightly, but she was stepping on to dangerous ground and she knew it, as her clasped fingers tightened painfully in her lap.

'It's never been a deliberate thing,' he said, after a pause. 'Until a year or so ago, hauling the company back from the brink occupied most of my time and energy. When the money men finally stopped scowling, I decided I could take life a little more easily. But that was all.

'Because I never pretended to the girls I dated that I was looking for any kind of permanent relationship. And most of them were looking for fun rather than commitment too, so we generally managed to reach a consensus that suited us both.'

She said, 'But there must have been some who hoped you would offer more.'

His mouth tightened, and he looked past her, his eyes suddenly remote. 'If so,' he said. 'That would be their problem, not mine.'

And one of those problems is locked away in a private hospital that's more like a prison, you unutterable bastard...

She said quietly, 'I shall consider myself warned.'

'That isn't what I meant, and you know it.' His tone was almost fierce. 'Give me the chance and I'll prove it to you. And whatever happened in the past is over—for both of us.'

The desserts appeared, and Tarn forced herself to eat the rich, creamy concoction with its sharp fruit counterpart with every sign of appreciation.

So where did the expensive diamond ring he'd given Evie feature in this no-commitment scenario? she asked herself. Or was that how he paid his women for services rendered?

She remembered a story she'd heard when she was a child about a girl finding the man she was to marry was another Bluebeard and exposing his guilt by flinging the severed and bejewelled ring finger of one of his victims on the table in front of him at their betrothal banquet.

If she could find Evie's ring, she thought, throwing it at him in some public place would make a splendid denouement for the moment when he finally learned the truth about her. When he discovered it was his turn to be deceived and callously dumped.

And now, she thought, steeling herself, it's time to proceed to the next stage.

So when coffee was offered, she declined, with an anxious glance at her watch.

'My flatmate will be wondering where I am.'

'You're not living at your cousin's place?'

'It's minute,' she said. 'My stuff would fill it, and I don't want her to come home and feel squeezed out, so I've moved in temporarily with a friend.'

'While you look for a place of your own?' Caz asked as he dealt with the bill.

'Perhaps. I haven't decided yet.' She picked up her bag. 'However—thank you for a wonderful meal. You've been—' she hesitated '—very kind.'

'And it's equally kind of you to say so.' There was a touch of wryness in his tone. 'My driver will be coming to pick me up in a few minutes. May I add to my good works and offer you a lift?'

'I think you've done enough,' she said. 'At least for one evening.'

The hazel eyes danced. 'Is that a hint that there may be another in the offing?'

'It's a promise to think about it,' Tarn said sedately. 'Nothing more.'

'Then I shall simply have to hope for the best.'

They were outside now, and he hailed a cruising taxi for her.

She gave the driver the address, burningly conscious that Caz was standing right beside her. Would he try to kiss her? She couldn't be sure.

But he merely opened the cab door and held it for her to climb in.

'That's dangerous thinking.' As she prepared to do so, she managed an impish smile. 'I might be the worst thing that's ever happened to you.'

He said softly, 'I'll take that risk.'

He handed the driver some money and stood back. As the cab sped off, Tarn wondered if he was watching, but nothing in the world could have persuaded her to turn and look.

You think the past is over? she whispered under her breath. *Oh, no, Mr Brandon, it's right here waiting for you. And I'm your unexpected nightmare.*

CHAPTER FOUR

'You had dinner with him?' Della stared at her, open-mouthed. 'With the Demon King? How—and why?'

Tarn shrugged. 'I was working late, he came back for his briefcase and we met. It was just—happenstance.'

'If one can believe in such a thing,' Della said with a touch of grimness. 'So tell me about it.'

'He took me to a wonderful restaurant, great food, fabulous wine—and he came on to me.'

'In what way?' Della leaned against the kitchen worktop. 'The direct approach? "My place or yours?"'

'Far from it.' Tarn poured herself some coffee, and refilled Della's beaker. 'A well-practised speech full of love, romance and "the first time I saw you" stuff.' She gave a contemptuous snort. 'My God, even if Evie wasn't involved, I'd want to see him get his comeuppance. It shows how little respect he has for women. He must think I'm a total idiot if he expects me to fall for that old routine.'

Della's eyes widened. 'So, your life has been punctuated by men laying their lives at your feet, is that what you're saying?'

'No, of course not.' Tarn frowned. 'But—oh, hell, you know what I mean.' She paused, then added casually, 'Besides, the entire world knows he's seeing Ginny Fraser from the "Up to the Minute" show.'

'Seeing each other's brains out, by all accounts,' Della

agreed cordially. 'Therefore you haughtily rejected his un-wanted advances and swept off into the night. Right?'

Tarn shifted uncomfortably. 'Not exactly.'

'What then?'

'He asked if he could have dinner with me again, and, natu-rally, I said I'd think about it.'

'Well, naturally,' Della echoed ironically. There was a si-lence, then she sighed. 'Tell me something, Tarn. If Evie didn't feature in this scenario, and you'd simply met Caz Brandon at a party and you'd spent time together, and he'd suggested an-other meeting, would you have said "Yes" to him?'

'No,' Tarn said passionately. 'Never in a million years. Because I don't go for arrogant, all conquering men.'

'Hmm,' said Della. 'Some might say you're being a trifle picky, but that's your choice.' She paused again. 'However, I've always had a bad feeling about this scheme of yours, and, somehow, it's getting worse all the time. So—if you do go out with him again—what then?'

'Nothing,' said Tarn. 'Not next time, the time after that, or any time at all. I give him enough encouragement to keep him interested, but he stays strictly at arms' length until he's ac-tually desperate. And then I choose the time and place to tell him that he's an uncaring swine and why I wouldn't have him if he came gift-wrapped.'

'But do you really think he'll care—given that he's appar-ently one of the major bastards of the western world? Maybe he'll just shrug and walk away.'

'That would depend on how many other people are around at the time. And mud sticks. He'll find himself being talked about in ways he won't like. So I hit him twice—firstly in his belief he's sexually irresistible. Secondly in his self image as the great publishing tycoon. He'll know I've been laughing at him all the time, and he's going to have to live with that for the rest of his life.'

'Sweet suffering saints,' said Della. She shook her head

wonderingly. 'You really intend to go to those lengths? A public denunciation?'

'Of course,' Tarn said defiantly. 'Ever since I re-read Evie's letters, and saw how much in love she'd been with him. When I realised exactly what he'd done. How appallingly he'd treated her.'

'And do you also realise how easily you could come unstuck?' Della demanded roundly. 'He's not a boy but an experienced and very attractive man, so you may not find him as easy to distance as you think. And when he finds he's been made a fool of, things could get even trickier.'

Tarn shrugged. 'It's a risk worth taking. Besides, as I've told you, he doesn't appeal to me.'

There was a loaded silence, then Della said quietly, 'Honey, it's still not too late to ditch the plan and run.'

'Don't tell me you're concerned for him!'

'I'm concerned for you. Tarn—this is all so out of character. You're not the vengeful type.'

'I'm learning to be.'

'Then stop now, while you can, before any real damage is done, to you or him. Hand in your notice, head back to the States, or, if you feel like a change, find a place to rent in Europe and resume real life.

'Evie may have had a rough time, but she might get over it much more easily if you're not there dispensing sympathy and muttering vengeance.'

'You didn't see her.' Tarn spread her hands. 'See the terrible state she was in—and all down to that utter bastard.'

'But you can't spend your future protecting Evie from unsuitable men,' Della objected. 'Or dealing with the consequences if she gets drawn in. She's got to learn to look after herself—to discriminate between the decent guys and the rats.'

'She hasn't anyone else.' *The same words she'd used earlier to Caz Brandon.*

'That is so not true,' Della said firmly. 'Actually, if you did but know it, she does have a mother. Who rang up earlier, as it happens, in a state over Evie's flat. It seems the landlord wants it cleared out if she's not coming back, and there's some rent owing too. Apparently La Mère Griffiths is passing up this belated but golden opportunity to take on some of the responsibility for her daughter and wants you to sort it out instead. So no surprises there.'

'It's not altogether her fault,' Tarn said, with a faint sigh. 'Uncle Frank took care of everything. Until he died, I don't think she'd ever had to pay a bill or speak to a bank.'

'And he passed the over-protective mantle on to you.' Della nodded. 'Well, that makes a kind of sense.'

'And Caz Brandon has got to learn that having power and money does not absolve you from all sense of decency,' Tarn added fiercely. 'Before he destroys some other poor girl's life.'

'Then I just hope you're not numbering Ginny Fraser among his unfortunate victims.' Della finished her coffee and rinsed the beaker. 'In the ruthless ambition stakes, she could probably leave him standing.' She moved to the door. 'Sweet dreams, honey, and tomorrow, please wake up cured. Or even slightly more sane would do.'

But if anything Tarn only felt more determined when she opened unwilling eyes in response to the radio alarm next morning. She'd had a restless night, interspersed with brief, uneasy dreams. Things she preferred not to remember in the light of day.

She paused while cleaning her teeth and studied herself in the bathroom mirror. There were shadows under her eyes, and her cheekbones looked stark in their prominence. Not really the kind of look to appeal to a would-be seducer.

I need to relax, she thought. Smile more, or he could change his mind and walk away. And I can't let that happen, because, whatever Della may think, he's asked for everything that's coming to him.

'Congratulations,' was Lisa's greeting as Tarn entered the
All Your Own editorial suite. She shook her head. 'You're the
original dark horse, my girl, just full of surprises and suc-
ceeding where others could only fail. I can hardly believe it.'

My God, Tarn thought shakily. Someone must have seen
me with him last night, and word's got round already. This was
not what I'd planned at all. The opposite, in fact.

She tried to speak steadily. 'What do you mean?'

'I mean, my pet, that you seem to have waved some kind
of magic wand and turned dear Annetta into a writer.' Lisa
picked up the draft script and waved it like a flag. 'This can
actually go into the schedules. In fact, I'm debating whether
we should build on this and do a whole series of celeb stories, that is if you're prepared to pick up the slack and spin the
straw into gold.'

'Chameleon' on a small scale, Tarn thought ironically. This
was getting rather too close to reality. And why hadn't she
seen it coming?

She marshalled a smile. 'That sounds a marvellous idea.
But do you think the accountants will wear it?'

'They will if Caz tells them to.' Lisa's expression was cat-
like. 'And maybe we can offer him a sweetener by including
Ginny Fraser on the list.'

Pain, sudden and astonishing, twisted inside Tarn like a
sharpened knife. But somehow she let her smile widen. Become
conspiratorial. 'Then let's go for it. What have we got to lose?'

Lisa nodded. 'I'll send a proposal up to him as soon as he
gets back.'

'Oh.' Tarn paused on her way back to her desk. She kept
her tone casual. 'Is he away somewhere?'

'Paris, Madrid, then Rome,' said Lisa. 'One of his usual
rounds.'

So much for forward planning, thought Tarn wryly. She'd
dressed that morning in a brief black skirt that showed off her
slim legs, teaming it with a scoop-necked white top that might

be deemed by the purists as a fraction too low for office wear, and she'd left her hair loose.

She'd been so sure he'd waste no time in finding an excuse for their paths to cross again, or press for an answer to his invitation in some other way. Had been bracing herself, in fact, for a summons. So, why hadn't he mentioned his trip the previous evening?

Because he didn't have to, she told herself, biting her lip as she stared at her computer screen. Because last night he acted on an impulse which he probably regretted just as quickly, and this is the cooling-off period. When he returns, he'll have other things on his mind and he can allow the whole thing to slide quietly into oblivion.

Which takes me right back to square one.

She bit her lip, and switched on her computer. She'd worry about that later when she'd finished work. Now she needed to concentrate.

But when the working day was over, there was Aunt Hazel to attend to. She'd phoned twice, the first time to make sure Della had passed on her message—'I thought she seemed very casual'—and the second to remind Tarn she'd need to call round and pick up Evie's key and the address.

When Tarn arrived at Wilmont Road, she found her foster mother peevish.

'I thought you were never going to get here.' She picked up an envelope. 'The rent money's in here. Six hundred pounds in cash, as he insisted.' She pursed her lips. 'How very unreasonable people can be, harassing me like this when he must know I'm half out of my mind with worry. But at least it means my girl will be coming back here to her own home when she's better.'

'I suppose he's entitled to be paid,' Tarn said mildly. 'And to look for another tenant.'

'Oh, poor Evie.' Mrs Griffiths shook her head, tearfully.

'She should never have gone to live in that flat. I knew no good would come of it.'

And this time, Tarn could only agree.

Evie had said that Caz had arranged for the move, so Tarn expected her cab to drop her at some smart apartment block. Instead she found herself outside a tall house in a busy street filled with identical buildings, many of which had clearly seen better days. She walked over chipped paving stones past a row of over-stuffed wheelie bins, wondering if Aunt Hazel had sent her to the wrong place.

But one of the keys fitted the front door, and she walked into a narrow hall. There was only one door clearly leading to the ground floor flat, where Mrs Griffiths had said the landlord lived, and most of the remaining space was occupied by a bicycle leaning against one wall, and a narrow side table littered with junk mail pushed against the other.

If he owns the place why doesn't he clear it up a little, thought Tarn pressing the bell. She rang twice and waited, but there was no reply, so she mounted the uncarpeted stairs to the next floor and Flat Two.

She unlocked the door with faint trepidation, wondering what she would find, but the interior turned out to be a distinct improvement. The small square hall was flooded with light from a big window overlooking some overgrown but attractive back gardens.

The bedroom, she saw, was directly opposite the entrance, its half-open door revealing an unmade bed and the kind of serious clutter a hurricane might leave in its wake.

Tarn wondered, with a faint shiver, if that was where Evie had been found, and hastily turned her attention to the comfortably sized living area with its galley kitchen, accessed by three shallow steps down from the hall.

The carpet and furnishings were not new but they looked clean and in reasonable nick. She'd seen very much worse in her travels.

But this was still far from the kind of love nest that she would ever have envisaged for Caz Brandon. Evie must have been totally blinded by passion not to realise she was being offered a pretty third-rate set-up.

But she wasn't here to speculate, she reminded herself, or even to build up her resentment and bitterness towards Caz, although this visit was simply confirming everything she'd thought about him. Her job was to clear out Evie's stuff.

There was an inventory pinned to the galley notice board, which demonstrated that Evie had been content to stick with what was provided and make no individual additions to the utensils, or the china, glassware and cutlery either. But then cooking had never been a big thing to Evie.

Nor had the living space benefited from her attention. Every cushion, picture, and sparse selection of ornaments was also listed.

So Tarn was forced to face the bedroom, and the cramped en-suite shower room which opened off it.

It was unlikely Evie would wish any reminders of the room, she thought as she stripped the bed, and bundled the bedding into a plastic sack, before filling a hold-all with Evie's clothes and shoes. Although, from a psychological point of view, she realised, it might be better to get rid of all of them too, and start again from scratch.

Emptying the wardrobe didn't take much doing. For a girl who'd been living the high life with a millionaire boyfriend, Evie didn't seem to have a lot of clothes, and what there was didn't rate highly on glamour, thought Tarn, wondering what had happened to the chiffon and lace wedding dress as she emptied the small tallboy.

The drawer in the bedside cabinet would only open fractionally, and she realised something was stuck there. After a brief struggle and a bruised knuckle or two, she managed to release it and extract the culprit, which turned out to be a square, leather-bound book.

Of course, she thought. It's Evie's diary. I should have known. And she must be missing it. In the past, she probably hasn't missed a day without writing in it. I wonder if they'd let her have it at The Refuge. It might be therapeutic for her.

She slipped it into her shoulder bag, then returned to the drawer. Small wonder it had stuck, she thought, discovering an envelope bulging with paperwork which she decided to take with her too, in case there was something incriminating about Caz among its contents. And under the envelope, she found a scrapbook. One glance told her that every single newspaper cutting and photograph that filled its pages featured Caz. And maybe all this material explained why there were no actual framed photographs of him in the flat. Unless, of course, Evie had never been given such a keepsake.

Whatever, this will not be going with me, she told herself grimly, adding the scrapbook to the bin bag.

Then, as she felt further towards the back of the drawer, she encountered something else—a small square jeweller's box covered in black velvet.

She opened it and gasped aloud at the blaze of the stones that glittered like ice-blue fire in Evie's engagement ring.

My God, she muttered under her breath. No wonder she believed every rotten lie he told her. Each of them must have cost an entire carat. But why on earth did he bother? Unless it had always been intended as a kiss-off payment, she thought, wincing.

She closed the box with a snap, and dropped that into her shoulder bag too.

The shower room was easily cleared, all the half-used toiletries swept into the bin bag along with the remains of the packs of painkillers, indigestion tablets and Evie's contraceptive pills, which were all that the small medicine cabinet over the washbasin contained.

No sign of the sleeping tablets Evie had used for her overdose.

She fastened the tie handles on the plastic sack and carried it back into the bedroom, where she stopped, gasping.

A man was standing in the doorway, thin and barely above medium height with very pale blond hair and light blue eyes, dressed in a grey suit with a faint silky sheen that whispered expensive.

He said softly, 'Exactly who are you? And what are you doing here?'

This, thought Tarn, recovering her breath, must be the troublesome landlord.

She said crisply, 'Quite obviously I'm removing Miss Griffiths' possessions as requested. But perhaps it's a trick question.' She paused. 'And I have your money.'

The fair brows lifted. 'Do you indeed? Well, that is good news.' He glanced around. 'Do I take it that Evie will not be returning?'

Tarn stared at him. 'But you know that already. You told her mother you wanted to re-let the place.'

'Ah.' The thin mouth stretched into a smile. 'I think there's a slight misunderstanding here. My name is Roy Clayton and I actually live upstairs, another of Bernie the Bloodsucker's hapless tenants. I heard someone moving around down here, came to investigate and found the door unlocked.'

'But you didn't ring the bell,' said Tarn.

'Er—no. Evie and I weren't on such formal terms.' He paused. 'And you are?'

'Her sister.'

'What a charming surprise. I didn't know she had one.' His smile widened a little. 'Such a dreadful thing to have happened. You must all be devastated. I was the one who found her, you know, and called the ambulance.'

'No,' Tarn said. 'I didn't know that.'

'So is she fully on the road to recovery? And can she have visitors, wherever she happens to be?'

'She's making satisfactory progress,' Tarn returned. 'But she's not up to seeing people yet.'

'What a pity.' He glanced round the room again, his gaze lingering on the suitcase and the empty bedside cabinet, while Tarn took a quick look at her shoulder bag beside the chest of drawers, checking that it hadn't been disturbed because Evie's ring was in there.

He added, 'Bernie should have told me that she wasn't coming back. I could have saved you a journey and a job, and cleared the place for you.'

'That's kind of you,' Tarn said untruthfully. 'But it's probably a task better suited to her family.'

'I'm sure you're right.' The curiously pale eyes rested on her. 'You mentioned something about money?'

She looked back at him, bewilderment mixing with her unease. 'Yes—but I thought you were the landlord wanting his rent.'

'Oh, dear, another disappointment,' he said lightly.

'You mean Evie owed you too?' She drew a dismayed breath, bracing herself. 'If you'll tell me what it was for and how much, perhaps something could be arranged.'

'Oh, I couldn't possibly put you to so much trouble,' he said. 'And it's really quite a trivial matter. Besides, I'm sure Evie and I will be running into each other again. One of these days. When she's better.'

He paused again. 'Now I'll leave you to your toil. Do tell Evie next time you see her that I was asking about her. You won't forget, will you?' Another swift smile, and he was gone.

Tarn stayed where she was, uncomfortably aware that her breathing had quickened, and the plastic sack in her hand seemed suddenly to be weighing a ton.

Oh, pull yourself together, she told herself sharply. He's just a concerned guy from upstairs. You're letting this whole Caz Brandon thing knock you sideways, make you imagine every man you come across is a potential threat.

On the other hand, as she went downstairs, she found the genuine article waiting for her, bald and tattooed in a football shirt and denim cut-offs.

'Bernie Smith.' He gave her a hard look. 'You're not the woman I talked to.'

'No, that was Miss Griffiths' mother.'

He grunted. 'Got the rent?'

Tarn handed over the envelope and watched him count it.

'Seems to be all there,' he said. 'Lucky I don't charge for having the place cleaned. And the inconvenience—paramedics and police swarming all over. Gives a place a bad name.'

'Difficult to see how,' Tarn said, giving the hallway a disparaging look before dropping the keys into his hand.

'No need to be so high and mighty,' he called after her, as she left. 'And I'll be checking that inventory, no danger.'

But I shall not, Tarn thought, as she hailed a cab, be mentioning any of this to Aunt Hazel.

'Are you sure you won't come to Molly's birthday bash tonight?' asked Della. 'She said you'd be more than welcome.'

Tarn shook her head. 'I'm going to have a long bath, wash my hair, and go through the stuff in the envelope yet again, in case I'm still missing something.'

'Like a proposal of marriage from Caz Brandon in writing?' Della wrinkled her nose. 'You can't sue for breach of promise any longer.'

Tarn sighed. 'I wasn't thinking of that. I'm just trying to make sense of it all. To correlate the weird flat with that amazing ring, the chainstore clothing with the millionaire lifestyle.'

'A noble ambition,' said Della. 'And I'm sure Evie would do just as much for you.'

Tarn bit her lip. 'But you must admit it's strange.'

'Strange is not the word. And at the risk of turning into Cassandra whose warnings were also ignored, I say again that you should drop the entire mess, and get back to your own life.'

She gave Tarn a minatory glance. 'A decision that Mr Brandon may also have made.'

'Apparently he was bankrolling her,' Tarn said unhappily. 'There were some nasty letters from the bank and a credit card company in the envelope, but a week later she's writing in her diary that she no longer has any money worries, "thanks to C."'

'Exactly,' said Della. 'He must have realised she was a total flake, especially where money was concerned, and that he'd be lucky if she didn't bankrupt him.'

'But he was going to marry her,' Tarn argued. 'Why didn't he sit down and talk to her if there was a problem? Try to work things out?'

Della shrugged. 'Maybe he did, and found it was stony ground.'

'There's also a load of stuff about the MacNaughton Company,' Tarn said, producing a sheaf of papers. 'Whoever they are.'

'Now there I can help,' said Della. 'They're a cleaning firm, incredibly high-powered, lethally expensive, and very discreet, exclusively employed by the mega-rich and famous. They appear like good elves, perform their wonders and vanish.' She frowned. 'But from what you've said, Evie's flat wouldn't be their usual stamping ground, even if she could afford them.'

'I gather from her diary that Caz Brandon fixed her up with them too,' Tarn said wearily. 'Though there wasn't much sign that professional cleaners had ever been there.'

Della was silent for a moment. 'The guy upstairs—was he attractive?'

'He gave me the creeps.'

'But you, honey, are not Evie. Could she have been two-timing her fiancé with the neighbourhood watch, do you suppose?'

'Never in this world,' Tarn said with emphasis. 'No-one who was seeing Caz Brandon would give Roy Clayton a second glance.'

'Is that a fact?' Della said affably. 'How very interesting that you should think so.'

She picked up her bag and walked to the door. 'If you get tired of your mysteries, Sherlock, we'll all be at the Sunset Bar,' she threw over her shoulder as she left.

An hour later, Tarn was wishing she'd taken up the offer. Wrapped in a towelling robe, her hair curling damply on her shoulders, she was ensconced in a corner of the sofa, re-reading Evie's diary and getting more depressed by the minute.

The contrast between the almost hysterical happiness at the beginning of her relationship with Caz and the agonised descent into despair when it ended was almost too painful to contemplate.

'What can I do? I can't go on?' were words repeated over and over again. But Tarn had an odd sense from the later entries that Evie was not just wretched, but frightened too, because *'What will happen to me? Where will I go?'* also cropped up with alarming frequency.

What did he do to her? she thought.

She reached for the beaker of coffee she'd made earlier, realising with a grimace that it was now cold. She closed the diary, put it on the floor with the envelope, and rose to go to the kitchen.

She was waiting for the kettle to boil when the door bell sounded.

Della must have forgotten her key again, she thought, although it seemed rather early for the birthday celebrations to have ended.

A teasing remark already forming in her mind, she walked to the front door and threw it open.

And stood, as if turned to stone, as she stared at her caller.

'Good evening,' said Caz Brandon, and he smiled at her.

CHAPTER FIVE

SILENCE stretched between them, threatening to become endless as shock held her motionless. Speechless. Yet she had to do something...

'You.' Her mouth was dry. She hardly recognised her own voice. 'What are you doing here?'

His shrug was rueful. 'I'd hoped to take you to dinner, but my flight was delayed, so my guess is you've already eaten.'

He paused, the cool hazel gaze sweeping over her. His expression did not change, but Tarn's instincts told her that he knew perfectly well that she was naked under the towelling robe. She had to resist an impulse to tighten her sash, and draw the lapels more closely to her throat.

He added, 'I seem to have called at an inopportune moment, so maybe a drink is out of the question too?'

She made no immediate response and his brows rose with faint mockery. 'Another loaded silence,' he remarked. 'I suppose I shall have to become accustomed to that.'

She went on staring at him. 'How did you find me?'

'Quite easily. Your contact details including your address are all logged at the office—as you must know.'

Of course she did, but she was playing for time, trying to pull her scattered wits together.

She said slowly, 'I'm not exactly geared up for going out. And we don't keep much in the way of alcohol.'

'I'd settle for coffee,' he suggested. 'I might even drink it here at the door, if you insist.' He went on softly, 'Although I promise I don't pounce, or, at least, not without a serious invitation.'

Her smile was brief and unwilling. 'I think it would probably be better if you came in.'

He followed her into the flat. 'You looked as if you'd seen a ghost,' he commented. 'Surely you were expecting me to make contact?'

'Not really.' She hunched a shoulder. 'Men often say things that they don't mean, or that appear less enticing the next day.'

'Then you must have been unlucky in your men friends.'

As she walked ahead of him into the sitting room, the first thing she saw was Evie's diary lying on the carpet by the sofa.

Oh, God, she thought. Having been involved so closely with her, he'll recognise that as soon as he sees it.

She said with a kind of insane brightness, 'It's so untidy in here. I must apologise.'

She moved quickly, gathering it up under the cover of the envelope that lay beside it, and pushing them both on to a shelf in the bookcase.

Caz was glancing round. 'This is a pleasant room.'

Better than the place you found for Evie...

Aloud she said, 'Thank you. Won't you sit down?'

'I have been sitting,' he said. 'On a plane, and then in the car that picked me up at the airport. May I help with the coffee instead?'

She hesitated, then led the way to the kitchen. It was a comfortable size, but tonight it felt cramped, as if by the simple action of turning from the sink to the worktop and from the worktop to a cupboard, she would brush against him.

She was almost surprised to discover she'd managed to assemble the coffee beans, the grinder and the percolator without any physical contact with him whatsoever.

Yet it was the mental awareness of him that she found so

disturbing. The consciousness that he was leaning against the doorframe silently observing her flustered preparations.

She said, holding up a bottle, 'I've also found some brandy, but I think it's what Della uses for cooking, so I can't vouch for it.'

He grinned. 'No point being snobs in an emergency. Where do you keep your glasses?'

'Top cupboard on your right.'

As she spooned the freshly ground coffee into the percolator and added boiling water, the aroma filled the air, replacing the faint, expensive hint of musk that she'd detected from the cologne he wore.

When she'd decided to let him in, it was with the fixed intention of provoking him into making a pass, and then reporting him to the police for sexual harassment.

But wiser counsels had soon prevailed. The fact that she'd admitted him when she was alone and only wearing a bathrobe would do her case no good at all, she admitted silently. Besides, he'd said he wouldn't pounce, so she would have to make all the running—another serious black mark against her.

And the fact that this was Della's flat, and her friend totally disapproved of what she was doing stopped her in her tracks, at least for tonight, and warned her to think of something else.

'I'm hoping this might relax you,' Caz remarked, handing her a rounded crystal glass. 'You look like a kitten caught in headlights—as if you don't know which way to run. Am I really so scary?'

'No,' she said. 'No, of course not. It was just—such a surprise. Besides, I'm not really dressed for entertaining.'

If she'd expected some leering riposte, she was disappointed.

Caz frowned slightly. 'I should have telephoned ahead. Warned you I was calling round, or maybe made a date for a more convenient time.'

'Then why didn't you?'

'Considering the amount of twitch in the air, maybe I should reserve my reasons for another time too.'

'I have a better idea,' Tarn said. 'Why don't we just—start again.' She held out her hand. 'Good evening, Mr Brandon. What an unexpected pleasure.'

'Change Mr Brandon to Caz,' he said, the warm strong fingers closing round hers. 'And it will become an unmitigated pleasure.'

And I'm an unmitigated fool not to throw this brandy over you here and now and scream what you've done to your face— tell you what a bastard—what a love rat you are. Although you wouldn't recognise or understand the word 'love.' And, any- way, you'd just shrug it off and walk away. Water off a duck's back. But some day soon, you'll be made to care...

She allowed her long lashes to sweep down in demure con- cealment, in case he read the truth in her eyes. 'Very well— Caz.'

'A moment I might have missed if I'd called in advance,' he said softly as he released her hand. He paused. 'So where's your flatmate this evening?'

'At a hen party. Someone's birthday.'

'You didn't want to go?'

She sent him a wry glance. 'I decided to settle for a quiet night in.'

'Which I've spoiled,' he said softly. 'However, your loss is my definite gain.'

She set a tray with cups and saucers, adding a jug of cream. Caz carried it into the sitting room, placing it on the small table in front of the sofa, and she followed with the percolator. She sat at one end of the sofa, and he occupied the other, stretch- ing long legs in front of him.

'I like the shampoo you use,' he commented unexpectedly. 'Apple with a hint of vanilla.'

Tarn busied herself pouring coffee, leaning forward so that

the swing of her hair could conceal the sudden warmth invading her face.

She said, 'You're—very perceptive.'

'I'm on a steep learning curve,' he said. 'Finding out about you.'

Her throat tightened nervously. Was he serious? Given his money and resources, if he really started to probe her background, what might he not unearth?

With a supreme effort, she kept her voice light, and her hand steady as she passed him his coffee. 'Well, that shouldn't take long. There isn't very much to discover.'

'On the contrary,' he said slowly. 'I suspect it could take a lifetime.'

He reached for his brandy glass and raised it. 'To us.'

She drank without repeating the toast. 'Isn't that still slightly presumptuous?'

'I hope not,' he said. 'I simply have to win you round to my way of thinking, that's all.'

Her breathing quickened. 'And if I can't be won?'

'Do you mean "can't"?' he asked. 'Or is it really "won't"?'

She moved a restive shoulder, replaced her glass on the table. 'Does it make a difference?'

'Not really,' he said. 'Whichever it is, you'll find I don't give up easily.'

There was a silence, then she said jerkily, 'Mr Brandon—Caz—this whole conversation is making me—uneasy. I think you should drink your coffee and leave.'

'I'm sorry if you feel uncomfortable with the situation.' He smiled at her. 'Now, I was thinking it was like a foretaste of the future. Me—back from business trip. You—with your hair just washed and no makeup. Both of us enjoying a nightcap together, knowing exactly how the evening will end, but content to wait. To savour every lovely moment.'

His gaze rested on her startled, parted lips then moved down to the flurried rise and fall of her breasts under the concealment of her robe.

He added with sudden roughness, 'For God's sake, Tarn. Don't you know that I'm nervous too. Have you forgotten what I said the other night?'

'No.' She paused. 'I—I haven't forgotten anything.'

'You said earlier that we'd start again, and that's what I'm asking for. A chance to prove to you that I mean what I say. And we'll go at your pace, not mine. That's a promise. When you come into my arms, it will be because you want to be there.'

His mouth twisted ruefully. 'Now relax, and drink your coffee, while we discuss our first real date.'

She gasped. 'You—really don't give up, do you?'

The hazel eyes glinted. 'You'd better believe it. And at the same time please understand that you have nothing to fear.'

No, she thought. You're the one who should be afraid.

She picked up her cup and drank, regarding him over its brim. 'So what do you have in mind for this date?'

'I thought we might go to the theatre. I have tickets for the opening of the new Lance Crichton play next Wednesday.'

Her brows lifted in disbelief. 'Heavens. Sprinkled with gold dust, I presume.'

'Almost,' he admitted. 'Are you interested?'

Her eyes danced. 'I think it's an offer I can't refuse. I saw Payment in Kind on Broadway and loved it.'

'Then I hope you'll tell him so. He got rather a mauling from some of the New York critics.'

She drew a breath. 'You mean I could meet him. Are you serious?'

'I'm sure it could be arranged.'

Tarn thought then shook her head regretfully. 'The play's quite tempting enough. I think that meeting Lance Crichton would turn my head completely.'

He smiled. 'You're not so easily overwhelmed.'

He drank the rest of his coffee and stood up.

'You're leaving?' The words were involuntary, and so, she realised with shock, was the note of disappointment in her voice.

'That was what you wanted a few minutes ago,' he said. 'If you remember. And I've got what I came for, so I'm quitting while I'm ahead. It's wiser and probably safer.' He paused. 'I'm sure I don't have to explain why.'

There was a sudden, odd tension in the room, making her skin tingle. Forcing her to catch her breath.

She made a business of scrambling to her feet. 'I—I'll see you out.'

'Fine,' he said equably. At the front door, he turned, looking down at her. 'If you asked me to stay, I would.' His voice was gentle, but the hazel eyes were asking questions for which, to her horror, she could find no answer. She looked back at him, mutely, pleadingly, and he nodded as if she'd spoken.

He said, 'Then I'll be in touch.' He took a strand of her hair and lifted it to his face. 'Apples and vanilla,' he said, and went.

Tarn leaned against the closed door, trembling. Dear God, she thought weakly, just for a moment there I was actually tempted. And he—*he*—let me off the hook. How shameful is that?

She washed up the cups and glasses, emptied the percolator and put everything away as if she'd spent the entire evening alone. She'd tell Della he'd been there—of course she would. But in her own time, which certainly wasn't tonight. She needed to get her head straight before she broached the subject.

In her room, she took off her robe and reached for her nightgown. But, on impulse, she let it drop to the floor, and slid into bed naked. The sheets were cool against her heated skin, the fabric a caress that tantalised, offering arousal without satisfaction.

Eyes wide, staring into the darkness, she moved restlessly, languorously, aware, deep within her, of a scald of yearning, as unwelcome as it was unfamiliar.

It was wrong to feel like this, she told herself feverishly. Wrong and hideously stupid. None of the men she'd met in the past had affected her in the same way. She'd enjoyed their company—even found it pleasant to be held—kissed—but never wanted more. Had not grieved when it ended.

At the same time, she'd wrinkled her nose derisively at the thought of Mr Right waiting patiently just off-stage.

Not that Caz Brandon would ever figure in that category for any woman, she added hastily. Unless of course it was Ginny Fraser. According to Della, they seemed well-matched. Another 'celebrity couple' in the making, smiling for the camera if not for each other.

And maybe, with the prospect of younger talent climbing the television ladder behind her, Ms Fraser would find a different kind of limelight sufficient compensation for her husband's practised womanising.

'They're welcome to each other,' Tarn whispered, turning on to her front and burying her face in the pillow. 'And, once this is over, I—I have my career to get back to.'

She tried to think of the next Chameleon project. A couple of tempting names had been dangled in front of her, but ghost-writing was a two way street. She would have to meet the subjects and talk to them. See if there was any kind of rapport which could develop into a platform of mutual trust and liking. A prospect that they would eventually open up to her completely, maybe even tell her things about themselves they hadn't guessed until then.

That was the best foundation, and while it was being established, either party could simply walk away. It happened, and sometimes she'd been sorry, but often relieved, scenting trouble ahead.

And now, suddenly, there was Lance Crichton, she thought. One of the most successful playwrights of his generation, yet a man who'd always shunned personal publicity, letting his work speak for itself.

But a man who undoubtedly had a story waiting to be told, if approached in the right way. Only she'd come across him at totally the wrong moment because she couldn't put out even the most discreet feeler without the risk of self-betrayal, she reminded herself, sighing. Until her work here was done, Chameleon had to remain another closely guarded secret.

And so did the way Caz Brandon could make her feel, she thought, and shivered.

'You found her diary?' repeated Professor Wainwright. 'May I see it, please?'

Tarn lifted her chin. 'I'd prefer to give it to Evie,' she said quietly. 'She's always kept a diary from being a small child. Written in it every day. It was almost an obsession with her. I thought that having it back might help with her treatment.'

'I think I am the best judge of that, Miss Griffiths. Her case is a complex one. But the diary could be useful in other ways.' He held out his hand and Tarn hesitated.

'First, will you tell me something, Professor?'

'I cannot guarantee that. What do you want to know?'

'Her mother told me Evie had taken an overdose but I didn't find anything like that when I cleared her bathroom.'

'The police removed them. They are a very strong brand, known abroad as Tranquo, and not legally available for sale in this country. I gather their possible side-effects mean that they never will be so licensed. However, supplies of this drug, among other illicit forms of tranquillisers and stimulants, are regularly smuggled in for sale on black market networks.'

'Smuggled in? By whom?'

He shrugged. 'No-one is quite sure, but people who travel abroad a great deal on perfectly legitimate business, and therefore have not attracted the attention of the police or customs authorities are natural suspects.

'It is believed a lot of them are bought by the rich and famous initially for their own use, but then recommended to their friends and acquaintances. Because these drugs work, Miss Griffiths, in spite of their inherent and serious risks.' He paused. 'They also cost a great deal of money.'

'But Evie couldn't possibly have afforded anything like that,' Tarn protested. But Caz could, she thought. And he travels constantly. Could it be even remotely possible…

And found her mind closing against the thought.

'Well, that is something the police will wish to discuss with her when she has recovered sufficiently.'

Tarn stared at him. 'And you think that's all right, do you? Have you forgotten that Evie's not a criminal but a victim, driven to total desperation. And you must know why,' she added fiercely.

'Let us say a clearer picture is beginning to emerge.' He was unruffled. 'Now, may I have the diary?'

She surrendered it reluctantly, and watched him place it in a drawer of his desk.

She said, 'And may I go and see Evie?'

'Not today, Miss Griffiths. I regret that you've had a wasted journey, but you are obviously upset, and it would be better to wait until you are calmer, and able to accept that what we do here is for your foster sister's ultimate good.'

She said, 'It may be a long time before I believe that.'

'Also I would prefer her not to know that we have her diary.' He paused. 'In future, perhaps you should telephone in advance and make sure your visit is convenient.'

'Yes,' she said, and rose from her chair. 'I shall. But let me assure you, Professor Wainwright, that nothing I've done or shall do for Evie will ever be wasted.'

The theatre bar was crowded, and alive with an excited buzz of conversation.

No doubt in anyone's mind that this was an occasion, thought Tarn drily as she waited for Caz to return with their interval drinks.

She'd felt as if she was strung up on wires as she'd dressed for the evening, choosing a plain black knee-length shift topped with a taffeta jacket striped in emerald and black. Her hair she'd fastened in a loose knot on top of her head, and she wore jet pendant ear-rings.

She looked, she thought judicially surveying the finished article in the mirror, the image of a girl ready for a date with the most attractive man she'd ever met.

Not at all like someone who'd spent her recent days and nights wondering whether or not that same man might be a drug smuggler, and if she should take her suspicions to the authorities.

Eventually, she'd told herself wearily that she was crazy. Because being a womanising bastard and love rat did not make Caz Brandon a felon, much as she might wish it. And watching him get his just deserts did not necessarily mean jail.

Della had arranged to be elsewhere when Caz came to pick Tarn up.

'I don't trust myself not to scream, "She's out to get you, and not in a good way,"' she'd commented candidly.

Tarn said with difficulty, 'Dell—this isn't a joke.'

'No,' Della returned. 'In my view, it has all the makings of a tragedy. But that's your choice, honey.'

Now Tarn watched as he threaded his way through the general melee carrying her spritzer and his own Scotch and water. It took a while because he was constantly being halted to respond to greetings.

When he reached her side, Tarn said, 'Do you know everyone here tonight?'

'I know some, but I think a lot of the others believe they know me because of some past introduction.' His voice was rueful. 'If I had to remember their names, I'd be in difficulties.' He handed over her drink. 'Here's to Act Two.' He added softly, 'And I don't necessarily mean the play.'

'Ah, but I do.' She sent him a smile. Made it teasing. 'It's absolutely wonderful—especially as I haven't the faintest idea what to expect next.' She gave a faint whistle. 'Lance Crichton certainly knows how to put the audience's emotions through the wringer.'

Caz nodded. 'When Bateman made that last entrance, I thought the woman next to me was going to fly out of her seat.'

Tarn shuddered. 'I thought I might too. Although I've never heard of the actor who plays him. Proving how out of touch I am.'

'Rufus Blaine? He did a season at Stratford in minor roles, and people at the time were saying he was a star in the making. I think this Bateman portrayal has confirmed that.' He paused. 'Curious, isn't it, how the wicked usually get far more interesting roles than the good?'

Tarn shrugged. 'It sometimes seems the same in real life.'

'Isn't that a little cynical?'

'Probably.' She added lightly, 'Blame it on Bateman, and the shocks in store for us. I can hardly wait.'

'I'm delighted to hear it.' He hesitated. 'I was afraid you were regretting having accepted my invitation.'

'What made you think that?'

'You seemed very quiet when I came to pick you up.'

'Did I? Perhaps I find dating the boss a daunting prospect.'

'Has it occurred to you that I might be a little daunted too?'

'Frankly, no. Why should it?'

He said slowly, 'Because you're different. There's something guarded—unfathomable about you, Tarn.'

Why—because I'm not a pushover, falling enraptured at your feet?

'A woman of mystery?' she asked, brows lifted. 'Flattering but untrue, I'm afraid. What you see is what you get.'

'I think,' he said, 'that only time will convince me of that.'

At that moment, the bell sounded to signal their return to the auditorium.

And she really had been saved by it, Tarn thought, quashing a sudden bubble of hysteria as she walked sedately beside him back to the stalls. Because Caz Brandon was going to be no pushover either. He was far too perceptive for his own good—or hers.

Dear God, she thought, I shall have to be so careful. So terribly careful.

CHAPTER SIX

THE word 'Careful' sang in her brain as she sat tautly beside him in the back of the car on the journey back to the flat, waiting for him to lunge at her.

But it didn't happen. Instead he chatted about the play, the performances, and the almost unbearable tension of the final act. And when the car drew up outside the apartment block, he dismissed her protests and escorted her to her door.

He watched as she fumbled in her bag for her key. 'Am I going to be asked in again for coffee?'

'My flatmate will be asleep,' she said, hoping that a wide awake Della wouldn't suddenly appear to make a liar of her. 'I—I don't want to disturb her.' She added, 'Besides, your driver's waiting.'

'Of course,' Caz said softly, and smiled at her. 'And I can wait too.'

His gaze travelled down to her mouth and she knew that he was going to kiss her. Knew as well that there was no realistic way she could avoid this. That she must, at least, appear willing if her long term plan was to succeed.

Her whole body stirred as he bent towards her, and she felt the slow, painful thump of her heartbeat echo through every nerve-ending in her skin. *Careful*...

His hands were gentle on her shoulders, drawing her towards him, then his lips touched hers, brushing them swiftly, lightly in a caress as fleeting as an indrawn breath. A tease that promised but did not fulfil.

Then he released her and stood back, the hazel eyes quizzical as they scanned her flushed face.

'Goodnight,' he said quietly. 'Sleep well. I'll be in touch.' And went.

As she walked on unsteady legs into the sitting room, she heard from the street below the sound of the car pulling away, and stood rigidly, one clenched fist pressed against her breast.

Clever, she thought stormily. Oh, God, he was clever. But she could play games too. And somehow—however difficult it became—she intended to win.

Her interior warning to take care continued to hang over her, as the spring days brightened and lengthened, and Caz's campaign began in earnest.

However Tarn soon realised that he seemed to be keeping it deliberately low-key, not crowding her or bombarding her with demands for her company. Certainly not trying to sweep her off her feet as he'd done to Evie with high profile dates. But a couple of times a week, they dined together, or visited a cinema, or went to a concert or another play, the arrangements invariably made through text or voicemail on her mobile phone.

It would have been much easier, she thought unhappily, if she hadn't been forced to remind herself quite so often that the time spent with Caz was simply a means to an end and nothing more. Because that should have been a given.

She didn't want to enjoy any part of these occasions, much less allow the reasons for them to slip from her mind, even momentarily. It worried her too that when she was alone, she sometimes found that she was smiling to herself, remembering something he had said or done, and was then forced to pull herself together, thankful that, knowing what he really was, she had the power and the will to resist his charm.

And, as she told herself, it was a relief that was all she had to fight. Because one element of their relationship did not vary. Each time he brought her home, he kissed her briefly, grazing her mouth with his, just once and departed. Leaving her restless and wondering what he was doing on the other five days and nights when she didn't see him, apart, of course, from the occasional glimpse at work, generally on his way to or coming from a meeting, and immersed in conversation.

Although Tarn was busy too. Lisa had been given the go-ahead on the celebrity short story series, and they were in contact with the 'A' list they'd drawn up, so she had little time in office hours to let her mind wander in his direction.

Which, as she reminded herself forcefully, was all to the good.

What was not so good was the realisation that she was actually enjoying the job she'd embarked on so carelessly. That she would regret having to resign in order to substantiate her harassment claim.

In connection with this, she'd expected that by now her involvement with him would have got around via the usually efficient office grapevine, adding weight to her eventual complaint against him.

Every day, she went in prepared for knowing looks, smothered grins, and whispered remarks. But there was nothing. If anyone knew or even suspected, they were keeping very quiet about it.

Maybe when he's going out with nobodies like Evie and myself, he prefers to keep his private life strictly under wraps, she thought, recalling that Evie hadn't featured in many of the pictures in the scrapbook. In fact, Tarn couldn't remember seeing even one, suggesting her foster sister had been told to stay off-camera when she appeared with him in public.

And she'd have been far too besotted to protest, or ask, 'Are you ashamed to be seen with me?' Tarn told herself bitterly.

She had phoned The Refuge several times, but the hoped-for permission to visit Evie was still being withheld, which worried her.

'That place really is like a prison,' she complained to Della, who shrugged.

'Maybe seclusion is what she most needs,' she returned. 'When my mother was in hospital last year, she said she'd have given every penny she possessed for a couple of days of peace, quiet and no visitors.' She added gently, 'I think, my pet, you have to give them credit for offering her the best possible treatment.'

'I suppose you're right,' Tarn conceded, sighing.

She wished very much that she hadn't left Evie's letters in New York. She'd have liked to check how long had elapsed between the first date with Caz, and that delirious weekend alone with him in the depths of the country.

However, it couldn't be much longer before he made his move, she thought, biting her lip. No matter how circumspect and restrained his behaviour towards her, his eyes often told a different story, sending the unequivocal message that he wanted her.

It was moments like that which kept her awake at night, and made her question uneasily whether the shivers that ran through her at the thought of seeing him again were solely caused by apprehension.

If he has this effect on me without even trying, she mused wretchedly, how will I manage when he decides to get serious? If he ever does.

It was a question for which she had to find an answer sooner than she'd thought.

She was on her way down to the art department the following day, when she came face to face with him in an otherwise deserted corridor.

Caz stopped a few feet away from her, and she felt the hungry intensity of his gaze touch her like an electric charge. She stared back at him, aware of the sudden clamour of her pulses, knowing that if she took even a single step forward she would be in his arms.

But Caz stood his ground. Kept his distance. She saw his hands clench into fists at his side and swift colour flare along his cheekbones. He said abruptly, 'Dinner? Friday evening—at my flat?'

The moment of decision had arrived, catching her unprepared and suddenly hesitant.

You don't have to do this, said an urgent voice in her head. *You can take Della's advice, abandon the whole idea and run.*

For a moment, she had to struggle to think of Evie as she'd been on that first visit to The Refuge, but knew she needed to remember the small, broken figure in the bed, with the scared voice who was the reason why she'd embarked on this course of action, and why she had to go on to the inevitably bitter end.

Her mouth was dry. 'Yes,' she said. 'If—if that's what you want.'

'You must know that it is.' He paused, drawing a deep breath. 'I'll send Terry to pick you up at eight.'

She nodded. 'Eight o clock,' she said huskily. 'Yes.'

She moved to one side of the corridor, he to the other, and they continued on their respective ways without saying more.

Tarn however by-passed the art department, heading instead for the women's cloakroom. She went straight to a basin, running the cold tap over her wrists, and wiping her face with a damp paper towel as she waited for her inner tumult to die down a little.

Two days and two nights, she thought, before she could achieve her aim and start the process which would make Caz Brandon the target of the contempt he deserved. He'd feature in some very different headlines before it was all finished.

She leaned against the basin, feeling faintly nauseated as she stared at her reflection in the mirror, face white, eyes glittering like a cat's.

She said under her breath, 'I look like a stranger. Worse than that—like someone I wouldn't want to know. I could even pose for a portrait—Nemesis, goddess of retribution.'

Only a few weeks ago, her life had been in place. Her career was fine, she was enjoying her sojourn in New York and she was in a relationship that might even have become love if she'd given it the chance.

Although at this moment, she found it hard to remember what Howard had looked like, let alone what it had meant to be held, kissed by him.

It seemed as if this thing with Evie had consumed her, leaving room for nothing else.

When it was over, she doubted whether she would return to the States for longer than it took to re-let her apartment and pack the rest of her things.

Maybe she'd take at least some of Della's advice and find a new home somewhere in Europe. France, maybe, or Italy. Or perhaps a Greek island. After all, the nature of her job meant she could work anywhere that she could set up her computer, so why didn't she take full advantage of the fact? Find her real self again in this new beginning.

But it was too soon to be making any decisions about the long-term when it was the immediate future which had to be foremost in her mind.

And right now, the art department was still waiting, so getting back to work was a priority. Time enough afterwards, when she got home, to consider all the implications of Caz's invitation, and how to deal with them.

She had the flat to herself on Friday evening, as Della was spending the weekend at her sister's house in Kent. She'd told her that she and Caz were having dinner but omitted further details, knowing exactly the objections that Della would raise. Knowing that nothing her friend could say would deflect her from her ultimate goal.

Tarn was glad too that she could be nervous without a witness, as she systematically tried on and discarded every dress in her wardrobe, eventually going back to her first choice, a simple wrap-round style in a jade-green silky fabric which clung unashamedly to her slender body.

She used cosmetics with a light hand, darkening her long lashes with mascara, and painting her mouth a soft, clear coral.

Nothing too overt, she told herself as she brushed her hair back from her face and secured it at the nape of her neck with an antique silver clasp.

Her legs were shaking under her as she walked down to the car. She sat huddled into a corner of the rear passenger seat, staring out at the busy London evening with eyes that saw nothing.

She wasn't even aware of the route Terry had taken, rousing herself only when the car drove through a security checkpoint and down a ramp to a private underground car park.

'The lift is here, madam. You press the button marked "P" for the penthouse, and "G" for the garage on your return. Mr Brandon will arrange for me to be waiting for you here by the lift gates.'

If his driver was staying on call, Caz could not be planning a lengthy seduction, she thought, her throat tightening. He must think he had her in the palm of his hand, she told herself, as she forced a smile and murmured her thanks.

She pressed the button and was swept smoothly and swiftly to the top floor of the building. As the lift doors slid open, she saw Caz descending a shallow flight of stairs at the other end of a carpeted corridor.

As he reached her, he said quietly, 'So you're here.'

'I thought you'd asked me.'

'I did. But with you I can never be certain.' He took her hand. 'Come and meet the others.'

Others? Tarn repeated silently, as she walked beside him. That was the last thing she'd expected to hear.

But, as they went up the stairs, she could hear music playing softly and the sound of voices.

She found herself in a vast lamplit room, and confronted by a huge picture window offering sweeping views of London by night.

On the right hand side of the room, two girls in neat black skirts and white blouses were putting the finishing touches to a circular table laid for four and gleaming with silver and crystal.

On the left hand side, three beautifully sculpted sofas upholstered in cream linen had been arranged round a fireplace, illumined by the glow of a gas fire.

All, she thought, exactly as Evie had described.

A tall fair man rose to his feet from one of the sofas, and waited smiling as Caz and Tarn approached. His companion was a dark, pretty girl, whose pale pink wool dress, although beautifully cut, did not completely conceal the fact that she was pregnant.

'Tarn, may I introduce the Donnells, two of my oldest friends. Brendan—Grace—this is Tarn Desmond.'

'It's good to meet you at last.' Brendan Donnell's handshake was firm, his blue eyes dancing. 'God knows, Caz has talked about little else.'

Tarn flushed. 'I'm sure that's an exaggeration.'

'Only a slight one,' said his wife. She patted the sofa. 'Come and sit beside me while Caz gets you a drink. I'm on the orange juice, sadly, although I'll allow myself a glass of wine at dinner, if Bren's not looking.'

Tarn was glad to sit, her mind still reeling from the scuppering of her plan for the evening. Before many minutes had passed, she'd learned that Brendan was managing director of the Lindsmore Investment Group, that they had recently moved out of London to a house in the depths of rural Surrey, and that Grace, currently on maternity leave, had been a corporation lawyer.

'I planned to go back when the baby was born,' she confided. 'But now I'm not so sure. The house needs work and I'm really enjoying getting it all organised. And we have a garden too, with a small orchard, which has always been my dream. I see a total change of career looming.'

She paused. 'What about you, Tarn? Have you always worked on magazines?'

'For much of the time, yes,' Tarn returned evasively.

'And you and Caz met when you were job-hunting,' Grace said musingly. 'Now there's a lucky chance.'

At that moment, Caz returned with the white wine she'd asked for, so she was saved from having to reply and was able to smile rather tautly and thank him instead.

What the hell was he playing at—introducing her to his friends? she raged inwardly. And without a word of warning either so that she couldn't think of an excuse. It seemed out of place as well as out of character. She certainly couldn't remember Evie referring to anyone called Donnell in her letters, or noticed the name in her diary. And could these really be the powerful friends she'd been warned against? That also appeared unlikely. So what was happening? And what had he been saying about her?

But almost before she knew it, she was no longer having to pretend her enjoyment of making a new acquaintance, because it was impossible to harbour resentment over the collapse of her scheming when she was having such a good time.

Certainly the evening she'd planned had never included helpless laughter. Or eating very much for that matter.

Yet the dinner supplied by the very efficient catering company was wonderful too, from the excellent clear soup, through the flavoursome casserole of spring lamb with baby vegetables to the wickedly rich chocolate mousse and splendid cheese board. In spite of herself, Tarn found she was doing the meal full justice.

Also it was clear that Caz had never had any intention of attempting to move their relationship to a more intimate level, because Brendan and Grace were not vanishing when dinner was over, thus leaving them alone together, but apparently spending the night in his spare bedroom.

'I have some baby shopping to do in the morning,' Grace confided. 'So, it's a dual purpose visit.'

And so was mine, thought Tarn bleakly. Finding some way of luring him to disaster.

She let herself back into the empty flat, tossed her bag to one side and sank down on the sofa. The evening had not turned out at all as she expected, or planned for. In fact, a degree of re-thinking was called for.

Because now there were other even more disturbing factors to add to the mix…

The evening had ended pleasantly with coffee and brandy and more conversation on topics ranging from the serious to the frankly frivolous, and she'd experienced real reluctance when she looked at her watch and said that she must go.

'But we'll meet again.' Grace hugged her. 'I'll get Caz to bring you down to the hovel. Are you any kind of a photographer? You could take some before and after pictures—of me and the house,' she added with a giggle.

A nice thought, Tarn acknowledged silently. What a pity it could never happen.

Using her need to 'freshen up' as an excuse, she'd seen the rest of the flat, even managing a look at Caz's bedroom. The bed was indeed vast just as Evie had artlessly confided, and for a moment Tarn had been assailed by a disturbing image of the two of them naked and passionately entwined, Evie surrendering eagerly to every sensual demand that he made of her.

Tarn found herself backing away hastily, shutting her eyes, a little gasp that mingled pain with horror rasping her dry throat.

But thinking of them together was perhaps something she needed to do, she told herself, in order to counteract the unexpected pleasures of the evening, and remind her of the real reason why she'd accepted this invitation.

'So,' Caz said as he walked with her to the lift. 'Am I forgiven?'

She was momentarily startled. 'For what?'

'For changing tonight's rules of engagement.' He shook his head. 'There was a moment as you arrived when you looked as if you were about to face a firing squad.'

'Oh.' She took a breath. 'Well—hardly. Your friends are charming.'

'I'm glad you think so. They were also charmed.' He sent her a frowning glance. 'Yet suddenly here you are at a distance again. Why?'

Her heart missed a beat. 'You—you're imagining things.'

Caz said softly, 'Prove it,' and took her in his arms.

For an instant, his face seemed to swim before her startled eyes, then his mouth came down on hers, and not in the customary fleeting graze of a kiss that she expected either. She'd learned to deal with that, after a fashion. But this time his intentions were clearly very different. He was there to stay.

Her first instinct was to brace her hands against his chest and push him away, because her own intentions were entirely different too. Yet what logical reason did she have to remain aloof? Reason indicated that by now she should at least appear to want to be in his arms, and that any form of resistance might simply lead to him giving up the chase, which would destroy her ultimate objective. Having come so far, could she really risk that?

Besides, in practical terms, the way he was holding her suggested that fighting him would be like trying to push over a brick wall.

Because his lips might still be gentle as they explored hers, but they were also warm and unashamedly determined, and they demanded a response. The desire she'd seen in his eyes had now become a physical reality.

Prove it...

Warning her quite explicitly that he was tired of waiting. That the next step was there to be taken.

In the full and certain consciousness of this, she let her mouth move under his slowly and sweetly, offering him a reply that was shy but willing.

His fingers were tangling in her hair, unfastening the silver clip and letting the scented strands tumble over her shoulders.

He sighed against her mouth and his kiss deepened, his tongue probing her lips, seeking her surrender to a new and disturbing intimacy.

Tarn was not aware of moving, but suddenly her body seemed to sink into his, one hand on his shoulder, the other cupping the nape of his neck as her lips parted for him.

Then, between one heartbeat and the next, she was lost, the scent of him, the taste of him swamping her astonished senses, as her tongue lapped almost frantically against his, and her teeth grazed his mouth in turn.

They swayed together, his hands sliding down to her hips, pulling her even closer. She could feel the hardness of him against her thighs, triggering a sweet drenching surge of longing in her own body, which sent shock waves to her reeling mind by its very intensity.

Caz raised his head, looking down at her, his eyes burning under half-closed lids as he studied her flushed face.

His hand swept the dress from her shoulder, and he bent to kiss her bared skin, his lips tracing the delicacy of her bone structure, before moving down to the lace which shrouded her breast, and closing on the deep rose of her nipple, suckling it with sensuous delight.

Tarn's head fell back and she moaned softly at this unfamiliar mingling of pain and pleasure. Every sense, every nerve-ending she possessed was in turmoil, warning her that if he was to push her back against the wall and take her, she would not be able to deny him.

And suddenly she was more afraid than she'd ever been in her life. More even than of being sent away from Wilmont Road as an unwanted child again. Because she had never felt like this before. Never experienced the blazing force of sheer physical need. The overwhelming urge to be taken and give endlessly in return.

But that would ruin everything. She couldn't jettison her aims for the brief satisfaction of the moment. She had to retrieve the lost ground and resist him. Had to...

'Caz—no.' Her voice was small and husky. 'Stop—please. You—I can't...'

For a breathless moment, she thought her protest was going to be ignored, then, slowly and reluctantly, he straightened.

Taking a deep, steadying breath, he restored her dress to order, then ran a finger down the heated curve of her cheek in a gesture that was as much reassuring as tender.

He said very quietly, 'Are you telling me you don't want me?'

Mutely, she shook her head, knowing it would be useless to attempt to lie.

'Then what is it? Has someone in the past treated you badly—hurt you?'

How can you ask that? she wanted to cry aloud. You of all people? Where was all the gentleness and concern for Evie?

'Tell me, sweetheart, was it this guy in the States?'

'Howard?' It was a struggle now even to remember his name, she thought with shame. 'No, it's nothing like that. Quite the opposite, in fact.' She swallowed. 'It's just that I don't... I haven't—ever...' She stumbled to a halt, staring down at the carpet. 'Ludicrous, isn't it?'

Caz said gravely, 'Do you hear me laughing?' He shook his head. 'My darling, being a virgin isn't some kind of stigma. And, anyway, I should have realised. It explains some of the contradictions I've sensed in you.'

He took her back into his arms, holding her close, his cheek resting on her hair. 'So, at some future time might I be able to persuade you to reconsider your present stance?'

'I don't know.' And that, too, was no more than the truth. 'I—I'm so confused.'

'Then it looks as if I'll just have to go on waiting,' he said. 'And hoping...'

Remembering his words, the wry husky tone of his voice, sent a slow voluptuous whisper of sensation rippling through her body. She found herself remembering his hands—his mouth. Felt her flesh stir—her breathing quicken...

'Oh, God,' she whispered. 'Of all the men in the world, Caz Brandon, why must you be the one to make me feel like this? When you're the one who needs to be driven crazy with unfulfilled desire.'

And knew that in order to defeat him, she faced the fight of her life.

CHAPTER SEVEN

'IT's not fair,' Mrs Griffiths complained fretfully. 'All this talk about human rights, and I can't even see my own daughter.' She gave Tarn a mulish stare. 'It's about time you did something.'

'I have tried.' Tarn made herself speak gently. She'd spent a restless night interspersed with wild and disturbing dreams, then woken very early when the sky was barely streaked with light to discover with shock that her arms were wrapped round her pillow, holding it closely to her body as if it were flesh and blood rather than feathers and down. And realised that she was glad she couldn't remember her dreams in detail.

She'd known from past experience that she would not go back to sleep, yet was unwilling to simply lie there, staring into space, while she reviewed yet again the events of the previous evening and tried to make sense of them. Or rationalise her reaction to them.

Instead, she'd got up, dragged on some track suit bottoms and a T-shirt, and conducted a cleaning blitz on the flat, losing herself in sheer physical hard work.

When she'd finished, the whole place gleamed and she surveyed it with a sense of real satisfaction.

She showered and washed her hair, then, with the faintest hint of gritted teeth, she reminded herself that she almost certainly owed her foster mother a visit and took a bus to Wilmont Road before heading off to the supermarket for the Saturday morning shop.

'But clearly you haven't tried hard enough.' Mrs Griffiths was like a dog with a bone, and not to be put off. 'I need her, and Evie needs me at a time like this. You have to tell those doctors so. You must.'

I can talk to the Professor until I'm blue in the face, but it won't make the slightest difference, Tarn thought, suppressing a sigh. Aloud, she said temperately, 'I'll go down there tomorrow and see what I can do.'

'I've bought her a dress,' Mrs Griffiths said. 'Her favourite turquoise. And I want to give it to her myself. Tell them that. Make it perfectly clear.'

Tarn nodded as she got up from the kitchen table and walked to the door, where she paused as a thought struck her. 'Talking of clothes, what happened to Evie's wedding dress? Is it here somewhere, because there was no sign of it at the flat. I don't want her to ask me about it, and not be able to answer her.'

Aunt Hazel shook her head. 'I don't know, I'm sure. I certainly never saw it. Another of her surprises, poor baby. But when she described it, I wasn't convinced that satin was the wisest choice she could have made.'

'I think that was probably the least of her worries,' Tarn said, then stopped, her brows drawing together in a swift frown. 'Did you say it was satin? I thought—she said in one of her letters that it was cream lace and chiffon.'

'Satin,' said Aunt Hazel. 'And oyster. I think she looked at quite a few before she made up her mind.'

'Yes,' Tarn acknowledged, still frowning. 'I suppose that must be it.'

'And you'll go down to see her. You won't let that Della talk you into doing something else.'

'Della's away this weekend, visiting her family,' Tarn said with faint weariness.

Mrs Griffiths sniffed. 'Well, aren't they the lucky ones. Of course, I should have insisted you stay here instead of moving in with that flighty piece.' She paused, giving Tarn a critical stare. 'As it is, you look as if you've been burning the candle at both ends for a week.'

Tarn bit her lip. 'I simply had a bad night, that's all.'

'Just the same, I expect you slept better than my poor girl, locked away like that,' was Mrs Griffiths' parting shot, accompanying Tarn down the hall to the front door.

What happened to Evie was not my fault, she wanted to shout back. *But I'm doing my damnedest to make amends anyway.*

Instead, she bit her tongue hard and went shopping.

An hour and two heavy bags later, she let herself into the apartment block and walked up the single flight of stairs to the flat. As she reached the landing, a tall figure moved away from the wall he'd been leaning against and came towards her.

'I was just about to leave you a note,' said Caz.

Tarn, aware that her jaw had dropped, hurriedly restored it to its proper level, thankful he could not hear the tattoo that her pulse was drumming.

As she'd pushed her trolley up and down the aisles, she'd been rehearsing what she would say, how she would behave when she next saw him. Now here he was, lithe and attractive in pale chinos and a dark blue shirt, its sleeves rolled back over his tanned forearms, its open neck revealing a dark shadowing of chest hair.

And suddenly her wits seemed to have deserted her.

She said with an assumption of cool, 'And what was the note going to say?'

'It's a lovely day. Let's spend it together.'

'Brief and to the point.' She swallowed past the dryness in her throat. The nervous twist in her stomach. 'But what about your friends?'

'They're going to have a short, sharp shop, then get back to Surrey. Grace tires easily these days.'

'Yes, I suppose she would.' Tarn forced a smile. 'The perils of motherhood.'

His tone was laconic. 'It's reckoned to have its compensations too.' He paused. 'So will you come with me?' He added softly, 'We can treat it as a journey of discovery.'

Tarn hesitated. 'I'll have to put my shopping away.'

'Of course.'

'And change.' She glanced down at her black cut-offs and crisp white blouse, thankful that the track suit and tee of her cleaning marathon had been safely consigned to the laundry basket.

'Unnecessary,' he said. 'What more do you need for a trip to the seaside? Apart from a jacket, maybe.'

This time her smile was genuine if a little startled. 'The coast? That would be lovely.'

'You unpack your groceries,' he said. 'I'll make coffee and we'll argue about whether to go south or east. The Channel or the North Sea.'

She nodded. 'Fine,' and unlocked the door.

'You've been busy,' Caz commented as he followed her into the spotless kitchen.

'I enjoy housework.' Which was just as well, she reflected, as she'd certainly done enough of it when she was living at Wilmont Road. She began to empty the first bag. 'If all else fails I can always apply to the MacNaughton Company for a job.'

'I used them at one time.' Caz filled the kettle, set it to boil and found the cafetière. 'But I'm not sure I'd recommend them. Anyway, who's talking about failure?'

She passed him the fresh pack of coffee she'd just bought, telling herself that Evie must have obtained the paperwork about the cleaning company from him. Something she should have realised. Aloud, she said, 'No-one can predict the future.'

'I can.' He took the coffee from her, and held onto her hand, looking down at the palm and tracing a line with his fingertip. 'And I foresee a long and happy life.'

His touch shivered through her senses as if his hand had stroked her naked body.

She detached herself with a self-conscious laugh. 'I don't believe in fortune telling.'

'Not even when the fortune is being arranged for you?'

'Particularly not then.' She made her tone crisp. Continued putting things away in cupboards. Did not look at him.

'In other words, I'm rushing you into something you're not ready for. *Mea culpa.*' He paused. 'Is that why you looked again as if you were confronting your worst nightmare when you saw me just now?'

'I was just surprised, that's all.' In order to reach the fridge, she would have to get past him, so she put the items for cold storage on one side. 'I—I wasn't expecting to see you so soon.'

The dark brows lifted sardonically. 'Really?' He spooned coffee into the cafetière. 'I thought I'd made my intentions pretty clear.'

Tarn shrugged. 'Perhaps I'm having trouble believing that you have any intentions.'

He gave her a swift grin. 'For someone who doesn't like to be rushed, lady, that sounds suspiciously like a hint for a declaration.'

'No—nothing like that.' Her protest was instant. 'It's just that— Oh, for heaven's sake, everyone knows that you're involved with Ginny Fraser. And how many others before her? How many so-called declarations have there been?'

Tell me about Evie. Offer some explanation—express some compunction for what you've done to her. I'm giving you this chance...

He said quietly, 'I've never pretended I've lived like a Trappist monk while waiting for the right woman to walk into my life. Ginny had her career and I had mine. Our relationship has been—convenient. It is now in the past.'

Consigned to oblivion—like Evie.

She watched him fill the cafetière with boiling water, her

hands curling into fists at her sides. She said, 'But Ginny wasn't the only one. What about the others? What happened to them?'

'You're beginning to make me feel like Bluebeard,' he commented unsmilingly. 'All I can tell you is that I never made any woman a promise I wasn't prepared to keep. And that, my lovely one, will also apply to you.' He paused. 'Now shall we relax a little and discuss how to spend our day?'

In the end, they drove to Whytecliffe, a village on the South coast set on a small bay.

She'd been surprised to find a sleek black convertible two-seater parked a few yards from the apartment block.

'No Terry?' she asked.

'A driver is more convenient on working days. But at weekends, I like to drive myself. And as I said—we're spending the day together.' He slanted a smile at her. 'Don't you trust me to take care of you?'

'Of course.' But, in truth, she wasn't altogether sure. This car looked to have a lot of power under its pared-down lines.

Hood down, they headed out of the city, and Tarn soon realised she hadn't the least cause for concern. He was a terrific driver, positive without being aggressive, treating other road-users with consideration.

'So where are we going?' she asked as they left the suburbs behind.

'It's a surprise.'

And a very pleasant one, she discovered, as they eventually wound their way through narrow lanes with the sea shining in front of them, and reached Whytecliffe.

It was small and sleepy in comparison to other nearby resorts, its harbour catering primarily for private sailing dinghies rather than the fishing smacks of the past, while further round the bay, at the foot of the chalk cliff, a row of brightly painted beach huts stood sentinel over the stretch of sand and pebbles leading down to the sea.

The village itself had a Norman church, and a pleasant main street, partly cobbled, which housed a few shops and cafés. They walked slowly, her hand in his because he'd reached for it and she couldn't think of a solitary reason to deny him, looking into the windows of the various antique shops, as they went and wandering round the small gallery displaying the work of local artists.

There was also a bistro-type restaurant which turned out to be only open in the evenings, but Caz declared that was unimportant and headed for the solitary pub overlooking the breakwater.

'The Smuggler's Chair.' Tarn looked up at the swinging sign above the door. 'That's a strange name.'

'And it goes with a strange story.' Caz had to bend to negotiate the low entrance. He guided Tarn down a tiled passage and through a door with 'Fisherman's Catch' painted on it.

She found herself in a wood panelled room, with old-fashioned settles flanking tables set for lunch, several of which were already occupied.

Caz ordered a white wine spritzer for her and a beer for himself, and they took the remaining table by the window.

The menu was chalked on a board, offering Dover sole, hake, crab and lobster, but they agreed to share the special, a seafood platter served with a mixed green salad and crusty bread.

'So tell me about the Smuggler's Chair,' Tarn said when their order had been given.

'Well, in the bad old days, the village had a reputation for being involved in free-trading,' Caz said. 'And cargoes from France were regularly landed here.

'The leader of the gang used to come here to drink quite openly—apparently he had an eye for the landlord's daughter—and he always sat in the same chair by the fire.

'An informer told the Excisemen who organised a surprise raid. When they burst in, there was this man sitting in the chair with his pipe and his pint pot, just as they'd been told. They ordered him to stay still, but he reached into his coat, and thinking he was going for his pistol, they shot him.

'However, when they searched the body, they found government papers authorising him to compile a secret report on the local free trade. It seems the smugglers had their own informers, and were expecting his visit.

'Which is why, when he arrived at the inn, he was made welcome—and offered the best chair by the parlour fire.'

'Nasty.' Tarn wrinkled her nose. 'What happened to the gang leader?'

Caz shrugged. 'Got away, scot-free, and presumably found somewhere else to drink, complete with some other obliging wench.'

'And the chair?'

'Oh, that's allegedly still here in the other bar, but it seems no-one fancied using it after the shooting in case the Excisemen returned and made a second mistake, so it was always left empty, and the story got around that it was haunted, and that doom and disaster would pursue anyone reckless enough to sit there. Even these days, it's given a wide berth.'

Tarn laughed. 'You surely don't believe that.'

'I heard the story at a very impressionable age,' Caz said solemnly. 'My parents used to rent a house nearby for the holidays. The then landlord used to offer a fiver to anyone who'd take the risk. I gather it's currently gone up to a hundred quid, but still no takers.'

Tarn took a reflective sip of her spritzer. 'It's quite a reward—just for sitting down. I think I might try it.'

Caz put down his glass. 'No.' The negative was sharp and held a note of finality.

'Oh, for heaven's sake,' she said laughing. 'It probably isn't even the same chair.'

'Possibly not,' Caz agreed. 'That doesn't change a thing.'

Tarn gave a provocative whistle. 'Palmistry, now superstition,' she marvelled teasingly. 'I would never have believed it. But you were quite right,' she added. 'This is certainly a voyage of discovery.'

'Nothing of the kind,' he returned. 'If you sit in the smuggler's chair and lightning fails to strike, you've ruined a perfectly good legend forever, and it'll be the landlord's curse you need to watch out for if you spoil his trade.'

'The pragmatic response,' Tarn said lightly. 'I'm disappointed. But I suppose you're right.'

'Besides,' Caz went on thoughtfully. 'Disasters I can well do without.'

'Ah,' she said. 'But I'd be the one to suffer.'

'Not any more,' he said. 'What happens to you, happens to me. That's the way it is, lady.'

Tarn looked down at the table, her heart hammering. *Dear God,* she said silently, *please don't let that work both ways. Not this time.*

The seafood platter was piled high with prawns, mussels, oysters, cockles, spider crabs and crayfish, and came with finger bowls and a pile of paper napkins.

Sharing it with him should have been a problem, an intimacy she could have done without, but in some strange way it was fine, even enjoyable, as if they'd been doing it all their lives.

And, at the same time, it was messy, funny and totally delicious.

Of all the meals we've eaten together, she thought suddenly, this is the one I shall always remember. And stopped right there, because she didn't want any memories of him to take, alone again, into the next chapter of her life. Because she couldn't afford that kind of weakness.

They decided to forego the desserts, choosing instead a pot of good, strong coffee.

'Shall we take a walk along the beach before the tide turns?' Caz suggested, as he paid the bill.

There was flat sand beyond the pebbles and shingle, and the

sea was just a murmur, its surface barely ruffled by the breeze. Tarn drew the clean air deep into her lungs as she lifted her face to the sun, wondering at the same time how things would be if nothing existed but this moment.

'So, tell me what you did in New York.' He spoke softly, but his question brought her sharply back to reality. Because it was clear he expected to be answered.

She shrugged. 'I suppose—pretty much what I do now.'

'Your editor was sorry to lose you.'

'I owe her a lot.' *Especially for that reference.*

'Will the job be waiting for you—if you go back?'

'That or another one. I've rarely been out of work.' She didn't want the interrogation to continue, so she bent, slipping off her loafers. 'I'm going to find out if the sea is as inviting as it looks,' she threw over her shoulder as she headed for the crescent of ripples unfolding on the sand.

'I warn you now—it will be cold,' Caz called after her, amused.

'You can't scare me. I've been to Cape Cod,' she retorted, speeding into a run.

He hadn't been joking, she discovered. The chill made her catch her breath and stand gasping for a moment, but an igno-minious retreat back to the beach was out of the question for all kinds of reasons. So she waded in a little deeper, finding that it grew more bearable with every step, until eventually it bordered on pleasure.

However, it was also bordering on the turn-ups of her linen pants, which was not part of the plan at all, so she opted for discretion over valour and walked slowly back to the shore.

Caz looked at her, shaking his head in mock outrage. 'Crazy woman.'

She lifted her chin. 'Chicken!'

'But not a chicken risking pneumonia. Or with wet feet and no towel.' Before she could stop him, he picked her up in his arms and carried her up the beach, scrunching over the pebbles before setting her down on a large, flat rock. 'I prefer my seas warm, like the Mediterranean or around the Maldives.'

He produced a spotless white handkerchief from a pocket in his chinos and unfolded it. 'I'm afraid this is the best we can do.' He dropped to one knee in front of Tarn and began to dry her feet, slowly, gently and with immense care. 'Like blocks of stone, as my old nanny would have said. Even your nail polish has turned blue.'

Forbidding herself to laugh, she tried to free herself. 'There's no need for this. I can manage—really.'

'Is it the reference to Nanny that's worrying you?' Caz looked up at her, his hazel eyes warm and amused. 'Do you think I'm going to revert to childhood and play "This little piggy"? Or are you afraid I'm a secret foot fetishist seizing his opportunity?'

'It's just—inappropriate,' Tarn managed lamely, aware that some totally foreign instinct was prompting her to wriggle her toes into the palm of his hand, and not just for warmth either.

'Is it?' He was grinning openly now. 'I do hope so. I'd hate to be politically correct at a moment like this.' He traced the delicate bone structure of her slender toes with the tip of a finger. Cupped the softness of her heel. 'They're adorable,' he said softly. 'Maybe these foot fetishists have a point.'

'Caz.' Her voice was husky. 'Don't—please.'

'Why not? Isn't this where women like to see men— kneeling at their feet?'

'I am not "women".' Tarn could feel that betraying heat spreading through her body again. 'And I want to put my shoes on.'

'In a minute. This is a new experience for me, and I like it.' He bent his head and kissed each instep, warmly and lingeringly. 'They taste of salt,' he whispered.

The breath caught in her throat. She said with difficulty, 'People—there are people coming. You must get up.'

Caz shook his head. 'And lose this perfect opportunity? Not

a chance.' He looked up at her, and there was no laughter in his gaze. It was serious and intent. 'Tarn, my sweet, my lovely girl, will you marry me?'

'You—you said you wouldn't rush me.' Her voice was a whisper too.

'I dare not wait,' he said quietly. 'After all, you came out of nowhere. I'm terrified that you may disappear in the same way.'

'No,' she said. 'I—I won't do that. But it's too soon. You must see that.' She spread her hands almost beseechingly. 'We—we hardly know each other.'

'Something I'm seriously trying to redress,' he said. 'Or hadn't you noticed? Sweetheart, we can catch up on the details as we go. But I think I knew from that first moment that you were the one. I guess it was too much to hope that you felt the same.'

He added almost harshly, 'But now that I've found you, Tarn, I can't let you go, and I won't. Not when I love you and want you to be my wife. You and no-one else for the rest of our lives.'

'This isn't fair...'

'I think there's a cliché that covers that—something about love and war.'

But this is war, she cried out silently, from the pain and confusion inside her. *It's just that you don't know it yet.*

Aloud, she said, stumbling over her words, 'I—I have to think. You must give me time. We have to be sure.'

Caz sighed ruefully. 'My darling, I am sure. Now, I just have to convince you. But I'll be patient. I won't even ask if you love me in return. Or not yet.'

He took her loafers and fitted them back on to her feet. 'There you go, Cinderella. They fit. Now you can't turn me down.'

'You may believe you're Prince Charming,' Tarn said, forcing herself somehow to speak lightly as she scrambled up from her rock. Struggling to behave as if the whole world had not

turned upside down. 'But this couple walking their dog probably think you're an escaped lunatic.'

Caz turned towards the elderly man and woman, walking
arm in arm along the beach, their Jack Russell scampering
ahead of them. 'Good afternoon,' he called. 'Isn't this a wonderful day?'

The man looked dubiously at the sky. 'I reckon we've had
the best of it, and it's clouding over for rain. The weather's always treacherous at this time of year.'

Treacherous, thought Tarn. Why had this man, this stranger,
chosen that of all words?

'Darling, you're shivering, and our coats are in the car.' Caz
spoke with compunction. He untied the sweater looped casually around his shoulders. 'Wear this.'

Obediently, Tarn pulled the enveloping softness over her
head, knowing as she did so that the freshening breeze from
the sea was not the problem, and that a dozen layers of cashmere would never be enough to alleviate the icy numbness
building inside her. Possessing her. Making her feel she would
never be warm again.

Oh, God, she thought desperately. What have I done? And
what am I doing? I don't seem to know any more.

Worst of all, I'm not sure I know myself. And that terri-
fies me.

CHAPTER EIGHT

IT WAS a largely silent journey back to London.

Caz was quietly attentive, asking if she was warm enough, or if she'd like to listen to some music. Tarn assented politely to both propositions, hoping that the second option would avoid any more discussion of his plans for their future. However, she declined a further suggestion that they should stop somewhere for tea.

She wanted to get back, she thought, because she needed to think. To work out what to do next. If that was possible.

The CD he picked featured a woman singer she did not recognise, with a deep, almost harsh bluesy voice, whose lyrics were, without exception, a disturbing exploration of love, and all its confusing complexities.

Something else Tarn could well have done without.

She told herself that everything Caz had said to her on the beach was entirely meaningless and just part of a well-worn routine. That he'd probably gone on his knees to Evie in exactly the same way.

Yet, in spite of all that, she could still remember how the look in his eyes had made her breathless and the way his smile had reached out to touch her. Could feel the clasp of his hand round hers as they returned to the car, strong and sure as if he would never let her go, and catch the familiar scent of his cologne on the sweater she was still wearing.

Which, of course, she could return. Disposing of all those other sensations was an entirely different matter.

How, she asked silently, was it possible for him to sound so sincere? To almost make her believe…

She stopped right there. That was not a line she needed to follow.

Although for him to want her had been, of course, an essential part of her plan. She'd intended to rouse him to a fever pitch of unsatisfied desire, before slamming him into limbo, harshly and very publicly. And thanks to Lisa, she'd already worked out the perfect occasion.

'Each June, there's a garden party at a house called Winsleigh Place,' her editor had told her. 'Everyone in the company is invited from the directors to the cleaners and catering staff. Coaches are laid on to take us all there and back, so no-one is tempted to drink and drive. There's a wonderful buffet lunch, with non-stop champagne, and in the evening, a dance, with more glorious food. And Caz provides it all.'

So the entire Brandon ensemble would hear the unpleasant truth about their supposed Lord Bountiful, Tarn had resolved, even as she smiled and said with perfect truth, 'It sounds perfect.'

But today's turn of events had thrown her scheme back into the melting pot. If she refused his proposal, she would have revenge of a sort, but it would be a private matter between the two of them, and she wanted more than that.

On the other hand, if she agreed, then she would almost certainly attend the garden party as his fiancée, and any attempt to discredit him would reflect just as badly on her. People would wonder how she could possibly have become engaged to him, knowing what she did.

And I wouldn't be able to answer them, she thought.

Unless, of course, he intended to keep her under wraps until he was tired of her, as he'd clearly done with Evie. A thought that twisted inside her like a knife.

But even that possibility seemed totally unable to negate any of the feelings towards him that had taken such an astonishing and unwelcome hold on her almost from the beginning, and intensified so alarmingly over the last forty-eight hours.

She felt as if two entirely different women were occupying her skin and fighting for the domination of her mind. And she had to make sure that the right one became the ultimate winner.

Because she could not let herself be beguiled by the sensuous passion of his mouth, or give way to the kind of impulse which had almost led her to stroke the dark silk of his hair as he knelt at her feet.

Nor could she allow herself to forget that, in the end, she'd been saved, not by her own strength of will, but by an amateur weather forecaster with a Jack Russell terrier.

And how shameful was that? she thought bitterly.

Della had once asked how she might have reacted to Caz if they'd simply met as strangers without Evie's involvement, and she'd replied dismissively, defensively.

If she asked me the same question now, she thought, I don't know what I'd say.

When they eventually reached her flat, Caz left the engine running as he turned and gave her a long, steady look. 'I'm not going to ask if I can come up with you,' he said quietly. 'Because I know damned well that I'd try a different kind of persuasion—in bed. And that wouldn't be right or fair.'

She bit her lip. 'Thank you. I want you to know that, whatever happens, you've given me the loveliest day.' She reached for the door handle, and hesitated. 'Oh—your sweater...'

'Keep it,' he said. His smile was faintly crooked. 'It looks far better on you than it ever did on me.' He paused. 'When you've made up your mind, whichever way it goes, call me.'

'Yes.'

'And I don't trust myself to kiss you either, in case you're wondering.'

Her own attempt to smile was a failure. 'You're—very strong-minded.'

'No,' he said. 'It's just that I feel I've put quite enough pressure on you already.' He ran a finger down the curve of her cheek. Touched it briefly to her mouth. 'Promise me we'll talk soon?'

She nodded, dry-mouthed, and left the car.

She didn't watch him drive away. She walked upstairs, aware that her legs were shaking. Fumbled the key into the lock. Closed the door behind her and leaned against it, staring blind-eyed into space, aware of little but the deep, rapid thud of her heart.

She was thankful that she was alone. That she could keep the day's events to herself, without having to offer excuses or explanations, because she could imagine what Della's reaction would be to this latest development.

Eventually, she forced herself to move. To walk to the kitchen and put on a pot of strong coffee to brew, while she took a shower. All sensible measures to dispel the ice which had apparently settled inside her.

But while the shower warmed her, it failed to make her feel any cleaner, so its comfort was, at best, limited, she thought wearily as she dried herself.

Wrapped in her dressing gown, she curled into a corner of the sofa, sipped her scalding coffee and tried to force her teeming brain to focus. She caught sight of her bare feet, and, realising that she was shivering voluptuously at the memories they evoked, hastily tucked them away under the skirts of her robe.

How was it possible, she wondered dazedly, for all that apparent tenderness, all that caring to be only an illusion?

She wished she still had the diary, which might give her some clue as to what to expect next. After all, didn't they say that forewarned was forearmed?

Unless his proposal was simply a ploy to get her into bed. A form of deception Caz hadn't needed with poor Evie, she thought bitterly. But if he thought she was merely playing hard to get, he would soon discover his mistake.

But just suppose that he means it, said a small sly voice in her brain. That, no matter what has happened in the past, you're the one that he truly wants. How do you deal with that?

I tell myself that it doesn't change a thing, she whispered under her breath. *And I keep saying it.*

Because if he was genuine, why didn't he tell me about Evie? Express some remorse for the way he treated her. Why didn't he say, 'Darling, I have something to confess. I was engaged once before to a sweet girl, but it didn't work out, and, although it's over, I know I hurt her terribly, and I shall always regret that.'

But he'd said nothing. Instead he's simply airbrushed her out of his life, she thought. And he could do the same to me. I must not ever let myself forget that.

She tried to divert herself by watching television. One of her favourite films was showing, something so familiar that she could almost repeat the dialogue by heart, but this evening it totally failed to engage her.

The scene on the beach unfolded, frame by frame, over and over again in her mind, eclipsing anything on the screen.

'Oh, to hell with it,' she muttered eventually. 'I'm going to bed.'

Her clothes were still lying on the bedroom floor, and she bent to retrieve them, tossing each item into the basket for laundering. Wondering, as she did so, whether she could ever bear to wear any of them again.

Until, at the bottom of the pile, she came upon Caz's sweater.

For a moment, she stared down at it, then, obeying some incomprehensible primal instinct, she gathered up its soft weight with both hands and held it against her breasts, her throat, her mouth, breathing in the scent of his skin, and drawing it deep into her lungs as if, by this means, she could somehow capture the essence of him and hold it within her forever.

A long, quivering sigh convulsed her body. A sigh of yearning, bewildering her with its strength. A sigh of loss and regret, and she felt her throat muscles tighten painfully as she tasted the first bitterness of tears. A low, animal sound rose from deep inside her and was torn from her parted lips.

And with it came chaos.

She sank down on to the carpet, still clutching the bundle of cashmere and pressing it to her face as if she hoped it could somehow staunch the tears that were pouring down her face, or silence the harsh, gasping sobs that were suddenly ripping her apart.

She seemed incapable of movement or even coherent thought as she crouched there, her body shaking uncontrollably.

I want him. I love him. Oh, God forgive me, I love him so much...

The words, unbelievable, unutterable, ran crazily through her head, piercing her with their shame.

When at long last there were no tears left, and her throat was aching with dry sobs, she got clumsily to her feet. She shed her robe and climbed naked into bed, spreading the damp sweater across her pillow and pressing her cheek against it. Knowing that it might be all she would ever have of him.

'From that first moment...'

His words, and she could see now that they were as true for her as he'd claimed they were for him. That she'd gone to the reception looking only to avenge Evie and come away with her mind in turmoil, no matter how much she might have tried to deny it.

She could recognise now that she'd been in one form of denial or another ever since.

Something which had to stop right here. Because there were choices to be made, and she would need a clear head to make them, she thought as she closed her eyes and allowed herself to sink down into the mattress. Aware that very soon her physical and emotional exhaustion would take her over the edge into temporary oblivion, and let sleep work its magic.

* * *

She woke the next morning feeling calm and strangely empty, but knowing exactly what she had to do.

She would visit Evie at The Refuge that afternoon, no matter what obstacles were put in her way, and break the news to her that she had changed her mind and abandoned the planned revenge. At the same time, she would also tell her that she was leaving Britain, probably for good, and returning to her own life.

Because Della had been completely right, of course, she told herself. She had no obligation to drop everything and run to their aid whenever Aunt Hazel or Evie sent out an SOS. As it was, her intervention, however well-meant, had led to her own heartbreak, and she would need time and distance for the healing process to begin.

Evie, too, was receiving the best treatment and would also recover. And both she and her mother would eventually learn to stand on their own feet too.

I've done them no favours by encouraging their dependency, she thought.

Ironically, it was Caz himself who had shown her the only solution to this maze of lies and unhappiness she was embroiled in. After all, he'd said yesterday that she'd come out of nowhere and might vanish in the same way.

And that was precisely her intention. To depart without trace. To find somewhere else to live and sink back into her work. To start over, a chameleon, invisible in her surroundings.

A clean break, she resolved, removing the necessity for any tortuous and impossible explanations which would not reflect credit on either Caz or herself. 'Least said, soonest mended,' she thought wryly, and all the other comforting clichés, which were no comfort at all.

And if, at the moment, the break felt more like an amputation, she knew that once the numbness had worn off, the pain would start in earnest.

But maybe she could arrange to be long gone by then.

And in the meantime, ordinary life pursued its prosaic path.

She showered, dressed, and breakfasted on toast and coffee before making a bacon and sweetcorn quiche for Della's return at suppertime, just as she'd intended to do before her life skidded sideways to disaster.

She had also determined to return Evie's engagement ring anonymously to Caz. A padded envelope with a London postmark would give no clues. It was a reminder of unhappiness that the younger girl didn't need, she thought as she looked down at the cold glitter of the stones, as well as an awful warning of how easy it was to be dazzled into believing the improbable.

A danger that she herself was avoiding by a whisker.

While Caz—he can hand it on to the next lady who takes his fancy, she thought sinking her teeth into her lower lip, as she closed the box.

Professor Wainwright regarded Tarn with open disfavour. 'I thought we had an agreement, young lady. No visits without a prior appointment.'

'Yes,' she said. 'But I really do need to see her.'

'You are not the only one. Her visiting time today is already reserved.'

'I could wait...'

'Miss Griffiths may well find the experience—unsettling, and will need to rest.' He looked at his computer screen. 'Perhaps next week.'

'That's too late. I may not be here.' She paused. 'Please, Professor. I must at least be allowed to say goodbye to Evie.'

'But not today.' His tone was final. He began to put papers into a file. 'Now you must excuse me. I have a meeting.'

'Is there really no other time for me to see her?'

He sighed, and looked back at the screen. 'Tomorrow afternoon might be a possibility.'

'Yes,' she said. 'I'll come tomorrow.'

'But telephone first,' he cautioned. 'Her condition will need to be carefully assessed.'

'Very well,' Tarn said tonelessly, and rose.

'Miss Griffiths.' She was halfway to the door when his voice halted her. 'Since our last meeting have you told anyone of Evelyn's whereabouts? Mentioned it inadvertently in conversation, perhaps?'

Tarn frowned. 'No, of course not.'

'Then there must be some other explanation.' He gave a brisk nod. 'I regret you've had another wasted journey.'

'Not really wasted,' she returned. 'Because I shall see Evie tomorrow.'

She could have walked back to the Parkway, but when she got to the main door, an elderly couple were paying off the station taxi, so she decided to ride there instead.

She had just settled herself into a corner of the back seat when another car came up the drive and stopped in a swirl of gravel.

More visitors, thought Tarn. And aren't they the lucky ones?

Then she saw the driver emerge and walk round to the rear passenger door, and stiffened incredulously.

Because she knew him. And the car. Knew, as well, with sick foreboding, exactly who his passenger must be.

She shrank back in her seat, every nerve-ending jangling, and pressed a clenched fist against her lips, stifling any hint of shocked and aching sound, as Caz got out and stood for a moment in the sunlight, clearly giving Terry instructions.

He was back to formality today, in a dark suit, and even carrying a brief case.

Legal documents? Papers for Evie to sign, enjoining her silence? Drawing a line under the past so he could look to the future with a free mind?

How can he? she whispered silently. *Oh, God, how can he do this to her? Force himself back into her life when she's trying to recover from the way he treated her. When what she needs more than anything is to wipe him from her memory forever.*

And I—how could I possibly have forgotten what he was and let myself be tempted by him, even for a moment?

She felt physically ill as she watched him walk up the steps and disappear inside the building. She hadn't been allowed in, Aunt Hazel was still barred, yet Caz, the man responsible for Evie's pitiful condition, as the staff must know, was apparently allowed unrestricted access. It made no sense. It defied reason.

'Unsettling' might have been Professor Wainwright's word for Caz's visit, but Tarn could think of so many others that were far more apposite. 'Cruel' for one, she told herself as her taxi moved off. 'Monstrous' for another. And, ahead of them all, 'Unforgivable'.

Because that changed everything. It had to.

I was going to leave her, she castigated herself, gazing at the passing hedgerows with eyes that saw nothing. Abandon her to the mercy of someone who plays games with women's hearts and minds in order to save myself.

But she's not a survivor as past events have proved. And I am. So I'm going to stay and keep my promise, no matter what the cost. There'll be no unfinished business on my watch.

'My mother sends her love,' Della announced exuberantly as she tucked into the quiche. 'Also a Dundee cake, which we could have for afters.'

'Your mother's a saint.'

Della gave her a shrewd look. 'And how are your equally sanctified relatives?' she queried. 'I ask because you're looking a little worn round the edges, my pet.'

'Nonsense.' Tarn managed an approximation of a cheerful grin. 'All's well.' She'd already decided to say nothing about the day's revelations, telling herself it would solve no useful purpose.

'If you say so.' Della took more salad. 'And the publishing tycoon? Seen much of him lately?'

'Why, yes,' Tarn said lightly. 'We drove down to the coast yesterday.'

'Indeed?' Della raised her eyebrows. 'Well, I can only hope you know what you're doing.'

'Oh, I do,' Tarn said with quiet emphasis. 'I've never been so sure of anything in my life.'

'Fine,' Della said equably. 'Then there's no need for me to remind you of the old saying that it's much easier to ride a tiger than it is to dismount?'

'None at all.'

'Then I won't mention it.' She waved a fork. 'The cake, by the way, is in that tin over there.'

They spent a companionable evening watching television and chatting on a variety of deliberately non-taboo subjects, but Tarn was conscious there was a distance between them and regretted it.

But Evie had to matter more, she told herself.

She went to work as usual the next day, but just before noon complained of a severe headache and said she was going home to drawn curtains and painkillers.

She arrived at The Refuge prepared to do battle, but it was unnecessary. The nurse she had met previously took her straight to Evie's room.

'How is she?' Tarn asked, and the other woman pulled a face.

'Yesterday did her no good at all, but it couldn't be avoided, and it probably won't be the last time. But it may cheer her up to see a friendly face.'

Evie was crouched in her chair, wan and red-eyed, nursing a box of tissues.

'Tarn.' She straightened. 'Oh, Tarn, it's been so awful. I'm so scared. You have to do something. You have to keep him away from me.'

'Yes.' Tarn pulled the other chair up beside her, and sat, taking her hand. 'I'll do my best, I promise, so try not to think about it. About him.'

'I thought I was safe here.' Evie swallowed. 'That he wouldn't know where I was.' Her voice rose slightly. 'I wasn't going to tell anyone about him—what he did. Truly I wasn't. He ought to know that. He seemed so kind, as if he wanted to look after me. I never realised what he was really like.'

'No, of course not,' Tarn said gently. 'Why should you?'

After all, I knew, she thought, and it made no difference. I still wanted him in spite of everything. So how can I blame you when I really ought to be disgusted with myself?

Tarn dragged herself back to the here and now. 'Evie—what actually happened yesterday? What was said?'

'I can't talk about it. I'm not allowed to. And, anyway, I'm sick of questions. I won't answer any more.' She began to cry weakly. 'I just want to get out of here. I know I've been a fool, but I don't see why I should go on being punished like this. You have to do something, Tarn. You have to take me home.'

Easier said than done, Tarn thought as she sat on the train back to London. Evie had continued in much the same vein for the entire visit, alternating recrimination with bouts of self-pity. Tarn had done her best to make her think more positively about the future, talking of new jobs and a possible holiday in the sun, and being careful not to mention Caz by name, but her foster sister had just stared at her, wounded, and told her she didn't understand.

It was almost a relief when the nurse appeared and said that visiting time was up.

'I'll deal with him, Evie,' Tarn said softly, as she rose to her feet. 'When I've finished, he won't bother you again.'

'And tell them I won't answer any more questions,' Evie called after her, her voice sullen.

I won't be telling 'them' anything, thought Tarn. Whoever 'they' were.

She sighed to herself. If she was honest, she could see no prospect of an early release for Evie. From what the younger girl had said, she was still confined to her room. Yet the other residents seemed to move round the house and gardens easily enough, under the watchful eyes of the staff, and the big board in the hall was crammed with notices about the various activity groups on offer. Surely joining with other people and finding new interests would contribute towards Evie's rehabilitation.

Whereas being made to confront her erstwhile fiancé would not. Especially as it seemed he might be exerting pressure on her to keep quiet about their relationship. And what were these so-called experts like the Professor thinking of to allow it?

Couldn't Caz see the state she was in? Tarn railed inwardly. Did he truly have no compassion or sense of guilt over the havoc he'd created in the life of someone who'd simply been too trusting and gullible for her own good?

And how, she asked herself almost helplessly, is it possible for him to be so different with me? Unless, of course, he's simply biding his time. Waiting until he's tired of me too.

And felt her whole body clench, as if warding off unbearable pain.

As she walked into the flat, the telephone was ringing.

'I heard you'd gone home sick,' Caz said. 'I was worried.'

Tarn took a deep breath. Steadied her voice. 'It was just a headache. It's gone now.'

'Then would you be free for dinner tonight—if I promise not to mention anything stressful?' There was a smile in his voice.

Tarn had the strange sensation that she was teetering on the edge of an abyss.

But it's not too late, she told herself desperately. Even now she could save herself. Step back to safety or…

Instead, she heard herself say huskily, 'I'd love to have dinner with you, Caz. And we can talk about anything you want.'

And threw herself into the waiting void.

CHAPTER NINE

HE TOOK her to the Trattoria Giuliana, as he said, 'For old times' sake.' They even had the same table as before.

As they sat down, he looked at her, his smile faintly rueful. 'Or am I being overly sentimental?'

'No,' she said. 'It's a lovely idea. I always hoped we'd come back here sometime.'

'Then why not make it a regular date,' he said, the hazel eyes caressing her. 'For the rest of our lives.' Then checked. 'But perhaps I'm being too optimistic. After all, I haven't had your answer yet.'

Tarn stared down at the tablecloth. 'I think you know what I'm going to say already.' And wondered how she could possibly sound so quiet and steady with the maelstrom of emotions raging within her.

'Or else you wouldn't be with me tonight?'

'Maybe,' she said. 'But I suppose I could be coy, and say I was still making up my mind.'

'You could.' His hand reached for hers across the table. 'But you won't. Will you?'

'No,' she said. 'I won't.' In spite of herself, the warm clasp of his fingers round hers was sending tendrils of sensation throughout her entire being. She paused, looking at him, and allowing her lips to part a little as if she was breathless. Except, she realised with shame, she did not have to pretend, because his lightest touch could do that to her. 'I—I will marry you, Caz. If you still want me.'

He said softly, 'More than I've ever wanted anything, my darling.' He signalled, and a beaming waiter arrived with champagne.

'My goodness.' She managed a laugh. 'You really were sure of yourself.'

'Not in the slightest.' He studied her for a moment, his expression quizzical. 'There's an elusiveness about you, Tarn. As I've said, I sensed it from the beginning. I'm wondering if it might not be wise to chain you to my wrist until we're safely married.'

He was too damned perceptive by half, Tarn thought. She raised her eyebrows. 'You regard marriage as safety? I thought it was an act of faith—a step into the dark.'

'Not for us.' He raised his glass. 'Here's to forever.'

He sounded so certain—so bloody sincere, she told herself as she responded to the toast and sipped her champagne. A man any girl would be glad to trust with her future. Unless, of course, she had the memory of Evie, cowering in her chair, to warn her and harden her heart against him. And she would need that every hour of every day.

Caz reached into an inside pocket and produced a small velvet box. He said, 'At the risk of seeming presumptuous, I brought you this.'

As he opened it, Tarn stiffened, expecting to be dazzled by another showy blaze of diamonds. But she was wrong. The diamonds in this ring were gleaming in discreet brilliance around an exquisite square sapphire in an antique gold setting.

The gasp that escaped her was of genuine wonder and delight. 'Oh—it's beautiful.'

'I'd hoped you'd like it,' he said. 'It's been in the family for a long time, and my grandmother gave it to me for this very occasion. It might have to be made smaller, of course. You have very slim hands.'

'No,' she said, dry-mouthed as he slid the ring on to her finger. 'It—it's quite perfect.'

'You're absolutely sure? It occurred to me you might prefer to keep this as a dress ring and have something modern for our engagement—a special design, maybe.'

She covered it protectively with her other hand. 'You couldn't give me anything lovelier.' Her response was instinctive—genuine. Because this could—should have been the happiest moment of her life, she thought with bewilderment. Yet, instead, she felt as if she was dying inside.

Judas, she said silently, *reborn as a woman.*

She took a deep breath. 'But I can't wear it, Caz. Not yet. Not in public.'

His brows snapped together in a frown. 'What are you talking about? Why the hell not?'

'Because I have a job to do,' she said steadily. 'Working for you in a section of one of your companies. That means a lot to me, and I don't want it to change, and it will, once word gets out about us.'

She forced a smile. 'Besides, when the news does break, it's bound to be a nine-day wonder, and I'm not sure I'm totally prepared for that. The fuss—the attention—stories in the papers. That's a lot to take on board—for me. So, can't we keep it as our secret—just for a while?'

'Now there we differ,' he said gently. 'Because I want to shout it from the rooftops. Tell the whole world what a lucky bastard I am.'

Tarn said with constraint, 'Are you certain that's what the whole world wants to hear?'

'Ah,' he said. 'I suppose we're back to Ginny again.' He took her hand again. 'My darling, the past doesn't matter.' His voice was warm and urgent. 'We can't let it—not when we have the future.'

And Evie? If she's part of your immaterial past too, why are you still harassing her? Why can't you leave her alone?

Now, if ever, was the time to ask these things. To come at him like a bolt from the blue and shock him, perhaps, into honesty. Even into contrition.

Before she walked away...

So why was she hesitating?

After all, she wanted to humiliate him. To let him know at first hand what it was like to be made a fool of and dumped. But a half-full restaurant on a Monday evening was not the public arena for the major victory she'd envisaged.

Better to bide her time, she thought, her throat tightening. Wait for the right moment and the maximum impact.

He said, 'You're doing it again, my love. Disappearing into some world where I can't follow.'

'Not really,' she said lightly, and paused. 'It's just that there's suddenly a lot to think about.'

'Then maybe we should start sharing some thoughts now,' he said. 'Do you want a big wedding?'

'Oh, no.' The negation was involuntary, and she'd have said exactly the same if this had been the beginning of their future, and the ceremony was to be a reality.

'You're very sure,' he commented, with faint amusement. 'I thought all women dreamed of floating down the aisle, wearing the obligatory meringue, in a country church crammed with well-wishers.'

Tarn wrinkled her nose. 'That's part of the problem. I'd have difficulty filling a pew.'

Caz pulled a face. 'And I know far too many people who would expect to be there, whether we wanted them or not,' he said. 'And someone I do want who, sadly, can't be there. So, why don't we do it quietly at a friendly neighbourhood register office? Will your cousin be well enough to act as one of the witnesses?'

Her heart skipped a beat. 'Well—no. At least she's not around,' she added hurriedly. 'She's gone away to convalesce. She needs absolute quiet, so she'll be gone for some time.'

Which at least was the truth.

'Your flatmate?'

She shook her head. 'She's away a lot. I'm not sure of her plans.'

'I see.' Caz was silent for a moment. 'Well, we could ask Brendan and Grace instead. I think you liked them when you met.'

'Yes,' said Tarn, despising herself for her faint feeling of desolation. 'Yes, I did.'

'And when the news of the wedding does get out, we shall have left on our honeymoon,' he went on. 'So we shall miss all the razzmatazz. And by the time we come back, everyone will be used to the idea. So it's a win-win situation for us.'

No, she thought. It will be a very different kind of victory. And you will be the loser. But she had no sense of triumph. Instead she felt as if everything within her had become a cold, aching hollow.

The food and wine were delicious, but, for Tarn, they might have been bread and water. Her energy and attention were fixed, as they had to be, on this new role she had to play—the happy and loving fiancée.

And, of course, on never letting herself forget that it was just a role. That it could never be anything else no matter what she might want or feel in her inmost being.

Because all that had to be suppressed. Pushed out of sight, and eventually—please, God—out of mind. No more walking round the flat with her arms wrapped round her body, damming back the pain. No more tears, even if she could manage to weep silently.

He said, 'You're very quiet,' and she looked at him, startled.

'I think I'm just stunned.' She made herself smile. 'It's been a hell of a forty-eight hours, and it takes some getting used to.'

'For me too, believe it or not.' He paused. 'What we need is some time alone and in private. Let's get out of here and have our coffee elsewhere.'

'But Della's at the flat...'

'Darling, I meant my place, not yours.' He smiled at her. 'Besides, it will give you the chance to have a good look round and tell me what you'd like to change.'

'Change?'

And I have seen it—all of it—the other night. And imagined you there with Evie...

'Of course. You're bound to have some ideas about your future home.' His grin was teasing. 'I'd be disappointed if you didn't.'

'Your flat,' Tarn said slowly. 'You'd want us to live there. I—I didn't realise.' One of many things she hadn't taken into account, she thought. The way he already had their lives mapped out in this straight and shining path. But she couldn't turn back now. She had to go on. Had to...

'I thought—to begin with at least,' he said. 'While we decide where and what our permanent home should be.' He gave her a searching look. 'You're not keen?'

'I hardly know.' She searched for an excuse. 'It's just that everything's moving so fast...'

'Not for me,' Caz said softly. 'Given the chance, I'd get a special licence and carry you off this week.'

She forced a smile. 'I think you'll have to be patient with me.'

'I can do patient.' His tone was rueful. 'Although I may struggle a bit.' He took her hand again. 'You'll have to make allowances too, my sweet. Promise?'

'Yes,' Tarn said and hated herself.

She stood in the centre of that vast living room, trying not to shiver as Caz took her wrap from her shoulders and tossed it over the arm of a sofa before discarding his own jacket.

'What do you want to see first?' His voice was teasing. 'The kitchen? After all, there's coffee to be made.'

She eased away from him. 'I think you can manage that perfectly well without my interference.'

'Then start the tour without me.' He slanted a grin at her as he headed off. 'I'll be asking questions later.'

She'd noticed the big vibrant canvases that hung on the pale walls during her previous visit, but tonight there were no friends or caterers to provide a distraction—or to act as a barrier, said a warning voice in her head—so she had time to look around properly—examine the pictures at her leisure.

Like Evie, she was no expert, but she could see they deserved attention, their colours and textures drawing the eye and invading the imagination, their effect enhanced by careful lighting.

But there were other, homelier touches too. She noticed some charming ceramics, not old enough to be valuable, on a table and walked over to look at a group of photographs on top of a bookcase. Her gaze travelled from a couple, not young, standing smiling in the sunlight in front of a wall, draped in wisteria, to some children on a beach with a black Labrador, and, lastly, standing by an elegant fireplace, an elderly woman whose white hair belied the command of a strong but beautiful face.

Looking down at the sapphire ring, Tarn wondered if this was the grandmother who'd planned for his marriage.

I'm sorry. She sent the message out into the ether. I'm so sorry, and I'm glad you can't know what's going to happen.

When Caz returned with the coffee, she was standing at the window, staring at the lamplit panorama.

'At sunset, it's truly spectacular.' He set down the tray. 'Come and sit down. Can I offer you some brandy?'

'Better not.' She kept her tone light. 'My head's whirling quite enough, I think.'

She took her place next to him and accepted the cup he handed to her, breathing the coffee's rich, heady aroma.

She said, 'I've been admiring your pictures.' She paused,

adding deliberately, 'You'll have to teach me what they're all about.'

He gave a rueful shrug. 'I have a mate called Adam who'd be a far better instructor. My choices are instinctive rather than informed, and he says I've been damned lucky not to have been taken for a ride so far. When you meet him, ask him anything you want to know.'

'But I understood you were a connoisseur.' She could not hide her surprise.

Caz's mouth twisted. 'Well, I can't imagine where you heard that, flattering though it may be.' He added, 'And I hope you're not disappointed, now you know the truth.'

'No,' she said quickly. 'Not a bit. Besides, your method is probably better than picking something that ticks a lot of boxes with art critics. And I'd rather hear why you chose them.'

'Let's save that for some long winter evening,' he suggested softly. 'We have other things to discuss tonight.'

Her heartbeat quickened. 'Yes—of course.'

'For one thing, you need to see the rest of the place, including the kitchen, even if I couldn't tempt you in there just now.' He paused, putting down his cup. 'My God,' he said. 'I never thought to ask. You can cook, I suppose.'

'Now there's a male chauvinist question.' Her glance held mock reproof. 'If I say no, will you want your ring back?'

'Far from it,' Caz said cheerfully. 'I'm not looking for a domestic slave. If necessary, I'll simply get the meals myself.' He paused. 'But I admit it would be nicer if it was a joint affair.'

'Much nicer,' she said. 'And I may as well confess right now that I love cooking.'

'Excellent.' He took her cup from her hand and set it down, then moved closer, sliding his arms round her and pulling her against him. 'And as love has been mentioned,' he murmured. 'Now might also be a good time for you to tell me how you feel about me.'

'I thought I'd already made that clear.' Her voice shook a

little as the warmth of him, the scent of his skin began at once to work their dark, insidious magic.

'All the same, my darling, I need to hear you say it.' He pushed back her hair from her face, letting his lips graze her temple. 'Would it be so very difficult?'

You don't know. Oh, God, you just don't know...

But at least, for once, she could speak the truth without evasion.

For this moment, she thought, just for this moment.

She said quietly, 'I love you, Caz. I think I did from the first, only I couldn't—I didn't want to admit it when there were so many reasons not to. So many reasons for me to keep my distance.

'But now it's said and I can tell you that I shall go on loving you for the rest of my life.'

The truth, the whole truth and nothing but the truth...

Heaven help me, she thought.

He said hoarsely, 'Oh, God, Tarn, my sweet, wonderful girl.'

He began to kiss her, gently at first, then with increased passion, his mouth moving on hers in urgent sensuous demand.

And Tarn responded, eagerly, helplessly, her arms around his neck, her breasts crushed against his chest, as her lips parted for him.

Just for this moment.

A moment when nothing else in the world existed but the sweet draining delight of his kisses. She found herself sighing her pleasure into his mouth, arching towards him as she felt the first heated explicit thrust of his tongue and offered him an equally candid response in her turn, clinging to him, drinking from the shared moisture of their mouths.

She smiled as she experienced the warmth of his lips caressing her closed eyes, the curve of her cheek, and the crazy throb of the pulse in her throat.

Caz pushed her back against the softness of the cushions, his hands moving slowly but very surely, skimming the delicate line of her shoulders, then sliding down to cup her breasts and stroke them gently through the silky top she was wearing, coaxing her nipples to rise to hard, aching peaks under the passionate certainty of his touch.

Tarn gasped, her head thrown back, her whole being consumed by the long, delicious shivers that were running through her, inspiring her to let her fingers in their turn begin their own exploration—discover the taut muscularity of his back and trace the long supple spine through his fine linen shirt.

To feel the heat of his body as it pressed on hers, and find it echoed in the giddy rush of her own blood stream, and in the deep, inner trembling of her ungiven flesh as she encountered the hardness of his arousal against her slender thighs.

The thin layers of cloth that separated them seemed suddenly too great a barrier. With a kind of desperation, Tarn wanted to be naked in his arms. Naked with him. To find herself at last possessed and know the rapture of his body sheathed in hers.

To understand why she had made herself wait all this time.

Just for this moment. Just for this man. Whom she could not have...

He was kissing her again, slowly, deeply, and she cried out softly in longing and despair, her voice breaking as she whispered his name against his mouth.

'My angel.' His voice was hoarse, his hand heavy on her bare thigh where he'd pushed her skirt aside. 'Tarn—stay with me tonight, darling—please. Give yourself to me.'

All she need do was remain silent and he would lift her and carry her to his room. And to the bed he'd shared with Evie...

It was that realisation that, somehow, forced her to clutch at her reeling sanity. Made her find the words that would save her. 'I—I can't.' She stared up into his eyes, lambent with desire. 'You—you said you wouldn't pressure me. You promised...'

'I did,' Caz said quietly after a pause. 'And I meant it. But I'm only human, my sweet, so you can't blame me for trying.'

He sat up, pushing his hair back from his sweat-dampened forehead while Tarn ordered her dishevelled clothing with unsteady hands.

She said, stumbling a little, 'Are you angry with me?'

'No,' he said gently. 'Why would I be? I want you very much, Tarn, but it has to be mutual.' He added ruefully, 'And for a few moments there, I thought it was.'

'It was.' Her voice shook. 'It is. You must believe that.' She hesitated. 'It's just—being here—in your flat. I don't know how to explain.' She swallowed. 'I can only say that it has—connections that I can't forget—and never will.'

Ask me, she thought. Ask me exactly what I mean and I'll tell you, so that I can put a stop to the whole thing once and for all. Because I can't bear to go on like this. It's ripping me in pieces.

'Ah.' He was silent for a moment, then sighed. 'I must be extraordinarily insensitive, my darling, because it truly never occurred to me that my bachelor indiscretions would come back to haunt me in this particular way.'

He took her back into his arms. 'But if that's how you feel, so be it.' His lips brushed her hair. 'You don't have to live here, sweetheart, or even spend one solitary night with me. I'll put this place on the market, and we'll find somewhere else—somewhere new, with no connotations from the past whatsoever. We can start looking this week.'

'You'd do that for me?' She turned her face into his shoulder.

'That and far more,' he said. 'How many times must I say it?' He paused. 'Tarn, I wish I knew what had happened in your life to make you so reluctant to trust me. Will you tell me—one day?'

'Yes.' Her voice was muffled. She was thankful she didn't have to look into his eyes. 'Yes—one day.'

When Tarn got back to the flat, she found Della curled up on the living room sofa in her dressing gown.

'Oh, hi.' Tarn checked in surprise. 'I thought you'd be asleep.'

'No.' Della rose to her feet. 'I had things on my mind, and I wanted to talk to you.' She took a breath. 'Tarn, are you engaged to Caspar Brandon?'

Tarn's lips parted in a gasp of shock. But she can't know that, she thought. Not possibly.

She said with perfect truth, 'I—I don't understand.'

'Nor do I—but I found this.' Della produced Evie's ring box from her pocket. 'It was on the sideboard and—well, I'm afraid I had a look inside. I had no right to do that, and you've every reason to be angry with me.

'But I want you to know that whatever you've said about him—everything you've believed is absolutely true. He is a love rat and a cheat, and this proves it. So please tell me that if you are engaged to him, it's for you own purposes and not because you've also been taken in by his charm and his lies.'

'Dell, slow down.' Tarn's head was whirling. 'What on earth are you talking about? That's Evie's engagement ring. Her diamonds, not mine.'

Della snorted. 'Diamonds be damned. They're cubic zirconia. Pretty to look at but worth a fraction of the real thing.' She shook her head. 'I admit I had my doubts about Evie because I've always considered her a total flake. But Caz Brandon is far worse. A bigger fake than his so-called diamonds.'

She sighed before continuing. 'I know I was against what you were planning, but you were right, and I was wrong. He dazzled that poor silly girl into his bed and dumped her when he was tired of her. And I've discovered something else. That place she's been locked up in—well, he's on the board of trustees. That's why it's so difficult for you to see her and talk to her. Because he put her there, conveniently out of his way.'

Tarn stared at her, the beat of her heart slamming slowly and heavily against her ribcage. She said in a whisper, 'Are you—quite sure?'

'I looked him up on line—not the social stuff—but the directorships and other connections outside his publishing empire, and found it. Then I checked back with The Refuge to make sure. Not just a trustee but listed as a benefactor. With his sort of money, you can get away with anything.'

Della took a deep breath. 'But I'm here now to say that he deserves everything that's coming to him, and if I can help you bring him down, I will.'

Tarn took the little box from her outstretched hand and opened it slowly, staring down at the icy glitter of the stones. Wondering how she could have been so deceived. Why she too hadn't recognised at once that they were not real diamonds.

But nothing about his relationship with Evie had been true, she thought. And he dared ask me to trust him...

Pain twisted to agony inside her as she re-lived the memory of being in his arms. He chooses his bait according to his victim, she thought. With Evie, it was all glamour and the high life. But with me, it was sex.

And I so nearly fell for it—for all the well-worn technique he's practised over the years. How could I have been so weak—so stupid?

She said, her voice harsh, 'I disliked this ring from the moment I saw it. It was too big, too showy, but I told myself that at least it seemed to prove that he'd really cared for her once.

'And even though I was wrong about that, I'll make sure that he cares eventually. That he'll regret to his dying day what he did to Evie.'

And for myself, she added silently. How much will I be left to regret—and for how long?

And knew that, in spite of everything, her regrets could last for the rest of her life.

CHAPTER TEN

THINGS, Tarn told herself, were moving altogether too far and too fast, as if she was a novice skier caught heading downwards on a black run.

Her first shock had been the sale of Caz's flat less than a week after it had gone on the market.

'There were four offers,' he told her that evening, with a tinge of ruefulness. 'Even the agents were surprised.'

'Well—it's a beautiful flat,' Tarn returned, glancing around her, and suppressing a slight pang of her own.

But she couldn't weaken now, she thought. He deserved to lose it. To know what it was like to be left with nothing.

'But sadly not beautiful enough to tempt you to forget my bachelor sins and stay here.' Caz lifted her on to his knee and held her close, his lips against her hair. 'Now we have to find somewhere for ourselves alone.'

The next shock had been to find herself being escorted round a whole series of the kind of properties she'd only ever imagined in her dreams and having constantly to remind herself that dreams were all they could remain.

She'd envisaged Caz becoming bored and possibly irritated at being involved in an endless quest which he must regard as unnecessary, but, however contrary her behaviour, and she remained consistently hard to please, his patience and good humour remained constant.

And their shared sense of the ridiculous provided her with

some awkward moments when his sardonic sideways glance when the agent was happily eulogising some terrible interior design excess almost reduced her to helpless giggles.

'It's lovely,' Tarn admitted, after they'd left yet another glamorous penthouse and returned to Caz's flat. 'But it's just a showcase. I bet no-one's so much as chopped an onion in that kitchen. And do we really need a hot tub in the roof garden?'

Caz took her in his arms and kissed her slowly and thoroughly. 'A shower big enough to share is quite enough for me,' he whispered. 'Maybe we should ruin the Realtor's day and ask to see rather simpler properties from now on.' He gave her a long look. 'And the sooner the better. You're beginning to look a little tense, my sweet. Is the pre-wedding pressure getting to you?'

If he only knew, thought Tarn, remembering the nights when she'd walked the floor unable to sleep, her mind trying feverishly to detach itself from recent memories of sitting curled up beside him on the sofa, watching television or listening to music together.

Reminding herself that none of it was real, except, perhaps, her involuntary response to the tender restraint of his lovemaking, the gentle arousal of his hands and mouth on her body which was all he would allow himself just before he took her home.

And that, to her shame, was where pretence stopped.

She forced a smile. 'Hardly. After all, we haven't actually set a date yet.'

'Something else we need to remedy.' He paused. 'Do you still want to keep our engagement a deadly secret, or shall we say "To hell with it" and surprise the world with an announcement in The Times?'

Tarn hesitated. She'd been wondering how to introduce the subject, and now he'd done it for her. Her chance had come, and she had to take it.

Now, she thought, or never.

She said, trying to sound casual. 'Actually, the garden party's next week. I was thinking we might go public then. That is—if you agree.'

Caz's brows lifted. 'I'd be delighted.' His tone was faintly quizzical. 'But are you sure?'

She shrugged lightly. 'Let's just say I'm becoming used to the idea.' She paused. 'Of course, I'll have to hand in my notice at work. I don't want to be regarded as a boardroom spy.'

'That's a pity,' he said quietly. 'When you're so good at your job. Won't you miss it?'

'Yes, but I'll have plenty of other things to occupy me.' Meaning, she thought edgily, the growing list of potential projects from her British and American agents, about which she would soon have to make some definite decisions.

Her Chameleon camouflage was right there, waiting for her to slip back into it as if nothing had happened and she'd never been away. And she should be feeling grateful for that, she told herself fiercely, instead of suddenly cold and bleak.

'So,' Della said when Tarn got home. 'Have you put a down payment yet on your future love nest? Or are you still prevaricating over these multimillion pads he keeps trotting out for your inspection?'

'Still managing to keep the whole issue at bay.' Tarn accepted the cup of coffee Della handed her.

'But for how much longer? Or are you planning for him to become homeless and be forced to occupy a cardboard box in some alleyway?'

'There's no chance of that.' Tarn sat down on the sofa as if her legs were too weary to support her any longer. 'Besides, the sale hasn't been completed on his present flat. He can always pull out.'

'True.' Della nodded. 'On the other hand, honey, if you're too choosy, he might begin to smell a rat.'

'He won't have time,' Tarn said harshly. 'He's going to announce our engagement in front of everyone at the company garden party next week, and that will be closely followed by my own special announcement. End of story.'

'Wow.' Della whistled. 'Short and extremely sharp. In other circumstances, I could almost feel sorry for him.' She paused. 'Have you told Evie what you're planning?'

Tarn shook her head. 'I haven't had the chance. She's strictly incommunicado again for some unknown reason. No doubt on my fiancé's orders,' she added jerkily. 'But I'll tell her when it's done, and before I leave. At least that beastly professor can hardly stop me from saying goodbye to her.'

'The whole place needs exposing,' said Della. 'One of the PAs at work has a cousin who's an investigative journalist. He might be interested.'

'A good idea, but I'd like to be out of the way first.' Her coffee tasted unusually bitter and Tarn put her cup down, unfinished, knowing it was not down to the brew but rather the fault of the nerves twisting in her stomach.

Nerves which Caz, of course, had noticed...

But I mustn't arouse his suspicions, she thought. Not at this late stage. Because nothing can go wrong now. I won't let it.

Tarn opened her eyes on the Saturday of the garden party to find bright sunlight streaming through the curtains. Clearly her waking dream that the whole event had been washed out by flash floods would not be coming true, she thought as she pushed the coverlet away and got reluctantly out of bed.

The dress she'd bought a few days earlier was hanging on the front of her wardrobe, cool and simple in white lawn with self-embroidery at the scoop-neck and around the hem of the full skirt.

'Bridal white, eh?' Della had asked, lifting her eyebrows when she saw it. 'Just to rub more salt into the wound, I suppose.'

'Actually no,' Tarn returned, a mite defensively. 'I just thought it looked pretty and summery.'

Looking at it now, however, she had to acknowledge that it could easily have been chosen as a dress for a very quiet wedding, perhaps with a small bouquet of pink roses. And stopped there, jolted by the path her thoughts had taken.

Out of the realms of fancy and down to earth, she scolded herself as she showered. She could have done with a pep talk from Della right now, but the other girl had been called away by her boss on a sales trip, standing in for a sick colleague.

So Tarn had been forced to make do with her erstwhile flatmate's warm hug and a fierce 'Good luck—and I'll be seeing you.'

Although it was not certain when that would be, she mused. Probably not for a considerable while, as she had tracks to cover. But Della fully understood that.

She towelled herself briskly and put on her underwear, then used a hand dryer to encourage her hair into its usual gleaming waves before donning mundane jeans and a T-shirt.

The rest of her clothes were already packed, and when the afternoon was over, and she'd paid her final visit to Evie, she would book in to some anonymous airport hotel until she could get a flight to the States.

She grilled bacon, scrambled a couple of eggs to go with it plus three slices of wholemeal toast. After all, there'd be no champagne buffet after she'd delivered her bombshell, so she probably wouldn't get another full meal until sometime in the evening, and she needed to keep her energy levels up for the task ahead of her.

Besides, once it was over, she wasn't sure when she would feel like eating ever again. Even now, she was having to force the food down into her churning stomach.

When she'd finished and cleared away, she went to her laptop to see what late deals there might be in hotel rooms, and found to her surprise that there was an item of mail waiting for her. From Caz.

She hadn't expected to hear from him. Unless, she thought, he was making a last attempt to persuade her to travel down to Winsleigh Place with him, instead of taking the coach with her colleagues.

She clicked on to his message, then sat, stunned, staring blankly at the few, hasty lines on the screen sent from his iPhone.

'Sweetheart,' he wrote. 'Something's come up and sadly I can't make it to the party. Have a great time yourself and I'll call you as soon as I get back.'

She said, 'No.' Then repeated it, 'No, no, *no*,' more violently each time, banging her fist on the table as she saw her great plan shatter into fragments around her.

The sleepless nights, she thought dazedly. The days of tension, always struggling against self-betrayal. The constant rehearsing of what she intended to say until she was word-perfect. And, more than anything, the pain of steeling herself against the moment when she would turn her back and walk away from him forever.

All of it for nothing.

She looked at her waiting travel bags. If she'd ever been the superstitious kind, she could tell herself it was a sign, cut her losses and run.

And paused right there, looking back at the screen. Reading his message again.

Because, she realised, there was, of course, another explanation. A totally different sign for her to ponder.

She had to face the fact that Caz had indeed been operating the same kind of pretence with her as he had with Evie, but was now bored with that too, and bringing the interlude to a close.

After all, Tarn thought, biting her lip until she tasted blood, he didn't fight too much when I asked to keep our engagement a secret, so perhaps that suited his purposes just as well as mine. And I was too taken up with my own plans to see it.

Besides, he doesn't have much to show for the past weeks of intensive courtship. He hasn't even succeeded in seducing me, unlike poor Evie, and now the deadline for losing his beloved flat is approaching. Maybe that's what's prompted him into thinking that the game isn't worth the candle and made him decide to walk away.

Because a public announcement in front of his workforce had turned out to be a step too far, even for him.

She felt deathly cold. She'd known from the start that it was a possibility, even a probability that he chose his women in much the same way as he'd purchase a new silk tie, and would subsequently discard them once their novelty value had dissipated.

Quite apart from Evie, the example of Ginny Fraser should have taught her that. Because she was in the past. He'd said so quite unequivocally, from the stance of a man who did not look back.

Oh, God, hadn't she told herself over and over again that falling in love with him was a weakness she couldn't afford. While believing, even for a moment, that he loved her in return was sheer madness.

The wishful thinking of a relatively inexperienced girl, beguiled beyond reason by an all-too-experienced man. Tempted out of her senses by the deceptive tenderness of his lovemaking.

How could I ever have pitied Evie, she thought, a faint moan rising in her throat, when the only difference between us is that he won't have to find a place for me in one of The Refuge's convenient recovery programmes?

Because I will survive this. I'll survive him.

And I shall be the one to walk away first.

But today, the only place I'm going is to a garden party. As arranged.

* * *

Winsleigh Place was just as beautiful as everyone had said. The house itself was Georgian, an elegant jewel in a magnificent setting.

'How on earth do we get to have a party in a place like this?' Tarn asked, turning to Lisa in disbelief as she surveyed the sculptured lawns, now dotted with colourful marquees, which led down to a small lake.

'As I said, we have Caz to thank,' Lisa said, shrugging. 'I gather there could be some distant family connection, or maybe he just has influence in high places, but no-one is really sure.'

'No,' Tarn said lightly. 'Probably not.'

'Pity he can't be here himself,' Lisa went on. 'Rumour has it that he's in France. One of the Parisian directors seems to be the world's most difficult man and Caz is always having to dash over and sort things out, usually to prevent some kind of mass walk-out. I guess history has repeated itself this weekend.'

'Perhaps.' Tarn shrugged. 'Whatever the reason, he's missing a treat, even if he did organise it.'

In one corner, a stage had been erected under a striped awning and here a jazz band was playing. Elsewhere there were old-fashioned sports like skittles, quoits, and even a coconut shy, while in another part of the garden a croquet tournament was taking place.

'There's a fortune teller too.' Lisa pointed to a brightly painted bow-topped vardo. 'Fancy a glimpse into the future?'

'I don't think so.' Tarn's smile was taut. 'She'd probably tell me I was going to meet a tall, dark stranger.'

'And that's bad?'

'It could be. Anyway, I'm not going to risk it.'

'Well, I have to look out for my own tall, dark stranger.' Lisa patted her arm. 'He was taking the children for lunch at my mother's first.' She paused. 'I have to say, Tarn, that you look absolutely amazing. I love that dress, and I find it astonishing that you haven't been snapped by some lucky guy long before this.'

Her smile was mischievous. 'On the other hand, maybe you'll have your encounter with destiny right here—even without the gipsy's warning.'

Left to herself, Tarn wandered across the grass, moving between the groups of laughing, chattering people, exchanging smiles and greetings with those she knew, and realising ruefully how comparatively few of them there were. And this was only a small section of the Brandon empire.

'It is Tarn, isn't it?'

She turned in surprise to see an older woman, in a dark blue linen dress, her blonde hair in an immaculate chignon, whom she recognised as Caz's principal PA, until now only seen from a distance in the office.

'Oh.' She hesitated. 'Good afternoon, Mrs Everett.'

'Make it Maggie, please.' The other's smile was relaxed and friendly. 'I was sure it must be you. I told myself there couldn't be two people in the UK company with quite that glorious shade of hair.'

Tarn flushed. 'Well—thank you.'

'Caz asked me to look out for you,' Maggie Everett went on and Tarn froze.

'He did?' she managed feebly.

'Why, yes. In his unavoidable absence, I have strict instructions to make sure you have plenty of champagne. Although there are loads of iced soft drinks, if you prefer.'

She was steering Tarn towards the largest marquee. And as there was no longer any need to keep a clear head, Tarn decided that champagne it should be.

Mrs Everett, whose husband, she told Tarn, was a successful barrister who believed that wives should pursue their own careers if they wished, proved an amazingly easy companion for someone who was dubbed Caz's Rottweiler by a number of the Brandon workforce.

Tarn couldn't figure afterwards whether it was the other woman's friendliness, her own emotional turmoil or the potent effect of a vintage wine that made her reckless, only that during a lull in the conversation, she found herself saying, 'I knew someone who used to work at Brandon a few months ago. Do you remember Eve Griffiths?'

Maggie Everett thought for a moment. 'The name rings no bells, I'm afraid,' she said eventually. 'Which department was she in?'

'I believe she used to work for Mr Brandon himself.'

'I really don't think that can be possible.' Mrs Everett frowned a little. 'I know everyone who has worked for all the board members during the past year, even on a temporary basis, and there's certainly been no-one called Griffiths. Your friend must have been employed elsewhere in the company.'

'Oh, she's hardly a friend,' Tarn said swiftly. 'Just—someone I met who said Brandon was a great company to work for. I probably assumed she worked for Caz—Mr Brandon, that is.'

Because that's what Evie said in all her letters, and I can't be wrong about it. I can't be...

Mrs Everett's grey eyes twinkled. 'There's no need to be so formal, I assure you, and certainly not with me. Anyway, relax—have some more champagne. You must be very disappointed that Caz can't be here,' she added. 'But I know it has to be for the very best of reasons.'

Whereas I, thought Tarn as her glass was refilled, no longer know what to think—about anything.

Wanting a quick change of subject, she said, 'That's a very good band.'

'All locals, who play here every year. But if you want a change of sound from Dixieland, there's a string quartet in the drawing room who specialise in Mozart. And, of course, another band for tonight's dancing.'

'All tastes catered for,' Tarn commented lightly.

'Caz likes his staff to be happy,' Maggie Everett returned.

At least until they're surplus to his requirements, thought Tarn. Thought it, but did not say it.

Her companion's mobile phone buzzed and she excused herself to answer it, moving away to a short distance.

When she came back, her eyes were dancing again. 'Shall we continue our stroll? See what else is going on?'

Probably wiser than staying where they were and consuming more champagne, Tarn thought ruefully as they emerged from the marquee. For a moment, she paused, dazzled by the sunlight, blinking as she reached hurriedly into her bag for her dark glasses because she was seeing things. She had to be, otherwise Caz was walking towards her across the lawn, smiling, and that couldn't be happening.

Because he couldn't make it. He'd said so, she thought, and only realised she'd spoken aloud when she heard Mrs Everett laugh softly.

'Nevertheless, here he is.' She gave Tarn a gentle nudge. 'Aren't you going to welcome him?'

Tarn took one faltering step, then another, still unable to credit that he was really here, believing it only when she found herself in his arms and held close while he kissed her.

'Surprised?' he whispered.

'Yes—yes, of course.' Her head was whirling. 'Someone said you were in France…'

'I was. That's where I called from. But the situation wasn't as bad as I thought so I got an air taxi back.' He let her go reluctantly. 'God, Maggie was right,' he said, his green gaze scanning her with delighted appreciation. 'She said you looked absolutely beautiful. But a bit forlorn too. She thought you were missing me.' He slid an arm round her waist and began to walk with her towards the band platform. 'I hope that's true. Still want to marry me?'

'Caz—I…'

'And the answer had better be yes,' he went on. 'Or I shall kiss you in front of all these people until it is. Now come on, sweetheart. We have news to break.'

The clarinettist stepped forward and helped Tarn up on to the stage while the trombonist handed Caz a microphone.

There was a pause while the trumpeter blew a ringing fanfare, then Caz spoke.

'First of all, I want to welcome you all here on this special afternoon.' His voice was clear and steady as people came forward, clustering round the edge of the stage. 'Many of you will already know Tarn as a colleague. However it's my great joy to be able to tell you that she'll soon be taking on another job—that of being my wife. We both wanted all of you here to be the first to know, although there will be a notice in The Times on Monday.'

Amid gasps and a ripple of cheering, he reached down and took the champagne flute that Maggie Everett handed him.

'So, I'd like you all to raise your glasses and drink to my adorable girl, the future Mrs Caz Brandon.'

The laughter and applause reached a crescendo, voices calling out, 'To Caz and Tarn. God bless them,' as the toast was honoured.

Caz took his grandmother's ring from his breast pocket and slipped it on to her finger. He said softly, 'Now it's there forever, my love,' and kissed her lightly and sensuously on the lips to even louder cheering.

Someone from the crowd who might have been Lisa shouted, 'Come on, Tarn. It's your turn. Speech.'

Caz handed her the mike. 'It's all yours, darling.'

Her fingers closed round it. She stared down at the sea of faces, all expectant, all smiling, and clearly all waiting for her to say—what? How happy she was? How much in love?

Yet somewhere in her brain, she knew, was a very different speech, one she had learned by heart for this actual moment.

So why couldn't she remember one word of it?

All she could think of was how her heart had lifted in a kind of astonished joy when she saw Caz coming towards her. How she'd found herself thinking as she stood in stunned disbelief, He loves me. He must do. Why else would he have dashed back to be with me? To do this?

A realisation that had thrown reason and emotion back into the melting pot.

She tried to visualise Evie, small and hunched in her chair, but could see nothing but the way Caz's smile lit his eyes when he looked at her. As he was looking at her right then, drying her mouth and making her heart thud unevenly.

And she knew then and there that what she'd intended—how she'd planned the afternoon to end was now quite impossible, even if it was for all the wrong reasons.

Someone called out, 'A silent woman, boss. Aren't you a lucky man.'

And on the roar of laughter that followed, Tarn found her voice.

She said shakily, 'I can't think of anything to say except— thank you for sharing this wonderful moment with us. I—I shall never forget it.' She turned towards Caz. 'And neither, I'm sure, will my fiancé.'

Because it's not over yet, she told herself silently, as Caz took the hand that wore his ring and kissed it. It's merely post-poned—to another time—another place.

And somehow—then—I'll find the strength and the will to go through with it at last.

CHAPTER ELEVEN

'BUT what happened?' asked Della.

Tarn shook her head. 'I don't know. It was the perfect opportunity, but—I—I couldn't say it.' She groaned. 'Not with everyone looking at me and smiling.'

'So what will you do at the wedding?' Della's tone was caustic. 'Take this man for your lawful wedded husband so that everyone continues to smile?'

Tarn flinched. She said in a low voice, 'There won't be any wedding. I admit that the date's been set and the register office booked, but that's where it will end.' She drew a deep breath. 'Everything I planned to say, I shall put in a letter to be delivered by courier just before the ceremony is due to take place.'

'I see.' Della was silent for a moment, then said more gently, 'Have you worked out why you don't want to confront him face to face?'

Tarn turned away. She said dully, 'Yes, I know. And I can't—I dare not risk it.' She swallowed. 'When he said he wasn't going to be at the garden party, I really thought he was going to dump me, just as he'd done with Evie. But suddenly there he was, and I realised I'd misjudged him and I felt—well, that doesn't matter—but that was another reason why I couldn't do what I'd planned.'

'That's exactly what I was afraid of.' Della sighed. 'Oh, God, what an unholy mess. Didn't someone once say that revenge was a two-edged sword?' She paused. 'I have to say that's the most beautiful ring, and definitely the genuine article this time.'

'Yes.' Tarn bit her lip. 'It is—very lovely. It will be enclosed with the letter.'

'I suppose so.' Della hesitated. 'Did he say why he'd cried off from the party originally?'

'Some problem at the Paris office, I think. He was going to tell me about it, then someone else came up to congratulate us, and afterwards, he said that, on second thoughts, it would keep.'

'Always supposing he gets a second chance,' said Della. She paused. 'Have you told Evie yet what you're going to do?'

'I haven't had the chance.' Tarn pulled a face. 'I wanted to see her the day after the garden party, but my request was turned down. And I wanted to ask her about her time at Brandon, too.

'You see, she told me she worked for Caz, but Maggie Everett his chief PA has never heard of her.'

Della shrugged. 'She could be under strict orders from above.'

'But that could hardly be applied to the entire workforce,' Tarn argued. 'And the fact is that no-one remembers her working there, not even Tony Lee from the Art Department who makes a routine beeline for every pretty blonde.

'He says there was an Emma who was a temp in the Finance section around that time, but she was Australian and engaged to a rugby player, so he backed off. But no Eve, Evie and Evelyn anywhere.'

She frowned. 'Which just seems—odd. Because where could she have met Caz except at Brandon?'

'Honey, the oddities about Evie and her mother, come to that, would fill several pages of A4.' Della paused. 'But isn't talking openly about Evie something of a risk?'

'I doubt anyone's going to report me,' Tarn said drily. 'And, as I'm not on the payroll but just working a couple of days a week now to finalise a project, it's probably my last chance.'

'Did The Refuge offer any explanation for barring you yet again?' asked Della.

'No, and when I explained there was something I needed to ask her, the Professor said very curtly that she'd answered enough questions.' Tarn sighed. 'Heaven knows what that was supposed to mean.'

'Her mother might know.'

'Yes.' Tarn's voice was rueful. 'That's another visit I have to pay. Aunt Hazel still can't understand why I haven't waved my magic wand and got Evie out of "that awful place". And her last message was so garbled, I could only pick out that she wanted me to help with some enquiries.'

'Approaching her MP, perhaps,' Della suggested. 'I can imagine my mother's reaction if I was shut up somewhere and she wasn't allowed to see me. Especially if my ex-boyfriend was responsible,' she added darkly.

'Yes,' Tarn said wearily. 'I haven't forgotten that—even for a minute.'

It was something that haunted her continually—the strange dichotomy between Caz's ruthless treatment of Evie, and his entirely different behaviour to herself.

She'd walked round the gardens at Winsleigh Place, her hand in his, floating on a cloud of good wishes. And later, she'd danced the evening away in his arms like an enchanted princess with her prince, as if, for them, midnight would never strike.

But it had, and here she was once more, facing the harshness of reality.

'Are you meeting him later?' Della asked.

'Yes, we're going to look at another flat this evening. The agent says it's an older property that's been completely renovated, and it could be the blank canvas we're looking for.' She bent her head wretchedly. 'Oh, God, I'm such a hypocrite.'

'Caz Brandon, of course, being squeaky clean.' Della gave her a straight look. 'Knowing what he's capable of, could you ever truly trust him or be happy with him? Be honest.'

Tarn smiled unhappily. 'Then, in honesty, I can only say—I don't know.'

But the certainty she could not bear to contemplate, she thought, pain wrenching at her, was the misery that would be waiting for her when he was no longer part of her life.

And how soon that day was approaching.

'Well, you've taken your time,' was Aunt Hazel's greeting, her plump face set in martyred lines. 'I told you it was an emergency.'

Tarn bent to kiss her cheek. 'I came as soon as I could.' She kept her tone gentle. 'What do you want me to do?'

'I want you to find out what's going on.' Aunt Hazel spoke with energy. 'What the police are doing with my poor Evie. It's not a criminal offence to try to kill yourself—not any longer, so why is she being harassed like this? If they want to chase someone, it should be the brute who drove her to it, and you must tell them so.'

Tarn was startled. 'Evie's involved with the police? Surely not.'

Mrs Griffiths nodded. 'Helping them with their enquiries, which is what they always say.' She snorted. 'Her father must be turning in his grave at the very idea.'

'But there must be some mistake...' Tarn began, but was testily interrupted.

'Well, of course there is, and you must sort it out, before she does something else desperate.' And Aunt Hazel began to cry, helpless, genuine tears running down her face.

Tarn found tissues, made tea and uttered comforting noises, but her brain was in free fall.

At least, she thought, a police investigation explained why visitors were being kept at bay. But what could Evie possibly have done to deserve it?

When the older woman was calmer, she said, 'Aunt Hazel, how did you find out—about the police, I mean.'

'Mrs Benson's nephew is a solicitor. You weren't doing any-thing to help, so he wrote a letter for me to that place, to in-sist on my being allowed to visit my poor little girl, and that's what he was told. He generally does wills and property, not police matters, so he didn't feel he could take it any further. But you must.'

Tarn said carefully, 'Aunt Hazel—was there anything going on in Evie's life that ever caused you concern—made you wonder?'

'Evie was always as good as gold.' Bright spots of colour appeared in Mrs Griffiths' cheeks. 'She had a wonderful life—until she met that dreadful Caspar Brandon creature who ru-ined it for her. I wish she'd never gone to work for his horrible company.'

'Do you know how long she was there—and what exactly her job was?'

'She was some kind of executive, and when she changed to that other place—the Scottish company—she was promoted to top management.'

'Scottish company?' Tarn echoed. 'What was that?'

'Oh, I can't remember. Mac something or other.' Mrs Griffiths hunted for another tissue. 'And why are you harping on about the past, when it's now that Evie needs help?'

But Tarn was suddenly remembering the paperwork she'd found at Evie's flat. She said, 'Was it the MacNaughton Company she went to?'

'It may have been.' Aunt Hazel sniffed. 'How can you ex-pect me to think about trivia at a time like this?'

'I don't.' Tarn gave her a quick hug. 'And I give you my word I'll try and find out what's going on,' adding silently, *In all kinds of ways.*

The MacNaughton company occupied smart offices in Clerkenwell.

'Good afternoon.' Tarn smiled at the blonde receptionist. 'I was wondering if you could supply me with some information.'

The girl gave her a dubious look. 'If it's about a job, I should warn you that the company demands very high standards from our domestic and office cleaners, and requires at least three references.'

'It's nothing like that,' said Tarn. 'I wanted to ask about a relation of mine who worked here quite recently, as some kind of executive.'

'I doubt that very much,' the other returned stonily. 'This is a family firm, owned and managed by Mr and Mrs MacNaughton, and their two sons.'

'But I'm sure I have the right company. My—cousin's name is Griffiths—Eve Griffiths.'

There was an odd silence, then the receptionist said, 'I can't help you, I'm afraid.'

'Is there someone else I could speak to—Mrs MacNaughton, perhaps.'

The girl shook her head. 'It's strict policy not to discuss past or present employees with anyone outside the firm. If you're related to Miss Griffiths, I suggest you ask her what you want to know. Good afternoon.' She opened a file on the desk in front of her and began checking figures with ostentatious care.

'Thank you,' Tarn said coldly. 'I will.'

But when I do, she thought as she left the building, will I find myself walking into yet another brick wall? Oh, Evie, what on earth have you been doing?

'I hear you've found a flat,' said Grace. She and Tarn were sitting in Fortnum and Mason's having tea. 'I'm amazed you could prise Caz out of his old one, but I suppose love will always find a way.'

Tarn smiled awkwardly. 'Oh, I don't think he minded too much.'

'Well, I wish we were having the same luck tracking down a wedding dress for you.' Grace poured the tea and proffered a plate of cream-filled pastries. She went on wistfully, 'Have you seen nothing at all you liked today?'

'I'm afraid not,' Tarn fibbed, adding more truthfully, 'But I feel really guilty dragging you all round London on a wild goose chase.'

'I'm glad of the exercise. I was beginning to vegetate quite seriously in our rural idyll.'

'Well, it seems to suit you. You look fabulous.'

'I look like a pumpkin on legs,' Grace retorted. 'I haven't bought a dress for your wedding either—just hired a small tent.' She paused. 'And while we're on the subject of appearance, if you'll forgive me for saying so, you're looking a little pale and heavy-eyed.' She gave a naughty giggle. 'Of course, there may be a very good reason for this, but you should be aiming for radiance on the big day.'

Tarn flushed. 'I think I'm probably suffering from bridal nerves. Even for the tiniest wedding like ours there seems so much to do.'

Grace nodded. 'Tell me about it. I decided quite early on that I was in a no-win situation over the arrangements, so I stood back and let the respective mothers slug it out. It worked perfectly—for me anyway.'

She was silent for a moment, then said, 'Tarn—I know it's not really my business to be asking, but he's Brendan's best mate from way back, and I think the world of him too, so I'm going to say it anyway.' She drew a breath. 'You—you do love Caz, don't you?'

Tarn was reaching for her cup, and her hand jerked, spilling some tea in the saucer.

She achieved a breathless laugh. 'Yes—yes, of course I do. Why do you ask?'

Grace shrugged uncomfortably. 'I suppose—because it's all happened so fast.'

Tarn used a tissue to mop up the spilled tea. 'Also girl marries boss is a terrible cliché,' she said quietly.

'Well, knowing Caz's views on romance in the workplace, it has come as rather a surprise. Besides…' She stopped abruptly.

'Besides, you thought he was going to marry Ginny Fraser,' Tarn supplied.

Grace sighed. 'Let's say we were afraid it might happen. Which was one of many reasons why we were so delighted when he found you.' She smiled. 'Brendan always said it would happen like that. That Caz would meet someone and fall head over heels. And clearly he has.'

'But you're wondering if I've done the same.' Tarn stared down at the table. 'And as his friend, you're probably entitled to ask.' She drew a breath, then said, stumbling a little, 'I may not wear my heart on my sleeve, Grace, but I do love him, more than I ever dreamed possible, although I tried hard not to. And if I'm not turning cartwheels, it's because, frankly, I'm feeling stunned.'

She gestured helplessly. 'He's a millionaire several times over, for heaven's sake. And he takes so much about his life totally for granted—whereas I…'

'Fit into it just perfectly,' Grace said gently. 'But things haven't always been easy for him, Tarn. He's rich and good-looking and that can act like a magnet for some women.'

She frowned. 'For instance, he had a problem earlier this year with some idiotic female making a complete fool of her-self over him.'

Tarn sent her a swift glance. 'Who was that?'

Grace shook her head. 'I don't know all the details, but Brendan says it was a real mess and took a lot of sorting.'

'Yes,' Tarn said bleakly. 'I'm sure it did.'

It was an effort to smile, but somehow she managed it. 'And now to prove my sincerity about my forthcoming nuptials, let's get a cab back to that place in Knightsbridge and take another look at that pretty cream silk. It's the only one that's really stayed in my mind, so maybe that's a good omen.'

They continued to laugh and chat all the way back to

Knightsbridge and the purchase of a dress that she knew, as she paid for it, she would not be wearing on any occasion in her life.

Twenty-four hours. That was all the time she had left.

Tarn felt shaken and bewildered when she considered how quickly she had reached this point.

So many staging points along the way. So many games of 'let's pretend' with herself as the only participant.

The miles of furniture showrooms traversed.

The gallons of paint chosen for the team of decorators waiting to transform a flat she would never occupy.

The party at Brandon to wish Caz and herself well and present them with a magnificent collection of crystal glassware.

Her ticket booked on a flight back to New York, in the first instance. And after that—who knew?

And now, the final act. The devastating, terrible letter that she had to write.

Closure.

Followed, presumably, by 'moving on'.

That comforting, meaningless phrase supposedly intended to salve the agony of a life torn up and thrown away, Tarn thought and shivered.

'I'm on my way.' Della emerged from her room with her travel bag slung over her shoulder.

She was taking two days of her holiday entitlement and spending them at her parents' home, because, as she said, she had no wish to be around when Caz Brandon came calling.

'That won't happen,' Tarn had told her, but Della had simply pursed her lips and said she preferred not to chance it.

Now, she gave Tarn a narrow-eyed look. 'Are you going to be all right?'

'Of course.' Tarn lifted her chin. 'After all, this is what I've been aiming for.'

'Have you booked a courier to deliver it?'

'Yes. It's all arranged.'

'And have you tipped off the Press, to make his humiliation as public as it gets? Put the icing on the cake, just as you've always said?'

Tarn didn't look at her. 'Not yet,' she said. 'I—I'll write the letter first.'

'Well, don't forget,' Della cautioned. She gave Tarn a bracing hug. 'Be brave,' she whispered. 'You know you're doing the right thing.'

Am I? thought Tarn, when she was alone. With so many questions still unanswered, I'm not as sure. But I can't allow doubts to creep in. Not at this stage. I have to go on.

But an hour later and on her third draft, she was struggling. Her first attempt had sounded regretful; the second, apologetic. And that wasn't what she wanted at all.

I have to become Chameleon again, she thought. I have to detach myself and speak with someone else's voice. Tell it as if it was someone else's story.

Then maybe I can bear it.

'Caz,' she wrote eventually. 'There will be no marriage between us today or ever.

'I am leaving you, just as you abandoned Eve Griffiths, your former fiancée and my foster sister a few months ago.

'Eve, as you know, was so heartbroken and traumatised by your rejection of her that she tried to kill herself, and she is now a virtual prisoner in The Refuge, where you are a trustee.

'Presumably, you thought that once she was out of sight, she would also be out of mind. But not so.'

That was the right tone. Cool and dispassionate. Just relating the facts.

'Because Eve wrote me letter after letter, talking about you and your relationship with her. She believed her passionate love for you was returned, and was overjoyed at the prospect of becoming your wife. She was even naïve enough to think that the stones in the engagement ring you gave her were diamonds.

'She did not understand that you were simply stringing her along and had no intention of marrying her or that you would abandon her once you were tired of the brutal game you were playing with her heart and mind.

'As soon as she realised that, she tried to destroy herself, which was when I decided your cruelty and arrogance should be punished, and that you too should discover what it was like to be humiliated and deserted by someone you trusted. So I came to England to find you.

'No doubt you are used to thinking yourself irresistible to women, so you were, of course, ridiculously easy to fool.'

Oh, Caz—Caz...

'But now I'm the one tired of pretending, and it's time to bring the whole charade to an end.

'I hope you will have the decency to allow my foster sister to be released so that she can start to rebuild her life without further harassment from you or the police.

'Goodbye.'

She signed her name, folded the sheets of notepaper and put them in a padded envelope large enough to accommodate the box with his grandmother's ring as well.

But she couldn't bring herself to take it off quite yet. Knew how accustomed she had become to the glimmer of the stones and how bare her hand would seem without them.

'You're being sentimental,' she said aloud. 'And you can't afford that.' But the words were spoken without emotion or even conviction. And the ring stayed where it was.

In fact, she felt strangely blank, as if putting her accusations against him down on paper at last had somehow purged her of all the anger and bitterness that had brought her to this moment.

The evening stretched ahead of her like a wasteland, yet, at the same time, the walls of the flat seemed to be closing round her, leaving her feeling cramped and uneasy. No matter where she looked in the room, the envelope seemed to be in her sight lines, waiting.

And there was something else that must go into it before it was sealed, she reminded herself. The key to the new flat.

She remembered their first viewing of it, the whole top floor of an apartment building from an earlier century with high ceilings and large windows. How she'd walked from room to room at his side, in spite of herself almost breathless with excitement. Imagining the flat neutral colours on the walls replaced by something with more depth and glow—a gleaming ivory in the sitting room perhaps as a backdrop for Caz's pictures.

Space and light, she thought. And, in the master bedroom's en suite, a shower big enough for two.

'I hardly dare ask,' Caz had said softly when the agent had withdrawn tactfully into another room. 'But do you feel about it as I do? Do you think we could make it into a home?'

For a moment, she was silent, recognising the enormity of what was happening. When she spoke, it was in a voice she hardly recognised, expressing a truth she could not avoid or dissemble.

She'd said simply, 'I could be happy here.'

And knew that her words concealed a world of regret.

She hadn't been there for several days, so she had no idea how it looked now that their decorating ideas had been put into operation.

'You've got to promise me you won't go and peek,' Caz had said, laughing. 'I want it to be a surprise.'

But I mustn't think about that, she told herself. Not any more, or I shall go crazy. And switched on the television, looking for distraction.

'Starting next,' a disembodied voice informed her, 'is a new series, The Body Politic, which will take a close look at parliamentary democracy in the whole of the United Kingdom. The presenter is Ginny Fraser.'

'Some distraction,' Tarn muttered, her throat tightening painfully as she reached for the remote control. 'And the last person I want to see.'

Caz would probably go back to Ginny in the end, she thought, finding consolation in taking up where he'd left off. Her mouth twisted as she visualised Grace's reaction.

Then she stilled. Brendan and Grace, she thought, imagining their shock and anger when she failed to show. What would Caz say to them? What explanation could he possibly offer? Or would it come as no surprise because they'd known about Evie and her part in his life all along?

She found she did not want to believe that.

Do something useful, she told herself as she got up restlessly and fetched her bag. The key to the new flat was in an inside pocket, and she held it in the palm of her hand, looking down at it. Struggling with herself as temptation beckoned.

Where would be the harm, she thought, in taking one last look? Caz's ban had not been serious. Besides, he would never know, she assured herself. It was the eve of his wedding, so he would be enjoying his stag night, celebrating what he supposed would be his last night of freedom.

And, anyway, she needed to say goodbye.

She slipped a thin jacket over her dress and went out to find a cab.

Even as she was paying off the driver, she was still hesitant, but at the same time knew there was little point in turning round and going meekly back to the empty silence she'd left.

She tapped in the entry code at the front door, and rode up in the lift to the top floor.

'There's a roof garden here too.' She could hear Caz's voice. 'But the tubs are filled with flowers, not hot water.'

She unlocked the door and stepped into the hall, pausing for a moment to inhale the clean smell of paint and newly varnished wood floors.

She went first to the sitting room, halting with an involuntary cry of pleasure. The furniture that they'd been told would take several weeks to arrive had been delivered and unpacked.

Only Caz's pictures, placed carefully in a corner, were still in their wrappings.

The image in her head had become reality and it was beautiful, she thought, swallowing.

She turned away, her eyes blurring suddenly. She was heading for the kitchen but on an impulse opened the door to the master bedroom instead.

Someone had been busy here too, she saw as she walked slowly forward, because the bed had been made up with the creamy linen they'd chosen, and the exquisite coverlet, like a golden sunburst, was folded neatly across its foot.

I could be happy here...

She closed her eyes and stood, motionless, her arms clasped around her body, until the sudden, tingling moment when she realised she was no longer alone.

She turned slowly and looked at Caz, leaning in the doorway.

He said, 'So you couldn't keep away.'

'Nor could you.' She was trembling inside, the blood singing in her veins. She spoke huskily. 'I—I thought you'd be out on the town with friends.'

'Getting blasted?' His own tone was faintly caustic. 'Not very flattering to one's bride, I've always thought. Anyway, I went out a few nights ago for a quiet dinner with Brendan and a few other friends.'

'Oh,' she said. 'I see.' She paused. There was tension in the room, warm and living like an electric current. She touched the tip of her tongue to her dry mouth, searching for something to say. 'They haven't hung the pictures in the sitting room.'

'No,' he said. 'I thought we'd do that together, when we came back from our honeymoon.'

'Yes,' she said. 'That's a—lovely idea.'

How can you look at me? she wanted to scream. How can you be so blind as not to see what I mean to do to you?

Aloud, she said, 'It all looks wonderful. Better than I ever dreamed.' She shook her head. 'But I'm sorry if I've ruined your surprise.'

He said slowly, 'You haven't spoiled a thing.'

She went on quickly, 'You see—I just needed so very much to see it.'

Caz moved away from the doorway and walked forward, halting a few yards away, the hazel eyes tender and hungry as he looked at her.

'How strange you should feel like that,' he said. 'Because, although I didn't know it, I also needed—so very much—to see you here.'

He held out his arms and Tarn ran to him like a homing bird, a sob rising in her throat.

Their mouths met and clung with a stark and heated urgency.

And when he lifted her and carried her to the bed, Tarn knew she could no longer deny him. Or herself.

CHAPTER TWELVE

THE mattress felt soft and yielding as Caz placed her gently down upon it. She stared up at him, aware of the thunder of her heart, and the soft trembling building inside her that she knew, in spite of her comparative inexperience, was born of excitement, not fear.

Yet as he turned to switch on the ivory-shaded lamp on the night table, she sat up, reaching for his arm. 'No—please.'

'Ah, but I need to see you, darling,' he told her huskily. 'I want you to look at me too. So—no darkness between us. Not tonight, Tarn, my love. Not ever.'

She watched as he began to strip, his movements totally un-self-conscious, until he wore only his shorts, the cling of the silk in no way concealing the stark reality of his arousal. And when he came at last to lie beside her, drawing her close, she went to him without reserve.

They lay, wrapped in each other's arms, bathed in the soft light falling across the bed, exchanging slow, sweet kisses. And when, at last, he looked at her, a question in his gaze, she lifted a hand and touched his cheek, sliding her finger along the firm line of his mouth. He captured its tip with his lips, suckling it gently, making her feel the heat building inside her, and the sudden frantic scald of desire between her thighs as she wound her arms around his neck, lifting herself towards him in mute offering.

He began to undress her, his hands moving without haste,

but with heart-stopping purpose as he dealt with the fastenings on her clothes and laid them aside, one by one.

When her last covering had gone, he stared down at her, his eyes rapt, almost wondering.

He said shakily, 'Oh, God, you're so lovely. More beautiful than I could have dreamed. I'm almost scared to touch you. Scared I'll lose control and ruin everything for you.'

'You won't,' she whispered. She took his hand and carried it in promise and reassurance to her breast, gasping as his fingers cupped the soft, scented mound. As he stroked her nipple with the ball of his thumb, arousing it to swift aching life. As his mouth took hers once more with deep and passionate urgency, parting her lips with his to allow the hot searching invasion of his tongue.

She touched him in her turn, running her hands along the hard muscularity of his shoulders, letting her fingers drift questingly down the long, lithe spine until she reached the band of his shorts and slid her hands under the silk to find his firm, flat buttocks, instinct guiding her in how to mould and caress them.

Caz uttered a sound between a laugh and groan, the breath catching in his throat as at last he moved, discarding the shorts completely, then lifted Tarn, placing her against the heaped pillows, bending his head to kiss her breasts, his tongue laving their tautly sensitive peaks in an exquisite and irresistible torment that forced a startled moan from her lips.

She could feel the hardness of him pressing against her and she reached down clasping the rigid, velvety shaft, shyly at first, then with growing confidence, as she ran her fingers along its proud length, cupping and caressing him, and felt his whole body shudder with pleasure in response.

His hands were exploring her too in intimate detail, spanning her waist, skimming the slender curves of her hips, smoothing the concavity of her belly, every stroke of his fingers on her skin a potent and erotic delight, taking him nearer and nearer to the soft, downy junction of her parted thighs.

Tarn's head moved restlessly on the pillow as she tried and failed to control an involuntary sob of yearning. An open and unmistakable sign of how much she wanted the total consummation of their mutual desire. How she longed to belong to him completely at last.

And heard him whisper, 'Wait, my sweet. Wait just a little.'

But it seemed an eternity before he touched her *there* at the sweet, melting, molten core of her. Before she felt the subtle glide of his fingertips penetrating the soft satin folds of her womanhood in lingering, unhurried incitement.

Tarn felt the startled flurry of her breathing as one by one she found herself surrendering all the barriers to her deepest senses that she'd carefully constructed in response to this new and powerful intimacy, her body boneless, her eyes shadowed as she stared up into the dark, intent and tender face above her.

As she felt his smile touch her lips and welcomed again the enticing flicker of his tongue against hers.

His hand moved, claiming her tiny hidden peak, stroking it deftly but so very gently that at first she was hardly conscious of what he was doing to her until she realised that his soft, rhythmic caress was creating a whole new world of delicate almost fugitive sensations.

Her bewildered mind and body sought them, held them captive, her concentration focussing almost blindly now on the exquisite play of his fingers, their pressure increasing now, circling on her with sensuous purpose, inviting her to experience a pleasure she had never known before, nor even imagined could exist.

Every inch of her skin seemed to be quivering, the blood pulsing almost audibly in her veins, her entire being enslaved by this new and devastating intensity.

She was like a leaf caught in a tide, carried inexorably towards some brink under the irresistible urging of his hands and mouth.

His name was a husky moan forced from her throat, and then, in the next second, she was lost, her last vestiges of control shattered, as she was lifted up by a mounting spiral of shivering, sobbing delight until her body convulsed into its first spasms of sheer rapture.

She cried out again into the heat of his mouth, her voice cracked and incoherent, her hands biting into his shoulders.

And in that moment felt him slide his hands under her hips and enter her, sheathing himself in the pulsating inner sweetness that he had so gently but so surely created.

Briefly, he was still, then he began to move, as if emphasising his possession, thrusting into her slowly and deeply, filling her again and again with his strength and power.

Gasping, Tarn lifted her legs, locking them round him, letting her own body echo the rhythm he had initiated, giving herself without restraint, taking him into her with utter acceptance—utter completeness. Absorbing—glorying in the total difference of this sensation to everything that had gone before.

Finding herself at last a woman in union with her man.

And when the pace of their joining quickened, she made his urgency her own, answering the fierce drive of his loins with her own passion. Hearing him call out to her, his voice almost agonised, as he came.

Afterwards, she held him, pillowing his head on her breasts and feeling the dampness of tears on her face.

He knew at once.

'Darling—I hurt you…'

'No,' she whispered. 'Don't you see? I—I'm crying because I'm happy. That's all.'

Caz was silent for a moment then he said huskily, 'That's everything. My dearest love.'

Tarn awoke to early daylight and silence. She stretched slowly, eyes still shut, her bewildered mind acknowledging that her body was glowing with a sense of acute well-being that she had never experienced before, or believed could exist.

And with that, memories—images—of the previous night and just how often they'd turned to each other in mutual, laughing joy, came swarming into her consciousness, and she understood exactly why she felt as she did, her lips parting on a startled sound between a gasp and a laugh, as she reached across the bed to find the creator of this miracle.

But there was no warm man sleeping there, and the space beside her was chilly as if it had been empty for some time. She sat up sharply, the sheet falling away from her naked body, as she stared around her, alert for the sound of movement elsewhere in the flat, yet hearing nothing.

It was then she saw the folded sheet of paper on the adjoining pillow, and opened it with fingers that shook slightly, to read the few lines he'd left for her.

'My darling,' he'd written. 'I was watching you sleep when I suddenly remembered it's supposed to be unlucky for the bride and groom to meet on their wedding day before the ceremony. I reckon we've blown that particular superstition to kingdom come, but have decided to avoid further risks.

'So, my sweet, I'll see you again very soon at the register office, although I have to tell you that nothing can make you any more my wife than you are at this moment.'

He'd signed it simply, 'Caz.'

Tarn read it again, then dropped it as if the paper had scorched her fingers.

She should be thankful, she thought, her breathing quickening, that he had decided to leave without waking her, or she might not have been able to let him go at all. She could well have clung to him, forgetting everything but the need to be with him. To stay with him, and be his woman, his wife for all eternity.

Instead, she'd been spared to do what she must. To finish what she'd started. And the time had now come.

For a moment the room blurred, but she fought back the tears. There was no place for them now. They must wait.

Twenty minutes later, washed and dressed, she was heading off. She'd fully intended to leave his note behind, but at the last moment, just as she reached the front door, something impelled her to go back to the bedroom and retrieve it.

'And how many kinds of fool does that make me?' she wondered unhappily as she pushed it into her bag.

The hotel she'd picked near the airport was big, busy and anonymous, all points in its favour. She checked in, arranged to hire a car for her visit to The Refuge the following morning, then went up to her room, where she remained, at intervals trying to read, or trying to doze or trying to watch television, but accomplishing none of these aims.

She ordered a meal from room service, and ate half of it. She opened some wine from the mini bar and drank none of it. She walked up and down the room, her arms wrapped round her body, trying not to think what would have happened earlier in the day at the register office, but unable to rid her mind of it.

At first, he'd probably thought she was held up in traffic, or exercising a bride's prerogative to be late. But then, as the minutes passed, he must have begun to wonder, until, of course, the arrival of the courier with her letter made everything more than clear.

But at least she hadn't notified the Press. In the end, she had spared him because she couldn't bring herself to twist the knife by making the necessary calls. So, in effect, no-one would know of his humiliation except Brendan and Grace, who would naturally say nothing.

And by the time the news got to the London office, Caz would no doubt have found some excuse for his continued bachelordom. He could say they'd discovered they weren't suited after all. Even that it had been a lucky escape on both sides.

Or he might employ the same reasoning that he'd used with

Evie, she thought, trying to fire up her anger and sense of self-justification.

Not easy, when all she wanted to do was cry until she had no tears left. But that couldn't be allowed yet.

Who ever said revenge was sweet? she asked herself, as pain lanced her. Because they were wrong. It was savage and bitter, and no-one could remain immune from its effects. Least of all, the person who had set the whole thing in motion.

I could have said 'Not my problem' and stayed in New York, she thought. But I promised Uncle Frank I'd watch out for the two of them. And fight their battles if necessary.

And I have to believe that this was a just war. I must. Because I have no choice.

So, tomorrow morning, I shall go to Evie and tell her that she's avenged. That Caz Brandon now knows in his heart and soul the damage he's inflicted, and is paying for it.

And that she has nothing further to fear from him, and can start on the road to complete recovery.

Whereas I—I have another road to tread, and I can see nothing ahead of me but desolation. And no way back. Starting with tonight…

'She's much better this morning,' Nurse Farlow informed her briskly as she led the way up to Evie's room. 'Quite chipper, in fact. Mind you, the police haven't been back this week, which helps.'

'I don't quite understand.' Tarn spoke carefully. Her head was aching and her eyes felt as if they had been scoured with grit. She had spent most of the night staring into the darkness, too emotionally exhausted to sleep, or attempt to make positive plans. But now there were things she needed to know. 'Why did they want to interview her in the first place?'

She received a faintly caustic look. 'That's something you need to ask her yourself—if she'll tell you. But don't count on it.'

The older woman paused. 'I gather we won't be seeing you again. That you're leaving England.'

'I never intended to stay,' Tarn said. 'I only came over for Evie's sake. And if she's on the mend, hopefully her mother can start visiting in my place.'

The response was a dubious shrug, and a muttered 'Perhaps.'

Not nearly as hopeful as I thought, Tarn told herself ruefully as they walked along Evie's landing. The door of her room was open, and a cleaning trolley was standing outside.

Tarn was mentally bracing herself for the coming interview when the air was suddenly split by a shrill, wailing scream, then the word, 'No!' shouted over and over again.

The nurse pushed past Tarn, throwing 'Wait.' over her shoulder.

But there was no way Tarn was going to stand meekly in the corridor when Evie was in trouble, and she rushed into the room on Nurse Farlow's heels.

Evie was crouched in her chair, shaking, hands over her face, making strangled guttural sounds. Beside her, a white-faced woman in a crisp overall was trying ineffectually to calm her by patting her shoulder.

'What's going on here?' Nurse Farlow demanded.

The cleaner shook her head, looking terrified. 'I don't know, nurse, I'm sure. I had my Daily Gazette on the trolley, and she asked if she could see it. I didn't see any harm so I gave it to her. Then all this started.'

The paper in question was lying scattered on the floor, as if it had been thrown there.

Tarn bent, gathering the sheets together. As she straightened, she found herself staring down at the front page. At a picture of a man walking down some steps from a building, his head bent. At the headline above it, proclaiming 'Billionaire's Wedding Shock'. And at the text beneath it.

'Publishing tycoon Caspar Brandon wanted a quiet wedding,' she read in horror. 'But what he got was total silence when his mystery bride, former employee Tarn Desmond, failed to show up yesterday for the ceremony at Blackwell Registry Office.

'Brandon (34) who has escorted a series of beautiful women in the past, including TV Personality of the Year Ginny Fraser, raised eyebrows at a recent company gala when he announced his engagement to the unknown Miss Desmond who worked as a junior editor on one of his magazines.

'As he left the registry office alone, the jilted groom refused to speak to reporters. And a representative from Brandon International issued a firm "No comment."

'Efforts to trace Miss Desmond have so far failed.'

But this can't have happened, Tarn told herself, feeling cold and sick. Because I didn't tell them. I didn't…

And only realised she'd spoken the words aloud when there was another hysterical screech from Evie.

'You've dared to come here, you bitch.' She was glaring at Tarn as if she loathed her, spittle on her lips. 'You of all people? You were supposed to be on my side, but all this time you've really been trying to take my Caz away from me. Marry him yourself.'

Tarn stared at her. 'But Evie—you know that isn't true…'

'I know that it's me he really wants, and it always will be.' The younger girl's face was ugly, mottled with rage, her eyes blazing. 'Now get out of here. Out of our lives.' Her voice rose. 'You'll never have him, because I won't let you.'

The quivering heap in the chair was suddenly transformed, launching herself at Tarn with the speed of a striking snake. Taken unawares, Tarn was knocked to the floor by the sheer force of the attack, and cried out in pain as Evie's nails raked down her face.

The room was suddenly filled with people, the Professor himself pulling Evie away, holding her firmly, her arms behind her back, while he spoke to her quietly and gently.

Tarn scrambled to her knees and then, awkwardly, to her feet, unable to believe what had just happened.

She said unevenly, 'Evie, I don't understand. What is all this? I was only doing what you wanted. What we agreed. You know that.'

The Professor glanced round at her, his expression impatient. 'Doctor Rahendra, will you please see to this young woman's face, then take her to my office? And I'd be obliged if you'd also ask my secretary to organise some coffee.'

A slim pretty girl in a white coat, with olive skin and a thick plait of glossy dark hair, came to Tarn and took her arm. 'If you will come with me.'

'No, not yet.' Tarn tried to tug herself free. 'I want to know what's going on.'

'The Professor will speak to you presently. Explain everything.' Doctor Rahendra's voice was kind but firm. 'But now you must leave here. Our patient finds your presence disturbing. And those scratches are deep. They need attention.'

In a spotless treatment room, Tarn winced as her cheek was bathed with antiseptic, and cream applied.

'They are a little unsightly, but they will heal more quickly without a dressing,' the doctor told her. She added. 'And you will not be scarred.'

Tarn bent her head. 'Am I supposed to find that a comfort?' she asked dully. 'There are worse things than scars.'

The other nodded. 'The reaction of Miss Griffiths has shocked you deeply. That is quite natural.' She sighed. 'And it is all the more unfortunate when we believed she was making progress at last. But clearly we were being too optimistic as the Professor has warned us all along.'

She walked to the door. 'Now I will take you to him.'

The Professor was standing looking out of the window when Tarn was shown into his room.

He turned and gave her a frowning glance. 'I permitted this visit in order for you to say goodbye, Miss Griffiths—

or should I now call you Miss Desmond. I did not intend it to provoke another crisis.'

Tarn lifted her chin. 'Nor did I. In fact, I thought my sister would welcome the news that our plan had succeeded.'

'And what plan was that precisely?' He came back to his desk and sat down, reaching for the coffee pot standing on a tray in front of him, and filling two cups.

'As you know, Evie was having a relationship with a very rich, very attractive man.' Tarn kept her tone impersonal, as she accepted her cup. Sipped the strong brew. 'She was actually planning her wedding when he suddenly terminated their engagement. I—I understood it was the trauma of that breakup that triggered her suicide attempt.'

She took a steadying breath. 'He'd treated her abominably and I decided he should undergo the same fate. Suffer the same humiliation.'

He nodded. 'Acting for the benefit of female humanity, I suppose.'

Tarn said hotly, 'You find this amusing?'

'No,' he returned. 'Tragic. And with a little frankness, it could have been stopped at the outset. And for that, I must blame myself.'

'It's gracious of you to admit it.'

'Oh, it's not on your behalf, Miss Desmond. If I'd spoken, I might have saved one of our respected trustees, Caspar Brandon from trial by tabloid, among other things.' He shook his head. 'All along some instinct told me I shouldn't trust you, but that was for a rather different reason.'

'How dare you criticise me.' Her voice shook. 'Everything I've done has been in good faith—and because Evie herself begged me to help her. I wasn't acting alone. She wanted him punished. Needed him to feel some of the agony he'd caused her, and I agreed because I—I thought that would help her recover.'

'And what cod psychology books have you been reading, Miss Desmond?'

'I don't need to read anything to know that she's terrified of your so-called "respected trustee",' Tarn retorted. 'I don't know what threats he's made to keep her quiet about their affair—apart from locking her in here for the duration, but they've certainly worked.'

She drew a breath. 'And if what happened just now is a result of your treatment, heaven help the rest of the poor souls being kept here.'

'Amen to that,' he said unexpectedly. 'Sometimes, I wish I could call on divine intervention. Usually I have to rely on common sense. Which I signally failed to use in this particular case.'

He gave a brief harsh sigh. 'But that stops now, because there are a few things you need to know about your foster sister. Firstly, she is not in this institution simply because she miscalculated the number of illegal pills involved in her supposed suicide attempt. She had already agreed to accept out-patient treatment here as an alternative to serious legal proceedings against her.'

Tarn was suddenly rigid. 'On what possible grounds?'

'There is a choice.' He ticked them off on his fingers. 'Theft, drug dealing, wilful damage, assault and, of course, stalking. There was talk of a restraining order among other measures.'

The words were like blows, thudding against her ribs, making it difficult to breathe. She said hoarsely, 'I don't believe you. Evie wouldn't do those things. She couldn't...'

'She could, Miss Desmond, and she did. You've been working abroad, I believe, so you've been out of close touch with your family for quite a while.' He paused. 'But you were clearly doing well, and that, we feel, was part of the problem. Eve also wanted your earning power and what went with it. But as you know, she had no real qualifications and found it hard to find work that paid decent money or indeed hold down a job at all.

'However, she eventually managed to obtain employment with a highly reputable cleaning firm.'

Tarn said faintly, 'The MacNaughton Company?'

He nodded. 'The very same. At first she worked in their office cleaning section, where her performance appeared satisfactory, then, at her own request, she transferred to the domestic field, where she worked for some very wealthy clients, not all of whom, I fear, were as careful with their possessions as they should have been. And as your sister was permanently short of money, she succumbed to temptation, and began to steal from some of them.'

He frowned. 'There was no actual proof, of course, but a couple of them took their suspicions to MacNaughton and Evelyn was dismissed.'

'But she was living at home,' Tarn protested. 'She couldn't have been that badly paid.'

'She wasn't,' said the Professor. 'But by this time, she'd moved into a flat she could not afford, so she needed an alternative source of income. And eventually, because of her MacNaughton connections, she found one.'

She stared at him. 'But I don't understand any of this. Surely Caz—Mr Brandon—was paying for the flat.'

He said with a trace of impatience, 'My dear Miss Desmond, I doubt whether at that point he was even aware of her existence, although that was soon to change,' he added grimly.

'Not—aware?' There was a hollow feeling in the pit of Tarn's stomach. 'I don't understand. He—they were lovers. Engaged to be married. You must know that.'

'No,' the Professor said more gently. 'I'm afraid all that was pure imagination on her part. She saw him while she was working at Brandon, fell for him and created a fantasy in her own mind, which she built up when she began cleaning his apartment until it reached danger levels, and beyond.'

He shook his head. 'Evelyn has never had a relationship

with Caz Brandon, Miss Desmond. She has been lying from the start to everyone—most damagingly to herself.'

He paused, then added heavily, 'But also, it seems, lying particularly to you. Her hated rival.'

CHAPTER THIRTEEN

TARN felt numb and deathly cold, as if she was seeing the Professor through a wall of ice. His words seemed to sting at her brain.

She said, stumbling a little, 'You're saying she hates me? But why? She only found out about what I've done to Caz just now, so it can't be that.' She swallowed. 'Surely it's not because I went to America—and have a career? She's jealous of *that*?'

'That's only part of it,' the Professor said quietly. 'She has always felt you were her father's favourite, and resented it. Both she and her mother apparently looked on you as an outsider— a cuckoo in the nest.'

Tarn bent her head. 'I think I always knew that. But he— Uncle Frank—was so good to me, and I knew he wanted me to make sure they were all right. So I tried to do that for his sake.' She spread her hands helplessly. 'Yet Evie wrote me all those letters detailing her affair with Caz. Why did she do that?'

'It was all part of the illusion. She needed to prove she could outdo you in one area at least. To make you jealous as well.'

'You mean—this whole horrible thing is my fault?' Her voice broke.

'Certainly not.' His tone was brisk. 'Your mistake lay in believing your foster sister was still the child you'd grown up with, and were fond of, and you can't be blamed for that.' He paused. 'Even though you've undoubtedly been culpable in other ways.'

SARA CRAVEN   175

Tarn thought of the newspaper photograph, with Caz's face drawn and haggard, and winced at the pain which tore through her.

She said in a low voice, 'And for that I'm being well and truly punished, please believe that.'

She paused, taking a deep steadying breath, because there was so much more she needed to know. 'What exactly did Evie do? To Caz, I mean?'

'Went through the things in his flat. Took some shirts, some underwear, a pair of shoes to keep at her own place, to bolster her fantasy that they were in a relationship.' He sounded almost matter of fact. 'Removed and probably destroyed photographs that appeared to relate to other women. Read his desk diary then followed him to social engagements, blagging her way in.'

Tarn tensed, feeling a swift wave of nausea as she remembered how she had first forced herself on his attention. 'Oh, God, that's so awful.'

'It gets worse.' The Professor pursed his lips. 'While she was working for MacNaughton, she'd had the keys to his apartment copied. When she was still unable to gain his attention in the way she wanted, she tried to hack into his computer, and when that failed, she took a hammer to it. Wrote messages in lipstick on his mirrors. Slashed a valuable painting.

'Eventually she began approaching him in public and making scenes, until finally, in a restaurant, she threw a glass of wine over his companion, who was not, and I quote, the dirty bitch he was screwing—but a visiting editor from Canada.'

He frowned. 'By that time the police were involved, of course.'

She bit her lip. 'I—I suppose he had no choice.'

'Oh, Mr Brandon didn't begin it.' His voice was reassuring. 'Miss Griffiths was already under investigation over the supply of illegal drugs. The husband of one of her former MacNaughton clients had become concerned about his wife's odd mood swings and found some pills hidden in a drawer.

'He showed them to his brother, a doctor who raised the alarm, and the wife confessed that she'd been obtaining private supplies of this particular tranquilliser from her former cleaner. At extortionate expense, naturally.'

Tarn shook her head. 'This is unbelievable,' she said, half to herself. 'How on earth could Evie—*Evie*—possibly have got hold of such things?'

'She'd been targeted by a dealer, of course,' said the Professor. 'While she was still working for MacNaughton and had access to bored, rich women who found their doctors unsympathetic to their problems. The ideal set-up from his point of view.' He paused. 'And from hers, especially as by this time her financial problems were pressing. In order to gain access to the kind of places Mr Brandon frequented, she needed an entirely new image—a wardrobe she couldn't afford.'

He shook his head. 'In such places, she was naturally able to find new contacts needing sleeping tablets, diet pills and tranquillisers. People who didn't ask questions or worry about the cost. Being young and pretty, she built up a remunerative business, but unfortunately she got greedy, and imposed a private surcharge of her own.

'However, when her supplier found out, things became— difficult for her.' He added flatly, 'Mr Brandon had offered to drop the stalking and malicious damage charges against her if she agreed to have therapy, but she was desperate for somewhere to hide, and this seemed the ideal sanctuary. So she deliberately staged the suicide attempt, knowing she'd be offered immediate residential care, but misjudged the dose.'

He smiled grimly. 'You assumed when she spoke of being frightened that she was referring to Mr Brandon, but you were wrong.'

'But her diary,' Tarn said desperately. 'She talked about him there too. You must have read that for yourself.'

'Ah,' he said. 'The references to "C", which you interpreted as Caz, but which was actually her former partner in crime.

A man who lived in the flat above hers called Clayton. Roy Clayton.'

Tarn stared at him in horror. 'My God, I met him once, when I cleared out her things.'

'Then perhaps you can understand why she was scared,' he said drily. 'A thoroughly nasty piece of work. He even managed to get a message to her in here reminding her that she owed him money, and warning her to keep her mouth shut.'

Tarn gasped. 'But how could that happen? Security's so tight.'

'Unfortunately through a member of the kitchen staff, who believed quite sincerely she was passing on a love letter from a boyfriend, and has since been dismissed.'

Tarn got out of her chair and went to the window, pushing it open and gulping deep breaths of sunlit air. Behind her the phone rang, and she heard the Professor murmur a few quiet words before replacing the receiver.

When she could speak, she said, 'I'm sorry. I know that I'm keeping you from your work. But, you see, I keep telling myself that none of this is true. That it's just a nightmare and I'll wake up soon. Please tell me I'm right.'

'I'm afraid I can't do that, Miss Desmond. It's all too real.'

'I suppose so.' She turned slowly. 'And Evie—what will happen to her now—and in the future?'

'A lot will depend on the assistance she gives to the police investigation over the drugs racket. But I shall do my utmost to ensure she remains here. As Mr Brandon so quickly and generously recognised, she needs help rather than punishment.'

He gave a sharp sigh. 'Unfortunately, she is still using her delusions about him as a shield and an excuse for the rest of her behaviour. I am only sorry that you believed her and were drawn in.'

Tarn forced a smile. 'She—seemed to need me. That was my delusion. Perhaps it always has been.'

'But at least you won't be fighting against your return to

reality, Miss Desmond, so your recovery should be swift and complete. And you'll find your own life is waiting for you.'

Tarn turned back to the window, her throat tightening. 'I'm afraid your prognosis is wrong, Professor. I was stupid and gullible, and because of that I've deliberately wrecked my life and thrown away the only chance of real happiness that will ever come to me.

'All I have left now is my career, and, believe me, that's no comfort.'

Her voice choked into a sudden uncontrollable sob and the sunlight blurred as the floodgates opened and she began to cry at last, tears pouring helplessly down her face, scalding her skin and burning in her throat.

A box of tissues was placed silently beside her on the window ledge, and a moment later the sound of the door closing told her the Professor had left the room.

She was thankful for it. She didn't require sympathy, counselling or criticism. She needed only to be alone to mourn the self-imposed destruction of her life. To face up to the fact that she'd been a fool and worse than a fool to take Evie's story at face value, or to think her concern and affection for her foster family had ever been reciprocated, at least by the female members.

And above all, she wanted to rage inwardly with grief and despair over the eternal emptiness ahead of her. Knowing— accepting that she had no-one to blame but herself, and would have to live with that for the remainder of her life.

Realising that Caz would never again take her in his arms. That she would have to forget the seductive warmth of his mouth, and the murmur of his voice as they made love. That she could not turn in the night and find him beside her.

That she would be—completely alone.

She yielded herself up to the storm of her misery, head bent, hands braced against the wall, her whole body shaking, gasping and choking, hearing herself making harsh, painful noises in her throat like a small wounded animal as the weeping tore her apart.

For an endless time, it seemed at the beginning as if she might never be able to stop, but, very gradually, the first desperate agonies of her remorse began to subside, leaving an aching emptiness in their place.

When at last she straightened, she had managed to establish a modicum of self-command, enough, anyway, to take a handful of tissues and began to blot her eyes and remove the worst ravages of grief from her face.

Not much, she thought, an occasional sob still catching her breath, but it was a start. A first step in a long, weary journey.

As she heard the door behind her re-open, she deliberately braced herself, her fingers grasping the window ledge as she took a deep, steadying breath.

'I'm sorry to have turned you out of your office, Professor Wainwright.' Trying to sound positive was difficult enough, but attempting to disguise the huskiness of her voice was quite impossible. 'I—I really didn't mean to lose control like that, but I seem to have been crying inside for so long now that I suppose it was almost bound to happen. You see I—I never thought it was possible to hurt so much.'

She paused. 'I know you must want to be rid of me, but before I go, may I ask for one last favour. You'll be seeing Mr Brandon at some point, in his role as trustee, and perhaps you could find a moment in private to tell him that I'm sorry—for everything. And that I don't expect him to forgive me, because I'll never be able to forgive myself.'

She hesitated again. 'There's so much else I want to say, but it's probably best to leave it at that. So, will you—could you do that, please? I'd be eternally grateful.'

'Professor Wainwright has been detained,' Caz said quietly. 'So perhaps it would be more convenient if you gave the rest of your message to me in person.'

The room seemed to shiver and tilt, but somehow Tarn kept

on her feet. A voice in her head was frantically whispering, 'No, oh, God, please no. I'm not ready for this. I can't bear it.'

Only now there were no more choices to be had, and she knew it, so she turned slowly and faced him across the room, her heart thudding against her ribcage like a trip hammer.

He was wearing denim pants and a dark blue shirt, open at the neck, and with the sleeves rolled up. He looked unutterably weary, the lines of his face deeply incised and he needed a shave.

She fought the tenderness rising within her, and the yearning to go to him, taking his face between her hands, and kissing the grim tautness of his mouth. Because as she'd been telling herself over and over again, it was all a million years too late, and there was nothing to be done but stand her ground and endure his justified anger and whatever penance he might exact.

She said, 'What are you doing here?'

'It seemed the obvious place to find you. I knew that you'd be paying a last visit to your sister to tell her how well your plan had succeeded before you finally vanished back where you came from, and Jack Wainwright confirmed it for me.' His tone was flat. 'But I also knew that it wouldn't work out as you expected, and now you know it too. Don't you?'

'Yes.' She was glad she had no more tears to shed because weeping in front of him might be construed as a plea for mercy, and there could be none. They were standing on opposite sides of some great abyss and she couldn't reach him.

He looked at her more closely, his eyes narrowing, his brows drawing into a frown. 'What's happened to your face?'

'I already told you. When I heard the truth about Evie, I— lost it for a while. Didn't your friend the Professor tell you he'd left me to get over my crying jag?'

'No, he came down because he had other things he needed to say to me. And I was referring to the marks on your face, not the fact you look half-drowned.'

She lifted a defensive hand to her cheek. 'Evie went for me when she saw the newspaper story. It isn't serious.'

'Ah,' he said. 'I think that might depend on one's point of view.'

Tarn moved swiftly, restively. 'Caz—I don't know how the Press found out about the wedding, but I swear I didn't tell them. I—was going to, but I changed my mind. Someone else must have done it.'

'Your missing flatmate perhaps?'

She bit her lip. 'I—suppose so. I think she realised I wouldn't go through with it. She'd never agreed with what I was doing before, and had argued with me about it, until she saw Evie's supposed engagement ring. She knew of course that they weren't real diamonds, and then she got angry too, and thought you deserved everything you got.'

'Of course she did,' he said. 'I'd never realised before how compelling circumstantial evidence could be.'

'Nor had I,' she said. 'Although I'm not offering that as an excuse for what I've done.' She drew a deep breath. 'Caz, I don't know why you followed me here, but please believe that there's nothing you can say to me that will make me feel any worse about what's happened. So won't you accept that I'll never forgive myself for what I've done to you and just—let me go?'

He said quite gently, 'No, Tarn. I'm afraid I can't do that.'

There was a bleak hollow inside her. She said, 'I suppose it was too much to hope for. And I can't really blame you for wanting retribution.'

'If I did,' Caz said slowly, 'one look at you would change my mind. You're hardly a glowing advertisement for the benefits of revenge, my sweet.'

She said hoarsely, 'You're laughing at me?'

'Christ, no.' His tone sharpened. 'I've never been further from amusement in my life. And, yes, I was angry and hurt and humiliated, and all the other miserable fates you wished on me for the sake of that pathetic girl upstairs. And if you'd asked me there and then if I ever wanted to see you again, I'd have answered in the negative with no expletives deleted.

'But spending last night wide awake and alone, I came to a number of very different conclusions. For one thing, I realised you could have no idea what Eve Griffiths was and what she'd done. You simply believed the tissue of lies she'd invented for herself.'

She said slowly, 'She wrote me letters about you. Reams of them telling me how wonderful you were—and how much in love she was. She was so pretty, yet she'd never really had any serious relationships before, so I was glad for her. And, if I'm honest, relieved too.'

'Because she was going to be someone else's problem?'

'Yes.' Tarn winced. 'How awful that sounds. I'm so ashamed.'

'Don't be,' he said. 'It shows your instincts were working well. You should have listened to them and washed your hands of her long ago.'

'But I couldn't,' she said in a low voice. 'Her father was good to me. I always felt I had to look out for her, and Aunt Hazel too, for his sake.' She shook her head. 'I never knew how much Evie had resented that. Resented me.'

'Because you didn't know her.' He spoke forcefully, his eyes searching her face. 'Don't you understand, my love? You were guilty of nothing except being too loving and too loyal, and those are wonderful qualities, even when they're aimed at the wrong target.'

He sighed harshly. 'My God, I envied her for that, and wished with all my heart that I'd been the recipient instead.'

He paused. 'But I think what concerned me most was that you never actually asked me about this alleged affair. Faced me and demanded the truth.'

'Because I couldn't,' she cried passionately. 'Don't you see that? When I first met you all I could think about was avenging Evie's heartbreak. I told myself she was all that mattered.

That knowing you'd been punished for your treatment of her might genuinely help her back on the road to recovery.

'Then when everything began to change and I fell in love with you, it was too late. Because you'd have wanted to know why I hadn't spoken before—why I'd been deceiving you about who I really was, and what could I say? I was trapped in all the secrets—all the lies, and going on seemed the only solution.'

She looked away. 'Besides, I was afraid what the truth might be. I could see how you might have become bored by her, and I was scared that you'd admit that you'd been using her after all. That you'd never given a damn about her but were making a fool out of a silly girl, simply because you could, and I—I couldn't bear that either. Because it might mean you could do the same to me. That you could break me and throw me away just as easily.'

Caz said almost helplessly, 'Oh, dear God.' He was silent for a moment, then: 'In all honesty, Tarn, I wouldn't have known what to say. I'd never taken stalking particularly seriously. Probably no-one does until it starts happening. Apart from saying "good morning" while she was working at Brandon, I don't think I said one word to Eve Griffiths. I certainly never saw her at the flat, and I'm not sure I even knew her name.

'Occasionally at social events, I was aware of being intensely scrutinised by a pretty blonde, but that's an occupational hazard for any bloke who's ever featured on a rich list.'

He shrugged, his mouth twisting ruefully. 'Some women come on to you, and you have to decide pretty early in life whether or not you'll allow that, and I decided against. I prefer to do my own chasing.

'In the end, it was only when the bad stuff started that the truth dawned on me, and for a while my life became hell on earth. At that time, I admit I would gladly have had her locked up and thrown the key away, so that part of your accusation was pretty much true.

'I thought once she'd agreed to have treatment, it would be

over, but Jack Wainwright warned me it was never that simple, and he was right. At the moment, her attitude to me swings like a pendulum from one extreme to another, but Jack hopes that, over time, that will resolve itself.

'She's giving the police a bad time too, co-operating one day and in total denial the next.'

Tarn gasped. 'Is there nothing I can do?'

'Why, yes,' he said. 'You can leave her to the experts. Jack and his team can and will help her, once she accepts that it's her problem and no-one else's, but it will be a long haul and, as you found today, your intervention only makes matters worse. So you do not get involved.

'Besides,' he added. 'You're going to have other things on your mind, my sweet.'

'I—don't understand.' Her tone faltered a little. He hadn't moved a step but Tarn had the curious sensation she had only to stretch out her hand to touch him.

'Then I'll explain,' he said. 'I realised last night that nothing that had gone wrong between us actually mattered—not if the alternative was spending the rest of my life without you.'

'Caz.' Her words seemed to trip over themselves. 'Oh, Caz, you can't still want me—not after what I've done…'

'No?' He shook his head, the stark look fading from his face, to be replaced by a pleading tenderness that made her tremble. 'Then hear this. I meant every word of the note I left for you, Tarn. We may not have had the ceremony, but, by God, we had the wedding. You're still the only girl I'll ever love, ever need, and when you gave yourself to me, you became my wife, body and soul.

'There was no deception in that, Tarn.' His voice shook. 'It was love, pure and simple, and nothing can change that—unless, of course, you've decided that, because of all the other stuff, we're better apart.

'And even then I'm not letting you walk away, because we belong together and we both know it.'

He drew a breath. 'So, no more secrets, my dearest one. No more pretence. Just an old-fashioned marriage. A home together. A family. Is it a deal?'

She was never sure which of them moved first, only that they were in each other's arms, bodies pressed together in passionate intimacy, smiling mouths warm and seeking.

And when at last Caz raised his head, Tarn still clung to him, nuzzling his throat, breathing the scent of his skin, joy unfolding inside her like the petals of a flower.

He said unsteadily, 'Jack's been very tolerant, darling, but I think he might draw the line at us making love on his carpet. Where are you staying?'

'An airport place.'

He grimaced. 'It sounds as inviting as the place I picked. Why don't we collect your things, and find somewhere with four-poster beds and great food so we can begin our honeymoon.'

Tarn played with a button on his shirt. 'We're not actually married—if you remember.'

He kissed the tip of her nose. 'A minor point and strictly technical. After the honeymoon, we'll seek out a church with a friendly vicar, get him to call the banns and do the deed in style. I'll even get Jack to give you away.'

'Oh, God, I've got a hire car,' Tarn suddenly remembered as they walked hand in hand to the door. 'I'll have to return it.'

Caz shook his head. 'I'll arrange for it to be picked up,' he told her firmly. 'Because, my darling, I don't plan to let you out of my sight for some considerable time—day or night.'

Tarn laughed as she reached up, drawing his head down to her. 'That's definitely a deal,' she said, a world of promise in her voice. And kissed him.

* * * * *

COUNT VALIERI'S
PRISONER

CHAPTER ONE

IT WAS QUIET in the lamplit room, the only sound the occasional rustle of paper as the man seated on one side of the vast antique desk went through the contents of the file in front of him. He was unhurried, his black brows drawn together in a faint frown as he closely scanned each printed sheet in turn, then laid it aside.

The grey-haired man sitting opposite watched him, under the guise of studying his fingernails. It was over two years since they'd had cause to meet face to face, and there was no longer even a trace of the boy he had once known in the dark, incisive face bent over the documents he had brought for him only a few hours ago.

He had been welcomed with the usual courtesy, conducted by the *maggiodomo* to the room where he would spend the night, after which he had dined alone with his host. The food had been delicious, and on the surface, it was all charm and relaxation, but he was under no illusions.

The real business of his visit was being conducted right here and now.

Eventually, his reading concluded, the younger man looked up and gave a brief nod of approbation.

'You have been more than thorough, Signor Massimo. I commend you. An entire life laid out for my inspection in every detail. Invaluable.'

His swift smile momentarily softened the hard lines of his mouth and brought an added glint to eyes that were almost the colour of amber, flecked with gold.

It was a proud face with a high-bridged nose, classically moulded cheekbones and an uncompromising chin.

But now too austere to be truly handsome, thought Guido Massimo as he inclined his head in polite acknowledgement. And too coldly purposeful. The face of a stranger.

He waited as the other took the photograph which was the last object remaining in the file and studied it. The girl looking back at him was blonde, her pale hair hanging in a sleek silken curtain almost to her shoulders. Her face was oval with creamy skin, her eyes a clear grey. Her nose was short and straight, her chin firm and the delicately curved lips were parted in a slight but confident smile.

'When was this taken?'

'A few months ago on the occasion of her engagement,' Signor Massimo returned. 'It appeared in a magazine published in the county where she was brought up.' He allowed himself a discreet twinkle. *'Che bella ragazza.'*

His comment received only an indifferent shrug.

'This cool Anglo-Saxon type has no appeal for me.' The other's mouth twisted. 'Which, under the circumstances, must be deemed fortunate.' He paused. 'But no doubt her *fidanzato* will have a very different view and will pay the required price for her safe return. Or we must hope so.'

Signor Massimo murmured politely, keeping his expression impassive. He was well aware that his host's tastes in women favoured the elegantly voluptuous, but it would have been unwise even to hint that he possessed such knowledge.

The younger man returned the photograph to the file with an air of finality and leaned back in his chair, frowning again. 'The wedding is scheduled to take place in two months, which means there is no time to be lost. However it will make the resolution of the matter increasingly urgent, which is all to the good.'

Almost absently he began to play with the heavy gold signet ring he wore on his right hand. 'Tell me more about this television company she works for. You say it makes programmes for various arts channels?'

'And with some success. She is currently a researcher with a desire to move into production, but it seems marriage will end such hopes. As I have mentioned in the report, her *fidanzato* has already made it clear that he does not want his wife to work.'

The other nodded. 'And this has a caused—a certain amount of friction?'

'It seems so. As yet unresolved.'

'Ambition versus love.' The cool, deep voice spoke more softly. Became almost meditative. 'Which will she choose, I wonder, when serious temptation is offered.' He paused. 'Are you a betting man, Signor Massimo?'

'On rare occasions only.'

'And where would you place your money in such a situation.'

Guido Massimo gave a faint shrug. 'A girl soon to be a bride. She will wish to please her groom, I think.'

'You are unexpectedly romantic, *signore*. But I feel you are mistaken.' His smile was a curl of the lips. 'Because I know the bait that will bring her to me.'

'If I can be of further assistance...' the older man began, but was stopped by a raised hand.

'I am grateful but I believe that from here it is better for your involvement to cease. What happens should be my responsibility, and I would not wish you to have to answer any awkward questions, so the less you know the better.'

His tone became brisker. 'Leaving just the matter of your fee to be dealt with.' He opened a drawer in the desk, extracted a bulky envelope and handed it over. 'For the same reasons, we agreed this transaction should be on a cash basis. You may of course count it.'

'I would not dream of such a thing.'

'As you please.' The other paused. 'Which means I have only to thank you once more and wish you a peaceful night. We shall meet tomorrow at breakfast.'

Guido Massimo rose, made a slight bow and walked to the door where he hesitated. 'I must ask this. You are—determined? Quite sure there is no other course? The girl, after all, is an innocent party in all this. Does she deserve to be treated in such a way? I only enquire, you understand.'

'I comprehend perfectly. But you must not distress yourself, my friend. Once I have what I want, your *bella ragazza* will be returned as good as new to her future husband.' He added unsmilingly, 'That is, of course, if she still wants him.' He rose too, tall and lithe, his hands resting on his lean hips. 'There is no necessity to pity her, I assure you.'

But I shall do so, just the same, Guido Massimo thought as he left the room. And I shall also pity the boy I once knew, and remember him in my prayers.

'Darling,' said Jeremy. 'Please tell me this is some sort of joke.'

Madeleine Lang put down her glass and stared at him across the table in the wine bar in genuine perplexity. 'A joke?' she repeated. 'I'm talking about work here and perfectly serious. Why on earth would I be joking?'

Jeremy gave a hollow laugh. 'Oh, just a small matter of a wedding for over two hundred guests to arrange. Or will that be put on hold while you roam round Italy on some wild goose chase?'

Madeleine bit her lip. 'Hardly on hold, with your step-mother so firmly in control. I doubt if my absence will even be noticed.'

There was an edgy pause, then Jeremy reached across and

took her hand, his expression rueful. 'Sweetheart, I know Esme can be rather managing...'

Madeleine sighed. 'Jeremy, that's putting it mildly, and you know it. Everything I want and suggest is just—brushed aside. I don't even feel that it is our wedding any more.'

'I'm sorry, Maddie.' Jeremy's tone was coaxing. 'But—it's a really big deal for the family, and Dad wants everything to be perfect. Times may be hard but Sylvester and Co is still riding high. That kind of thing.'

'If it only was a family affair,' Madeleine muttered. She sat back, reaching for her glass. 'For one thing, where have all those guests come from? I've never even heard of two thirds of them.'

'Clients of the bank, business associates, old friends of my father.' Jeremy sounded rueful. 'But believe me it could have been very much worse. What we have now is the shortlist.'

'I don't find that particularly reassuring,' Madeleine told him candidly.

'Oh, come on, it's not that bad.' Jeremy paused awkwardly. 'But it could be if you persist with this Italian nonsense.'

She said slowly, 'I can't believe you just said that. First it was a joke, now it's nonsense. Jeremy, we're talking about my work here...'

'It used to be your work.' His tone was defensive. 'But very soon now it won't be, so what is the point in your shooting off across Europe in pursuit of some musician no-one's ever heard of?'

'But people have heard of her,' Madeleine fired back. 'Floria Bartrando was said to be the most wonderful young soprano of her generation. It was predicted she was going to be another Maria Callas, and then suddenly, with no explanation, she dropped off the edge of the world. It's been a major mystery for thirty years and now I have the chance to solve it.'

'But why you?' Frowning, he refilled their glasses. 'You're not the only researcher on the team.'

'Apparently the Italian contacts saw the programme on Hadley Cunningham's last symphony,' Madeleine said levelly. 'The one no-one knew he'd written. I did most of the research on that. So Todd offered me this.'

Jeremy's frown deepened. 'Frankly, darling, when you said you had something to tell me I assumed you meant that you'd handed in your notice as we'd agreed.'

'I said I'd think about it,' Madeleine said quietly. 'Having done so, I'm not walking away from a job I love without good reason.' She added, 'But I have booked out our honeymoon weeks as holiday.'

Jeremy stared at her as if she'd grown an extra head. 'And I'm supposed to be grateful for that?' he asked sarcastically.

'Well, you should be,' she said cheerfully. 'After all, you'd hardly want to go to the Maldives on your own.'

'I'm sorry, but I don't find this particularly amusing.'

'And nor do I. In fact I'm perfectly serious.' She gave him a rueful look. 'Jeremy, please try to understand.'

'What's to understand?' His shrug was almost petulant. 'Clearly finding material for minority interest television channels matters more to you than being my wife.'

'And now you're talking nonsense,' Madeleine retorted hotly. 'It's the twenty-first century, for heaven's sake, and most women combine marriage and a career these days in case you hadn't noticed.'

'Well, I want you to regard our marriage as your career,' Jeremy said, his lips tightening. 'I don't think you appreciate how hectic our social life will become, or how much entertaining we'll have to do. And I mean full blown dinner parties, not you rushing in at the last moment with a takeaway.'

She gasped. 'Is that how you see me? As some ditsy incompetent?'

'No, my sweet, of course not.' He was back in placatory

mode. 'It's just that we're not sure you realise how much you'll be taking on, or how stressful you might find it.'

Maddie sat back in her seat, and gave him a straight look. 'I presume that's not the royal "we" you were using there? That you're quoting your father?'

'Naturally it's been discussed.'

She bit her lip. 'Jeremy—the wedding may have got away from us, but this is our marriage, and you must make him see that.' Her voice deepened in intensity. 'I have no intention of letting you down, or failing to provide you with the support you need in your career. All I ask is that you do the same for me. Is that so very hard?'

There was a silence, then he said, 'I suppose—not when you put it like that. I'll talk to Dad again. Which reminds me...' He glanced at his watch and pulled a face. 'I should be going. I'm due to meet him with some people at The Ivy.'

He paused. 'Sure you won't come with me? It's no problem.'

Maddie got to her feet, forcing a smile as she indicated the slim-fitting jeans and white shirt she was wearing. 'Except I'm not dressed for dinner at a top restaurant, which might create its own difficulty. Another time, darling.'

'So what will you do?' He sounded anxious.

She shrugged on her navy and white checked jacket and reached for her canvas shoulder bag. 'Oh—have a girlie night in, washing my hair, giving myself a manicure.'

And I have just told my fiancé, the man I love, my first deliberate lie. Because actually, I'm going back to the office to do some more work on Floria Bartrando, but I doubt it would be politic to say so at this juncture.

Jeremy pulled her to him and kissed her. 'We mustn't fight,' he muttered. 'We can work things out. I know it.'

'Yes,' she said. 'Of course we can.' And kissed him back.

Outside the wine bar, she watched him hail a cab, then waved goodbye before beginning to walk slowly back towards the street where the Athene television production company was based.

She supposed that the recent confrontation had been inevitable, but knowing that made it no easier to handle. Somehow, she had to convince Jeremy that she could succeed as a working wife, a task handicapped from the outset by his father's forthright and openly expressed opinions to the contrary.

Maddie had known the Sylvesters pretty much all her life. Beth Sylvester, an old school friend of her mother, had been her godmother, and, as a child, Maddie had spent part of every summer at Fallowdene, the Sylvesters' big country house.

It had always seemed idyllic to her, but in retrospect she could see there'd been undercurrents which she'd been too young to pick up.

But somehow she'd known instinctively from the first that while her godmother would always be 'Aunt Beth', her husband would remain 'Mr Sylvester' and never become 'Uncle Nigel'.

Fallowdene was not in itself a beautiful house, yet to Maddie it had always seemed an enchanted place, especially when Jeremy, the Sylvesters' only son, seven years her senior and light years older in every way, was there to be shadowed adoringly.

But she'd never allowed him to get away with any implication that they'd been childhood sweethearts.

'Arrant nonsense,' she'd teased, the first time it was mentioned. 'You thought I was a total pain in the neck, and went out of your way to ignore me.'

'But I've made up for it since,' he'd whispered, drawing her close. 'Admit it.'

Yet her most abiding memories were not of Jeremy at all, even though her initial crush had lasted well into her early teens.

What she recalled very vividly was the way the atmosphere of the house underwent a subtle change when Nigel Sylvester came home.

He was a man of just above medium height, who somehow gave the impression of being much taller. He had gone prematurely grey in his late twenties, or so Jeremy had told her, adding glumly, 'I hope it doesn't happen to me.'

Maddie had stroked his cheek, smiling. 'You'd look extremely distinguished.'

But if she was totally honest, she'd always found Nigel Sylvester's silver hair, which he wore slightly longer than was fashionable and swept straight back from his forehead, to be in odd and disturbing contrast to his curiously smooth, unlined face, and dark brown heavy-lidded eyes.

Nor was it just his appearance that used to unnerve her. His standards were exacting, he missed nothing, and although she had never heard him raise his voice in displeasure, Maddie often thought it would have been better if he had shouted occasionally.

Because, there was something about his quietness which dried Maddie's throat when he spoke to her, and made her stumble over her words. Not that she ever had too much to say to him. She'd divined fairly soon that her presence at Fallowdene was tolerated by him, rather than welcomed, and tried to keep out of his way.

It wasn't too difficult. She'd been given the old nursery as her room, and this contained a glass-fronted bookcase, crammed with children's books by well-known authors in a range that appealed from tots to teens.

At first, when she was very young, Aunt Beth had read them as bedtime stories. Later, she'd been happy to while away solitary hours in their company.

But her happy childhood had been brought to an abrupt and tragic end one terrible winter night when an icy road and a driver who'd drunk too much at an office party had fatally combined to take both her parents from her.

She'd been staying with Aunt Fee, her mother's younger sister, at the time, and her aunt had immediately assumed charge of her, only to be approached after the funeral by Aunt Beth with an offer to adopt her god-daughter.

But the offer had been refused. Instead Aunt Fee and Uncle Patrick, her big genial husband had been quietly adamant that Maddie belonged with them, and she'd been loved, allowed to grieve then eventually find healing in their comfortable untidy house.

Her visits to Fallowdene, however, continued as before, although the question of adoption was never raised again and, in hindsight, Maddie was sure that Nigel Sylvester had probably opposed the idea from the outset.

She realized since that, although she'd been too young to recognize it at the time, he had represented her first brush with real power.

And she'd often wondered what had persuaded her godmother, with her quiet prettiness and sudden mischievous, enchanting smile, to marry him.

She had been in her first year at university when Aunt Beth died very suddenly in her sleep of a heart attack. She'd attended the funeral with her aunt and uncle and haltingly attempted to express her sorrow to Mr Sylvester, who'd muttered an abrupt word of thanks, then turned away.

And she was realistic enough to know that she would no longer be welcome at Fallowdene.

A week or so later she was astonished to receive a letter from a law firm informing her that Aunt Beth had left her a sum of money substantial enough to get her through her degree course without having to seek a student loan, with an additional bequest of the entire book collection from the nursery, which somehow meant far more than the money.

'Oh, how wonderful of her,' she'd said softly, wiping her eyes. 'She always knew how much I loved them.' She paused. 'But won't Jeremy want them?'

'It seems not,' Aunt Fee said rather drily. 'I gather if you'd refused the bequest they'd have gone to a charity shop.' She pursed her lips. 'No doubt they reminded Nigel too much of the wonderful career he'd interrupted.'

'Career?' Maddie repeated. 'Was she a writer once?' She frowned. 'She never told me.'

'No, that wasn't her talent. She was a very successful editor with Penlaggan Press. She found the authors of all those books, encouraged them, and published them.

'Your mother told me Penlaggan did their best to coax her back on numerous occasions, even offering to let her work from home.' She shook her head. 'But it never happened. Sylvester wives, it seems, do not work.'

'But if she was so good at her job...'

'That,' said Aunt Fee somberly, 'was probably the trouble.'

It was an insight into Aunt Beth's marriage that Maddie had never forgotten. And now it had a renewed and unpleasing resonance.

Well, I'm good at my job too, she thought, and I'm damned if I'm giving it up whatever Jeremy or his father may say about it.

She still felt raw when she remembered how Nigel Sylvester, having mourned for barely a year, announced his engagement to a widow called Esme Hammond and married her only a month later.

But then, quite unexpectedly, she'd met Jeremy again at a party in London. He'd expressed delight at seeing her and asked for her phone number, but if she felt this was more out of politeness than serious intent, she soon discovered she was wrong. Because he'd not only called but invited her to dinner. After which, events had seemed to snowball, she remembered, smiling.

Jeremy had changed a great deal from the taciturn, aloof boy who'd so consistently avoided an annoying small girl. He seemed to have inherited much of his mother's charm, but in spite of three years at university and a spell at the Harvard Business School before joining Sylvester and Co, he still seemed under his father's thumb.

But while Maddie did not delude herself she would have been his daughter-in-law of choice, at least Nigel Sylvester had not openly opposed the engagement.

But she still didn't call him 'Uncle Nigel', she thought, pausing at the office's street entrance to punch in her entry code. Nor, after the wedding, would he ever morph into 'Dad', 'Pa' or 'Pops'.

And he had put a spoke in their wheel in another way.

If Maddie had assumed that Jeremy would immediately want her to move into the company flat with him, she soon found she was wrong..

'Dad says he needs to use the flat himself on occasion,' he told her. 'And it would make things—awkward if you were there. And anyway he feels we should wait to live together until we're actually married.'

Maddie had stared at him. 'But who on earth does that nowadays?'

Jeremy shrugged. 'I guess he's just old-fashioned about these things.'

But Maddie was convinced 'hypocritical' was a better description, and would have wagered a year's salary that his father and the glamorous Esme had been sharing a bed even while Aunt Beth was alive.

'And what happens after the wedding?' she asked. 'Because, we'll be living there then, or will your father expect me to move out any time he plans to stay overnight?'

'No, of course not,' he said impatiently. 'He's talking of taking a suite at a hotel.' He pulled a face. 'And, believe me, sweetie, it could be worse. When it began, Sylvester and Co was Sylvester, Felderstein and Marchetti. You could be having all sorts of foreign directors dropping in.'

'Might have been fun,' Maddie said lightly. 'So why aren't there any now?'

Jeremy shrugged again. 'The families died out, or started new ventures of their own. That's what Dad said, anyway. We only became fully independent in my grandfather's day.'

Since when Nigel Sylvester had achieved success in the corridors of power, joining various government think-tanks and advising on banking and economic affairs.

So much so that, rumour had it that he would be offered a life peerage in the next New Year Honours' List.

I wonder if he'll expect me to call him 'My lord' she mused as she took the creaky elevator to her office on the first floor. Or curtsy when we meet. While Esme will be even more insufferable when she's Lady Sylvester.

But I'll deal with that when I have to, she told herself. For now, I'm concentrating on this dream assignment that's come my way.

Italy in May, she thought with an ecstatic sigh. Boy, I can hardly wait.

CHAPTER TWO

IT WASN'T UNTIL the plane had taken off that Maddie really believed she was going to Italy.

In view of the events of the past ten days, she would hardly have been surprised if Nigel Sylvester had found some way to have her bodily removed from the aircraft.

It had all come to a head over dinner at the company flat. She had believed with pleasurable anticipation that she and Jeremy would be alone, and was shaken to find his father and Esme waiting for her too, with Mr Sylvester telling her, with his thin-lipped smile, 'We feel we should all get to know each other a little better, Madeleine.'

Heart sinking, as she realised Jeremy was avoiding her gaze, she'd replied, 'By all means,' and accepted the dry sherry she was offered.

Conversation had been light and general over dinner, but she'd only picked at the excellent meal, cooked by the housekeeper Mrs Palmer, and watched with trepidation as the good woman was thanked and dismissed once the coffee and brandy were on the table.

The door had barely closed behind her when Esme leaned forward. 'I think, Madeleine, if the men will forgive us boring them with feminine affairs, we need to discuss your wedding dress as a matter of urgency.'

Maddie put down her coffee cup, bewildered. 'But that's all in hand.'

Mrs Sylvester's arched brows lifted. 'Indeed? I am not sure I understand.'

'I've chosen my dress and it's already being made by Janet Gladstone, who owns the bridal shop in the village. You must have seen it.'

'Not that I recall.' Esme's tone suggested she had not noticed the High Street either. 'And, anyway, I've made an appointment for you with Nina FitzAlan in three days' time.' Her smile was complacent. 'As I'm a favoured client she has agreed to drop everything in order to supply us with a gown of her own exclusive design. But there is no time to be lost.'

'That's very kind of you,' Maddie said evenly. 'But I'm afraid I can't possibly alter my arrangements, especially as Aunt Fee and Uncle Patrick are paying for my dress, and those of the bridesmaids.'

'And naturally you feel that a top London designer is beyond their reach, financially.' The older woman nodded. 'Well, don't concern yourself about that. Nina's bill, of course, will be sent to me. There is no need for your aunt and uncle to be bothered.'

'But they will be bothered. And so will I. Very much so.' Maddie ignored Jeremy's pleading glance from the other side of the table. 'Because I'm getting exactly what I want. White wild silk embroidered with silver flowers. I've already had two fittings, and it's going to be beautiful.'

Esme allowed herself the small, tinkling laugh that made Maddie's teeth ache. 'I don't think you have quite grasped, my dear, that you are dressing for a very important occasion. And a village-made frock, however pretty, just will not do.' She paused. 'So we will have a preliminary meeting with Nina at ten thirty on Thursday, after which you will hold yourself available for fittings at her salon whenever required.

'And as you've mentioned bridesmaids,' she went on. 'Perhaps this is the time to say that while I admire your loyalty in wanting your flatmates Sally and—Tracey, is it...'

'Trisha,' said Maddie.

'I think I told you.' Esme swept on, 'that Nigel would like his godsons' little ones to be your attendants. Two pigeon pairs—so convenient—and, I thought, in Victorian dress. Those charming caps for the boys, and frilly pantaloons for the little girls.'

Maddie's hands were clenched tightly in her lap. 'And I think I made it clear that I would not, under any circumstances, have very small children following me up the aisle. Especially ones I have never met, but, I gather, are barely potty-trained. Which,' she added, 'would make me fear for the pantaloons. Besides, Sally and Trisha are old college friends as well as my flatmates, so they will be my bridesmaids—the only ones.'

She paused. 'And, as, I'm going to be working abroad shortly, I couldn't be available for fittings with Ms FitzAlan, even if I wanted to.'

'On the contrary,' said Nigel Sylvester in a tone which made Maddie feel she'd been stranded naked on a polar ice cap. 'I think it is full time you recognised that you have responsibilities to my son that far outweigh your obligations to this—tin-pot job of yours, and hand your company a week's notice.'

Maddie lifted her chin. 'And you must also recognise I have no intention of abandoning my career.'

'Career?' he repeated almost meditatively. 'I think, my child, that you're deluding yourself.'

He then proceeded to deal quite mercilessly with her qualifications, her abilities and her ambitions, holding them up to ridicule, and dismissing them with quiet contempt, and all of it uttered with a smile like a naked blade held to her skin.

While all she could do was sit, head bent, in silence until it was over.

'How could you?' she flared at Jeremy when they were back in her own flat and alone, Sally and Trisha having taken a swift look at her white face and blazing eyes and tactfully disappeared to bed. 'I thought we'd already dealt with this. So how could you just sit there and let him speak to me—treat me like that?'

'I've told you time and again how he feels about working wives,' Jeremy said unhappily. 'And I've also tried to explain how Dad sees the importance of this wedding.'

She was about to hit back when she saw how wretched he was becoming and took a deep, steadying breath. It's not his fault, she reminded herself. His father has bullied him all his life. You know this.

'Darling,' she said. 'Esme and your father may have taken over most of the arrangements, but they're not adding me to their bag. I shall wear the dress I want, and have Sal and Trish as my backup on the day itself. No toddlers in sight. Not negotiable.'

He said slowly, 'But there's Italy. If I begged you not to go, would you think again?'

'I don't want you to beg,' she said more gently. 'Just to understand how much I want to research the Floria Bartrando story. I'll be gone a matter of days, that's all. It's not a problem.'

'It already is.' He shook his head. 'Dad's totally vitriolic on the subject, as if he's got a down on the entire Italian nation.'

'Your father simply has a down on not getting his own way at all times,' Maddie told him candidly. 'It wouldn't matter if it was Italy—or Outer Mongolia. However I can't and I won't give way to him, because that would set an unacceptable precedent. You must see that.'

She paused. 'Of course, we could always elope. Get a special licence and do the deed somewhere with a couple of strangers as witnesses.'

Jeremy looked at her with blank horror. 'You can't be serious.'

She hadn't been entirely joking either, she thought, suppressing a sigh.

She forced a smile. 'Alternatively, you could always come with me to Italy. Take a few days of all the leave you're owed and explore the delights of Liguria.' *And we could be alone as lovers again with no-one to interfere or disapprove. Get back to the time when we first fell in love. Wouldn't that be good?*

She added, 'And if I had you as an escort, that might placate your father about the trip in general.'

His mouth tightened. 'No,' he said. 'It wouldn't. And now I'd better go.' He took her in his arms and held her tightly. 'Oh, Maddie, I hate it when we quarrel.'

And I hate it when we have quarrels forced upon us, thought Maddie, fighting her disappointment as she kissed him and said goodnight.

And in the morning, she mused as she closed the door behind him, I shall have to tell the others it was a lovers' tiff. Pre-marital nerves or something. And see if they believe me.

Ironically, soon afterwards it began to seem as if Nigel Sylvester might get his own way after all.

Because Todd, her boss at Athene came within a whisker of calling the whole Bartrando project off.

'We need to know why a young singer with the world at her feet should simply disappear for thirty-odd years,' he'd said, frowning, at one of the morning conferences. 'We were promised a preliminary interview with Floria Bartrando herself, yet now they seem to be fobbing us off with a small provincial opera festival instead.' He snorted. 'And that's not worth the expense of the airfare, even if it is being sponsored by some local bigwig.'

'Perhaps she's making her comeback at this festival,' Maddie suggested, trying not to sound too anxious. If it all fell through, she could imagine Nigel Sylvester's triumph and the increased pressure to fall in with all future plans as a result.

Todd shrugged. 'Then, in that case, why don't they say so? I'm worried that this whole Bartrando thing could simply be a publicity stunt, and you'll end up being shown a grave in a cemetery and told that the festival's in her memory.'

'In which case, I use my return ticket, and we bin the entire project.' Maddie tried to sound upbeat. 'But I'm sure it's all going to work out.'

And a few days later when Todd summoned her to his office, it appeared she was right.

'I did the festival sponsor an injustice,' he announced, tapping the letter on the desk in front of him. 'He's written to us, in person, snail mail. His name's Count Valieri and he's apparently the link with Signorina Bartrando, so you'll be liaising with him.

'He'll have you met at the airport in Genoa and taken to the Hotel Puccini in Trimontano, where the festival will take place later in the year. And he'll contact you there and set up a meeting with the mystery lady.' He grinned. 'Maybe you should pack a posh frock if you're going to be hobnobbing with Italian aristocracy.'

'I'm more likely to be palmed off on some private secretary,' Maddie returned unruffled. 'But I'd better find out a bit about him, to be on the safe side.'

'I've already had a quick look online, and there isn't much.' Todd frowned. 'Just that the Valieri family actually started the festival over fifty years ago, so he's probably quite elderly, although there's no picture. And the family money now comes mainly from olive oil and ceramics. Apart from that—zilch.'

'Then it's fortunate we're not planning to tell his story.' She hesitated. 'Did he drop any hints about Signorina Bartrando?'

'Not one. Here, you'd better have it.' He handed her the

sheet of elegant cream notepaper and she read the two short paragraphs.

The Count used black ink, she saw, and his handwriting was crisp and incisive.

Back in her office, she checked the hotel he'd booked for her on the internet and saw it had an impressive number of stars, and its food and comfort were highly praised by recent guests.

So far, so good, she thought, wondering if Puccini's name was significant. After all, Floria Bartrando's first important role had been Musetta in 'La Boheme'. She'd received rave notices, completely eclipsing the woman playing Mimi. In fact, several critics thought she'd been miscast, and that her voice was more suited to the dramatic coloratura range of the leading part.

And her short but starry career had fully justified their opinion.

So maybe she simply disappeared because of death threats from other sopranos, thought Maddie, faintly amused.

But there'd been little to smile about since then. Jeremy had reacted badly to the news that her trip was definitely going ahead, and there'd been a definite coolness between them ever since. But that, she told herself, was probably due to his father giving him a hard time.

She had really hoped he would relent sufficiently to see her off at the airport, but there was no sign of him.

In the departure lounge she'd sent him a text— 'You'd better be pleased to see me when I get back', adding a row of kisses, but there'd been no response to that either and she'd boarded the plane, edgy and with the beginnings of a headache as she fought her disappointment.

When the trolley came round, she bought some orange juice and took a couple of painkillers, then settled back in her seat, deciding to close her eyes for a few moments.

But when the next sound she heard was the captain's voice

announcing they had begun their descent to Cristoforo Columbo Airport, she realised, startled, just how tired she must have been.

As the plane turned inland, she caught her breath as she saw ahead of her, in fold after jagged fold, the peaks of the Apennines, some of them still streaked with snow.

She knew, of course, that in Italy, the mountains were never too far away, but these seemed almost too near. In some strange way—almost alien.

But she would begin an even closer acquaintance with them when she reached Trimontano, she reminded herself as the aircraft touched down.

While visualising them as threatening in some way was being over-imaginative, and showed the kind of stress she'd been under lately.

And which she'd come here to escape.

As she emerged from Arrivals, she was approached by a uniformed official.

'Signorina Lang?' His smile reassured her. 'I have been asked to escort you to the Count's car. Camillo, his driver, speaks no English.'

'Oh,' said Maddie. 'Well—that's very kind.'

This Count must be a real force to be reckoned with, she decided, as she was conducted through the terminal and out into the warm May sunlight to what appeared to be a private parking area, where a grizzled man in a chauffeur's uniform was waiting beside a limousine.

Well even if this turns out to be a journey to nowhere, Maddie thought with slight hysteria, as he inclined his head unsmilingly and opened the rear passenger door for her, at least I'll have travelled in style.

She'd been right, she told herself, leaning back against the cushions, to opt for a trim navy skirt rather than her usual jeans, although her jacket, which had received a faintly disparaging glance from Camillo, was denim. But she was glad of it once the car moved off, and the air conditioning came into play.

In front of her was a square leather case, which on investigation proved to be a cold box, containing bottled mineral water and fruit juice.

Every comfort, in fact, she thought. However, it would all have been rather more pleasant if Camillo had only spoken some English and she could have questioned him about their route and Trimontano itself.

He might even have been able to tell her something about Floria Bartrando's connection with this area, especially as the singer had been living and working far away in Rome just before her disappearance, and winning plaudits for her interpretation of Gilda in 'Rigoletto'.

But perhaps this should be left to the Count.

The port and its environs were soon left behind, the car powering its way through heavy traffic on a broad, busy road. Then, after about fifteen minutes, they turned on to another much narrower road, and, as if someone had flicked a switch, the landscape changed. No more urban sprawl or industrial development, but chestnut trees, olive groves and scrubby pastureland covering the foothills of the mountains, and the occasional scattered hamlet, clinging to the slopes.

The traffic they encountered now consisted mainly of farm wagons, groups of hikers sweating under large rucksacks, and packs of red-faced cyclists pounding up the increasingly steep ascent.

Maddie, drinking some water from the silver cup provided for the purpose, was ignobly glad not to be of their number.

At the same time, she became aware that the brightness of the day had faded, and that heavy clouds were massing round the peaks in a frankly ominous way.

Bad weather would be disappointing, she thought with an inward shrug as the vision of sun-kissed villas and cypresses silhouetted against an azure sky began to fade, but, after all, she wasn't here as a holidaymaker.

Nor had she expected Trimontano to be quite so remote—not when it was the centre of an annual opera festival. The audiences would need to be serious music lovers to make this kind of journey.

And what had possessed Floria Bartrando to forsake the world stage and bury herself among these mountains?

There had to be a real story here if only she could unravel it, she thought, impatient to get to her destination and make a start.

A few minutes later, the car reached a fork in the road, and Camillo turned off to the right and began to descend into a valley, shadowed by a group of three tall peaks.

And there, suddenly, was Trimontano, like a toy town cupped in the hand of a stone giant.

Maddie leaned forward, eagerly scanning the clustering red roofs below her, noticing how a tall bell tower rose out of the midst of them, startlingly white and pointing towards the darkening sky like an accusing finger.

And at the same moment, like a warning voice reverberating between the mountains, came the first long, low rumble of thunder.

Heavens, thought Maddie, sinking back in her seat. That's a hell of an introduction. Good job I'm not superstitious, or I might just be having second thoughts.

It had already begun to rain when the car finally came to a stop in front of the massive portico of the Hotel Puccini in the main square.

A uniformed man, holding an umbrella, came down the steps to open the car door and shelter Maddie on her way into the hotel, while Camillo followed with her solitary bag.

Which should, of course, have been a matched set of Louis Vuitton, Maddie realised as she looked around at the expanse of marble, mirrors and gilded pillars which made up the hotel foyer. She turned to thank Camillo and found herself watching his retreating back.

He's clearly used to a better class of passenger, she told herself ruefully as she walked to the reception desk.

But the receptionist's greeting passed no judgement, and the formalities were dealt with swiftly and efficiently.

'And there is also this, *signorina*.' He handed her an envelope along with her key card.

'From Count Valieri?' she asked.

'*Naturalmente*. On whose behalf, I am to welcome you to Trimontano.' He smiled, making a slight bow. 'You are in Number 205, *signorina*. The lift is behind you, and your luggage is already in your room. If you need further assistance you have only to ask.'

Rule one in a strange town—know the right people, Maddie thought as the lift took her smoothly to her floor.

Her bedroom was more modern than she had imagined, with an impressive range of fitted furniture in an elegant pale wood, together with the widest bed she had ever seen.

The bathroom was breathtaking too, tiled in white marble, streaked with gold. It had a large sunken tub with two cushioned head-rests, and a walk-in shower also big enough for dual occupation, and then some.

The ultimate in togetherness, Maddie thought, suppressing a pang of regret that she was there alone. But even if Jeremy was far away, at least she could talk to him.

She went back in the bedroom and retrieved her mobile phone from her bag, only to discover to her dismay that there was no discernible signal.

'Let's hope that's because of the prevailing weather conditions and not a general rule,' she muttered, as she dialled reception from the bedside phone and asked for an outside line.

But she had another disappointment when, after a struggle to get through, Jeremy's voicemail informed her he was out of the office.

Sighing, she replaced the receiver without leaving a message. After all, she'd nothing to tell him about her trip that he'd want to hear. The important thing had been to hear his voice, even if it was only a recording. Crumbs from the rich man's table, she thought ironically. Speaking of which...

She reached for the Count's envelope and tore it open.

'And if this is to say that Floria Bartrando won't see me, then I'll know bad luck really does run in threes,' she said as she unfolded the single sheet of paper it contained. As she did so, another smaller, flimsier strip of paper fluttered to the carpet.

Maddie picked it up and found she was looking at a ticket for the opera that night at the Teatro Grande. 'Verdi's 'Rigoletto,'' she whispered to herself in excitement. 'Floria's last appearance. This has to be significant.'

The accompanying note, written in the familiar black ink said only 'Until later', and was signed 'Valieri'.

A man of few words, the Count, thought Maddie joyfully. But what does that matter, bless every grey hair on his probably balding head?

And she kissed the ticket and laughed out loud, because it had proved to be third time lucky instead and she was in business.

CHAPTER THREE

As the curtain fell on Act Two, Maddie sank back in her seat with a breathless sigh. She had forgotten how dark the plot of 'Rigoletto' was with its curses, vendettas, seductions and betrayal, and the hunchback jester seeking vengeance on his lecherous master. But she'd certainly never forgotten Verdi's glorious music.

And the beautiful aria *'Caro nome'* where the doomed Gilda rhapsodises about her lover's name was still singing in her head as the lights came up. It had featured on one of Floria Bartrando's few albums, and Maddie had acquired a second-hand CD, playing it constantly while she was preparing for her trip, and bringing it with her.

The Teatro Grande wasn't quite as large as its name suggested, but its Baroque styling was magnificent, she thought, glancing up at the semi-circle of ornately decorated boxes above her.

During the first act interval, she had been convinced that someone up there was watching her, and had looked up, scanning the boxes eagerly in the hope of catching a glimpse of the Count, or even Floria Bartrando herself.

If she had been the subject of scrutiny, she hoped she'd passed muster. Wisely, she'd brought her favourite and most expensive dress, a simple black knee-length shift, square-necked and sleeveless, relying totally on cut and its heavy silk fabric for its stunning effect.

She'd left her hair loose but swept back from her face with silver combs, and apart from the silver studs in her ears, her only jewellery was Jeremy's diamond solitaire on her engagement finger.

She followed the rest of the audience to the small crowded bar and took her double espresso to a small table with a single chair in a quiet corner. As she sat, she noticed the picture on the wall above her. It was a large oil painting in a heavy gilded frame, its subject a seated man, white-haired but still handsome with a calm, proud face. A small plaque read 'Cesare Valieri'.

So this is my host, she thought. And where is he?

She leaned across to the attendant, clearing a nearby table. 'Count Valieri—is he here tonight?'

He hesitated, his glance sliding away. 'He came, *signorina*, for a brief time, but has gone. I am sorry.'

Well, it didn't really matter, she told herself, suppressing a pang of disappointment. They would meet eventually. And at least now she knew what to expect.

And her instinct about being watched might well have been correct, so it seemed odd that he had not used the opportunity to make himself known to her.

She settled back in her seat for Act III, waiting for the tragedy to reach its culmination, with Gilda sacrificing herself to save the villainous Duke who had seduced and betrayed her.

Shivering as Rigoletto tells his hired assassin 'He is crime and I am punishment.'

And feeling tears prick at her eyelids as the jester realising he has brought about the murder of his own child, flings himself, heartbroken, across her dead body.

The applause at the end was long and generous with cries of '*Bravo*' from all over the auditorium. It took a while for the stalls to clear and Maddie hung back, unsure what she should do.

Her best bet, she supposed, was to go back to the hotel and wait for instructions. Because she was sure there would be some.

In a way, she hoped they'd arrive tomorrow. It was late, and she felt suddenly very tired, as she walked out into the rain-washed street, hugging her cream pashmina around her. The stress of the past weeks coupled with the flight and the long car journey were clearly taking their toll.

I need sleep, she thought longingly, not an interview.

But the Count clearly had other ideas, she realised, recognising the unmistakable shape of his limousine, parked just across the street from the theatre, with its chauffeur in his dark uniform standing beside it holding the rear passenger door open for her.

And not Camillo this time. This new man was altogether taller and leaner. Younger too, she thought, although his peaked cap was pulled down shadowing his face, denying her a good look.

'Signorina Lang—you will come with me, please.' His voice was quiet, but it seemed to convey an order rather than a request, and Maddie hesitated.

'You're taking me to the Count?'

'Who does not like to be kept waiting.'

Slightly brusque for a paid employee, she thought as she climbed into the car, but at least he spoke English, so that was a step forward.

Not that any conversation was likely, however, while the glass panels between the front and rear seating remained firmly closed.

On the other hand, she didn't really feel like talking. The effect of the coffee had worn off and waves of drowsiness were sweeping over her.

But I can't go to sleep, she told herself firmly, suppress-

ing a yawn. *I have to stay awake and totally alert. This is an
important evening.* And made herself check once again that
her little voice operated tape machine and spare batteries
were safely in her bag.

What she really needed was the caffeine rush from another espresso, she thought, helping herself to some of the
chilled mineral water, in the hope that it would clear her head.

She began to rehearse some of the questions she needed
to ask, but instead found the words and music of the opera
still teeming through her brain.

I am Crime. He is Punishment. Except that was wrong,
surely. It was the other way round. *He is Crime...*

Wasn't that the way it went? She wasn't even sure any
more. But she could remember Rigoletto's despairing cry,
'Ah, the curse' and shivered again.

She wanted to knock on the glass and ask the chauffeur
not to drive quite so fast, but it was too much effort. Somehow it was much easier just to lean back against the cushions,
and let them support her until the jolting over the cobbled
streets ceased.

I'll close my eyes for a few minutes, she told herself,
yawning again. *A little catnap. I'll feel better then. Wide
awake. Ready for anything.*

And let herself slide gently down into a soft, welcoming
cloud of darkness.

Her first conscious thought was that the car had stopped
moving at last, and she no longer felt as if she was being
shaken to bits.

Her next—that she was no longer simply sitting down, but
lying flat as if she was on a couch. Or even a bed.

With a supreme effort, she lifted her heavy lids and discovered that she was indeed in a bed.

Oh God, I must have been taken ill, she thought, forcing
herself to sit up. *And I'm back at the hotel.*

But just one glance round the room disabused her of that notion.

For one thing, the bed she was lying in, though just as wide and comfortable as the one in Room 205, was clearly very much older with an elegant headboard in some dark wood, and a sumptuous crimson brocade coverlet.

For another, there seemed to be doors everywhere, she realised in bewilderment as she tried desperately to focus. Doors next to each other, in some impossible way, in every wall all round the large square room. Doors painted in shades of green, blue and pink, and interspersed with shuttered windows.

I'm not awake, she thought, falling limply back against the pillows. I can't be because this is obviously some weird dream.

She wasn't even wearing her own white lawn nightdress, but some astonishing garment in heavy sapphire silk with narrow straps and a deeply plunging neckline. And it was the faint shiver of the expensive fabric against her skin that finally convinced her that she wasn't dreaming. And that she hadn't fallen down a rabbit hole like Alice either.

The bed and this extraordinary door-filled room were not Wonderland at all, but total, if puzzling, reality.

Go back to your first conclusion, she told herself. You became ill in the Count's car, and you were brought here to recover. That's the only feasible explanation, even if you don't remember feeling unwell—just terribly sleepy.

And you've been looked after, although a room liable to give one hallucinations was perhaps not the best choice in the circumstances.

Thinking back, she seemed to remember a phrase which described this kind of décor. *Trompe l'oeil*, she thought. That was it. She'd come across it during some of her preliminary research on the Ligurian region, but had decided it was irrelevant.

However, it occurred to her that she was growing a little tired of mysteries and enigmas, whether verbal or visual, and would relish a little straight talking from here on in.

She would also prefer to get dressed, she thought, if only she knew where her clothes were.

She wondered too what time it was—and that was when she realised, with shock, that not only was she no longer wearing her wristwatch, but that, even more alarmingly, her engagement ring was also missing.

And it's not just my clothes, she thought frantically, as she shot bolt upright, suddenly wide awake as she stared round the room. Where's my bag? My money, passport, credit cards, mobile phone, tape recorder—everything?

Suddenly, the fact that she was next door to naked in a strange bed, in a strange house in the middle of God only knew where, took on a new and frightening significance.

And even if there was a perfectly innocent explanation, the noble Count Valieri was going to have some serious explaining to do—when they finally met.

The next moment, Maddie heard a key rattle, and a section of the wall opposite the bed swung open, revealing that, in this case, it was a real door and not a pretence.

But it was not the man in the portrait, her expected elderly host who entered. Her visitor was male but younger, tall, lean, olive-skinned and, in some strange way, familiar. Yet how could that be? she asked herself, perplexed, when she was quite certain that she'd never seen that starkly chiselled, arrogant face before in her life, or those amazing golden brown eyes, currently flicking over her with something very near disdain.

'So you have woken at last.'

It was the voice that jogged her memory. The cool, peremptory tones she'd last heard ordering her into the Count's car outside the opera house. Only now, instead of the chauffeur's tunic and peaked cap of their previous encounter, he was wearing chinos and a black polo shirt, unbuttoned at his tanned throat, this casual dress emphasising the width of his shoulders, the narrowness of his hips and his long legs. He looked strong and tough without an ounce of excess weight.

A factor that only served to increase her unease, which she knew she must be careful not to show.

However, realising how much of her the sapphire night-gown was revealing in turn, she made a belated snatch at the embroidered linen sheet.

'Obviously,' she returned with a snap, angrily aware of a faintly derisive smile curling his hard mouth. She paused, taking a deep, calming breath. 'You're the Count's driver, so presumably you brought me here.' *Wherever here is.*

'*Sì, signorina.*'

'The problem is I can't quite remember what happened. Have I been ill? And how long have I been asleep?'

He shrugged. 'About twelve hours.'

'Twelve hours?' Maddie repeated. Then, her voice rising, 'That long?

That's impossible.'

'You fell asleep in the car. And you were still *morta*— sleeping like the dead when we arrived.'

'Then how did I get here—like this?'

'I carried you,' he said. Adding, 'And you continued to sleep quite happily in my arms as I did so.'

Her mouth went dry as she assimilated that. 'I don't be-lieve you,' she said hoarsely. 'There must have been some-thing—in the coffee. Or that water in the car. You drugged me.'

His mouth tightened. 'Now you are being absurd,' he stated coldly.

She waved an impatient hand. 'Well—maybe. But I don't understand why you didn't take me back to my hotel.'

'Because the Count wished you to be brought here.'

'Well, that was kind of him—I suppose. But I prefer to

stick to my own arrangements. Perhaps you would thank him and tell him I'd like to leave.'

'That will not be possible. You are going nowhere, *signorina*. You will remain here until arrangements for your release have been concluded with your family in Britain.'

There was a taut silence, then Maddie said unevenly, 'Are you telling me that I've been kidnapped?'

'Yes,' he said, adding laconically, 'I regret the necessity.'

'Oh you're going to have regrets all right,' she said, her voice shaking. 'When you find yourself in court. And don't think a plea of insanity will spare you.'

'I would not think of offering one, even if there were to be a court case—which I guarantee there will not.' He paused. 'And I am completely rational, I assure you.'

'In which case,' Maddie said stormily, 'you can prove it by returning my belongings and arranging for that other man—Camillo—to take me to Trimontano for the rest. Instantly.'

'That is not going to happen. Your possessions have already been collected from the hotel and brought here.'

Maddie gasped. 'Who decided this?'

'I did.'

'Then here's a decision that I've made,' she said icily. 'I came to Italy to interview a woman who was once a singer called Floria Bartrando. I don't suppose you've heard of her.'

'The name is familiar.'

'You amaze me.' She gave him a stony look. 'Your boss, Count Valieri was supposed to be acting as go-between, and I understood there was a need for a measure of secrecy about the project. But this—abduction—this is total madness. And it stops here.

'The deal over the Bartrando interview is off, and I'm leaving as soon as I get my luggage back.'

'And I say that you stay as you are and where you are.' He added softly, 'Until I choose otherwise.'

He walked towards the bed, and, in spite of her previous resolution, Maddie found herself shrinking back against the pillows. She said, 'Don't come near me. Don't dare to touch me.'

He halted, his mouth twisting contemptuously. 'You flatter yourself, *signorina*. Let me assure you that your body is of no interest to me, except as a commodity to be exchanged when my negotiations with your family are complete.'

She was silent, thoughts scurrying through her head. She knew of course that people were taken hostage, but these were mainly wealthy tourists who'd strayed into dangerous places. Not a TV researcher looking for a lost soprano in a supposedly civilised backwater.

She said slowly, 'You—you really mean you're holding me for ransom? That I'm your hostage?'

He frowned. 'A crude term. Let us say instead that you will remain here as my guest until the deal is done.'

'Then I'll be here for a bloody long time,' she flung back at him. 'My God, now I know you're crazy. My family haven't that sort of money. My uncle's the headmaster of a school, and my aunt helps in a local nursery. So they couldn't pay you in a hundred years.'

'But I was not talking about them. I was referring to the family you are about to marry into—who are rich,' he said quietly, sending a chill down her spine. 'And it will cost them a great deal to get you back—unharmed.'

Maddie stared up at the dark, cold face, her lips parted in shock.

She thought, 'He wants money from Jeremy and his father? But why? Just because they're wealthy?'

She said, her voice shaking, 'You can't possibly mean this.'

'Have I not made it clear that I do?'

'But you can't have thought about the consequences,' she persisted. 'You'll get years in jail when you're caught. Your life will be wasted.'

She saw his mouth harden, and his eyes fill with unutterable bleakness. He looked, she thought, as if he too had been carved from limestone like the nearby mountains.

He said, 'Then I would not be the first. But you argue in vain, *signorina,* because no charges against me will ever be brought.'

'But what about the Count? He's a respected man. A businessman. A patron of the arts.' She spoke almost wildly, clutching at straws. 'You can't tell me he knows what you're doing.'

'You are wrong. He knows everything.'

'And condones it?' Maddie shook her head. 'No, I don't— I won't believe it.'

'Then ask him,' he said. 'At dinner this evening. I am here to invite you to join him.'

'Then you can both go to hell.' She glared at him. 'Do you really imagine I'd sit down to a meal with someone who treats me like this? I'd rather starve.'

'Do so, then.' His tone was indifferent. 'If your future husband responds swiftly to my demands, you should not have to endure many days of hunger.'

'You mean—you wouldn't care?'

'That you wish to behave like a fool? That is your choice. But I think you would do better to accept the situation, so that you look like a woman and not a skeleton on your wedding day.'

He paused. 'There is a bell beside the bed. Ring it and a maid will come, and bring anything you require.'

'All I want,' Maddie told him tersely, 'is a way out of here.'

'That, I fear, she cannot provide. And she is loyal to the Count, like the rest of his staff,' he added. 'So do not ask.'

She said shortly, 'I'm hardly in a position to bribe anyone.' She hesitated. 'Nor am I exactly dressed for dinner— even with a geriatric kidnapper. Will I get my clothes back?'

'You will be provided with adequate covering,' he said. 'Be content with that.'

Which was another way of saying 'no', Maddie thought as he walked back across the room and the door—a blue one— closed behind him, becoming just part of the wall again.

She lay staring at it while she counted to fifty slowly, to make quite sure that he'd gone, before she pushed away the coverlet and swung out of bed, treading across the marble floor to try the handle. But the door was locked, as she'd known in her heart that it would be.

However, that could not be the only real door in the room. And now she would find the others.

The first she came across gave access to a large walk in closet, lined on one side with drawers in the same dark wood as the bed-head, all empty, with a matching series of wardrobes filling the opposite wall.

Maddie pulled open each door in turn, but the interior rail held nothing but a robe that matched the nightgown she was wearing, and a pair of velvet slippers in the same deep blue.

'His idea of adequate covering, no doubt,' she muttered as she closed the door again and went back into the bedroom.

What she really needed to find was the bathroom, but naturally she wouldn't have lowered herself by asking him where it was. And her dogged search revealed it behind a pink door a couple of doors away from the closet.

The dark green marble walls, she thought, made it gloomy, although that might have reflected her own mood, rather than the décor, while the bathtub and shower were both distinctly old-fashioned.

However, the water was hot and the plumbing worked. There were plenty of towels and a basic selection of toiletries, none of them her own.

There was also a full length mirror on one of the walls and she stood for a moment staring at her reflection.

Your body is of no interest to me...

Out of all the things he'd said to her, why on earth should

she remember those words in particular? Impossible, she thought, to fathom.

At the same time she could not help noticing, albeit unwillingly, how the deep bodice of the nightgown gently cupped her breasts and the way the cling of the fabric swirled as she moved, the silk hem just brushing her insteps.

No interest. Yet the right size, she thought, and the right length. And although the colour and style of the nightgown were not something she would ever have chosen for herself, she could not deny that it was becoming, making her fair hair look almost silvery.

What was more, she would swear it was brand new, and she wondered, as she turned away, who it had been bought for originally.

But, she reminded herself briskly, she had far more pressing matters to consider. Her priority was to get out of this crazy, dangerous situation and somehow reach Genoa, the airport and safety.

She knew now which were the real doors and which the false, and accepted that there was no opportunity for escape there. So, she started on the windows. The first two sets of shutters opened on to glorious oil-painted landscapes—one showing a sylvan lake overlooked by a rococo palace—the other depicting rolling meadows studded with poppies and edged by cypress trees.

The Italy I was expecting to find, she thought wryly, walking on to the next window, and catching her breath as she flung back the shutters.

Because there were the mountains as far as her eyes could see, confronting her, surrounding her like a cage of rock. And, in spite of the sunshine, as tall, harsh and inimical as her jailer, she thought, feeling suddenly cold.

While one gingerly downwards glance told her that below the window was a sheer drop to heaven knows where.

And there was no sign of Trimontano, or any other human habitation apart from the prison she was standing in.

She left the shutters open, and went back to lie on the bed, heaping the pillows up behind her as she began a serious attempt to evaluate her equally serious position.

Her only hope seemed to lie with Count Valieri himself, who surely could not know that an actual crime was being perpetrated in his name. Not unless the younger man had some hold on him too and was forcing him into it.

If this was the case, then maybe they could work together to stop things before they went too far. Unless of course the Count was older and feebler than his portrait at the theatre suggested.

But that couldn't be true. His handwriting suggested a forceful and determined personality, so he might well be acting against his better judgement for some reason.

So, she would simply have to talk him round, she thought. Tell him frankly that Nigel Sylvester was also a forceful and determined man, and certainly not someone you would wish to have as an enemy, and to treat him as prey would undoubtedly have a dangerous backlash.

She could also warn the Count that she wasn't Nigel Sylvester's favourite person and, if it was left to him, he probably wouldn't give a brass farthing to get her back.

Perhaps not in those exact words, she thought ruefully. But at least I can let him know that if this madness continues, he'll have a fight on his hands that he can't possibly win.

While I, she thought, her throat tightening nervously. I could end up caught helplessly in the middle. And what will happen to me then?

CHAPTER FOUR

SHE SEEMED TO have lost all track of time. But maybe that was a deliberate policy of disorientation on the part of her captors.

Eventually, of course, she had rung the bell, unable to ignore her stomach's wistful rumblings any longer, and recognising, too, that she needed to keep her strength up.

A maid had appeared so promptly she might have been waiting outside the door, and carrying a small table which she placed beside the bed. She was followed by another girl in a starched white overall, her hair covered by a cap, and carrying a laden tray. After which they nodded, smiled, wished her *'Buon appetito'* and left.

And this time, she actually heard the key turn in the lock.

And they'd behaved as if it was perfectly normal to serve a strange girl locked in a bedroom, wearing nothing but a nightdress in the middle of the day. A realisation which did nothing to lift her spirits.

Sighing, Maddie investigated the tray and found a tureen of vegetable soup, steaming and aromatic with herbs, a linen napkin containing freshly baked rolls, a plate of cold meats, and, in a covered glass dish, a scarily rich dessert that seemed to be composed from chocolate truffles. There was also a small jug of red wine, a bottle of mineral water and a pot of excellent black coffee.

It would have been more dignified to pick at the food, but Maddie fell on it as if she hadn't eaten for a week.

Last night's dinner was a long time ago, she told herself as she wiped out the few final delicious drops from her soup bowl with a crust, and tonight's confrontation was unlikely to be relaxed or festive. So she'd make the most of what there was, although she was sparing with the wine, knowing that later she would need to keep her wits about her.

But it took a very long afternoon to get to that point. When the maid returned for the tray, she brought with her a lamp with a pretty glass shade which she placed on the table. But when Maddie asked if she could have a book to read, the girl murmured an apologetic *'Non capisco,'* and left.

So there was nothing to do except allow the same weary thoughts turn like a treadmill in her brain, and watch the afternoon light begin to fade from the sky.

She even took a bath, just to break the monotony, but the warm water failed to have its usual soothing effect.

It was disturbing to consider how carefully her capture must have been planned and executed. And know it was her connection with the Sylvesters that had condemned her to this nerve-racking experience.

But I shall be blamed for it, she told herself. Because I insisted on coming to Italy.

Suddenly she had lost control of her life, she realised as trailed back into the bedroom, swathed in a towel. And the knowledge made her feel vulnerable. And scared.

Although the Count's henchman had said she would be returned 'unharmed'. And that was the word she had to cling to, hoping against hope that her captors meant it.

But all those trick doors were a reminder of how completely she was trapped. And if she was going to be left to vegetate all day and every day, she'd be stark raving mad by the time the ransom was paid. If indeed that ever happened…

The next time the real door opened, it was already quite

dark and she'd lit the lamp. She sat up nervously, wishing she was wearing more than a towel, but it wasn't her kidnapper but another maid, a short stocky girl, who'd brought with her Maddie's own hairbrush and cosmetics bag.

But nothing else.

The girl gave her an unsmiling nod as she walked into the bathroom, emerging a moment later, her face set in lines of disapproval as she shook non-existent creases from the nightgown Maddie had left on the floor after her bath. She placed it carefully on the bed, then fetched the matching robe which she laid beside it.

She said, 'You dress please, *signorina*.' Her English was halting and heavily accented, but at least it was communication, thought Maddie, wishing it had been the girl who smiled.

'Willingly,' she returned. 'When I get my clothes back.'

The girl pointed at the gleaming blue silk on the bed. 'This—clothes for you. Is time to eat, so please hurry.'

'Of course, the Count doesn't like to be kept waiting. I almost forgot.' Maddie's tone was sarcastic. 'Perhaps it would cause less inconvenience if I left him to dine alone.'

'*E impossibile*.' The other spoke firmly. 'He asks for you. Not good to make angry, *signorina*.'

'You mean he might send his enforcer to fetch me?' Maddie saw the girl's bewildered look and shook her head. 'Oh, it doesn't matter.'

Besides, she needed to talk him round not provoke his anger, she reminded herself as she went into the bathroom to change. So she would do as she was told—at first, anyway.

Once it was on, she discovered that the robe was cut on severe lines with high lapels and a full skirt, which revealed very little. Once Maddie had wound its long sash twice round her slender waist and fastened it with a secure bow, she felt rather better about her unorthodox appearance. She used no make-up, and simply brushed her hair loose on her shoulders.

She looked pale, she thought, wrinkling her nose, as she turned away from the mirror. But it would be impolitic to go in with all guns blazing, and besides, with a subdued approach, the Count might see her as a victim and take pity on her.

'Some chance,' she muttered under her breath as she returned to the bedroom, where the maid was waiting with ill-concealed impatience.

'*Fa presto, signorina,*' she said, leading the way to the door.

Following, Maddie saw a bunch of keys attached to the girl's belt, half hidden by her apron. She considered the chances of snatching them and running, and decided they were poor. Even if she took the girl by surprise, her adversary's sturdy build would make her difficult to overpower, while the other side of the door was unknown territory.

Be patient and bide your time, she told herself. It will come.

At the door she paused. 'What is your name?' she asked.

'Domenica, *signorina.*' The reply was brusque. '*Andiamo.*'

Maddie walked out into a long passage, dimly lit, with a short flight of steps at its end, and a curtained archway at their foot.

Domenica set a brisk pace, and Maddie, in her trailing skirts, struggled to keep up with her. At the end, the girl waited, tight-lipped, holding back the curtain for Maddie to pass in front of her.

She stepped out on to a wide galleried landing, and found herself looking down at a room as large as a medieval hall, panelled in wood, and reached by a broad, curving staircase.

In the centre was a vast refectory table, surrounded by high-backed chairs, while a pair of dark brown leather sofas flanked a stone fireplace where logs were burning.

One of the few cheerful signs she'd encountered so far,

she thought. As was the imposing bird cage hanging from a bracket in one of the corners.

And at the far end of the room was a grand piano, indicating the Count was not just an opera patron, but musical himself.

But, at the moment, the room was clearly unoccupied and she hesitated, glancing at Domenica who pointed expressionlessly at the stairs, then turned and disappeared back the way she'd come.

Like someone else on the Count's staff, her people skills could use some work, thought Maddie, lifting her skirts slightly in order to descend the stone treads in safety.

And if her host was such a stickler for punctuality, why wasn't he waiting there to offer an explanation for this outrage? To be followed by profuse apologies and offers of generous redress for the fright and inconvenience she'd suffered.

Nothing less would do, as she would make clear when he eventually showed up, she thought, noting thankfully that only two places had been set at the table.

And while she was waiting, she could take another and more thorough look round this amazing room.

But it didn't take long to realise that her eye had been tricked all over again because there wasn't a genuine inch of panelling anywhere, only skillfully applied paint. Even the splendid birdcage with its resident macaw was a clever three-dimensional deception.

And of the pair of imposing double doors flanking the staircase, only one would ever open—or it might when unlocked, Maddie acknowledged, vainly twisting the wrought iron handle.

But at least the fire was a living thing, she thought, and it might help to dispel the inevitable chill of tension. As she walked across the room, her attention was caught by the massive painting hanging over the mantelpiece.

An initial glance suggested that it was one of the Count's

favourite dogs—a German Shepherd immortalised in oils as it stood, king-like, on a high, flat rock against a grey and stormy sky. But then she realised that the shape of the head, the length of the snout, the colouring were all wrong. That this creature was far from being anyone's loved domestic pet. Nor would it ever be used to guard sheep, or not by a shepherd with a brain.

My God, she thought incredulously, staring upwards. It's a wolf.

And didn't realise she'd spoken aloud until a voice she recognised said softly, '*Sì, signorina*—you are quite right. Allow me to bid you a belated welcome to Casa Lupo. To— the House of the Wolf.'

Maddie swung round with a gasp, aware that her heart seemed to be beating a warning tattoo against her ribcage.

He was standing a few yards away, as a whole section of the false panelling closed noiselessly behind him.

He was slightly more formally clad than earlier, but that was little comfort when his elegant black pants fitted him like a second skin, and his white silk shirt was unbuttoned sufficiently to display several inches of bronzed chest. In fact, in some inexplicable way, it served to make him look even more formidable.

Maddie had to make a conscious effort not to take a step backwards.

'What are you doing here?' she demanded.

The dark brows lifted. 'I intend to have dinner. What else?'

She lifted her chin. 'Does the Count usually dine with his staff?' she asked coldly.

'If he wishes,' he said, unfazed. 'Why not?'

'Isn't it perfectly obvious?' She glared at him. 'Because I hoped—I really hoped I wouldn't have to see you again.'

His slight shrug conveyed indifference. 'Then let us both

hope this is the worst disappointment you have to suffer,' he retorted.

'But the Count will be joining us surely?' She could not hide her dismay.

'Perhaps later, if he so chooses. Is it important?'

'Of course it is.' Her voice was husky. 'I need to talk to him—to persuade him to see reason.'

'A waste of breath. Your views will not affect his plans in any way.'

'So you say.' Maddie's tone was ragged. 'How do I know he isn't just another of your victims, banged up for ransom somewhere.'

'Your imagination is running away with you. The Count Valieri is a free agent conducting his own affairs. Therefore I suggest you relax and trust that your *fidanzato's* family act quickly to effect your release.'

'And if they don't?'

He shrugged again. 'Then, unhappily, pressure will be brought to bear.' His deliberate pause allowed her to consider the implications of that. 'But let us hope for the best.'

There was a rattle of the door at the back of the room, and the smiling maid came in wheeling a trolley laden with bottle and glasses.

'So why not relax,' he continued. 'And join me in an *aperitivo.*'

'Thank you, but no.' Maddie gave him a scornful look. 'This is hardly a social occasion.'

'I believe you enjoy white wine with soda,' he went on as if she hadn't spoken.

And exactly how had he come by that scrap of personal information? Maddie wondered with a sudden thud of the heart.

Aloud, she said, 'It's not just your alcohol that I find unacceptable, but your company. Strangely, I've no wish to spend any more time with the Count's hired thug. I'd have thought he could have spared me that.'

'He tends to leave such decisions to me.'

'His mistake.' Maddie glanced towards the stairs. 'But it need not be mine. So, I'd like to go back to my solitary confinement. Right now.'

'You will remain here,' he said. 'In fact, I insist upon it.'

He turned to the maid and gave her a softly voiced instruction in their own language.

Almost within seconds a perfectly made spritzer was placed in Maddie's reluctant hand.

Childishly, she wanted to throw it over him. To watch it drip from his hair and soak his shirt, and see that cool impassivity splinter into something relatively human.

Except that provoking him into any kind of humanity might not be the wisest choice she'd ever made.

Instead, she gritted her teeth and said, '*Grazie.*'

'*Prego.*' The girl beamed as she poured a measure of Scotch into an elegant crystal tumbler and handed it to Maddie's companion, before whisking herself away through the door at the back of the room.

Leaving them alone again.

There was an odd silence, then he raised his glass. '*Salute.*'

Maddie paused, then responded with such open reluctance that the hard mouth slanted into a grin.

'Let me guess,' he said. 'Instead of drinking to my health, you would prefer to see me dead at your feet.'

She shrugged. 'Why should I pretend?' She paused. 'You speak very good English. Acquired by preying on tourists, I suppose.'

His grin widened wickedly. 'If they permit me to do so—why not?'

She felt an odd, unwelcome tingle of sensation feather down her spine.

She hurried into speech. 'May I ask you something?'

'Perhaps. Unless it is another request to see the Count. I am beginning to find your persistence in this matter a bore.'

'Well, we can't have that, can we?' Maddie said, poison-ously sweet. 'The Count mustn't be kept waiting. You mustn't be bored. I'll try to remember.'

'It would be a favour.' He paused. 'What do you wish to know?'

'I would like to know where all my possessions have gone.' She gestured almost helplessly. 'Particularly my engagement ring and my watch. They could surely be returned. I—I miss them.'

'And you must continue to do so, I fear. Along with certain documents, they are on their way to London as additional proof that you are in our charge.'

'How can you do this?' Her voice shook. 'Jeremy will be devastated—out of his mind with shock and worry.'

'A further incentive for the Sylvesters to come quickly to terms,' he retorted. 'If they do so, your diamond should be glittering safely on your hand again very soon.

'As for your watch,' he added, his tone faintly caustic. 'You will find the hours pass in much the same way without you keeping track of them. They may even go faster.'

'But you surely can't have sent my clothes to London as well, and I want them. I need them.' She gestured at herself. 'You can't expect me to wear these things all day and every day. It—it's degrading.'

'Degrading?' he repeated. 'I do not think you know the meaning of the word. However your own clothing will be returned when I feel you will no longer be tempted to escape and not before.

'Besides what you are wearing covers you from your throat to your ankles,' he added, the amber gaze sweeping her. 'Quite unlike the dress you wore to the opera yesterday evening, if I am permitted to say so.'

'Yes, she said. 'My dress and—other things.' She took a deep breath. 'You carried me to my room, but I'd like to know—who undressed me?'

'I am tempted to pretend,' he said silkily. 'But I shall not do so. It was Domenica.'

She bit her lip. 'I suppose I must be grateful for that at least.'

'And for much else, let us hope. You will find that the Count employs an excellent cook.'

Restive under his gaze, Maddie moved away down the room, stopping to look up at the painted cage and its silent inmate. 'Why is nothing as it seems in this house?'

'It is a style of decoration much favoured in this part of the world. You will become accustomed to it.'

'I trust I'll be away from here long before that can happen.' She took a sip of her drink and wandered over to the baby grand. 'At least this is real.' She played a note and paused. 'Is the Count a pianist?'

He shrugged. 'He had lessons in childhood, but he would tell you that he is no virtuoso, and plays for his own amusement. Why do you ask?'

She swung round, staring at him defiantly. 'Because it baffles me how a man with any claim to culture could behave in this barbaric way.'

'That might depend on how you define barbarism,' he said softly. 'You may have heard it said that the end justifies the means.'

'Oh, really?' she asked scornfully. 'And what possible justification can there be for abducting a total stranger?'

'You are far from that. A great deal about you is known. Your age, your work, your relationships, your size in clothing. Even your preference in drinks.'

He added, 'And it is a question of reparation. You are simply unfortunate in being the instrument by which this can be achieved.'

'And that gives you the right to keep me as a prisoner?' Maddie's tone bit. 'I don't think so.'

'You are merely being caused some minor inconvenience,

signorina.' His voice was equally curt. 'You would find genuine captivity far worse, believe me.'

'Something you and your boss will experience at first hand very soon, I hope.' She drew a jerky breath. 'You'll find to your cost that Mr Sylvester is a very unforgiving man.'

'But so is Count Valieri. Which is something he has had to wait a long time to prove.' He paused, then added quietly, 'Maddalena.'

The breath seemed to catch suddenly in her throat. 'That,' she said huskily, 'is not my name.'

'Not in your language perhaps, but in mine.'

'Well, I did not give you permission to use either version.'

'*Che peccato.*' He drank some whisky, watching her reflectively over the top of the glass. 'Whereas you, *naturalmente*, are entirely free to call me Andrea, if you wish.'

She lifted her chin defiantly. 'And here's another well-known saying for you, *signore.*' She laid stress on each individual word. 'In—your—dreams.'

That grin was playing about his lips again. 'I think my dreams are already stimulating enough,' he drawled. 'But I will bear your suggestion in mind.' He paused. 'And now, perhaps, you will join me at the table. Our dinner is being served.'

In some other dimension, she might have sat stony-faced, refusing everything put in front of her. In the real world, to her shame, she ate everything put in front of her from the dishes of *antipasti*, to the fillets of fish in their creamy sauce accompanied by asparagus spears, and the delectable veal casserole, fragrant with wine and tiny spring vegetables.

Finally, there was cheese, and rich *pannacotta* served with a thick red berry sauce.

And, of course, wine. A crisp Orvieto to begin with, and a full-bodied Montepulciano to follow. While, with the coffee came *grappa,* innocently colourless yet heart-stoppingly potent in the tiny glasses as Maddie discovered with her first cautious sip.

And all this regardless of the sardonic gaze of the man lounging in the high-backed chair at the head of the table.

It occurred to her reluctantly that she could not fault her captor in his role as stand-in host. No matter how monosyllabic her replies, he continued to chat as if this was a normal dinner party and she the guest of honour.

Good manners, she asked herself wryly, or just unmitigated gall?

The opera was one of the topics touched on.

'You enjoyed it?'

'It's a dark, grim story,' she returned. 'Perhaps it should have been a warning to me.'

He laughed. 'You think you will be disposed of and stuffed into a sack like Gilda?' He shook his head. 'What a tragic waste that would be.'

'Am I supposed to find that reassuring?'

He shrugged. 'It is the truth. Make of it what you will.'

She played with the stem of her glass. 'When does the Count expect a message back from London?'

'He has received one already, but merely to say that the papers and the evidence that you are his guest have been safely delivered at their destination. Now the matter rests with your *fidanzato* and his father.'

She gasped. 'Then I could be out of here in forty-eight hours.'

'It is possible.'

'My God,' she breathed and laughed out loud. 'Which means I shall be free—and you and your boss will be under arrest. Because my first port of call will be the nearest police station to press charges.'

'Your attitude may have changed by then.'

She said crisply, 'Not a chance, *signore*.' And paused, as

a thought occurred to her. Be proactive, she told herself, instead of reactive. Test his loyalty to this unseen aristocrat.

She took a deep breath. 'Unless, of course, you're prepared
to get yourself off the hook and do a deal.'

The dark brows rose. 'What precisely are you suggesting?'

So, she wasn't being dismissed out of hand, Maddie
thought, exultancy stirring within her.

'That if you let me go in the morning—drive me back to
Genoa, I'll say nothing about all this. No police, no charges,
no jail. My silence in exchange for my freedom. What do
you say?'

'I say—that it is not much of a deal.' He looked her over
slowly, his eyes lingering cynically on her mouth, and the
swell of her breasts under the lapels of the robe. His insolent smile seemed deliberately to graze her skin. 'Have you
nothing else to offer?'

It was suddenly difficult to breathe. And useless to pretend she did not understand. She steadied her voice. 'I—I
thought you said that I did not attract you.'

He shrugged. 'This is an isolated spot,' he drawled. 'My
choice in such matters is, of necessity, limited. So I am open
to temptation.'

'But I am not,' she said between her teeth. 'Because you
disgust me, and I hope you rot in jail forever, you bastard.
I shall tell the authorities everything about this—House of
the Wolf and the wolves that run it. The story will hit the
headlines worldwide.'

He said quietly, 'I fear you will find the outcome rather
different.'

'You're the one who should be afraid.' She pushed her
chair back and rose shakily. 'It was a bad day for the Count
when he decided to cross swords with Nigel Sylvester. He'll
be sorry he was ever born for keeping me here, I swear it.'

There was a silence as their glances clashed—anger and

defiance meeting faint amusement—and something far less easy to define.

At last he spoke. 'For once, Maddalena, I suspect you could be right. Now, run away to bed before I am tempted to reconsider your offer.

'And do not ask me what I mean,' he added softly. 'Because that is something we both already know. So do not annoy me by playing more games. Just—go.'

And Maddie found herself obeying him, walking to the stairs with all the dignity she could muster, holding up the skirts of her robe so she didn't stumble, trying to steady the judder of her heart against her ribcage.

As she reached the gallery, she found she was glad of Domenica's stolid presence waiting for her, and, above all, relieved that her strange prison cell possessed one door that would lock.

CHAPTER FIVE

TODAY, THOUGHT MADDIE, staring sightlessly out of the window. Surely it has to be today. It's got to be.

Because it should have been yesterday. Or the day before. Or the day before that. In fact, I was so absolutely certain it would be that I kept waking in the night, imagining I heard Jeremy's voice. But it was either a dream. Or wishful thinking. Or more probably a nightmare, because I'm sure at some point he called me 'Maddalena'.

To her annoyance, she felt her face warm, and her hands tightened on the windowsill.

But I won't let myself think about that, she told herself firmly. Because I will be free, even if it is nearly a week later than I hoped. Which is nothing really. Flights can be a problem, let alone transferring large sums of money at zero notice.

She sighed and turned away. The mountain view was no more welcoming now than the first time she'd seen it. While the second window she'd found at the other end of the room looked down on a small enclosed courtyard, apparently unused.

What she'd been allowed to see of the house itself told her it was large, but gave her no real idea of its layout, or how many people lived in it, apart from the Count and the jailer he employed to watch over her.

Andrea, she thought, her throat tightening as an image of

him swam, uninvited, into her mind. A predator, as dark and dangerous as the wolf this house had been named for. Her enemy, himself as much of an enigma as the reason she'd been brought here.

Someone it was best not to think about, she told herself, returning to her original musings. Presumably, she would be taken somewhere else for the handover, and probably blindfolded so she couldn't report back on her temporary jail, and why she'd been shown so little of it.

She seemed to be shut away in a forgotten corner, and sometimes she felt that even if she could open any of the other doors that surrounded her, she would find they all led nowhere.

Stir crazy, she thought, with a sudden shiver. That's what's wrong with you, lady, and the sooner you're out of here the better.

She climbed on to the bed and stretched out, disposing the folds of her robe and nightgown around her. These were in a wonderful shade of amethyst, while yesterday's set had been deep ruby, with others in turquoise and indigo. In different circumstances, this would have been spoiling to the nth degree, and she wondered, smiling, what Jeremy would make of these dramatic jewel colours in clinging satin and the additional sheen they seemed to give to her hair and skin, suggesting she might actually rethink her trousseau a little.

As for tomorrow's choice—well, hopefully, I shall never need to know, she thought, crossing her fingers.

Yet the Count who'd paid for all this charming nightwear had never seen any of it. And she'd given up on the hope of seeing him too. She'd even stopped asking for him, as it was clearly a waste of time and temper.

So, let him behave like the Invisible Man, she told herself defiantly. He's simply ashamed to face me, that's all. Mortified to have to acknowledge what he's done. And whatever happens to him, he has only himself to blame for abandoning me to his henchman, who has no finer feelings to lacerate.

Not that she'd been much in his company either, except at dinner, where she was no longer alone with him, thank Heaven.

A manservant in a neat dark suit called Eustacio, who spoke a modicum of English, now served them at table and poured the wine, and the smiling maid whose name, Maddie had learned, was Luisa, assisted him.

While the meals generally took place in near-silence. No discussions on opera or anything else, and a return to strictly formal terms.

Maddie wouldn't permit herself to ask if there was any news from London. Because to appear anxious would allow him a minor victory in the unspoken war between them, which seemed to assume an extra dimension each time they met, no matter how little was said.

The memory of those final exchanges between them on that first evening was always with her, like an unhealed wound. As was the fact that he hadn't made the slightest attempt to apologise since.

And her continued lack of conventional clothing only added to her mental discomfort.

She sighed. She supposed she really should have made more effort to find some way out of her predicament. After all, it was pretty spiritless, lounging around in a negligee, however glamorous, waiting to be rescued. On the other hand, it wasn't exactly ideal attire for a fugitive either. He was right about that, she thought bitterly.

But unless one of the staff could be bribed, her chances of getting hold of something less noticeable seemed less than zero. And when she wasn't actually locked in her room, she was always under scrutiny.

But, as a cell, it was now a little more comfortable than it had been. For instance a pretty brocaded armchair had suddenly appeared to stand beside the courtyard window, and there was also another larger table where she ate her breakfast and usually her lunch. Today's had been a warm chicken salad, followed by a wonderfully rich pasta carbonara, and a tiny filigree basket filled with strawberries. This had been accompanied by a small carafe of white wine, and the inevitable coffee pot.

Whatever else, she had no complaints about the food, she admitted. And her imprisonment had become slightly more stimulating too, because, on her second night, she'd swallowed her pride and asked if she might at least have the book she'd bought at the airport returned to her.

'I wouldn't want to affect your negotiations by dying of boredom,' she'd added sweetly.

She'd received a stony look, but he had silently inclined his head, and the thriller in question was on her bedside table when she went upstairs.

And last night, as she'd risen and bade him goodnight, he'd said to her amazement, 'You may borrow more books from the Count's library, if you wish. Domenica will escort you there to make your choice.'

'Oh.' Maddie hesitated. 'Well—thank you. But couldn't someone else do that?'

His brows lifted. 'Why?'

She shrugged. 'I don't find her particularly congenial.' *Which was putting it mildly. The girl seemed to radiate resentment and disapproval.*

'It is not essential that you should,' he said. 'What matters is that her family has served the Valieri faithfully for years.' He added coldly, 'I remind you of this in case you are considering the offer of another deal.'

Leaving her to retreat upstairs fuming.

And, once back in her room, to wonder why his boss had decided to make such a concession at this particular time.

Unless, of course, he was hoping some slight act of kind-

ness and consideration on his part might persuade her to
speak on his behalf at some future point. If so, he would be
severely disappointed.

He is Crime. I am Punishment.

I never realised before that I could be so vindictive, she
thought. But perhaps I never had sufficient cause.

She was roused from her reverie by the sound of voices
outside and the rattle of the key in the lock. The door opened
and Domenica came in, lips pursed in annoyance, accompanied by the girl from the kitchen who'd come for the lunch
tray.

She looked flustered today, a strand of dark hair escaping
from her cap, and a faint pink stain like fruit juice smudged
right across the front of her white overall.

Maddie deduced from the brief exchange that it was the
girl's less than pristine appearance that had aroused Domenica's disapproval.

Domenica handed the girl the tray, then turned to Maddie. 'You wish for books, *signorina*?' she enquired without
enthusiasm. '*Andiamo.* Let us go.'

She chivvied the kitchen girl out of the room, with Maddie following. Halfway along the corridor, she paused, nod-
ding at a door and giving some terse instruction.

As the door opened, Maddie could see over Domenica's
shoulder that it was a storeroom for household linen, but that
one section of the floor to ceiling shelving seemed to be devoted to staff uniforms. There were the neat black dresses
and pretty organdie aprons worn by the maids, and next to
them, grey and scarlet waistcoats, dark trousers and white
shirts which suggested there were indeed male indoor staff,
even if she'd never seen them.

Maddie wondered caustically if Andrea the Thug came
here for his gear and decided it was unlikely.

There were rows of shoes and boots too, but the largest
section by far was occupied by the starched white coveralls

and caps for the kitchen staff, where the hapless girl, now sniffing a little, was making her selection.

Maddie turned away, tightening her sash. Clothing, she thought, biting her lip. Heaps of clothing behind an unlocked door offering a perfect disguise, and only a matter of yards away. If only she'd known. Yet what could she have done? Broken down her own door to reach it?

Besides, it hardly mattered now. Not when she was leaving anyway.

She heard the storeroom door close again. When the girl had disappeared, she said quietly, 'Weren't you a little hard on her?'

Domenica shrugged. 'She is *sciatta*. Untidy. His Excellency would be angry to see her wait on you so.'

'But he hasn't,' Maddie pointed out. 'He didn't.' *Because he's never around, as I know to my cost.*

Domenica's mouth curled. 'His Excellency sees everything.' Her tone brooked no argument, while her expression suggested that Maddie should mind her own business.

When they reached the gallery, Domenica ignored the staircase descending to the *sala* below, leading the way instead to the far end where another archway waited with a narrow corridor beyond.

They appeared to have reached a dead end, but Maddie was beginning to know better and was unsurprised when the stone wall ahead turned out to be another door.

It would take a ball of string to find my way out of this labyrinth if the opportunity ever occurred, she thought ruefully, as she was conducted down a winding flight of stone steps. *Thank God I won't need one.*

At the foot of the steps, the passage divided. In one direction, Maddie could hear the distant sound of voices and the kind of clatter that indicated the kitchens. In the other, there was yet another curtained archway waiting to change into a door.

Maddie's head was beginning to spin as they passed through into a wide corridor. Halfway down, Domenica paused and knocked on a pair of double doors which, by some miracle, were exactly what they seemed.

A man called, '*Entrare,*' and she opened one of the doors and stood aside to allow Maddie to precede her into the room. It was large and square, every wall apparently lined with books just as you'd expect in a library.

But, she thought, she was taking nothing for granted any longer.

Because the voice had already warned her who was waiting for her, wearing a blue denim shirt and pants today, and seated behind a massive desk, his dark head bent over the letter he was writing, his hand moving smoothly across the paper.

Cream paper, she saw. And black ink. Both of them horribly familiar. As was the handwriting...

Maddie's lips parted in a silent gasp. I should have guessed, she thought wildly. Should have known. Because nothing is as it seems in the House of the Wolf. Nothing—and no-one.

Without looking up, he said, 'Take a seat, *signorina.*'

'Shouldn't I remain standing?' she asked bitterly. 'Your Excellency?' She added, 'Now who's the one playing games?'

He shrugged a shoulder. 'I realised you would have seen the late Count's portrait at the Opera House, and found the temptation to conceal my identity irresistible.'

'Yes,' she said. 'That's what this place is all about. Deception and pretence. Why stop at a few painted walls?'

'If you wish to see it like that.' He gave her a cold smile. 'But I had other reasons. You can tell much about someone from the way they treat their supposed inferiors.'

'I didn't think of you as inferior,' she said, stonily. 'Just as a blackmailing criminal. I still do.'

'Unfortunate,' he said. 'When you and I, *mia bella,* are

destined to continue to enjoy each other's company for a while.'

She said slowly, 'You mean I'm *not* leaving yet? But why? What's happened?'

He signed his letter. Blotted it. 'There has been no contact from your *fidanzato*'s family.' His voice was as cool as if he was telling her that rain was expected. 'It seems your immediate release is not their first priority, and they are considering their other options.' He paused. 'Such as they are.'

'I don't believe you. You're lying.' Her voice rose. 'Jeremy would never leave me here like this. You don't understand.' She banged her fist on his desk. 'We're going to be married—very soon.'

'*Sì*,' he agreed almost casually. 'In six weeks. However, I expect this matter to be settled before then.'

She said hoarsely, 'What makes you think that?'

'I have stated my terms. All they need do is accept them.' He lifted his hands. 'It is simple.'

'Not where Nigel Sylvester is concerned.' Her voice shook. 'You don't dictate to a dictator, *signore*.'

'No,' he said. 'You defeat him in battle.'

'No matter what happens to the innocent parties involved?'

'Ah.' He leaned back in his chair, his gaze reflective. 'You refer to yourself? But I have removed you from the conflict.'

'But perhaps I don't want that.' She glared at him. 'Maybe I want to be with the man I love, fighting at his side.'

'Then you will be disappointed.' He indicated a table at the other side of the room, where an open cardboard box was waiting. 'And there is a selection of English books for you, to pass the waiting time more pleasantly.'

'Damn you,' Maddie said fiercely. 'And damn your books. I want nothing from you.'

'Now you are being irrational,' the Count said calmly. 'I will have the books taken to your room. If you choose to throw them down the mountain side, *naturalmente,* you may do so. But if your *fidanzato*'s family prove obdurate, you may regret it.'

'And please stop calling him by that outlandish name,' Maddie flared. She was beginning to tremble inside as the full horror of her situation dawned on her. They couldn't intend to leave her here indefinitely—they couldn't...Could they?

She added, 'He's Jeremy.'

Say his name. Conjure up his face in your mind—his voice. Hang on to every wonderful memory you've shared and believe that you'll see him soon—very soon.

'And I am Andrea,' he drawled. 'A name that you are reluctant to use—Maddalena.' He was watching her through half-closed eyes. 'I know now that the photograph of you I was once shown did not do you justice, *mia bella*. It made you look *convenzionale*—even a little dull.'

He nodded slowly. '*Sì*, passion suits you. It gives fire to your eyes and colour to your skin. What a pity I have so far only seen anger have this effect, turning the serene English rose into a tigress.'

She clenched her fists in the skirts of her robe, forcing herself to breathe calmly and evenly. To regain some measure of control.

'Please don't imagine I find your offensive remarks flattering, *signore*. Or that I intend to listen to any more of them.'

His mouth curled in amusement. 'What is offensive about telling a woman that arousal makes her beautiful?' He paused. 'Has this man—this Jeremy never told you so?'

'My relationship with him is no business of yours.' Maddie lifted her chin. 'And now I am going back to my room.'

'I shall not stop you.' He reached for his pen. 'For one thing I have other letters to write. For another—the time is not yet right.' He added quietly. 'But that will change.' And looked up at her.

Their gazes met. Clashed. Became caught in a new and

tingling awareness. Making her conscious that there were golden flecks in his eyes, like tiny flames, dancing.

Maddie, shocked, found she had to force herself to look away. She said raggedly, 'Never—do you hear me? Never in a million years.'

She whirled round in a flurry of amethyst silk and stormed to the door, flinging it wide, startling Domenica, who was waiting outside with her arms folded.

She set off, almost running, in spite of the fact that her legs were shaking under her, desperate to reach the nearest thing to safety that she had in this chaotic dangerous world that held her trapped.

And she fought back the stricken tears already pricking at her eyes and aching in her throat.

Yes, she wanted to cry—to scream—to beat on the walls with her fists. But for all those things, she needed to be alone where no-one could see and mock her distress. Or realise how alone and isolated she felt. Or how scared she was—mostly for reasons she did not even want to contemplate.

So, she would break down in front of no-one—especially Andrea Valieri and his sour-faced spy, now struggling to keep up with this headlong dash.

When she reached her door, she flung it open, marched in and kicked it shut behind her. She half-expected it to open again to admit Domenica with the shrill tirade she was sure had been burning on her lips, but there was only a long silence, followed by the sound of the key turning in the lock. Something that, for once, she welcomed.

She threw herself across the bed, her fingers digging into the coverlet, and buried her face in the pillows as the first harsh sob rose in her throat.

Now that the tears had come, they were scalding, uncontrollable, and she welcomed that too, sensing somehow that she was weeping away all the tensions and fears that she'd been trying to suppress since this nightmare began.

That this was a catharsis that she needed.

When the storm passed, she felt limp and empty. She sat up slowly, pushing the damp strands of hair away from her face. She had to think about this latest development, she told herself, and think clearly too.

She'd been counting too much on other people. Taken it for granted that instant aid would be on its way, and that freedom was a foregone conclusion.

She took a deep breath. Well, she knew better now. And one of the uncomfortable facts to be faced was that Nigel Sylvester might indeed refuse to rescue her, regarding it as her own wilful disobedience that had led to this predicament in the first place.

'She put her career before you,' she could hear him saying to Jeremy. 'As she always will. And this is where it's led. She'll never make the wife you need and deserve, and it's time you came to terms with this. Admitted that marrying her will never work.

'Besides, she won't come to any real harm. When the kidnappers realise we have no intention of giving in to their demands, they'll have to let her go.'

In return, Jeremy would protest that he loved her, that she was the girl he wanted. Of course he would. But his hands were tied. His father controlled the money, and there was no way he alone could raise the kind of ransom being demanded. Whatever that was.

I wonder what I'm valued at in hard currency, she thought bitterly.

Even so, whatever the terms of her release, she knew that Nigel Sylvester would still see her as a liability, and do his best to have the wedding postponed at the very least.

Therefore, she could no longer afford to let matters drift. Somehow, she had to seize the initiative and try to engineer her own escape.

There were elements on her side. She knew now where

there was a change of clothes that might prove an adequate disguise, and she had seen more of the house, including where the kitchens were sited. It might not be much, and there was still this locked door to be dealt with, but it was a start.

She would not allow Andrea Valieri's scheming to threaten everything she held dear in life, she told herself, her heart jolting painfully.

But perhaps she was being unduly pessimistic. Maybe moves were already afoot to trace her secretly. To use some kind of professional negotiator, a fixer to arrange a compromise deal.

She had to believe that, in case her jailers were too watchful and self-reliance proved inadequate. Had also to pin her faith on Jeremy fighting for her. Coming to find her.

'Oh, darling,' she whispered brokenly. 'I need you so badly. For God's sake hurry.'

And just managed to stop herself saying, 'Before it's too late.'

CHAPTER SIX

As SHE SHOWERED away the signs of distress and weakness, Maddie decided that, to begin her campaign, she should try to regain some of the ground she'd lost earlier.

It had been unwise to lose her temper, and let him see how much this lack of response from London disturbed her. And sheer folly to over-react to his more personal remarks, she thought broodingly. Far better to have kept her cool and shrugged it off as trivial banter.

But from now on she would remain impassive in the face of any news, good or bad, and display total indifference to his sexual teasing. And if he persisted, she would tell him quietly that his behaviour was a breach of the good manners his birth entitled her to expect. Shame him into silence.

Although instinct warned her that he would not shame easily.

He would probably be anticipating more fireworks at dinner, but he would be disappointed, she thought as she dried her hair. She would conduct herself impeccably, speaking when spoken to and refusing to rise to any bait. And that's how it would be, however long she remained in this place.

At the same time, she would be looking all the time for a way out. Any chance, however slight, would do. And somewhere she would find help. There had to be a village around, albeit a small one, with communications to the world at large.

She wrapped herself in a fresh bath sheet and trod back into the bedroom for the siesta which had become part of her ritual. And when she awoke a new nightgown and robe would be waiting. As usual.

Emerald this time, I suppose, she thought as she stretched out on the bed. Although that's not my colour. I wonder if he'll realise that.

She bit her lip. That was not a train of thought, frankly, that she needed to pursue. He was hardly likely to have gone into some shop and chosen these frankly intimate garments himself. He'd have got some hireling to do so. But it was quite bad enough knowing that he'd given the order for her to spend her time dressed—or undressed—like this.

And if he'd seen her photograph, that meant he already knew her colouring and Heaven knows what other details about her, she thought, her face warming.

That was what she was finding so unnerving. All the research and planning that had gone into trapping her, of which she'd been so blithely unaware. The unseen power that this man—Andrea Valieri—had been able to exert to achieve it.

The feeling of helplessness, as if this deliberate removal of all her personal things had also wiped away her identity.

Added to that—the terrible realisation that she was merely a pawn in some game being played out by two arrogant men, and that pawns were easily sacrificed...

Stop that right now, she told herself with swift determination as a shiver curled the length of her spine. That's defeatist thinking and I'm not going to be a victim or a puppet any longer.

I'm taking my life back.

She slept eventually, and woke to a room full of evening shadows. As she'd expected, she'd had silent visitors while she was sleeping, and the new robe and nightgown were waiting for her, laid across the foot of the bed. But, this time, she discovered, they were black instead of the anticipated green.

Different styling too, she thought as she held them up, frowning. The robe had a revealingly deep square neck and was fastened down the front with large buttons embossed elaborately in velvet. And the nightdress was made from chiffon so sheer it was hardly more than a thin veil, with only narrow ribbon straps supporting its tiny bodice.

Sending her, Maddie realised furiously, an unmistakable message. A sensuous offering with deliberate provocation in every inch of fabric.

Well, it won't work, she silently informed her unseen antagonist. I'll wear the damned things as if they were towelling and flannelette.

As she glanced around, she saw the box of books on the table, and lying next to it her CD player with the disc of Floria Bartrando's favourite arias.

Another concession, she thought, biting her lip uneasily. It was hardly a charm offensive, but it was disturbing just the same. Although it made no difference. Nothing he could say or do would ever change her attitude towards him. Her mind and her body were immune to his overtures.

He was her enemy, and, once she was free of him, he would suffer for the way she'd been treated.

If Jeremy didn't kill him first, she thought, viewing her reflection with disquiet. The robe's tight bodice enhanced the slenderness of her waist and showed far too much of the creamy swell of her breasts. While those buttons which were supposed to keep it fastened seemed much more invitation than protection, she thought, hating the sudden colour that flared in her face.

Tonight it was Luisa who came to escort her downstairs, her eyes and mouth round with astonishment as she looked at her.

Whatever you're thinking, you're wrong, Maddie muttered savagely under her breath, grabbing up the CD as she passed the table.

She was halfway along the corridor when she heard the music. A piano playing something soft and lilting—and not far away. She paused to listen, wondering, then drew a deep breath as she remembered.

He had lessons in childhood. Andrea Valieri's casual words. *Now he plays only for his own amusement.*

And doesn't he like to amuse himself, she thought scornfully, as she walked out on to the gallery. He doesn't miss a trick. What will it be next? Mandolin serenades under my window?

She stopped halfway down the stairs, looking down the length of the room, watching him, her hand resting lightly on the stone banister, her body taut under its light draperies.

And the music was certainly beguiling, played in a minor key, dancing joyfully along one moment, wistful and plangent the next.

His dark head was bent over the keys. He seemed intent—oblivious, but she wasn't fooled. He was as aware of her as she was of him. Even at this distance she could feel it, like the stroke of a fingertip over her bare skin.

She realised, shocked that her nipples were lifting and hardening against the chiffon that cupped them. Recognised her body's desire to sway with the rhythm of the music. To let it take her down the stairs and towards him, the black silk floating around her.

Recognised it and fought it. So that when the final chord rippled into silence, she was able to applaud slowly, almost languidly, making him look at her directly. Letting him register the silent challenge of her pose.

'*Bravo, signore.*' She moved then, descending the remaining stairs. 'And I thought you said you weren't a virtuoso.'

He rose. 'Flattery from you, *signorina*?' he queried sardonically. 'I am astounded.'

'I think it would take a good deal more than that to surprise you.' She paused. 'I didn't recognise the music. What was it?'

'It is something quite new, composed by someone I was at school with, Gianfranco Deloria. He has been collecting old forgotten folk music from this area and giving it a contemporary twist.'

'Well, it's—beautiful.'

'He would be pleased to hear you say so. His first album is coming out quite soon, and he will give a recital in Trimontano in the autumn.'

'Ah, yes,' she said. 'The festival. Which reminds me— thank you for the return of my player, but you may keep this.' She put the Floria Bartrando CD on the dining table. 'I don't want any souvenirs of my time in this place.'

'And yet she is what brought you here.'

'As if I needed reminding.' She allowed a trace of bitterness in her tone. 'However, that's when I thought I was researching for a television programme. Now I doubt that Floria Bartrando still exists, let alone has plans to resume her career.'

'On the contrary, she is alive and well,' he said after a pause. 'And she does intend to sing again one day—when the time is right.'

'Then she'll do it without any help from me.' Maddie shrugged. 'Does she know you involved her in your scheming?'

'I would not have used her name without her permission.'

'So you do occasionally have scruples. Now I'm amazed. And especially about Signorina Bartrando,' she added musingly. 'How can someone with the voice of an angel lend herself even marginally to an extortion racket? Has she fallen on hard times?'

'She lives in perfect comfort.'

'And so do you.' She glanced around her. 'Or have you

been hit by the global economic downturn? Are the olive oil and ceramics markets heading for the rocks?'

His brows lifted. 'No, they are not. But your research has been thorough.'

'But clearly I didn't look deeply enough,' Maddie said. 'For instance, I found no mention of the late Count's death.'

'He wished it so,' Andrea Valieri returned. 'He was a very private man.'

'Then perhaps it's as well he's not here to see you drag his name through the dirt.' She sent him a challenging look. 'Or, like you, did he consider himself above the law?'

'No-one is that, *mia bella*.' His sudden smile touched her like a kiss, and she had to overcome the urge to take a step backwards. Because that would be a damaging act of self-betrayal that she could not afford.

But she could not control the faint breathlessness in her voice. 'Don't—call me that.'

'You think it is more deception?' he asked softly. 'I promise it is not.' The amber gaze studied her, lingering on her breasts then travelling slowly down the rest of her body as if he was imagining what he would see if the robe were gone. 'You were lovely before, Maddalena. Tonight you are breathtaking.'

'And stop talking like that.' Her words were falling over each other. *Stop looking at me. Stop standing only a few feet away. And, dear God, stop smiling as if you already knew—everything there is to know about me. Because that scares me far more than any number of hours in a locked room.* She rallied. 'You have no right—no right at all.'

'I have any rights I choose to impose,' he drawled. 'But there is no need for such panic. I was paying you a compliment, not attempting seduction.'

'Seduction?' She lifted her chin defiantly. 'Don't you mean—rape?'

'No,' he said with sudden harshness. 'I do not, and you

insult me and the ancient name I bear by such a suggestion. Because I swear on the honour of my family, that I have never in my life taken a woman against her will.' He paused. 'And you, Maddalena, will not be the first.'

His eyes narrowed. 'If you are honest, surely you must know that? Or is it possible that you are still an innocent with no experience of how a man expresses his desire?'

'Of course not.' She took a deep breath, adjuring herself silently to get a grip. 'You know quite well that I'm engaged—and about to be married.'

He shrugged. 'Sì. But one thing does not necessarily rule out another. And you seem—curiously untouched.'

'Curious indeed,' she said, crisply. 'As Jeremy and I are deeply and passionately in love. But I suppose I have to endure your unpleasant sexist speculations along with everything else you've inflicted on me.'

'That will not be necessary. I have already drawn my own conclusions about the depth of passion you have experienced.' He paused. 'But tell me, *mia cara,* have you never wondered if there could be more?'

'No.' She glared at him. 'Because loving someone and wanting to spend your life with them isn't all about sex.'

'Ah,' he said. 'A cynical man might say you had just condemned yourself, Maddalena.' He paused. 'So where is this devoted and passionate lover? If you belonged to me, I would be here, beating at the door, offering everything I possessed in the world to get you back into my arms. Except...'

'Yes,' Maddie prompted coldly. 'I'm sure there'd be an exception.'

'Except I would never have permitted you to travel into the unknown without me,' the Count said harshly. 'I would not have allowed you out of my sight by day and would have made sure you were safe in my bed each night. Why did he not do the same?'

Safe in *your* bed? thought Maddie. In what alternative reality would that be true?

'Jeremy has an important career.' She faced him defensively. 'He had other things to do than follow me round Italy.'

His mouth twisted. 'In other words, *mia bella,* he was obeying his father's orders. No, do not attempt to deny it,' he added as her lips parted indignantly. 'My research has also been thorough.'

'And, like mine, incomplete, because you don't know my future father-in-law,' she flashed back.

'Nor, Maddalena, does he know me. You seem to forget that.'

She moved a hand impatiently. 'Because it makes no difference.' She paused. 'Oh God, how can I convince you that he'll never give into your demands. I expect Interpol are searching for me right now.'

'I would not count on it,' he returned calmly. 'Nor should you.'

'I'm counting on one thing only,' Maddie said fiercely. 'Getting out of here damned quickly.' And managed, just in time, to stop herself adding, 'And as far away from you as it's possible to get without leaving the planet.' Because, although true, it was altogether too much of a revelation.

The sound of the door and the rattle of the trolley announced Luisa's timely arrival with the drinks, and Maddie turned away, drawing a relieved breath.

She was tempted to ask for mineral water, but instead accepted her spritzer without comment. Everything as usual, she thought, in spite of him.

When Luisa had poured him his whisky, she was quietly dismissed and they were alone again.

Needing a neutral topic of conversation, if there could be such a thing in these circumstances, she wandered towards the fireplace, taking a closer look at the oil painting that hung there.

'A strange subject for a picture,' she commented lightly. 'Is that the actual wolf the house was named for?'

'No, he was merely a symbol, painted from photographs. Originally, this house was called *Casa d'Estate*—the House of Summer. My great grandparents named it that because they spent their summers here to escape the heat of the coast.

'It was my grandfather who made the change. Forty years ago, studies revealed that the Apennine wolf was in danger of being wiped out. He had always found them interesting animals, brave loyal and with close family bonds, and he was among those who worked to protect them. They are now on the list of endangered species.'

Maddie frowned. 'But they're dangerous themselves, aren't they?'

He shrugged. 'To smaller animals, certainly. They are carnivores, *sì*, but they also eat berries and plants. My grandfather had to battle with local shepherds and the hunters who saw the wolves as trophies. He had the painting done and re-named this house to demonstrate to the world which side he was on.'

'That can't have made him very popular.'

'It did not. But to the local people he was the *padrone* and the Valieri have always been good landlords who did not ill-treat or exploit their tenants, so they grumbled but respected his wishes.'

He smiled reminiscently. 'And when people argued with him, he told them never to forget that the Roman empire owed its existence to the she-wolf who suckled Romulus and Remus.'

'And did they accept that?' Maddie found she was smiling too.

'Not for a moment,' he admitted. 'But it usually ended the debate. He was a very determined man.'

'A trait he has obviously handed down.' Maddie spoke lightly, and, to her surprise, saw his face change, harden.

'It may seem so,' he said, after a pause.

'Ah,' she said, hiding her surprise at his response. 'Could that mean that, even now, you might be open to persuasion? After all, you've made it clear you don't need the ransom money.'

'But it is not a question of money,' he said quietly. 'And never has been.'

She stared at him. 'What then?'

'I could tell you,' he said. 'But at present you are too hostile, too suspicious, Maddalena, to believe anything I might say. So explanations must wait for a more favourable time. As you must also wait for the Sylvesters' response. I wonder which will come first.

'And no persuasion you can muster, however tempting, will cause me to change my mind,' he added softly. 'So do not try.' He paused. 'Unless, of course, you are looking for an excuse to share my bed. Although that is not necessary,' he added musingly. 'I promise that "Andrea, I want you" is all you need say.'

They were several feet apart, but the atmosphere between them was suddenly charged—electric with tension.

Maddie's breathing quickened. She said unsteadily, 'How dare you insult me like this. It's disgusting.'

'Let me ask in return how you dare be such a hypocrite, *mia bella*,' he retorted, his mouth twisting cynically. 'I am simply acknowledging that the desire between us is mutual. Which you know as well as I do.

'Besides,' he added. 'The choice will always be yours.'

'Then I choose not to be alone with you again!' Her voice was stormy.

'You will have your wish,' he said calmly. 'At least for the next few days. I have business elsewhere.'

'More helpless people to kidnap?'

'I hope,' he said, the amber eyes glinting in that disturbing way, 'that you are not describing yourself in those terms, Maddalena.'

'But supposing there's a message from Jeremy and his father, offering terms. You won't be here to get it.'

'Have no fear,' he said. 'If there is any breakthrough, which I doubt, I shall be informed.'

'But I shan't be,' Maddie protested furiously. 'I'll have to stay locked up here in total ignorance when anything could be happening.'

'You are still hoping perhaps that your future father-in-law will pull strings in Whitehall and have the British SAS parachute in to rescue you?' He sighed. 'A vain hope.'

'But there's another factor in all this that you've overlooked,' Maddie said tautly. 'The television company I work for, who sent me here. They're expecting regular reports on my progress with the Bartrando research. If they don't hear from me, they'll become concerned and start making enquiries.'

'But they have received several texts from your mobile phone assuring them that all is going well,' he said gently. 'They will be disappointed if you eventually return empty-handed, but that is all.' He paused. 'Now that I have set your mind at rest, let us have dinner.'

'No thank you,' she said, putting down her half-empty glass. 'I'm going to eat in my room. Perhaps you'd arrange for someone to bring a tray. Some pasta and dessert will be fine. I'm not hungry.'

He shook his head. 'That is a banal reaction and not worthy of you, *carissima*,' he commented. 'But if that is indeed what you want, I will give the necessary orders. I shall also summon Domenica to escort you back.'

He went to the fireplace and tugged at the embroidered bell pull. 'However,' he continued, 'I hope you will continue to dine down here during my absence.'

She was already on her way to the stairs, but she turned

looking at him almost blankly, as she recalled there were at least two exits from the room. 'You trust me that far?'

'No,' he said. 'But Eustacio will be here, and I trust him to look after you on my behalf.' He watched her bite her lip and added silkily, 'Besides, it will give me pleasure while I am away to think of your beauty gracing my table. And to imagine a time when we shall not part for the night once the meal is over.'

Sudden, helpless warmth flooded her face, and was echoed by the slow torment of the heat slowly uncurling inside her. The betraying sensuality of that deep inner ache, telling her unequivocally that all her protests were lies and how it would be all too easy to say 'Andrea—I want you', instead of the biting riposte which would silence him now and forever.

Her nails scored the palms of her hands, as, to her eternal shame, the words of angry dismissal failed to materialise.

And as she climbed the stairs towards Domenica's solid bulk in the shadows, she could feel the Count's gaze following her as if he were walking with her, his hand on her waist, and his lips grazing her hair.

And heard his voice, faintly mocking. 'Until we meet again, Maddalena. Believe me, *carissima,* I shall count the hours.'

And found herself praying silently that she would not do the same.

CHAPTER SEVEN

MADDIE READ THE last page of her book, sighed, and tossed it away from her. She swung herself off the bed and began to walk up and down the room in the mid-afternoon sun.

Andrea Valieri had been gone for two days now, and when she'd forced herself to ask Domenica when he was expected back, the other woman had shrugged with sour malice before informing her that the business which detained him was a girl in Viareggio. 'His *amante*,' she'd added unnecessarily. 'And very beautiful, so who knows when he will return.'

All the same, Maddie knew, with every hour that passed, that her chances of escape, already slim, were becoming positively skeletal.

Of course, he hadn't been serious about counting the hours until he saw her again. He'd simply been winding her up, and she knew that. Told herself so continually.

Nevertheless, the news about the girl in Viareggio had shaken her to the core, and she'd had to work damned hard to conceal her inner turmoil from Domenica's sly scrutiny.

She found herself wondering just how much the maid had heard and understood of the exchanges between her master and his prisoner while she was on escort duty and what deductions she might have made.

Another good reason for getting out of here, Maddie thought biting her lip with unnecessary savagery.

Because, if she'd been frightened before, she was now in a completely different kind of danger. And she was petrified.

She had spent the last forty-eight hours striving to convince everyone at the house that she was resigned to her fate, at the same time sticking resolutely to her decision not to dine or eat any other meal downstairs.

Eustacio had visited her that morning, looking anxious, to tell her His Excellency would be distressed to hear she had not left her room, even to pay another visit to his library.

'And I'm equally distressed at being made to stay here,' she'd returned quietly and he had retired, shaking his head.

She'd hoped, in Andrea Valieri's absence, that there might have been a more relaxed attitude to her detention, but it hadn't worked out like that. Wherever he might be—and whoever he might be with, she thought, biting her lip hard, the Count's presence still loomed over the Casa Lupo, and she seemed to be watched more closely than ever.

Today's bright spot was that Domenica, the prison wardress, had so far not put in an appearance. No doubt busy making herself a new broomstick, Maddie thought bitterly. Though she was probably being unfair to a woman simply doing her job.

It was just the manner of it that was bewildering. Maddie was at a loss to understand why she was so unremittingly hostile. After all, the other staff weren't like that. Luisa and the girl from the kitchen, whose name was Jolanda, were always smiling and pleasant in spite of the language barrier, while Eustacio was courteous in the extreme.

Just a clash of personalities, I suppose, she told herself with another sigh. And while nothing could make her enforced stay agreeable, it would be easier if she was able to have a normal conversation sometimes with the person she saw most often.

And with that she heard the rattle of the key in the lock.

But it was again Luisa who led the way into the room, carrying clean towels over her arm, followed by Jolanda who'd come, albeit belatedly, to collect the lunch tray, Maddie having finished her meal more than an hour before. She surveyed them in faint surprise. 'Domenica?' she queried.

The girls exchanged glances, then Luisa performed a brisk and realistic imitation of someone being violently sick.

'Oh,' Maddie said slowly. 'What a shame.' Then, remembering the scanty Italian derived from her phrase book, *'Che peccato.'*

The girls nodded then Luisa headed for the bathroom, while Jolanda picked up the tray and left the room with it, leaving the door open.

Maddie stared at it, swallowing. This was the first time it had ever happened. Domenica invariably locked the door as soon as she was inside it. But it might be the nearest thing to a chance she would get and she had to take it.

She took one uncertain step then halted as a shattering crash and a shriek of pain came from the passage.

Without further hesitation, Maddie ran out and found a sobbing Jolanda picking herself up from the floor amid a welter of broken glass and crockery.

She was nursing one hand in the other, a deep cut across the palm oozing blood.

Groaning inwardly, Maddie helped the girl to her feet, and examined the wound, which was clearly a nasty one. She heard a horrified squeak and turned to find Luisa standing behind her, mouth open.

'Get a towel,' she directed, and as the maid stared at her in bewilderment, she pantomimed drying herself.

When Luisa returned with one of the small linen towels, Maddie wrapped it tightly round the injured hand.

'Now take her downstairs to the kitchen. *La cucina,*' she added as she received another uncomprehending stare. 'She needs to go to hospital. *Ospedale,*' she reiterated. *'Presto.* Her hand may need a stitch.' She demonstrated the action of sewing which drew agonised yelps and cries of '*Santa Madonna*' from both girls and renewed sobbing from Jolanda.

'And I'll see to that,' Maddie went on crisply, seeing Luisa gazing in consternation at the mess on the floor. 'You take care of her. *Attenzione,* Jolanda.'

Luisa nodded distractedly and led the other girl away, an arm protectively round her shoulders.

As they disappeared from sight, Maddie released her indrawn breath. Luisa would ultimately remember that the room had been left open with the prisoner free to roam, and she could only pray it would be later rather than sooner.

The keys were in the door, and to buy a few extra minutes, she locked the door from the outside. Picking up her skirts, she jumped across the debris of her lunch tray and ran to the store room. She picked out a white overall that approximated to her size, grabbed one of the elasticated mob caps and a pair of low-heeled black shoes. She stripped off her robe and nightgown, thrusting them, with the keys, into a hamper for soiled linen at the side of the room, then dressed swiftly.

The overall's starched linen felt coarse and uncomfortable against her skin, making her feel even more naked than usual. Something else that Andrea Valieri would eventually pay for, she told herself, struggling to fasten the buttons.

But at least she was covered, and beggars could not be choosers, she thought as she crammed her hair into the cap and pulled it down so that, hopefully, not a blonde wisp was showing.

Then, slipping her feet into the clumpy shoes, she set off along the passage, rehearsing the route in her mind, and listening all the time for the alarm to be sounded. She tiptoed along the gallery, through the arch and made her way to the false wall, feeling for the door handle.

When she reached the foot of the steps and the spot where the passage divided, she turned towards the kitchens, keeping close to the wall, head bent, not hurrying too much. Just another girl getting through the working day, anonymous in her uniform.

As she got nearer, she could hear the hubbub of excited voices, and, rising above them, the sound of Jolanda protesting tearfully. The volume doubled momentarily as a door opened and a man emerged, carrying a box of bottles and jars. He sent Maddie a brief, incurious look and went on down the passage.

My disguise works, she thought, her heart thudding. He must be going to the garbage bins, and all I have to do is follow him.

She maintained a discreet distance, watching as he rounded a corner, and was rewarded by the screech of hinges and a sudden influx of sunlight up ahead.

Not ideal when compared with the dimness of the passage. But her luck was holding, because when she reached the open doorway, he was nowhere to be seen.

Maddie stepped out into a walled courtyard lined with outbuildings. There was a gate in the far wall—or was this just more *trompe l'oeil*—designed to trap her in another part of the house?

But there was no imitating sunshine and fresh air, she thought with relief as she sprinted across the yard. And the gate was real, its heavy bolts sliding open, and the heavy ring handle turning with well-oiled ease.

She squeezed through the gap, then closed the heavy timbers carefully behind her. No need to leave clues to her chosen exit.

For a moment she stayed still, controlling her flurried breathing as she attempted to get her bearings.

The mountain that she'd seen every day from her window was over to her left, grey, monstrous and impenetrable as it loomed over the valley at its foot. Straining her eyes, Maddie could see far below the gleam of water and the pale line of a road that followed it—leading where?

Well, to civilisation, presumably, by the most direct route. The obvious choice for someone who needed to get away fast. But too obvious. She would be spotted miles away on that long curving descent. And even more easily by anyone returning...

The alternative route lay straight ahead of her. A rough track rising steeply into dense woodland which seemed to be composed mainly of chestnut trees. Not very appealing, dressed as she was, but at least the canopy of foliage would hide her as she travelled, and the thick trunks offer cover if necessary.

She started up the slope, pulling off the cap and stuffing it into her overall pocket. As she shook her hair loose, she silently cursed her unsuitable footwear. Better than going barefoot, she told herself, but only just.

Once safely in the shade of the trees, she paused again briefly to look back at her erstwhile prison. It was even larger than she'd supposed, not so much a house as a *palazzo*, with an imposing square tower at its centre, and she wondered if there were already faces at some of those innumerable windows scanning the countryside for a glimpse of her.

A great block of immutable stone, she thought, taking a last look over her shoulder, totally in keeping with its remote landscape, and certainly not her idea of a *casa d'estate*— a summer house. Its latter name, the House of the Wolf, suited it much better—as well as matching the character of its owner, she added with something of a snap, and plunged into the forest.

The path was narrow and heavily overgrown in places, but still reasonably discernible, indicating it had once been in regular use. So it could lead eventually to a hamlet or at least another house where there might be a telephone.

She tried to maintain a steady pace but it wasn't easy with all the fallen branches and foliage underfoot, or with the ill-fitting shoes she was wearing. She could almost feel the blisters springing up.

In spite of the shade, it was hot, and she was already growing thirsty. Pity there'd been no bottled water in the storeroom, she mused, wondering how soon she'd find some sign of human habitation. She seemed to have been walking for at least an hour or more, but without her watch, how could she tell? Yet surely the sun was considerably lower than it had been when she set out?

But she'd find water soon, she assured herself. There were bound to be streams feeding the river she'd seen in the valley, and she'd just have to risk their purity.

She couldn't, however, estimate her progress. She was no great judge of area, and these woods could well spread for acres.

There'd been plenty of woodland walks near her home when she was a child, but none of them like this. The trunks of the trees were thick and twisted, like something from an Arthur Rackham illustration. She could almost imagine gnarled arms emerging to seize her as they'd done in a scary Disney version of 'Snow White' she'd watched when she was little.

Shut down the imagination and stick to practicalities, she adjured herself. They're just trees. The real nightmare is behind you. And you can't be caught and taken back—for every kind of reason.

The forest was full of noises too: the whisper of leaves above her in the faint breeze, the rustling sounds in the bushes that flanked her path indicating the unseen presence of what she hoped were very small and friendly animals, and the shrill calling of birds which ceased abruptly at her approach.

Like a tracking device, she thought, with a faint grimace, easing her shoulders inside the stiff constriction of the linen.

And then she heard another noise, louder and more alien

than anything else around her. The sound of an approaching helicopter.

Maddie gasped, shading her eyes as she stared upwards through the tangle of leaves and saw the gleaming silver body passing almost directly overhead. The increase in volume from its engine told her all too well that it was coming in to land, and she knew, heart sinking, who was almost certainly on board.

Oh, trust Andrea Valieri not to have done the conventional thing and travelled by car, she raged inwardly. And why had it never occurred to her that Casa Lupo might have a helipad?

He couldn't possibly see her, in fact he would assume she was still safely his prisoner, but she suddenly felt as exposed as if she'd been tied naked across a rock in the sunlight.

And it wouldn't be long now before he discovered the truth, she thought, a knot of panic tightening in her stomach. And then, like a wolf, he would begin to hunt her down.

Not immediately, of course, she told herself, trying to be optimistic. He might well think that she was hiding somewhere in the house, until someone discovered her robe and nightgown and forced him to refocus.

All the same, the path no longer seemed a blessing, but quite the reverse. She tried to calculate how long it would be before he came to look for her, and how far she could get in that time and find some kind of shelter, but her head was whirling like the blades on the helicopter, and nothing made any sense.

'Maddalena.' Another trick of the imagination seemed to bring her name to her on the breeze, and she shivered uncontrollably.

She thought, 'I can't let him find me. I can't…' And knew it was not simply the fear of being locked up again that was driving her on with such desperation.

Determinedly, she dismissed her aching leg muscles and sore feet and quickened her pace. Inevitably, the track began to climb more steeply, and along with the forest floor debris, she also had loose stones to contend with.

She wasn't in condition for this, she told herself, panting as she paused to wipe the sweat from her eyes. And before too long she'd be getting dehydrated, and seeing things.

If that wasn't happening already, because the branch of a tree hanging down across her path seemed in some weird way to be moving, and turning upwards as if it was climbing itself.

'I'm going mad,' she said aloud, then stopped with a sti-fled cry as she realised what she was watching was a large snake, recoiling itself on to the tree limb above it.

A snake. For a moment, Maddie stood motionless, rigid with revulsion, then she flung herself sideways into a bush. For a brief moment, she was held there by twigs and thorns, until, with the sound of snapping wood, the bush gave way and she found herself rolling helplessly downhill in a welter of earth, leaves and stones.

She just had time to think, 'This is where it ends,' only to find her rush halted as she collided breathlessly with a fallen tree trunk. Gasping and choking for breath, she remained where she was, wondering how many bones she'd broken in those few crazy, terrifying seconds.

And when she did sit up, slowly and gingerly, her first act was to look cautiously round her in case the snake had followed.

'I didn't know Italy had such things,' she wailed inwardly.

She moved her arms and legs with care, but they seemed to be working reasonably well, so she hauled herself to her feet, using the fallen tree as a lever, and stood for a moment, wincing. She was scratched, grazed and would be bruised tomorrow, and she'd certainly twisted her ankle, but she'd managed to escape serious injury.

But she was damaged in other ways too. Two buttons were now missing from the top of her overall, now covered in earth and leaf stains, while the left-hand side of its skirt had been ripped open from mid-thigh downwards, taking it, she realised wretchedly, to the edge of indecency.

She sat down limply on the trunk and, fighting back her tears, waited until the worst of the shock had worn off and she'd at least stopped shaking. Knowing that she had to set off again and soon.

It was chillier now, reminding her that sunset could not be far off. And there was no way she wanted to be still in this forest at dusk.

Glancing around, she selected a suitable branch, using it as a walking stick to propel her back to the top of the slope. It might also be useful as a weapon, she decided, thankful that the snake was nowhere to be seen.

But there was no point in pretending she could pick up the old pace again. She felt a protesting twinge in her ankle at the very idea, so she was reduced to limping sedately, cursing her luck with every awkward step as she resumed the long and tricky ascent.

The forest was quieter now. Even the birds were oddly silent.

I probably frightened them away with the noise I made crashing down that hillside, Maddie thought, grimacing. Not to mention screaming at the snake.

At the crest of the slope, the track forked sharply, leading downwards in both cases.

Maddie paused, leaning on her improvised cane as she considered her options. The right hand path was marginally better kept, whereas the one on the left gave the impression it had been abandoned long ago. She had no coin to spin, so again she obeyed her instinct and ignored the more obvious choice.

She had been walking for about half an hour when the tangled greenery suddenly thinned out, and, her heart lifting, she saw below her in the sunset a cluster of stonework and slate roofs.

Houses, she thought, wanting to whoop with joy. People. I picked the right way after all.

She made her way carefully down the steep gradient, emerging into a village street lined with houses.

It was very quiet. No smoke came from the chimneys. No neighbours stood gossiping at their doorways. And as Maddie got closer she realised that most of the houses lacked doors and windows, and the slate roofs were sagging and in holes.

Whoever the inhabitants had been, they were long gone.

Except for one. A dog who came trotting out of an alley and stood in the middle of the street looking at her.

So where do you belong? Maddie wondered as she halted too. Because you're obviously not starving. So—take me to your master.

And then she looked again, and the beginning of her smile faded as she realised exactly what she was seeing. As she recognised the size of the animal. Its colour and weight. And, most tellingly, the shape of its muzzle.

Remembering as she did so, the picture over the fireplace back at the house and its savage subject, here and now confronting her in the flesh.

Oh God, she whispered silently. Oh God help me.

She took a cautious, shaky step backwards, then another while the wolf watched her, unmoving, the yellow eyes intent.

A voice in her head was telling her to be steady—be calm. That she had a stick to defend herself and the last thing she should do was turn and run.

On which, she dropped the stick, turned blindly and ran, cannoning into the hard, strong body standing right behind her. Feeling muscular arms go round her, grasping her firmly. Inexorably.

'So Maddalena,' said Andrea Valieri with soft satisfaction. 'We are together again at last. What a delight.'

CHAPTER EIGHT

SHE COULD NOT even feel surprise. Just a trembling sense of the inevitable.

As he held her, she was aware of the scent of his warm clean skin, mingled with the musky fragrance of the cologne he used.

She felt something unfold inside her like the opening of a flower and began to struggle all the more, beating at his chest with clenched fists. But it was like trying to push over that damned mountain and his grip on her did not relax for an instant.

'Let go of me.' She gasped the words frantically. 'Oh God, can't you see? Are you blind or just crazy? There's a wolf...'

'There was,' he said. 'It has gone now.' He turned her to look back down an empty street. 'See?'

She saw. Realised also that she had escaped one predator only to fall back into the power of another, and that she had been living in a fool's paradise during these past few hours to think she could really get free of him. That he would not find her.

The Count held her at arm's length, surveying her frowningly. '*Santa Madonna*, what have you done to yourself?'

She could well ask him the same, she thought, dressed as she'd never seen him before in cord pants and long boots, and

wearing what appeared to be a canvas jacket with an array
of pockets over a dark shirt.

She lifted her chin defiantly. 'I had an accident. There was
a snake hanging from a tree right in front of me, and I was
terrified so I ran, and fell down a slope.'

He said tersely, 'My sympathies are entirely with the
snake. Have you injured yourself?'

'Just my ankle.' Trying to run had been stupid and the
joint was throbbing badly now.

He said something under his breath, then reached for her,
swinging her up into his arms and carrying her towards one
of the crumbling houses.

She began to struggle again. 'Put me down.'

'*Basta!* Be still.' It was an order not a request, and she
subsided unwillingly against the strength of him.

As they neared the house, she saw that, unlike its neighbours, it had a door, even if it was no longer attached, but
merely propped against an outside wall.

And as he carried her inside, she discovered it was furnished in a rudimentary manner with a table, two chairs, a
sink served by a single tap, a fireplace and a decrepit stove.
Also that, at the rear, an archway half-covered by a ragged
curtain led to another room, equipped even more basically
with a mattress on the floor.

She also noticed a large, serviceable backpack leaning
against the wall, and next to it, a long case that quite clearly
contained a gun.

He placed her on a chair and went down on one knee. 'Let
me see your ankle.'

She jerked her foot backwards, stifling an instinctive cry
of pain. 'Don't touch me.'

He gave her a long icy look. 'Attempting to escape was
the act of a fool. Why compound your stupidity by refusing
help that you clearly need?'

Oh, don't let him guess the reason. Please—please don't let him guess...

For a moment, she was silent, then she nodded as if defeated, and sat back, hurriedly dragging her torn skirt together over her bare thigh as he removed her shoes. He examined the blisters on her toes and heels, his mouth compressed into a hard line.

When he touched her ankle, his fingers were firm but gentle.

'There is no fracture,' he diagnosed eventually.

'I could have told you that,' she muttered, aware that her skin was tingling at his touch. Despising herself...

'Just a slight sprain,' he went on as if she hadn't spoken. 'It needs ice, but Giacomo has no freezer, so we must use what is available.'

'I didn't know you had medical training,' she said. 'In addition to all your other talents.'

'I don't,' he returned brusquely. 'Instead I have common sense. Permit me to recommend it.'

He looked her over again, frowning as she shivered suddenly, then stood up and went over to the fireplace, taking a box of matches from one of his jacket pockets and lighting the small pile of kindling in the hearth. Once it had caught, he added more wood from a sagging cardboard box, picked up a pot like a witch's cauldron and filled it at the sink before hanging it from a hook over the flames.

Then he went into the adjoining room, returning with a tin hip bath which he set in front of the fire.

Maddie drew a sharp breath. 'You have to be joking.' Her voice wobbled.

'No,' he said. 'Some of those scratches need attention, and must be cleaned first. But do not distress yourself,' he added with a faint curl of the lip. 'I shall not insist on witnessing the process.'

He opened a rickety cupboard under the sink, and produced some stubs of candles in chipped pottery holders, making her realise how quickly the light was fading

'Does this Giacomo actually live here?' she asked as he set the candles on the table, and lit them. 'He must find it lonely.'

He shrugged. 'He is a shepherd. He is accustomed to his own company, and he finds this place useful when he has sheep or goats to move.'

'And he doesn't mind visitors?'

'In this region, we help each other.' He looked at her with the first glimmer of a smile. 'It was Giacomo who told me he had seen you today and where he believed you were heading. Later Aldo, who was out looking for wild boar with his son, confirmed what he had said, and I came to find you.'

Maddie gasped. 'You mean I was being watched? All the time?'

'You think a blonde with hair like sunlight would not attract attention?' he countered, adding drily, 'The description is theirs, not mine. Besides, they were concerned for you. This is no country for someone without proper clothing or footwear.'

She bit her lip. 'Or anything to drink.' The admission cost her. 'I'm so thirsty.'

'*Dio mio.*' He cast a despairing glance at what was left of the roof before going to his backpack and producing a bottle of still water and a tin cup. 'Drink it slowly,' he cautioned as he filled the cup and gave it to her.

She sipped. 'But how did they let you know they'd seen me?' She added with constraint. 'After all, you were away.' *In Viareggio. With your mistress. Something that shouldn't matter because I'm in love with Jeremy—engaged to him— soon to be married. And I can't let myself forget that even for a second.*

And gulped some more water.

'I returned just as it was realised you were missing,' he said. 'And Giacomo and Aldo contacted me by radio.'

'Radio?' she repeated. 'Up here?'

'*Sì.*' He nodded. 'Hunting parties use them all the time to communicate with each other. The latest have a range of over ten kilometres.'

'How efficient of them,' Maddie said bitterly.

'It is for the best,' he said, shrugging again. 'You would not have wished to spend the night alone up here, even in surroundings as comfortable as this,' he added drily. 'What would you have done, *per esempio,* if you had found you were sharing your accommodation with a scorpion?'

She put the cup down. 'Is there one?' Her voice was hollow.

'No,' he said. 'But they often come in at night.'

'Scorpions,' she said unsteadily. 'Wolves. Snakes. It's a jungle out there.'

'It was probably a rat-snake if it was hanging from a tree.' He sounded infuriatingly casual. 'They are not particularly venomous, and prefer to crush their prey.'

'Wow,' she said. 'How fascinating. I only wish it had explained that to me before I ended up at the bottom of a hill.'

She paused. 'And how did you manage to get here before I did? You certainly didn't pass me on the way.' Otherwise, somehow, I would have known, she thought and controlled another shiver.

'There is another road,' he told her. 'Camillo left me there at the crossroads, and I walked across country to wait for you.'

'You mean the car's not far away?' She closed her eyes. 'Thank heaven for that.'

'You are so anxious to return to your jail?' He was pouring water again, this time into the bath using a jug from the sink cupboard, before adding the contents of the cauldron.

'On the contrary.' Her denial was instant, her tone defiant. 'But at least it's better than this.'

'I am glad Giacomo cannot hear you insult his hospitality.'

He indicated the tub. 'Your bath awaits, *signorina*. I regret there is no soap or any towel. You will have to dry yourself on what you are wearing.'

She flushed. 'But that's impossible. It—it's all I have.' *As he knew perfectly well.*

He took off his coat, hanging it on the back of the other chair, then began to unbutton the charcoal grey shirt he wore beneath it.

She said hoarsely, 'What are you doing?'

'Calm yourself. I am not planning to join you in the bath.' He stripped off the shirt and tossed it to her. 'Wear this when you have washed.'

His skin was bronze, the sculpting of bone and muscle strong yet, at the same time, intrinsically elegant. His chest was shadowed with hair which arrowed down into the waist-band of his pants.

Unlike Jeremy, whose skin was smooth and paler in spite of assiduous tanning. And whose shoulders were less broad. Less powerful...

She looked away hastily, dry-mouthed.

'I—I couldn't possibly...'

'Don't be foolish.' The amber eyes swept her. Lingered ironically. 'You will certainly find it more modest than what you are wearing now.'

Her face burned as she watched him walk to his back-pack, produce a thin wool sweater with a roll-neck and pull it over his head.

Finally, he took out a small jar and placed it on the table. 'Antiseptic cream,' he said, and disappeared into the street.

Swallowing, Maddie shed the overall, and stepped into the bath. It was one of the strangest she'd ever taken, but, whatever her misgivings, it felt warm and infinitely sooth-ing as she sat, knees to chin, carefully washing away the smears of earth, before standing up and letting the water pour in small, blissful rivulets from her cupped hands down her aching body.

She kept a careful eye on the doorway, but there was not so much as a shadow to disturb her.

When she had finished, she turned the overall inside out and patted herself dry with the cleanest part. She applied the cream to the worst of her grazes, then, slowly and reluctantly, she picked up his shirt and put it on.

The scent of him lingered quietly in its folds, as potent as when he'd held her in his arms, making her fingers clumsy as she struggled with the buttons, fastening them from throat to hem.

He was right, she conceded unwillingly when she'd finished. Its covering was more than adequate—longer in fact than some of the dresses she'd worn recently in England. The sleeves hung over her hands, and she rolled them back to her elbows.

Then, taking a deep breath, she called, 'I've finished.'

But the immediate response she'd expected did not come. The doorway was filled only with the gathering darkness. Wincing, she ran to the door, peering out.

Calling, 'Andrea,' her voice high and urgent.

And saw his tall figure taking solid, reassuring shape among the clustering shadows as he approached.

'Is something wrong?' he enquired as he came up to her. 'Another snake, perhaps?'

'No.' She felt foolish. Angry too that she'd betrayed her vulnerability yet again. 'I didn't know where you were.'

'I took a walk,' he said, adding drily, 'As I am not a saint, I decided to remove myself from temptation.'

She knew she was blushing again, and was glad of the darkness.

She hunched a defensive shoulder. 'I—I thought the wolf might have returned. And you didn't take the gun.'

'Because there is no need,' he said calmly. 'You are quite

safe.' He put a hand gently on her shoulder, turning her back into the room. The warmth of his touch seemed to penetrate every bone in her body. 'Now, if you sit, I will attend to your blisters.'

She sat, hands folded in her lap, waiting while he carried the bath outside to empty it, before returning to the backpack and taking out a roll of bandage and a small tube.

'This is a gel,' he told her. 'It acts as an artificial skin.'

'Will it hurt?' My God, she thought. She sounded about five years old.

'A little,' he said. 'But it will help.' He added drily, 'I hope you heal quickly, *mia bella*. When I promised to return you undamaged, I had not bargained for how reckless you might be.'

Return you...

She said quickly, 'Is there news from London? Am I going home?'

'They have made no reply of any kind.' He was deft with the gel, but it stung all the same, giving her an excuse for the sudden tears welling up in her eyes.

She said huskily, 'And if they never answer, what will happen then?'

'You need not consider that,' he said. 'They will respond eventually, I promise.' He put the cap back on the tube. 'You will have to be patient, Maddalena.' He paused. 'And take no more stupid risks,' he added as he began to strap up her ankle swiftly and efficiently.

'Oh, that's so easy for you to say.' She wiped away an errant tear with an angry fist.

There was a silence, then he said quietly, 'You will feel better, *mia cara*, when you have had some food.'

She rose. 'Then please take me back to the house. I'd prefer to eat in my cell—alone.'

'You will be very hungry by tomorrow,' he said. 'We will eat now.'

'Tomorrow,' she repeated, her voice rising. 'Tomorrow? You don't mean that. You can't imagine I'd spend the night here.' She didn't add, 'With you.' She didn't have to.

She saw his face harden. '*Purtroppo,* I fear that neither of us has any choice in the matter.'

'But Camillo brought you by car. You said so.'

'And I sent him back.'

'No.' Maddie's stomach was churning. 'No, I don't believe it. Why would you do that?'

'Because the road here, like the village, has been abandoned, and is dangerous. I would not ask Camillo to take such a risk in fading light.

'So he will come for us in the jeep tomorrow.'

He added bleakly, 'And you, Maddalena, must live with the consequences of your own foolishness.'

She sank back on to the chair. 'What's so foolish about wanting to be free?' she asked bitterly. 'To be back with the man I love?'

His voice was equally harsh. 'Nothing. But for the moment, there is only soup, bread and sausage. You may eat or go hungry as you wish.'

She sat, arms folded defensively round her body, watching his preparations. He added more wood to the fire, refilled the cauldron, coaxed the rusty stove to light, poured soup from a jar into a metal pan produced from his pack and set it to heat.

While it was doing so, he unrolled what she now saw was a sleeping bag attached to his pack, and took it into the other room. Maddie noticed uneasily that he was unzipping it completely and arranging it across the bare mattress as a coverlet. Turning it into a double bed.

She stiffened, feeling her heartbeat quicken. Oh God, no, not that…

Then she smelt the wonderful aroma coming from the stove, and her mouth began to water, rendering other considerations secondary, even if only on a temporary basis.

He shared the soup, thick with chicken, herbs and vegetables, between two tin basins, and brought it to the table with wooden spoons that had clearly been hand-carved, and a platter of bread and sausage cut into chunks with his hunting knife.

In spite of her apprehensions, Maddie ate every scrap put in front of her, and even managed a constricted '*Grazie, signore,*' when she had finished.

'*Prego,*' he returned laconically. 'And earlier you called me by my given name.'

So, he had noticed after all, she thought, vexed with herself.

She said shortly, 'A slip of the tongue. I was—nervous.'

'*Che peccato,*' he said lightly. 'My hopes are dashed once again.'

She kept her voice cool. 'Given the situation, you can't be hoping for very much.'

'No? But every man is allowed, surely, to dream.'

Instinct warned her that Andrea Valieri's dreams should remain strictly a no-go area.

She shrugged. 'Yes, if he has time to waste.'

'Yet don't you dream, *mia bella*, of the day, the hour, the minute when you will become a bride? And do you consider that a waste?'

Did she still dream, she wondered, startled, or had it all become swallowed up by swathes of fabric, floral decorations and place cards? Subsumed by the ongoing battle with Esme over every detail?

She couldn't be sure any more. Only certain that she wanted this conversation to stop.

Back at the House of the Wolf, she would have made some excuse and gone to her room. Here she did not have that luxury, and she was acutely conscious the only thing waiting for her was that mattress and its makeshift quilt. Which might well be waiting for him too.

She pulled herself firmly together. 'But my dream is coming true, *signore*. That makes a difference.' She paused. 'How is Jolanda's hand? Did it need stitches?'

'How good of you to ask,' he said mockingly, letting her know that the abrupt change of direction had been duly noted. 'It has already been attended to at the nearest clinic.' He added softly, 'A little drama, of which you took full advantage, *mia cara*.'

'Perhaps, but I can still be concerned. And I hope Luisa won't get into trouble for forgetting to lock me in.'

'She has been reprimanded.' He added grimly, 'And Domenica too will have something to say when she returns.'

'No surprise there,' Maddie said crisply. 'Does she really have to be so obnoxious?'

'She has another side. She is, *per esempio,* devoted to my mother.'

That startled her. 'Your mother's still alive?'

His smile, tender, affectionate, lit his entire face. Suddenly he was someone she had never seen before but wanted very badly to know, she realised, as her heart turned over.

He said, 'Very much so, I assure you.'

'Oh,' she said. 'I—I just assumed…'

'Of course,' he said ironically 'Because to ask about my family, and use my given name would be to treat me as a human being, and it is easier to think of me as a monster.'

She looked down at the table. 'Hardly that. In spite of everything, you've been—kind tonight.'

'You are important to my strategy, *mia cara*.' His response was brusque again. '*Percio,* I cannot afford to let you go. Matters have gone too far for that.'

Too far, she thought, hazily as the candle flame seemed to swim in front of her eyes. But no further. She realised she was going to yawn, and tried to stifle it behind her hand, but, of course, he noticed.

'You have had a trying day, Maddalena. It is time you went

to bed.' His voice was expressionless. 'I regret the other facilities are only a hut outside the back door, but I have a torch.'

She said too quickly, 'I'll be fine right here.'

The dark brows lifted. 'Tired almost to death, *mia bella*, yet still fighting me? *Tuttavia*, I must insist. The mattress can easily accommodate us both, and I prefer to keep you beside me. I am sure you understand why.'

She said, stumbling a little, 'If I promise not to run away again, will you sleep out here?'

'No,' he said, adding with faint grimness, 'because, thanks to you, I too have had a wearing day, so you are in no position to make terms.'

Maddie got to her feet. 'But you said—you told me that you wouldn't do this. You promised.' She drew a swift sharp breath. 'I should have known I couldn't trust you—you bastard.'

'I said I would not take you against your will,' he corrected her. 'And I am in no mood to test your resolve tonight. I desire sleep, not pleasure.'

Her voice shook. 'You are—vile.'

'And you, *mia carissima*, are a painful and persistent thorn in my flesh,' he said harshly. 'Which I pray to God I shall soon be rid of.'

'Amen to that,' she shot back at him.

For a moment they glared at each other across the table, then suddenly and unexpectedly he burst out laughing.

'Now we have said our prayers, Maddalena, we can indeed go to bed.'

He paused. 'Can you walk, or shall I carry you?'

The question hung in the air between them for what seemed an eternity. Her mind was suddenly empty of everything but memories—the strength of his arms—the scent of his skin. His smile...

So much that was best forgotten. That should never have existed in the first place. That she should have fought from

the start with every atom of strength she possessed before
it took her unawares. Turned her world—her certainties to
chaos.

She said huskily, 'I—I can manage.'

'Then do so.' His tone was briskly impersonal. He went
to his pack and retrieved the torch which he handed to her.
'I will clear up here and wash before I join you.'

She nodded wordlessly and made her way carefully into
the other room. Thanks to the strapping, her ankle was not
aching nearly as much, she thought as she braved the few
feet of darkness beyond the narrow back door.

As he'd said, it was just a hut, and primitive was a compliment. Also she was unnerved by the rustlings and scratch-
ings she heard all around her, which the wavering torchlight
did not dispel.

She was almost glad to be back inside the house. The mattress was old and smelt of straw, but it was marginally better
than the floor. She put the torch down beside her and lay for
a moment, looking up at the stars which were plainly visible through the holes in the roof, trying to control her inner
trembling. Waiting.

The candles in the outer room were extinguished, signalling his approach, and she turned hurriedly on to her side,
seeking the furthest edge of the mattress, and digging her
fingers into its sagging contours to avoid rolling off.

Her eyes were closed so tightly that coloured lights danced
behind her lids, but she was fiercely aware of him just the
same. Every sense telling her that he had come round to her
side of the mattress. That he was standing above her, looking down at her. Oh God, bending towards her...

His voice was soft, its tone sardonic. 'I will take charge
of the torch, *mia bella*. It occurs to me it is a heavy one and I
have no wish to wake with a fractured skull. So now you may
stop pretending and sleep well.' He paused. '*E sogni d'oro.*'

He moved away, and she felt the mattress dip under his

weight. In spite of his assurances, she was rigid with tension, waiting for him to reach for her. But his only movement was to turn on his own side away from her, and a short while later, his deep, regular breathing told her that he at least had fallen asleep.

Slowly, gradually, she relaxed her grip on the mattress. She pillowed her head on her arm, breathing him again, as his shirt sleeve brushed her face, absorbing the male scent of him with a sudden, passionate hunger, which she could no longer dismiss or even deny.

The shame of it was corrosive. She'd known him only a matter of days, during which he'd been her jailer—her enemy. Anger and fear should have kept her safe. So why had nothing protected her from this strange turmoil of confused emotion?

I told myself I just wanted my freedom, she thought, her throat tightening. To get back to England, whatever the cost.

But it was never that simple. Because what I've really been doing is running away from myself. And from *him*.

And now there is nowhere left to go.

CHAPTER NINE

IT WASN'T EASY, as Maddie soon discovered, to lie wide awake next to a sleeping man, whom you were desperate not to disturb.

Especially when it was the first time she'd ever shared a bed for the entire night, she thought, wondering what would happen if her imitation of a statue was interrupted by an attack of cramp. Or sneezing. Or if she simply fell asleep and turned over...

Don't even think about it, she adjured herself grimly. Concentrate instead on the stars you can see through that hole in the roof.

But although her body was still, her mind remained restless.

Wasn't there some psychological syndrome, she wondered desperately, that caused victims to become physically attracted to their kidnappers?

Surely just knowing that would help her to fight this dangerous obsession. To overcome this bewildering, illogical need to move closer to the warmth of him, and the false security his arms seemed to offer.

Because she couldn't jeopardise her future—her marriage and all her dreams of happiness for what could only be a brief and sordid fling with a—a serial womaniser. A man, after all, who had spent the last two days and nights with another girl in some love nest in Viareggio.

A man who had surely done enough damage already to the Sylvesters, without enticing her—a promised wife—into this ultimate and disgraceful betrayal.

Think of Jeremy, she urged herself feverishly. Focus on him, and only on him. Think of being reunited with him, when all this will seem like a bad dream. Imagine being in *his* arms and belonging to *him* again.

At which point she paused, because, if she was honest, her sense of belonging had occasionally faltered in the past months.

And she found herself remembering unhappily how hurtful it had always seemed when Jeremy had dressed and left immediately after lovemaking, which had also been rushed and quite often less than satisfying—for her at least.

'You make me feel like a tart,' she told him one night while he was hurrying into his clothes. She tried to make it sound as if she was teasing rather than complaining, but he'd glanced at her defensively.

'Don't, darling. You know how things are.'

'Well, yes.' *Nigel Sylvester's shadow seemed to hang over them even in their most intimate moments.* She controlled a shiver, again, trying to sound jokey. 'But surely your father isn't having you watched.'

'Of course not, but he expects me to be first into the office each morning. So I need to leave from home.' He came over to the bed and kissed her. 'We'll soon be married, Maddie. We just have to be patient, that's all.'

And I have been, she thought now as she had then. In all sorts of ways. But for how much longer?

She looked back at the stars, trying, as a last resort, to count them, but always somehow getting the total wrong, and having to begin again. Until, eventually, she closed her eyes against their dazzle, and her mind to the numbers whirling in her head, and let sleep claim her at last.

The next time she opened her eyes, she saw above her a patch of sun-brightened blue sky signalling morning.

For a brief moment, she struggled to figure out where she was or what had woken her, and then, destructive as a tidal wave, memory came rushing back, and slowly and carefully, she turned her head.

Andrea Valieri was lying less than a foot away from her, propped up on one elbow, his mouth curving in a faint smile as he watched her. The sleeping bag had slipped down from his body, revealing that, apart from a pair of silk shorts, he was all bronzed skin. His hair was tousled, and he needed a shave, but neither of those circumstances detracted one iota from his sheer physical appeal.

'*Buongiorno.*' His voice reached her softly. '*E come stai?*'

Dry-mouthed, Maddie stared at him, trying to make her voice work, and at the same time wondering what in the world she could possibly say...

He tutted reprovingly. 'Have you not learned how to respond when the man in your bed wishes you "good morning"? Then permit me to show you.'

He moved then, reaching out to scoop her closer as he bent and let his mouth brush hers.

It was the lightest of touches, but all the same Maddie was aware of it in every inch of her skin, every nerve-ending. But most of all in every pulse of the soft inner trembling building inside her.

A trembling which could so easily become an ache— which she could not afford.

Only to feel her resolve slipping away as Andrea kissed her again, his mouth moving on hers, still gently but with a growing insistence as the seconds lengthened into minutes.

Maddie felt the flicker of his tongue probing her lips, searching for the inner sweetness they protected. At the same time his fingertips were stroking back the damp, dishevelled hair from her forehead, then tracing the contours of her face down to the curve of her throat where they lingered.

Her breath caught in mingled apprehension and excitement as his lips followed the same path softly kissing her eyes, her cheeks, the tremulous corners of her mouth, before feathering his lips over the pulse in her throat, making it leap in anticipation.

When, at last, he raised his head, Maddie's face was burning, forcing her to stifle a gasp as she registered the sudden tumult in her blood.

Now was the moment—if ever—to push him away. To hang on to some atavistic notion of survival and test his given word that he would not force her.

She was not a virgin but, at the same time she felt so inexplicably nervous and insecure that this might indeed have been her first time with a man.

Her body seemed to belong to a stranger, its reactions, responses to his mouth and hands, alien and bewildering, as if she was balanced on some brink as enticing as it was dangerous.

But when her hands lifted to his chest, it was not in the planned rejection. Instead, she found her fingers splaying across the muscular hair-roughened warmth of his torso, her palms pressing against the harsh thud of his heartbeat, knowing it echoed her own.

And as if responding to some unspoken invitation, Andrea sought her mouth again, his kiss deepening into passion, commanding a response, gathering her closer, as her lips parted at last to grant him the access he wanted.

And offer the surrender that she herself craved. No right—no wrong any more, she realised dazedly. Just this man and this moment. She could deny it no longer as she relinquished—released every pent-up sensation born of the tension that had been building between them since their first meeting.

Her nipples were pebble-hard under the concealment of her only garment, desire scalding between her thighs as their mouths explored and clung with heated, hungry delight. As their tongues met—mated in rising sensual urgency.

Eventually, Andrea lifted himself away from her, putting her back on the mattress, before leaning over her to unfasten, button by button the shirt she was wearing, his hand travelling downwards without haste, pushing the edges of the fabric apart so that his mouth could follow the warm, naked path he'd created, and seek the soft roundness of her uncovered breasts.

Maddie stroked the tangled black hair, her eyes closing as she savoured the delicious rasp of his chin against her bare flesh. Gasping with the pleasure that lanced through her as he cupped her breasts and raised them to his lips, capturing the dark-rose of each excited nipple in turn, and suckling them with delicate eroticism.

She could feel through the silk of his shorts the scorching strength of his arousal pressing against her, and her loins ached with the need to have all the male power of him sheathed inside her. To give herself completely.

But as her fingers sought his erection, Andrea halted her.

'Not yet, *mia bella*,' he told her huskily. 'For now I wish this pleasure to be for you.'

He unfastened the remaining buttons, and, for a long moment, looked down at her naked body, his eyes glowing like molten gold. He moved so he was kneeling at her feet, lifting them carefully to his gentle kisses, while his hands stroked her slim legs, sliding them beneath her to caress the sensitive area at the back of her knees, sending a long shiver down her spine, before travelling up to her flanks and slowly and sensuously moulding the swell of her buttocks.

Then his hands firm and purposeful, he lifted her towards him, letting his mouth drift enticingly over her slender thighs, before he reached the soft shadowing between them and kissed that too.

Maddie made a little sound between a sigh and a whimper and heard him murmur, '*Sì, carissima,*' as if he was answering some question she could not find words to ask.

He parted her legs, his fingers exploring her, pushing into the hot, sleek wetness of her. Seeking the tiny, tactile mound of her clitoris and teasing it with a fingertip to aching, quivering arousal, before bending his head, and possessing her with his mouth, his silken tongue flickering on her at one moment, then circling slowly and voluptuously the next.

Making her moan and writhe as he slowly and wickedly increased the exquisite pressure, coaxing her with devastating expertise towards her release.

She could hear a voice she hardly recognised as her own sobbing, 'Oh God, there—please. Yes—yes—now...'

And as her driven body finally reached the utmost pinnacle of pleasure and throbbed into climax, she cried out his name in joy and astonishment.

Afterwards, they lay wrapped in each other's arms, Andrea murmuring to her in his own language between kisses.

Nothing, she realised in wonderment, had prepared her for this moment. Had warned her of how he might make her feel, or the overwhelming sensations he would be able to exact from her eager flesh. She'd never denied she was capable of the normal female responses, but Andrea's lovemaking had taken her to a different dimension, quite outside any past experience. And her instinct told her this was only the beginning.

He'd truly said this time had been for her, she thought, her body still tingling in the aftermath of her delight, but now she wanted to pleasure him in turn.

Or as well, she amended, smiling against his skin as she

asked herself, astonished, how she could possibly want him again so soon.

He said softly, 'I have marked you a little, *mia cara,* I should have shaved. I will do so next time.'

She stroked his chin with the back of her hand. 'It doesn't matter.' And next time, she thought, was now...

She raised herself a little, leaning on one arm, then reached down, her fingers playing with the waistband of his shorts, deliberately tantalising him before she began to ease them down over his hips. And Andrea laughed softly, lying back in acquiescence, his arms linked behind his head, his whole attitude an invitation to take—or give—whatever she wanted.

And then between one breath and the next, everything changed. Andrea was no longer relaxed in sensuous anticipation, but jack-knifing into a sitting position, head bent as if he was listening for something.

'What is it? What's the matter?' Surprised, Maddie sat up too. He silenced her with a gesture and then she heard it. The distant blare of a vehicle's horn, succeeded by the faint noise of its approaching engine.

'Camillo,' he ground out. '*Dio mio,* I did not expect him so soon.' He pushed himself up from the mattress, jumping to his feet, and raking a hand irritably through his hair.

'Stay there,' he directed abruptly, heading for the outer room. 'I shall dress and deal with him.'

In spite of the curtain which he'd tugged into place as he left, she had a perfect view of Andrea, once more discreetly clad in his cord pants and sweater, moving the barrier from the doorway and walking out into the sunshine.

Leaving her there in a tangle of mixed emotions, with disappointment, embarrassment, and physical frustration leading the pack, as with unsteady fingers, she tried to fumble the shirt buttons back into their holes under cover of the sleeping bag.

Knowing that having tasted rapture in his arms, she'd

wanted the full banquet. And that she should be relieved that
Camillo had signalled his approach and not caught them *in
flagrante*.

And stopped right there, the breath catching in her throat.
What was she thinking of? she asked herself incredulously.
Because she had other far more cogent reasons for welcom-
ing the interruption.

I nearly made the biggest mistake of my life, she thought
frantically. Oh God, how could I have been so stupid?

Yet, if she was honest, she knew exactly why. The plain
fact was she'd been subjected to the attentions of a practised
seducer, and, in spite of all her brave words and pious res-
olutions, she hadn't even put up a struggle. Because she'd
wanted him. Wanted to know and be known completely. And
how shameful was that?

Count Valieri, she thought, swallowing. That was how she
must revert to thinking of him now. Her kidnapper—and not
the glamorous and alluring lover whose hands and mouth had
wrought such havoc with her senses only a little while ago.

She should have been warned when he'd told her he'd
never taken a woman by force. Because, of course, he didn't
have to.

I must have been his easiest conquest ever, she thought
bitterly. His experience would tell him exactly how I was
feeling. And he—he was unexpectedly kind.

But how could she ever face Jeremy again, knowing she'd
committed the ultimate in betrayal by having a one night
stand with his enemy?

But for Camillo, she would be in the Count's arms now,
answering any and every passionate demand he might make
of her. Oblivious to the nightmare of anguish and regret that
would surely follow when she came back to her senses.

Except that it was her senses that had deceived her in the
first place, turning her into this unrecognisable creature—
this *wanton* who'd shown Andrea Valieri a hunger she'd not

known could exist—until that moment. And who'd sobbed and begged for a piercing, soaring satisfaction wholly outside her wildest dreams.

Just as he'd known it would be, because he had no illusions about her level of sexual sophistication. Which was yet another humiliation to add to the growing list.

'Next time,' he'd said. Well, there would be no next time—just as there should have been no 'this time'. Because, she was back in control—of her mind as well as her body. And she would not allow herself to become his plaything again.

She heard the sound of voices, and shrank further under the sleeping bag. People talked about the cold light of day, she thought, and they were right. Because she was discovering that even bright sunlight had the power to make you shiver.

The curtain was pushed aside and Andrea came in, his face set.

'Camillo has brought you this,' he said, and placed her travel bag on the foot of the mattress.

She said slowly, staring at it. 'My things? Really—my own things? You've given them back to me?'

A faint smile dispelled some of the grimness from his mouth. '*Sì, davvero.*' He paused, then added crisply, 'There is water heating for you to wash, but I would recommend that you make haste. Camillo tells me that the weather will change, bringing storms, and the road is already dangerous enough.'

She nodded. 'I—I'll be quick.'

'And I must pack this.' He bent and gathered up the sleeping bag into his arms leaving Maddie with no covering except the half-buttoned shirt. Which, suddenly, was not nearly enough.

With a swift nervous gesture, she huddled it around her as best she could, seeing the astonishment in his face turn to something more disturbing and much colder until, without a word, he turned on his heel and left her.

Maddie got up slowly from the mattress, aware she was shivering. She still ached from her fall, but the bruises were beginning to come out, and she could at least put her foot to the ground without hobbling.

The bag did not contain everything she'd brought to Italy, but it held a complete change of clothing, including underwear, and her toiletries, so she wasn't going to quibble. Even, she discovered, her watch had been returned. Her phrase book too, but not, of course, her passport, wallet or tape recorder. That was too much to hope for.

But what, she wondered, as she made her swift and rudimentary *toilette*, had brought about this change of heart in her captor? Because that was how she must regard him from now on. Keep all the wrongs he'd done to her firmly in the forefront of her mind.

And be thankful it had been no worse, she thought, as she zipped up her black cut-offs and pulled her flowered black and white tee shirt over her head.

She had thought wearing her own clothes would make her feel less vulnerable, but she was wrong about that too. And knew that she would never feel really safe until she was back in London. And maybe not even then.

It took every scrap of courage she possessed to walk out of the hut to where the jeep was waiting, but the two men were clearly more concerned with the heavy cloud already gathering above the mountain tops than her sensitivities.

She received a slight, formal inclination of the head from Camillo, as he took her bag and opened the rear door of the jeep for her. Andrea merely sent her a brief, unsmiling glance with his curt, '*Andiamo*. Let's go.'

She soon realised it was not a journey she would want to make twice in a lifetime.

Because the Count had not been exaggerating about the state of the road. In places, it was only just wide enough for the jeep, and deeply pot-holed with a serious drop on one

side, which Maddie, sitting with her hands tightly clenched
in her lap, wished she hadn't seen, especially when she heard
the sound of stones and earth falling down into the valley
as they passed.

She was sorely tempted to close her eyes, but that might
have been interpreted as a sign of weakness, so she kept them
open staring rigidly at the back of Andrea Valieri's dark head,
only to remember with startling suddenness how thick and
vibrant his hair had felt under her fingers.

Which was an equally dangerous road to take, she realised, when her body began to tingle with other memories.
The awakening of fresh desires.

And better to be considered a coward than make an abject
fool of herself all over again, she decided resolutely, leaning
back and shutting her eyes tightly.

After a while, the jolting grew steadily less until, with a
final lurch that brought her heart into her mouth, the jeep
swung to the right and Maddie sat up to discover they had
emerged on to a reasonably decent road, descending between
the hills.

'*Mai piu*. Never again.' The Count turned, giving her a
crooked smile. 'I shall arrange to have that track closed *im-
mediatamente*. Anyone wanting Giacomo in future will have
to reach him on foot.'

'How nice,' she said. 'To have that kind of power.'

The smile vanished. 'Especially when one can use it to do
good, Maddalena.' He paused. 'But perhaps you have only
encountered the other kind.'

And he turned away, addressing some quiet remark to
Camillo.

Which will teach me, Maddie thought, savaging her lip
once more, to try and score points.

She stared out of the window trying to concentrate on the
spectacular scenery, striving to rebuild the barriers in her

mind and make them unassailable. To somehow recover some shreds of self-respect and decency to take back to Casa Lupo.

Out of the corner of her eye, she saw a flash followed almost immediately by a low, threatening rumble of thunder. At the same moment, the first heavy drops of rain hit the windscreen. The threatened storm had arrived in all its malignant force.

Maddie caught her breath as she watched the lightning forking down into the peaks as if it planned to tear them apart. And the crash of the thunder made it seem as if the mountains themselves had indeed succumbed to the eerie force and were beginning some lethal collapse, sweeping away everything in their path.

She'd never thought she'd be glad to see the house again, but, after nearly twenty minutes of driving, half-deafened, through the equivalent of a river, Casa Lupo's solid bulk seemed, absurdly, like a beacon of hope instead of a prison.

High iron gates swung open on to a short drive leading to the main entrance where Eustacio waited anxiously in the shelter of a huge black umbrella.

He rushed forward as the jeep halted, holding the umbrella over Maddie as he escorted her into the house, bombarding her with a stream of Italian which left her floundering.

'He is glad you are safe,' the Count supplied drily as he followed her into a massive hallway with a wide marble staircase at the far end.

'Oh,' said Maddie, forcing a smile. '*Grazie,* Eustacio.'

'He says too that Alfredo kisses your hands,' he added.

'Am I supposed to know who Alfredo is, or why he should want to do such a thing?' she inquired tautly.

'He is the father of Jolanda, now recovering at home. In the eyes of her parents, you are a heroine, Maddalena.'

'Hardly that.' She flushed.

'Perhaps not,' he returned silkily. 'But let us leave them their illusions, *mia cara.*' He beckoned and a sheepish Luisa came forward, and took charge of Maddie's travel bag. 'She will escort you to your new accommodation.'

'Where this time? A dungeon?' She extended her wrists. 'Won't I need handcuffs?'

'A delicious thought which we might discuss in more detail later,' he said softly and unpardonably, and her flush deepened hectically.

'The only thing I wish to discuss with you, Count Valieri,' she said between her teeth, 'is the time of my flight back to London.'

And with all the dignity she could muster, she followed Luisa up the marble staircase, instinct telling her that he was watching her every step of the way. And warning her at the same time not to look back.

CHAPTER TEN

MADDIE FOLLOWED LUISA along the broad gallery, quivering with what she told herself was sheer temper, and nothing else.

Because he was not irresistible. That was what she had to keep telling herself. That was why she had to banish from her brain every one of those dangerous, intrusive memories, reminding her how his hands and mouth had swept her away to that endless moment of sweet, pulsating rapture.

She took a deep breath, clenching her hands in the pockets of her cut-offs. Yes, she'd behaved stupidly—in fact, unforgivably—earlier that day, but she was not about to disgrace herself a second time. And she had to stop beating herself up about it. Transfer her anger to him instead.

From now on, she told herself angrily, he could keep his questionable remarks, along with the smile in his eyes and its unspoken promise of future delight for the girl in Viareggio, or whatever other floozie might happen to take his fancy, as he seemed incapable of being faithful for even twenty-four hours.

And that was the end of it.

Her dungeon reference had not been serious, but after her escape, she'd expected to find herself shut up somewhere even more remote and twice as secure as the room with the doors had been.

Yet halfway along the gallery, Luisa had turned into a

wide corridor and was briskly leading the way to a room at its end.

Maddie desperately tried to recall the Italian for 'Where are we going?' but without success. She really needed someone, she thought, to explain what was happening, even if it was in dodgy English with attitude.

'*Dov'e* Domenica?' she inquired. 'Is she still…?' She mimed someone throwing up.

Luisa shrugged and burst into a flood of incomprehensible speech, leaving Maddie none the wiser.

By this time they had reached the doors, and the girl flung them open and stood aside for Maddie to precede her into the room beyond.

She paused, catching her breath as she looked around her at a small but charming sitting room furnished with delicate sofas and chairs, all brocade-covered in blue, green and gold, grouped round a pretty marble fireplace, and a few elegant pieces of furniture including a writing desk at least two centuries old.

The walls were panelled in silk, and a cushioned seat ran the length of the long window.

I suppose this is more *trompe l'oeil*, and I'm really standing in a cupboard, Maddie thought, taking an uncertain step forward.

But the window, when she touched it, was the genuine article, looking down on to a formal garden, its geometric beds and gravelled paths now lit by a watery sun, making the stones and leaves sparkle.

She turned. 'It's lovely. *Bella*.'

Luisa beamed, then indicated the open door behind her.

Maddie walked past her into a large bedroom, occupied by a massive canopied bed curtained in dark blue silk. The headboard and posts were made from some rich golden-brown wood, intricately and beautifully carved with festoons of leaves, flowers and grapes.

The same wood had been used to build the row of fitted closets which framed another doorway. Beyond it, Maddie could see the gleam of ivory tiles, and the glimmer of gold fittings. A bathroom, she thought, with a sigh of longing. Warm water to wash the bits of dried leaf, dust and whatever insects had inhabited last night's mattress out of her hair, then to stretch out in and relax.

It felt like a wonderful dream. In fact, almost too wonderful...

She looked round at Luisa, who was placing the travel bag at the foot of the bed.

'For me?' She pointed to herself incredulously. 'I am to sleep—*dormire*—here?'

The girl nodded vigorously, her eyes dancing. She went to the closets and opened a couple of the doors, letting Maddie see that the rest of the clothes she'd brought to Italy were hanging there, or neatly folded in the adjoining drawers and shelves.

While in the next cupboard were the jewel-coloured nightgowns and robes which were all she'd had to wear up to now.

Side by side, Maddie thought, swallowing. These two different people that I've somehow become and their very different lives.

One of which had to go, and soon, because she was convinced that her enforced stay at the Casa Lupo had to be nearing its end, and that she would be returning home to sanity.

When Andrea Valieri would undoubtedly be hoping she would tell Jeremy and his father that she'd been treated well during her captivity.

Why else would she have been moved like this from her former room to what had to be the best guest suite?

Although she had to admit that, apart from last night, for which she had only herself to blame, she'd been kept pretty much in the lap of luxury from the start. She'd even become quite fond of all those doors.

She swallowed. Whatever she said when she reached London, she would have to choose her words with great care. After all, the Sylvesters would also be looking for revenge.

And I wanted him punished, she reminded herself, feeling suddenly as if a knife was twisting slowly in her gut. *I wanted them to lock him up and throw away the key—which could still happen. Only now, I'm not sure how I feel—or if even that is the truth...*

'*Signorina*?'

She realised that Luisa was watching her anxiously and summoned a smile.

'*Grazie*, Luisa. I want nothing more.' She spread her hands. '*Niente*.'

The girl nodded, showed her the embroidered bell pull beside the fireplace in the sitting room, then whisked herself away.

Left alone, Maddie headed for the bathroom with her toiletries and a change of clothing.

While the vast tub was filling, she stripped, then slid into the gently steaming water, submerging herself completely. She sat up with a gasp, pushing back her drenched hair and wincing a little as she felt the sting of the heat on her grazes.

Most of the bruising had emerged too, making her look rather like a piebald pony, she thought ruefully. Not the ideal image for the long-awaited reunion with Jeremy. On the other hand, it was precisely because of the wait that she'd been forced into desperate action. And so she would tell him. Or would she...?

She found she was examining her body more carefully, as if searching for tell-tale fingerprints. A different mark of Cain left by Andrea Valieri to betray her. Or to remind her how close she had been to betraying herself.

But she wouldn't think like that, she told herself, reaching with determination for the shampoo. She couldn't afford to.

In the end, it took three washings and a lot of rinsing with the hand spray before her hair felt really clean again.

As for the rest of her, she thought, switching off the spray, then gathering her hair into a rope and wringing the water from it, well—that might be a different matter.

She heard a faint noise and turned her head.

Andrea Valieri was standing framed in the doorway, his expression arrested, intent as he watched her, his eyes glowing with inner fire.

He said softly, '*Che bella sirena,*' and took a step forward.

For a moment, Maddie was transfixed. When she found her voice, she said hoarsely, 'Don't come any closer.' She lifted her hands to cover her breasts, all too aware that she was being absurd, and hearing her tone become stormier in consequence. 'How dare you just—walk in here like this. Get out. Get out now.'

He halted, his brows lifting. '*Dio mio*—I am here to bring you this.' He held up the jar of antiseptic cream he'd used the previous evening. 'I thought that you might need it.'

She took a deep breath. 'Then kindly put it down and go.'

He complied with the first half of the request. 'Why so agitated, *carissima*?' he asked softly, as Maddie sat rigidly, hands still clamped to her chest. 'Your body is hardly a mystery to me.'

'I don't need any reminder of that,' she said, adding bitterly, 'To my abiding shame.'

'Ah.' Andrea was silent for a moment, then gave her a level look. 'For my part, I remember only delight. But you had only to say "No", Maddalena.'

'I'm aware of that.' She bit her lip. 'Do you imagine it improves the situation?'

'At this moment, I doubt that anything could,' he returned with faint dryness. 'So, why did you not stop me when you had the chance?'

'Because I'd had a terrible time in your beastly forest,'

she flung back at him. 'And seeing that wolf was the final straw. I was scared—stressed out and you—you took advantage of me.'

'Why, Maddalena, what a little hypocrite you are,' he said softly. 'If we had not been interrupted, any advantage would have been mutual, and you know that, so do not pretend.'

'I wasn't thinking straight. I didn't know what I was doing,' Maddie defended a mite feebly. She rallied. 'Unlike you, *signore*. You, of course, had your own agenda.'

He shrugged. 'I wanted to make love to you, *mia bella*. It is hardly a state secret.'

'Is a few hours of celibacy really such a strain?' she asked witheringly. 'You'd only just got back from your lady in Viareggio when you came after me.'

'Portofino,' he corrected evenly. 'I was visiting a lady in Portofino not Viareggio.'

Maddie gasped. 'You think the location actually makes some difference?'

'When making accusations, I find it is better to be factually accurate.' He paused. 'I have noticed that you do not seem to share my view.'

'I have no wish to share anything with you, Count Valieri,' she said stormily. 'And that includes this roof. When will I be free to leave here?'

'I regret that the decision still remains in other hands than mine, *mia bella*. Or is that something else you prefer to forget?' He reached down the white towelling bathrobe hanging on the back of the door, and held it out to her. 'That water must be getting cold, Maddalena, and I would not wish you to take a chill.'

He absorbed her mutinous expression, sighed, then, draping the robe over the side of the tub, he turned his back and walked to the door.

Maddie could not pretend to be sorry as she scrambled out of the tepid depths of the bath, and huddled herself into the robe. It dwarfed her, reaching to her ankles, and the sash went twice round her slim waist before being tied in a secure knot.

As she rolled up the sleeves, a disturbing thought struck her. She said, 'Is this robe yours?'

'*Sì.*' He turned. 'But it has been laundered, so you will escape contamination.'

She remembered other things—like that handsomely carved bed in the other room, and her mouth dried. She gestured round her. 'And this bathroom—these other rooms are yours too?'

'*Naturalmente.*' He leaned casually against the doorframe. 'The whole house belongs to me, so how could it be otherwise?'

She said, 'That—isn't what I mean, and you know it.'

'No,' he said. 'You are concerned that you are sharing my private suite.'

'Not concerned,' she said. 'Furious. Are you surprised?'

'I think there is little more you could do to surprise me, Maddalena. So, let us rather say—disappointed.'

'Why?' Maddie lifted her chin. 'Because your nasty little scheme isn't going to work?'

The dark brows lifted. 'Is that how you regard my wish to be your lover?'

'Now who's being a hypocrite?' she demanded stonily.

'My desire for you is real and genuine, Maddalena.' He smiled suddenly, and she felt her heart thud. He added softly, 'Let me join you for the siesta later and I will prove it.'

'And that's really the only thing on your mind, Count Valieri?' Fighting the sweet seductive wave of warmth his words had induced, Maddie shook her head. 'I don't believe it.'

'With you in my arms, *carissima,* how could it be possible for me to think of anything else?' He paused. 'And it might be that I also wish to keep you close to me to avoid any further unwise attempts at escape.'

'Or you might also be looking for another way to punish

the Sylvesters,' she said. 'Or at least Jeremy. Which seems
far more likely.'

'Why—when I have done what is necessary already?'

'Because they haven't responded to your blackmail.' She
drew a painful breath. 'So taking me, and letting my fiancé
know about it, would be a very special form of revenge. The
stiletto through the ribs, up to its hilt.'

In the silence that followed, Andrea was no longer smiling.
'What a vivid imagination you have, *mia bella*,' he drawled.
'So what do you think I would say to him? That you indeed
have hair like the sun, but your body is sheer moonlight. That
you have a tiny mole on your right hip that I have kissed. That
you taste of honey and roses. All the exquisite intimate details about you that he must already know and which would
hurt him the most to hear from another man?'

'Yes.' Maddie felt as if she was burning all over. 'If—if
that's how you wish to put it.'

'I do not.' The words hung harshly in the air. 'I take the
reparation owing to me and no more. What you suggest is an
insult—to yourself, Maddalena, as well as to me.'

'Then let me go back to that other room.' *Away from here.
From you.* She added with difficulty, 'Please…'

'But it does not please me,' he said curtly. 'You will stay
here, but only as a matter of security. You will sleep alone.
I shall use the bedroom that adjoins yours.'

She lifted her chin. 'Does the door between us have a
lock?'

'*Sì.*' He paused, his mouth twisting. 'But no key.'

'And I'm expected to believe you—trust you?' she asked
raggedly. 'Not a chance, *signore*. But I promise you this. That
if you dare to come near me again I'll fight you. And next
time it will be with every breath in my body.'

'How quickly things can change,' he drawled cynically.
'But your vow will never be fulfilled, Maddalena. Because
in this next time you speak of, my moonlight girl, you will

come to me, of your own free will and giving yourself completely. And that, too, is a promise.'

He walked out, closing the door behind him, leaving her to stare after him, a hand pressed to her throat.

It soon became a very long day.

Maddie began it sitting on the edge of the bath, waiting for her inner trembling to subside. Or for Andrea to return...

When it became apparent this would not happen, she rose slowly to her feet, took the hand-dryer from the wall and carefully attended to her hair, smoothing it into shining order once more.

Hair like the sun...

Her heart pounded as she remembered the other things he'd said. Not that they bore any real relation to herself. They were simply the well-worn phrases of a practised womaniser, and she should treat them with the contempt they deserved.

His parting shot would have been unforgivable if it had not been so ludicrous. As if she would ever offer herself in that way. So why had it reduced her to stunned silence? she asked herself shivering.

But it was his query 'Why did you not stop me?' that she found beating in her brain, because pleading 'temporary insanity' was no excuse at all, and she knew it.

At the same time it occurred to her that if Jeremy had ever thought her body was like moonlight, he hadn't mentioned it.

She applied the antiseptic cream Andrea had brought her, then, leaving the borrowed robe in a crumpled heap on the tiled floor, she dressed in a plain blue skirt, and short-sleeved white top, and made her way back to the sitting room, curling up on the window seat.

Honey and roses.

She closed her eyes, emptying her mind, forcing away, with the words, memories of the magic of his lips and hands.

Trying to restore herself to the rational world, but without success.

It was almost a relief when a tap on the door signalled the arrival of Eustacio with her lunch—soup and a baked pasta dish in a delicious sauce, followed by fresh fruit. After making sure she had everything she needed, he informed her in his stilted English that his Excellency the Count had been called away on urgent business, but hoped she would do him the honour of dining with him that evening.

She could produce all kinds of feasible and dignified excuses to make it quite clear to her host that she didn't wish to be alone with him under any circumstances. For heaven's sake, the list had to be endless, with self-preservation at the top.

Instead she found herself murmuring her acquiescence.

And as she ate her meal, she wondered where the urgent business had taken him. Viareggio—or Portofino?

Not that it was any of her concern. What mattered were his negotiations with the Sylvesters, because surely this situation couldn't go on much longer.

Please, she whispered under her breath. Please let it be so. Because I have to get out of here. I must…

As afternoon passed into evening, she changed into the black dress she'd worn at the opera, and was back, sitting on the window seat, looking down into the darkening garden when Luisa came to fetch her.

She followed the girl back down to the hall and watched as she pressed a section of panelling which immediately swung inwards.

Easy when you know how, she thought, bracing herself as she walked into the *salone* beyond. And stopped, staring at the empty space above the fireplace.

For a moment, she thought she was being subjected to yet another trick of the eye. That if she blinked, or moved slightly to left or right, the picture that usually hung there would be in its accustomed place.

But as she moved closer, she realised all that remained was a slight discoloration on the surrounding wall.

'I had it removed.'

Maddie swung round and saw Andrea standing in the doorway. Unsmiling, he was wearing an elegant dark suit, and, apart from his loosened tie and the open top button on his shirt, looked remote and powerful as if he was about to chair some vital board meeting.

There was certainly no trace of the lover who had shown her a glimpse of Paradise that morning. But that had to be a good thing...

She experienced a sensation like a fist slowly clenching in her stomach, and hurried into speech.

'Removed? But why?'

He shrugged. 'After your encounter with a live wolf in the village last night, it seemed wiser. A reminder of the experience might cause you more fright—more stress,' he added pointedly. 'And neither of us would wish that.'

Maddie flushed, struggling to keep her voice steady. 'But the protection of the species—all the work that's been done— is part of your heritage.'

'To Count Guillermo, the cause was admirable,' he said. 'However its purpose has been achieved, and my own interests lie in other directions. Please believe that the absence of the picture is no hardship. I would prefer this place to become again what it was intended to be—the House of Summer.' He gave a faint smile. 'You have provided the incentive.'

'The House of Summer,' she repeated slowly. 'That sounds—really lovely.'

'I shall make it so.'

In the pause which followed, Andrea's eyes met hers and the silence between them suddenly began to change. To shim-

mer with tension, and an awareness as endless as the space
between them.

So why did it seem that just one small step would take her
into his arms? As if some unseen, unknown magnetic force
was drawing her to him.

Drawing her to her own destruction...

A realisation that gave her the strength to act. To break
the spell that held her before it was too late.

She moved, swiftly and restlessly, tearing her gaze from
his and staring down at the floor as she wrapped her arms
round her body in a gesture of total negation. And heard
across the room the harshness of the brief sigh that escaped
him.

A sigh that found an echo in the depths of her being, but
was not uttered aloud.

Instead she heard herself say with quiet intensity, 'Let me
go. You have to let me go. You boasted once that you'd never
taken a woman by force, yet that's how you're keeping me
here. It can't go on like this, and you know it.'

'I do indeed know,' he said. 'But it will not continue for
much longer.'

Her throat constricted painfully. She made herself look
up. Look at him. 'You mean there's news? You've heard from
London?'

'No,' he said. 'I have not.'

'Then end it,' she said passionately. 'Cut your losses and
send me back. Because he—Jeremy's father—will never give
in. You don't know what you're up against.'

'You are wrong, Maddalena. I have known for a long
time. Almost my whole life. And I too do not—give in.' He
paused. 'And you? Are you still determined to marry into
this family?'

She lifted her chin. 'I'm marrying the man I love. Not his
family. A very different proposition.'

His mouth curled. 'I am glad you think so. I hope you

will not be disappointed.' He walked to the drinks trolley, and mixed her a Campari soda, pouring whisky for himself.

He handed her the drink, and Maddie took it, being careful to avoid brushing his fingers with hers.

He raised his glass, his mouth twisting. 'To your future happiness, *carissima*.' He added sardonically, 'Whatever form it takes.'

He swallowed half the whisky, and turned away.

'To happiness,' Maddie echoed huskily, and found the pungent taste of the Campari turning sour in her throat as she drank.

CHAPTER ELEVEN

DINNER WAS AN awkward meal, interspersed with silences that neither of them seemed to wish or be able to break.

But when, at the end of the meal, Eustacio, following a signal from his master, brought a bottle of grappa to the table and placed it beside him, Maddie hastily finished her coffee and excused herself.

And tried to ignore the soft taunt, 'Running away, *mia bella?*' which followed her as Eustacio conducted her to the hidden door and back to her room.

The bed had been turned down, on one side only, she saw with relief, while her own lawn nightdress had been fanned out across the coverlet.

But she still felt uneasy about the unlockable door which was all that separated them, especially if it was Andrea's intention to drink himself to extinction on that potent Italian spirit before coming to his room.

Her brave words about fighting him off might just come back to haunt her, she thought, biting her lip.

But her rest was untroubled, and the next time she opened her eyes, she found sunshine filling the room and the ever-smiling Luisa bringing her a breakfast tray.

On which was a note in a familiar hand.

She fortified herself with coffee and hot rolls spread with honey before opening it.

'Forgive me for last night,' it began abruptly. 'I spoke churlishly. But this is a new and beautiful day and I shall be driving to the coast later this morning. I hope that you allow me to make amends by agreeing to be my companion, and joining me downstairs at eleven o clock.' It was signed with his initials.

Maddie read it twice, her brows creased. Was 'I shall be driving' to be taken literally, or would Camillo once again be behind the wheel?

Common sense told her that to spend a whole day in Andrea's sole company would be playing with fire.

On the other hand, refusing his invitation was tantamount to admitting as much. Telling him she was scared of being alone with him.

And not because she feared he might break his word and try to make love to her, she thought unhappily. On the contrary, it was because she couldn't trust herself.

Something that, for her own piece of mind, she couldn't allow him to suspect. Ever...

So when Eustacio came for the tray, she handed back the note saying quietly, 'Please thank Count Valieri and tell him I shall look forward to it.'

He repeated the words carefully, bowed slightly and left.

Leaving Maddie to review her limited wardrobe.

In the end she chose a plain white linen skirt teamed with a black tunic-style top, fastening her hair at the nape of her neck with a silver clip.

Neat and businesslike rather than seductive, she reassured herself as Luisa conducted her downstairs to meet him.

Andrea, in cream chinos and a dark red polo shirt, was standing in the hall, clearly issuing some last-minute instructions to Eustacio, but he broke off at Maddie's approach, looking up at her, the smile in his eyes jolting her like a sudden electrical charge.

For a second she hesitated, telling herself it was not too

late to change her mind and scurry back to her room for a dull but safe day reading.

Except that this was probably her only chance to see something of Italy. She could not imagine Jeremy permitting her to return any time soon, if ever.

So, she completed her sedate descent, just as if her heart was not hammering fit to break out of her ribcage, and walked across the tiled expanse of the entrance hall to join him.

She said, 'Isn't this rather a risk?'

His brows lifted. 'In what way?'

'By inviting me to go with you, back into the real world.' Maddie swallowed. 'Aren't you afraid I'll run away again?'

He gave a faint shrug. 'There is certainly that possibility. But will you?'

They looked at each other, Andrea's gaze intense, questioning as it locked with hers.

And she heard herself say, 'No.'

He gave a slight nod. 'Then let us go.'

It was a car she had never seen before, a sleek open-topped sports model, instantly confirming that Camillo would not be with them, either as driver or chaperon.

Maddie settled herself into the passenger seat, tying a scarf over her hair and hoping she looked more composed than she felt as the engine purred into life like a waking lion.

They took the road that snaked down into the valley. She found that he drove well, if rather faster than she was used to, but this was, after all, a familiar road with only local traffic, and very little of that.

She said, 'I'm glad the storms have gone.'

'They will return.' He shrugged a shoulder. 'But not too soon, I hope.'

'Or at least until I've gone home.' She kept her tone light but positive. Making it clear that was her real focus. Her main concern.

'*Naturalmente.*' Andrea's voice was silky. 'Yet who knows when that will be?'

'And how my life will be when I get there.' She spoke half to herself as all the doubts and fears of her first days at Casa Lupo suddenly returned. As she pictured Nigel Sylvester's fury at having to pay to rescue her, and felt cold inside.

'What do you mean?' He was frowning.

Maddie bit her lip, vexed at that involuntary moment of self-revelation. 'For one thing—will I have a job to go back to? I vanish off the face of the earth for days on end and come back empty-handed. That's hardly a good career move.'

'But you are going to be married,' he said. 'Therefore such considerations can hardly matter.'

She gasped. 'I can't believe you just said that—that blatant piece of male chauvinism. You should be ashamed.'

'But I was just echoing a familiar viewpoint, *certamente,*' he said softly. 'Or are you going to tell me that your *fidanzato* approves of your becoming a working wife? Because I warn you, Maddalena, I shall not believe you.'

She turned her head sharply, staring at him. When she could control her voice, she said, 'Is there anything about me that you don't know?'

'*Sì,*' he said. A smile touched the corners of his mouth. 'One last secret that I have yet to make mine. As you are already aware, *mia bella,* so let us not pretend.'

'At least,' she said huskily, 'there is something that I can keep from you.'

'*Forse sì, forse no.* I would say, *carissima,* it is all in the lap of the gods. And I can still hope.' He paused. '*Tuttavia,* there is so much you could learn about me, so much I wish to tell you, yet you never ask.'

She clasped her hands tightly in her lap to conceal the fact that they were trembling. 'I would prefer to change the subject.'

'*Certamente*. What would you like to discuss?'

'You said—the coast.' Geography should be safe enough. 'But I know very little about this area,' she went on brightly. 'So, where exactly are you taking me?'

'Oh, did I not say?' He shot her an amused glance. 'I have business in Portofino.' He added, mockingly, 'Private business.'

There was silence. Maddie sat staring straight ahead of her, rigid with temper and disbelief.

What in hell was he trying to prove? That the women in his life were so amenable they didn't mind sharing his favours turn and turn about?

And was that what he'd had planned for her too—if she'd committed the ultimate folly and become his lover?

Well, she thought, her throat tightening, at least she'd been spared that particular humiliation. But being forced to meet his current mistress was quite another story. And cruel to them both.

A sharp unfamiliar pain was twisting slowly inside her, tying her into trembling knots. At the same time, she was aware of an almost uncontrollable desire to scream, hit him, and burst into tears.

My God, she thought incredulously. I'm jealous. For the first time in my life, I'm jealous. This is how it feels, and I hate it. I hate myself. After all, it isn't as if—as if...

And closed her mind as the inner pain deepened, intensified.

One day she would be leaving all this behind, forgetting it as if it was a bad dream. That's what she had to believe. To cling to.

And if it taught her to value the happiness waiting for her even more, well—that was all to the good too.

Just the same, she would have given anything to be able to order him to turn the car round and take her back to the house, but she knew any such request would be laughed at then ignored.

So, she dug her nails into the palms of her hands and prepared to endure.

It was a quiet journey.

Apart from asking once or twice if she was comfortable, Andrea said nothing, and it occurred to Maddie, as she replied politely and briefly in the affirmative, that he too might be having second thoughts about the wisdom of this trip.

At first, she'd been able to concentrate fiercely on the spectacular scenery. When they eventually joined the major road, there was little to absorb her but the busy and fast-moving traffic. And it wasn't enough.

Her anger had subsided, leaving a deep, aching hollow in its place, with tears never too far away. She could feel them pricking at her eyes, and burning in her throat, but she wouldn't allow as much as one drop to fall.

At the same time, she knew she had no right to feel so wretched—so desolate, and she was disturbed by the intensity of her own emotions, and reluctant to contemplate what this might signify.

Knowing only this trip was a mistake, and she wanted it to be over.

Portofino occupied the edge of a small peninsula, and the road leading to it was narrow and twisted like a snake.

Just as if she wasn't nervous enough already, thought Maddie.

'There is no need for concern.' He must have noticed the tense clasping of her hands in her lap. 'I know this road well.'

'I'm sure you do.' She instantly regretted the slight snap in her tone, adding with cool if inaccurate civility, 'And I'm not at all worried.'

'*Certo che no*!' he returned. 'Of course not.' He paused.

'Cars are not allowed into the village, so we will have to park and walk a little way.'

'A walk would suit me very well,' she said. 'A long one, perhaps, while you transact your private business.'

'Ah,' he said softly. 'But for that, *mia bella,* I need you at my side. Did I not make that clear?'

She gave him a bitter look. 'Yes,' she said. 'But I hoped for everyone's sake that you might have changed your mind.'

'But mine is not the mind that needs to change, Maddalena.' There was an oddly harsh note in his voice. 'As I intend to prove to you very soon.'

He turned the wheel and swung the car into a small crowded parking area overlooking the bay, slotting it expertly between two four-wheel drives. He walked round to the passenger side and opened the door for her to alight, extending a helping hand which she ignored.

She stood for a moment, straightening the creases in her skirt, and smoothing her hair, released from the scarf, with unsteady fingers.

'*Andiamo.*' Andrea's hand was firm on her arm.

She tried to hang back. 'Please—I can't do this. I'm not ready...'

'Ready or not, it is time you knew the truth. Learned why you were brought here.' He paused. 'And some of the reasons why I have not let you go.'

They set off down the steep hill, but turned off after a couple of hundred yards on to a lane, little more than a track.

'Where are we going?'

'To pay a visit to the Villa Gabriele.'

She said hoarsely, 'Do you realise how cruel you're being—to her?' Almost adding, 'And to me,' but stopping herself just in time.

'This is not cruelty,' he said. 'But necessity.'

They rounded a bend, and the house was in front of them, honey-coloured in the sunshine behind its wrought iron gates.

Large, too, and surrounded by flower gardens, and with charming balconies to its upper floor windows.

No expense spared, thought Maddie, a fist clenching in her chest. And is this trip designed to show me what I'm missing by turning him down as a lover? Is there another villa, somewhere, waiting for a mistress? The new name on the list?

Andrea took her up the path, and the short flight of steps to the front door, where he rang the bell.

Almost before Maddie could draw breath, the door opened and she found herself confronted by Domenica. She greeted Andrea with a bob of her head and a polite murmur, but for the astonished Maddie there was just the usual unfriendly glance.

What on earth is she doing here? Maddie asked herself as they walked through an airy hall into a large *salone* at the rear of the house, and out on to a terrace overlooking Portofino and the sea.

A woman dressed in black was standing by the stone balustrade, and she turned quickly. But this was not the sexy blonde or the voluptuous brunette of Maddie's imagination.

This woman was older, her dark hair, drawn back into a heavy chignon, streaked with silver. Her face was still beautiful because of its exquisite bone structure but at the same time it was strained, even haggard, her wide amber eyes fixed on Maddie with the same inimical expression used by Domenica.

She turned towards Andrea speaking rapidly in Italian, the sun creating sparks of fire from the diamonds on her slender hands as she gestured angrily.

He said gently, 'Mammina, it had to be. You know this. Now speak English or Maddalena will not be able to understand.' He looked down at Maddie standing like a statue beside him. '*Carissima,* I wish you to meet...'

'But I know who it is,' she said hoarsely. 'It's Floria Bartrando. The missing opera singer I came to Italy to interview. I—I can't believe it.'

'She is also my mother,' he said. 'The Contessa Valieri.'

Maddie felt as if she'd been winded. 'How—how do you do,' she managed.

But her greeting was not returned, and the Contessa did not offer a hand to be shaken.

'I had no intention of ever speaking to you, *signorina.*' It was a rich, lovely voice still, in spite of its overt hostility. 'We meet now only at my son's insistence. I do not willingly receive a young woman who openly allies herself with my enemies.'

Maddie's stunned astonishment was fading fast to be replaced by indignation as she registered the contempt in the older woman's tone.

'Enemies?' she repeated. 'What do you mean? If you're talking about my fiancé and his father, they knew exactly why I was coming here, and it was obvious they'd never heard of you.'

Yet, at the same time, hadn't Jeremy told her that his father was violently opposed to the idea of her visiting Italy...

'No,' said the Contessa icily. 'Andrea's father took great care that they should not do so. He knew trouble was coming and he was afraid of how it might end, so he insisted our secret must wait for better times in order to protect me. To protect my reputation. My career.'

'I don't understand any of this,' Maddie protested. 'What trouble?'

'Perhaps it would be better to start at the beginning,' Andrea suggested quietly. 'This is a time for explanation, not to create further misunderstandings.' He took his mother's hand and kissed it. 'Mammina, please try to accept that Maddalena is innocent of all blame in this affair.'

'All blame?' The Contessa pursed her lips. 'I wonder. But let us deal with the matter, *figlio mio,* as you suggest.'

She waved to a table and chairs set under a striped awning. 'Shall we be seated?'

Maddie hesitated. She didn't want to be here, she realised. She didn't want to hear what they might be going to say. She felt suddenly scared, as if she was standing at a door which might lead to a bottomless abyss, where only one unwary step could lead to her destruction.

Turn back, an inner voice was prompting her. You don't have to hear these things. You're the innocent party in all this, as he's just said. So, refuse to listen and turn back to safety.

Yet in her heart, she knew she had forfeited safety from the moment she'd decided to research the story of a lost soprano. From that moment on, she'd simply been a puppet, manipulated by forces she had never encountered before like hatred and revenge.

And, if she was to be wholly honest, haunted—torn apart by a sexual desire that was also totally outside her experience.

I have to know, she thought, a faint shiver running through her in spite of the sun's warmth. I can't spend the rest of my life wondering why this happened to me.

When they were seated, Domenica appeared carrying a tray with glasses and a tall jug of fresh lemonade, clanking with ice cubes.

She's like a different person, Maddie thought, observing the warm smile that transformed the other's features when she spoke to the Contessa. But not with me, she added ruefully, finding herself once more on the receiving end of another surly glare as Domenica retreated indoors.

Accepting the lemonade Andrea had poured for her, she said, 'I'm ready to listen.'

He was silent for a moment. 'I must begin with a question,' he said at last. 'During your time with the Sylvesters, have you ever heard the name Marchetti?'

Maddie frowned. 'Yes—once. Jeremy was saying that

Sylvesters used to have foreign directors on the board. I'm sure that was one of the names.'

He nodded unsmilingly. 'It was. The last to serve was Benito Marchetti, but his poor health did not allow him to play an active part. That role was taken by his son Tommaso. He had spent much of his boyhood in England, and had even been to school with Nigel Sylvester, with whom he had become friends. Great things were expected of him. Accordingly, when he was told there were problems with the branch in Milano, he decided to investigate personally.'

He paused again. 'While he was there, he met a girl, a young soprano who was also making a name for herself, and who had come to the city for some specialised coaching by a Maestro Benzano before returning to Rome to sing the role of Gilda in "Rigoletto".

'We fell in love,' said Floria Valieri. The harshness had gone. Her gaze was remote, tender. 'It should not have happened. It was madness. We were too young, just starting our careers. Yet suddenly nothing mattered but each other. We were overwhelmed by our feelings, our need for each other.

She shook her head. 'I had never realised that sometimes it can be like that. That in a moment two lives can change forever.'

She smiled faintly. 'We told no-one, but Tommaso's great friend who had introduced us guessed somehow, and promised to keep our secret. He did so his whole life long.'

Maddie's voice was barely more than a whisper. 'You mean—Count Valieri?'

'*Sì.*' Andrea took up the story. 'They decided that when her season in Rome was over, they would be married. But Tommaso returned to London in order to make enquiries into some of the things he had learned in Milano.'

'What kind of things?' Maddie's heart was beating an alarm.

'Sums of money,' he said. 'Lost in a labyrinth of transactions that led nowhere. Currency deals that could not be traced. Other apparent irregularities. All the evidence suggested that one person was responsible, but Tommaso could not—did not want to believe it.'

He sighed. 'He told Cesare Valieri, who warned him to be careful. But it was too late. Soon after his return to London he himself was arrested and charged with embezzlement. All those strange elusive deals he had discovered were suddenly being traced back to him.'

'How much was he supposed to have stolen?' Maddie's mouth was dry.

He shrugged. 'In the region of half a million pounds. At his first hearing, bail was refused and he had to await trial in prison. While he was there, he wrote a letter to his *fidanzata*, telling her that he had been framed and promising he would prove his innocence very soon. He told her that she must not go to England or become involved in any way, that she must continue with "Rigoletto" and write to him only through his lawyer.

'He also wrote to Cesare, imposing the same sanctions and begging him to take care of his beloved, if the worst happened.

'He told them both that he had no doubt that the case against him would be dismissed and the real embezzler brought to justice. He also told them the culprit's name.'

Maddie stared at the Contessa. She said thickly, 'I know what you're going to say, and I can't—I won't believe it.'

'Nor did Tommaso—at first.' The Contessa sipped some lemonade. 'The man had been his friend. It seemed impossible that he should steal and lay a trail to a false bank account so my Tommaso would be blamed. *Tuttavia,* it was the truth.'

She looked back at Maddie, her gaze unwavering. 'Understand this, *signorina*. Nigel Sylvester is a criminal. A thief— and, in the eyes of God, a murderer too.'

CHAPTER TWELVE

'No.' MADDIE WAS on her feet, her glass overturned and the remains of her lemonade dripping on to the flagstones of the terrace. 'No, that I will never believe. Not even he...' She stopped with a gasp as she realised what she was saying.

'I said a murderer in the eyes of God.' The Contessa's tone was austere. 'No, he did not do the deed himself or hire someone for the purpose. I acquit him of that. But it was Nigel Sylvester's plotting to cover his own crime that caused my Tommaso to be in jail, and in that way he was responsible for his death.'

'There was a fight in the prison,' Andrea explained bleakly. 'Two men attacking someone smaller—weaker. Tommaso went to the victim's aid, but one of the assailants had a piece of sharpened metal, and, in the struggle, my father was stabbed in the throat, it seems accidentally. He bled to death before help could come.'

'Your father?' Maddie asked hoarsely. 'You're saying *he* was your father? But I thought...'

The Contessa lifted a hand. She said heavily, 'I had told Tommaso that I was to have his child before he went back to London. And I was glad I had done so, telling myself I had given him a reason to fight to prove his innocence. As he would have done, if he had lived,' she added, pressing a lace-edged handkerchief to her lips. 'But the case died with him, leaving this unjust—this unforgivable stain on his name—his character.'

Maddie sank back on her chair, her legs trembling.

She said, 'But what can you do?'

The Contessa's eyes flashed. 'I can make Nigel Sylvester pay for what he did. A poet once wrote that the mills of God grind slowly, and that one has only to wait in patience for vengeance to be accomplished.'

'But you can't actually prove anything,' Maddie argued. *The man's going to be my father-in-law, for God's sake. I have to defend him.* 'Besides Signor Marchetti might have been mistaken and blamed the wrong man. It's quite possible.'

She took a deep breath. 'You loved him. You want to believe the best of him, and I understand that. But his innocence doesn't necessarily make Nigel Sylvester guilty.'

'But there is proof,' said the Contessa. 'Tommaso wrote down every detail of his investigation, and hid the papers under the floorboards in his London apartment.'

'He told only Cesare what he had done,' Andrea said quietly. 'And his friend found the files while he was settling my father's affairs, even though the flat had been searched by the police and later ransacked again—by someone else.'

Maddie swallowed. 'But if the Count had this evidence, why didn't he use it then and there?'

'Because the case was officially closed. And also he knew that my father had not trusted the policeman leading the investigation. He feared the files might simply—vanish.'

'But above all he was thinking of me,' said the Contessa. 'Because when I heard the news, I was suddenly in this dark place where I could not think—where I could barely speak. I could certainly not sing. Not then. Not since. For a while, I even thought I would lose my baby.'

Maddie felt the breath catch in her throat.

Involuntarily, her eyes turned to Andrea—to the cool,

proud face, its austerity contradicted by the golden glow of his eyes. The firm mouth that could curve into a smile to wrench at her heart, and bring her to the edge of surrender with its beguiling warmth. The potent sensual promise of the lean, muscular body, once so briefly yet unforgettably close to hers.

A cold hand seemed to touch her, turning her blood to ice as she thought, 'You might never have been born. I might never have seen you. Never been held in your arms. And I can't bear to think about it. I can't...'

'Cesare had been asked to protect me,' the older woman continued. 'A promise he took most seriously. He felt that I needed peace and a safe sanctuary in which to recover, to regain my strength and my sanity. And somehow find acceptance.'

Her sudden smile was unexpectedly tender. 'All these things he gave me and more. Finally, he offered his name to me and to the child I was expecting, asking for nothing in return. We were married in secret at a church in the hills above Trimontano and went back to live at Casa Lupo, where Andrea was born and raised as Cesare's own child.'

'But surely people must have been looking for you,' Maddie protested. 'You were already famous and you just—disappeared.'

The Contessa shrugged. 'But no-one knew where to look.' She added coolly, 'You would not have done so either, *signorina*, had you not been led here.'

Maddie bit her lip. 'I need no reminder of that.' She paused. 'But you had the most beautiful voice. How could you bear to give up singing?'

'For a long while, I felt as if I was drowning in my unhappiness. But as time passed, and my son was born, my life changed for the better. I became a wife to the husband who loved me and in this new contentment, my voice began to return a little.

'But I made a solemn vow that I would never sing publicly again until Nigel Sylvester had paid for what he did. Nor will I, although I am now hoping my return in concert will not be too long delayed.'

'Which was how you tempted me.' Maddie sighed. 'What would you have done if the company had sent someone else?'

'It was not our only plan. We would simply have begun again.' The Contessa gave her a thin smile. 'Perhaps in the Maldives.'

Maddie drew a shaken breath. 'You actually knew where I'd be going on honeymoon?'

'The Sylvester family has no secrets from us,' the Contessa informed her calmly. 'My late husband decided to have them watched, and over the past few years the surveillance has intensified.'

Maddie bent her head. 'I see.'

'There was no personal enmity towards you,' said Floria Valieri. 'But we felt you could be useful. As it has proved.' She paused. 'If not altogether wise.'

'I can promise you that,' Maddie said coldly.

'You can certainly hope.' The Contessa shrugged again. *Tuttavia,* it was the information that Nigel Sylvester was to become a member of your House of Lords that gave us the opportunity to take from him the very thing he has worked and schemed for. The supreme accolade for his life's work. A career founded on greed, betrayal and deceit.' She almost spat the words.

'And you really think he will let that go?' Maddie asked incredulously. She shook her head. 'Never in this world.'

'He has no choice.' Andrea spoke. 'Among my father's papers is a letter in the man Sylvester's own hand, begging him for the sake of their past friendship and the bank's good name not to continue with his exposure of the fraud, and offering to put matters right. He must have assumed it would never be found.'

'But if you have this evidence, why did you need me?' Maddie spread her hands. 'It makes no sense.'

'Because we require more from him.' Andrea's tone hardened. 'He must write another letter to us admitting his guilt, not just for the fraud, but for the betrayal which led to my father's death.' He paused. 'In addition, he must refuse the life peerage that has been offered to him.'

Maddie looked away. She said bleakly, 'Then I'm not surprised he hasn't replied. You—you're really asking for your pound of flesh.'

The Contessa's brows lifted. 'I would call it natural justice, *signorina*. You blame us for this?'

'No,' Maddie said dully. 'In the circumstances, I don't think I can.' She swallowed. 'But maybe you can also understand that I wish I'd never heard of you.'

She rose and walked over to the balustrade, its stone warm under her hands as she looked down at the view—the tumble of houses among the vivid green of cypresses, cedars and palm trees leading down to Portofino's horseshoe harbour lined with buildings in yellow, ochre and cream, and, beyond that, the restless azure glitter of the sea.

She wondered how anything could be so beautiful, so brilliant, when everything in the safe world she had longed to return to had become so dark and so ugly.

Be careful what you wish for, she thought, because it might come true. Isn't that the old saying? Maybe I should have remembered that.

And it occurred to her that a simple ransom demand would have been far easier to bear.

And thought, I don't know what to do...

Behind her she heard a murmur of voices, and then the receding click of high heels across the flagstones, signalling that Floria Valieri had returned to the house.

Andrea came to stand beside her. 'Forgive me, Maddalena.' His voice was gentle. 'But it was time you heard the truth.'

She went on staring down at a vista that had become strangely blurred.

'Jeremy knows nothing about all this,' she said, her voice trembling. 'Nothing, I tell you.'

'*Naturalmente.*' His tone was wry.

She turned on him. 'You don't believe that?'

'It is what you believe,' he said. 'That is enough.'

There was a note in his voice that troubled her, making her heartbeat quicken.

Swiftly, she changed the subject. 'So Domenica really works for your mother. Well that explains the hostility. And now I've met the Contessa, I can understand the devotion too.'

She bit her lip. 'I wish I could have known her under different circumstances.'

'A desire that I share.'

Heartbeat still hammering, Maddie hurried on. 'And I'm glad she found happiness with your—stepfather.'

He inclined his head gravely. 'He was the best of men.' He paused. 'He loved her from the first, but when she met Tommaso, one look was enough to tell him he had lost her. He told himself then that a better man had won.'

Maddie stared at the horizon. 'Perhaps he should have spoken up anyway,' she said. 'Not been so noble.'

'But how can we truly judge at this distance?'

'Isn't that exactly what you're doing now?' she asked stonily, and turned towards the house. 'May we leave, please.'

'Not yet,' he said. 'We are to have lunch with my mother.'

'I couldn't eat.'

'Starving yourself is not the way to deal with bad news.' He took her arm. 'Come.'

The brush of his fingers scorched her to the bone. She shook him off. 'Don't touch me.'

He stepped back, his mouth tightening. 'As you wish, Maddalena. But my mother and the food are waiting. You will obey me in this at least.'

She preceded him into the house where Domenica waited to conduct them into the cool dimness of a formal *sala da pranzo*. Long crimson drapes had been half-drawn to exclude the sunlight and, in the centre of the room, a large ceiling fan turned with silent efficiency.

The circular table in some dark wood was set with silver, crystal and exquisite lace mats, and the long sideboard which matched it was almost groaning under the weight of several ornate silver candelabra, a heavily chased antique coffee service, and a range of elegant silver-topped decanters.

It made the huge dining hall at Casa Lupo seem almost rustically simple, thought Maddie as she took the indicated high-backed chair.

After the *antipasti*—a delicious selection of spiced meats, sausages and tiny platters of seafood—came *linguine* served simply with *pesto,* which, as Maddie had learned at Casa Lupo, had been invented in Genoa.

The main course was fish, baked in a sizzling cheese and herb sauce, and this was followed by peaches in red wine.

Domenica was waiting at table, and Maddie fully expected to find one of the courses being served straight into her lap, but the worst that came her way was the usual surly glance.

She managed to eat some of everything put in front of her, although her usual appetite had deserted her.

Conversation, unsurprisingly, was also fairly stilted. Andrea said little, lost in his thoughts, so it was left to the Contessa to ask civil questions about Maddie's work at Athene and receive equally polite replies.

'I hope your experiences here will not give you a distaste for Italian opera,' the Contessa remarked at last as coffee was served. 'I noticed that you seemed to enjoy "Rigoletto".'

Maddie stared at her, remembering the curtained box. 'You—were there too?'

'*Certamente.* I was as curious to see you, *signorina*, as you were to see me, although for very different reasons. As for the performance, I thought Ernesto Brazzoni lacked that spark of the devil that makes the Duke so interesting—and so attractive to all those unfortunate women.'

Maddie drank some of the rich fragrant brew in front of her. She said coolly, 'Not a trait that holds any appeal for me, I'm afraid. I think a member of the aristocracy should show more discrimination.'

Andrea roused himself from his introspection. He said softly, 'But if he did, Maddalena, there would be no story.'

She lifted her chin. 'And the girl who truly loved him would be saved from misery and a wretched ending.'

'Ah,' he said, his mouth curling cynically. 'True love. I bow to your greater experience in such a matter.'

The breath caught in her throat. And you, she thought. How much would you have taught me about heartbreak if I'd given myself to you, body and soul? How long has that girl in Viareggio spent lately, wondering where you are? Waiting for you to call?

At which point, Domenica came back into the room. She went straight to Andrea, speaking to him quietly, but Maddie caught the word '*telefonata*' and realised her stomach was churning suddenly in mingled excitement and dread.

Calm down, she told herself. It could be anything—some business matter—a problem at the house.

Then watched him get to his feet and pause briefly to place a hand on his mother's shoulder before striding from the room, and knew that it was not just—anything.

The Contessa sat rigidly, staring in front of her, the tension in the room almost tangible as the minutes ticked endlessly by.

Maddie looked down at her hands, clenched so tightly in her lap that her knuckles were white.

This is the moment you've been waiting for, longing for, said a small stony voice in her head. You should be thinking of your reunion with Jeremy and smiling, bubbling with joy inside at the thought of seeing him again. Of returning to normal. Resuming the preparations for your wedding.

But today has changed all that. Now you no longer know what to expect—except there's bound to be confrontation—fallout. Because you've learned things you'd rather not have known. Stuff you have to try and live with.

And felt herself shiver.

Andrea came back into the room, closing the door behind him.

His voice was quiet, almost flat, without a hint of triumph. 'A visitor has arrived from England and is waiting at the house. It appears he has brought with him the letter we have been waiting for.' A muscle moved in his throat. 'It is over at last.'

There was a silence, then the Contessa's icy control snapped and she burst into tears. Andrea's arms went round her, drawing against his shoulder as he whispered to her in his own language.

Maddie rose silently, went to the door and let herself out. As she paused in the hall, Domenica reappeared.

'Why are you here?' she demanded aggressively. 'Did Her Excellency invite you to look round her house? I think no.'

'I wish to find a bathroom,' Maddie returned. 'I suppose that is permitted.'

Domenica muttered something under her breath, and led the way upstairs to a spacious room tiled in pale blue and silver.

'I wait here,' she announced, stepping back into the passage.

In case I try to make off with the towels, thought Maddie, trying to derive some humour from the situation, and failing utterly.

She had a strong desire to emulate the Contessa and find release for her confused and troubling emotions in a flood of weeping.

Her legs were trembling so much she had to lean against the marble washbasin, while she splashed cold water over her face and wrists. Her reflection in the mirror above the basin was no comfort either. She looked as white as a ghost, her eyes hunted—haunted.

It was shock, she told herself. Shock mingled with relief that her ordeal was coming to an end at last. That was all.

And when she got to Casa Lupo and found Jeremy waiting for her, she would be fine again, and they'd face the inevitable problems together.

So why was it suddenly so difficult to form an image of him—let alone to remember the sound of his voice, or the feel of his arms around her?

A brief tap on the door made her snap out of her reverie. Domenica was clearly becoming impatient.

'*Uno momento,*' she called back, combing her hair back from her face with shaking fingers and struggling to refasten the clip.

'Do you want to search me?' she began as she opened the door, then stopped, her face warming with embarrassment as she saw it was not Domenica but the Contessa waiting outside. 'Oh—I—I'm sorry.'

'There is no need.' The Contessa's eyes were red, but she was back in control. 'My son has asked me to say that he wishes to leave as soon as possible.'

'Yes,' Maddie said, swallowing. 'Yes, of course.'

'And I sent my maid away so that I could speak privately to you,' the older woman added. 'I have an apology to make to you, *signorina.* I thought you must know the true nature of your future father-in-law, but were prepared to overlook this because of his wealth and position. Therefore, in my eyes, you were one of them.'

She paused. 'Having met you, I no longer believe this, and accept that you had a right to know the reason for your involvement, and that you should hear it from me.'

'My relationship with Mr Sylvester has never been easy,' Maddie admitted. 'And now it's going to be more difficult than ever. I—I accept that too.

'But, on the other hand, I've always told myself that I was marrying Jeremy, not his father, and I know my fiancé is just another innocent party in all this.' She gave a determinedly bright smile. 'We can work things out. I'm sure of it.'

There was a brief silence, then: 'Your loyalty is commendable,' said the Contessa, adding wryly, 'and so is Domenica's in a different way. She has always been ferociously devoted to me.'

'I only saw the ferocious bit.' Maddie hesitated. 'Is she like that with all outsiders, or just me?'

'Her grandmother was said to have the sight—the ability to see into the future,' said Floria Valieri. 'It seems she predicted that a fair-haired woman from across the sea would bring about the end of the House of the Wolf. Domenica was convinced from the first that it was you.'

Maddie shook her head. 'She's quite wrong. I'm sure I won't be the last blonde foreigner to cross Andrea's path.'

She forced another smile. 'I know I made a lot of threats at the start and meant them, but that's all over now.' She took a breath. 'And I promise that I shan't make trouble for him when I get back to London. So you mustn't worry about that.'

'I am grateful for the reassurance.' The Contessa gave her a meditative look. '*Tuttavia, signorina,* I fear it may be too late and the damage may already be done.'

She gave a brief, harsh sigh. 'So be it. And now we must not keep Andrea waiting any longer.'

CHAPTER THIRTEEN

HE WAS IN the hall, pacing restlessly, his face strained and brooding. He came across to his mother, took her hands and kissed them, and then her cheek.

'And now I deal with what remains to be done, Mammina.' He looked down at her searchingly. 'I proceed as we agreed? You have not changed your mind?'

'Justice will be done,' said the Contessa. 'That is what matters. And our decision is made.'

He bent his head in affirmation, and Maddie felt a faint shiver pass through her.

He is Crime. I am Punishment.

She'd thought Andrea didn't know what he'd taken on with Nigel Sylvester. She now saw that the boot was on the other foot.

As they left the villa to walk back to the car, Maddie glanced back and saw a familiar face peering at her from a front window, her clenched fist extended.

'What does this mean?' She demonstrated.

Andrea frowned. 'It is the *mano cornuto*,' he said brusquely. 'Protection against the evil eye. I suppose it is Domenica?'

'Yes, but I think she's being a little over-cautious.' She tried to speak lightly. 'After all, she's never going to see me again.'

'I am sorry she ever saw you at all,' was the harsh return. 'I put her in charge of you because my mother taught her to speak English, and I thought it would make matters easier. I see now that it was a mistake.'

'Your mother's English is wonderful,' she ventured.

'She learned languages as part of her training. She is also fluent in French, and can speak some German.'

She was silent for a moment, then said with constraint, 'If the letter does what you want, do you think she will sing again?'

He shrugged. '*Non lo so.* Who can tell?'

Which closed another conversational avenue, thought Maddie, her throat tightening. But why should that matter when Jeremy was only a relatively short drive away from her and they would be going home together? As soon as I see him, she told herself restlessly, as soon as he takes me in his arms, everything will be all right again. Besides, I can stand up to his father now, which will make our future together so much easier.

I know it.

And she kept whispering these three words under her breath like a mantra as they drove swiftly and silently back to Casa Lupo.

At the house, a strange car was waiting at one side of the drive, its driver leaning against the bonnet and smoking a cigarette.

Eustacio was standing on the steps, his expression frankly anxious, as he watched his employer's car come to a halt. As Andrea left the vehicle, he was greeted by a flood of Italian, and he paused for a clearly soothing word before allowing Maddie to precede him into the house.

In the hall, she paused, staring at the wall of panelling, the final barrier, and heard Andrea just behind her say very quietly, 'Maddalena.'

She had a crazy, terrifying impulse to turn and fling herself into his arms, to beg him to hold her and keep her safe forever, and found herself fighting it with every atom of resolve she possessed.

'My name is Maddie,' she said. 'Maddie Lang. And I'd like to see my fiancé, please.'

Watching him open the door into the *salone,* Maddie's heart was thudding painfully and she was conscious of a slight feeling of nausea.

She thought, Jeremy's waiting for me but I don't want to go in there. I don't want to face him, yet I must. I must...

Then adjured herself sharply for being a fool, because this was the moment she'd been waiting for over all these long days and nights. This and nothing else...

It had to be.

Head high, she marched past Andrea into the room and stopped dead, her hand flying to her mouth, because the man rising from a chair beside the fireplace was not Jeremy at all but a complete stranger, of more than medium height and corpulent with thinning grey hair and a florid face.

He said, 'You'll be Miss Lang. For a supposed kidnap victim you seem to be kept on a pretty loose rein. Do you know how long I've been waiting?'

Andrea said evenly, 'If we had known of your arrival, *signore,* the inconvenience could have been avoided.'

The newcomer looked him up and down. 'I'm here to make a delivery to a Count Valieri, while you, young lady, pack your things. We're catching an evening flight from Genoa.'

Maddie stiffened, but Andrea was intervening courteously. 'I think your name is Simpson, *signore.* May I welcome you to my home?'

'We don't have time for that,' the older man said sharply. 'My instructions are to do the business and leave with the girl.' He turned to Maddie. 'Hurry up, dear. You've caused enough trouble without making us miss that plane.'

She said in a shaking voice, 'How dare you talk to me like that? And where is Jeremy, my fiancé? Why isn't he here?'

He pursed his lips. 'You think my client would allow him to walk into another extortionist trap? Oh, no, sweetheart. Your little escapade has cost quite enough.

'And I've been retained to collect you, safe and unharmed as promised by your kidnapper and return you to London.'

He opened a briefcase beside his chair and extracted an envelope. 'As for the so-called Count, he gets this in exchange for you. And I want a receipt.'

Andrea's smile was icy. 'I hope you will not object if I check the contents of the envelope before I release Signorina Lang into your custody.'

He took the envelope from the other's reluctant grasp and walked to the window at the far end of the room, standing with his back turned as he scanned its contents.

Maddie stared at the fireplace where a small fire was burning, wishing the cheerful flames could melt the block of ice inside her.

She thought, Supposing—supposing it doesn't say what they want? What he's expecting? What will happen then?

And remembered Floria Valieri's words, 'Justice will be done.'

But he came back looking cool and unruffled, the envelope in his hand.

'Your client has kept his word,' he said. 'I shall keep mine. I will arrange for Signorina Lang's clothes and other possessions to be packed and brought down immediately.'

'I think,' Maddie said coldly and quietly, 'that is for me to decide, so please both of you stop talking about me as if I wasn't here.' She turned to the older man. 'I shall not be travelling with you, Mr Simpson, tonight or at any other time. Explain to your client that I arrived alone and I shall go back alone when I choose to do so, using my own return ticket.'

'Those aren't my client's instructions.'

'You're paid to do his bidding,' said Maddie. 'I, however, am not.' She added crisply, 'And if he wished me to comply, he should have sent a messenger with a different attitude. Tell him that as well.'

'But he'll be waiting…'

'And I've been waiting too,' Maddie returned. 'For quite a long time, considering I expected to be out of here in forty-eight hours at most. Maybe you should also mention that.'

Mr Simpson turned on Andrea. He seemed to be swelling visibly. 'This breaks the agreement.'

Andrea shrugged. 'How can that be?' he drawled. 'I have released Signorina Lang. She is no longer under my control—or that of anyone else, it seems. Nor can I force her to return with you.' He paused meditatively. 'You could, I suppose, drag her to your car, but I would not recommend it.'

'Nor would I,' said Maddie.

'I'm beginning to think you're in this with him,' Mr Simpson said glaring at her. 'Maybe I should take that envelope back.'

'Then think again, because you will not get it.' Andrea's tone was ice. 'Let us not stray into the realms of fantasy, *signore*. The *signorina* and I met for the first time on the night she was brought here and she has been held against her will ever since. Only two days ago, she risked her safety and her health by trying to escape. She will rejoin her future husband when she chooses to do so.'

'And what guarantee does he have of that?' Mr Simpson demanded.

'My sworn promise,' Andrea said quietly. 'Which once again he will have to trust.' He crossed to the door and opened it. '*Addio, signore.* I cannot pretend it has been a pleasure.'

Mr Simpson hesitated, as if searching for a reply, then contented himself with grabbing his briefcase and storming out. A moment or two later, his car was heard to roar off down the drive.

Maddie said roundly, 'What an obnoxious little toad.'

Andrea closed the door and walked back to where she was standing. 'Even so, that was not wise, Maddalena.'

She stared at him. 'You think I should have gone with him?'

'You have told me many times that you only wished to be free,' he countered harshly. 'To prove it you ran away. Now it is over, and you have the chance to leave and every reason to do so, but instead you stay. Why?'

The enormity of the question and its implications made her reel inwardly, grasping at straws to answer him. Didn't he know? Hadn't he sensed her emotional turmoil? Guessed the reason for her inner confusion?

'I—I suppose I was a bit thrown.' Her voice was uneven. 'I was so sure that it would be Jeremy here today. That he would come for me himself. I—I was counting on it.'

Which was certainly the truth.

He said flatly, 'I am sorry your faith was not rewarded.'

She swallowed. 'But I'll go tomorrow, if Camillo can be spared to drive me to Genoa. I'll find a hotel there, until I can get a plane home.'

Unless you ask me to stay...

'That will not be necessary. I shall make arrangements for you to be on the next convenient flight tomorrow.' He held out the envelope. 'As this is the reason for your recent ordeal, you should read it.'

He added quietly, 'It will confirm everything you learned earlier today. So take it, Maddalena, *per favore.*'

The single sheet was hand-written, the pen in places almost gouging narrow channels in the expensive paper.

Maddie found she was holding it with her fingertips, as if to avoid contamination as she scanned the closely written lines, beginning 'I, Nigel Walton Sylvester...'

He admitted everything, without excuse or apology. The money had been taken from dormant foreign accounts to finance his private share deals. These high-risk investments had been unsuccessful, and he had not been able to conceal what he had done by repaying the money.

He had realised Tommaso Marchetti's investigation into irregularities in the Milan branch would lead to his disgrace and an inevitable jail sentence. Determined to save himself at all costs when the other man refused to help cover up his illegal activities, he had deliberately laid a false trail, implicating his former friend as the real thief.

In court, it would have been a matter of one man's word against another's and he was confident that the evidence he had fabricated would lead to a conviction, when the case came to trial.

In the event, because of the prison stabbing, this belief was never tested.

But he now declared that Tommaso Marchetti was innocent of all the charges brought against him.

This was followed by his signature and the date.

Maddie drew a deep breath as she handed the letter back. 'Your father was his friend,' she said. 'Yet he doesn't say one word of regret or remorse about his death.'

'The letter was written under protest, Maddalena, not out of decency. He wished only to stop me making public the evidence I already possessed.'

'When—when did he learn about that?'

He shrugged. 'Forgive me, but I do not remember.'

'No?' She smiled bitterly. 'I bet it was when you discovered that he wouldn't lift a finger to get me back, and you needed to exert some real pressure.'

'*Non importa.* He has confessed, and my father has been vindicated at last. That is what matters.'

'But it can't end there,' Maddie protested. 'You have his confession. You must intend to use it.'

'We wished for reparation,' Andrea said simply. 'He has made it. Also, he has had to refuse the great honour intended for him. For such a man that is punishment enough, I think. So now, I will take the action agreed with my mother.'

He tore the letter across, walked to the fireplace and dropped the pieces on to the flickering flames.

'Oh God,' Maddie said appalled, and would have made a grab for them if he hadn't restrained her. 'What have you done? Have you gone completely mad? You've destroyed your most valuable piece of evidence.'

'But how will he ever know?' Andrea asked quietly. 'Unless you tell him.'

She said slowly, '"Justice will be done."' She sighed. 'I understand now what your mother meant.' She paused. 'It—it's been quite a day. I think I'll go to my room for a while.'

'As you wish.' He crossed the room and opened the door for her. 'Can you remember your way, or shall I send for Luisa?'

'I can manage.' She glanced at him under her lashes. 'By now I could probably find your hidden doors, if I was pushed.'

'Or those you have seen, at least.' His smile was swift and polite.

Treating her, she thought, as if she was a guest—nothing more. And a guest who had outstayed her welcome. But then what else had she really expected…?

He added, 'Until later, then.'

And Maddie nodded, smiling back, and left him, her hands clenched by her sides to conceal the fact that they were trembling.

When she reached the suite, she went into her room and threw herself face downwards across the bed, pressing herself into the mattress as if it might open up and hide her.

She thought, 'What am I going to do? Oh God, what am I going to do?'

Somehow she had to get through the rest of the day—and

the night—without revealing the seething turmoil within her. To deal with the stranger that Andrea had suddenly become.

It was almost better when he'd been her enemy, she thought. Then, at least, he had looked at her as if she was human.

No, she amended quickly and guiltily. He'd looked at her as if she was a woman. She'd sensed it from the beginning, responded to it, at first against her will, then quite deliberately in an attempt to ameliorate a dangerous situation.

But only to be caught in her own trap, finding herself drawn to him and wholly unable to resist his attraction. This urgent, aching need he'd somehow awoken in her. And which he'd seemed to share.

Yet now…

She buried her involuntary moan in the pillow.

I never meant it to happen, she whispered silently, as if placating some unseen malevolent force. And I should have believed him when he said it was over. Should have made myself leave with the hateful Simpson.

Because she knew now that nothing—*nothing*—could be worse than inhabiting this—limbo she'd been consigned to.

At last she got up wearily, loosened her hair, removed her skirt and top and, after a brief trip to the bathroom to wash her face and hands in cool water, slid under the coverlet and tried to sleep.

It was not easy. Image after image chased through her mind, and all of them Andrea—devouring her with his eyes as she descended the stairs towards him, kneeling to attend to her blistered feet, and, above all, pleasuring her with such potent lingering sweetness that she ached at its memory.

Memories that were all she would have to take with her when she left.

Eventually, the pictures in her head began to blur and slip away and with them, if only for a little while, went the tension, the hurt and the unspoken yearning as she slept.

There were shadows in the room when she opened her eyes, but as she sat up she realised there was light coming from the bathroom together with the sound of the bath filling, and the next moment Luisa appeared in the doorway.

She checked. '*Scusi, signorina.*' She indicated her watch. '*E l'ora di cena.*'

She went to the closet and extracted the black dress, but Maddie shook her head.

'No, *grazie.* I will choose—*decidere.*'

Luisa's expression as she hung the dress back in the closet plainly asked 'What choice?' But she ducked her head in assent and left Maddie to her own devices.

Her sleep had done her good, she thought, as she went into the bathroom. She had woken, seeing things much more clearly, knowing herself far better than she'd done an hour or so ago.

And, as a result, she'd reached a decision. One last throw of the dice, she told herself. Make—or break.

She sniffed at each of the array of bath essences and picked one with the scent of clove carnations, adding a generous capful to the steaming water.

After she'd bathed and dried herself, she used the matching body lotion rubbing it lightly and sensuously into her skin. She gave a slight grimace as the mirrored reflection of her nakedness showed that she was still bruised from her recent adventure, although the grazes were healing well.

But there was no time for the marks to fade, she thought, as she returned to the bedroom. She had to act now. Tonight.

Besides he already knew what she looked like without her clothes, bruises and all, she reminded herself, her skin warming at the recollection.

She opened the adjoining closet and took the black nightgown and robe from the rail. As she slipped the gown over her head, the delicate fabric, so sheer it was like a dark mist, touched her like a caress.

It hid almost nothing, of course. But wasn't that exactly why he'd chosen it? And if she'd worn it the first time to throw his challenge back in his face, this time she intended it to be total enticement, she thought with satisfaction as she slid her arms into the sleeves of the robe, and fastened its buttons.

She brushed her hair into its usual smooth fall, before darkening her lashes and emphasising the curve of her mouth with her favourite soft coral lustre.

This time, she made her own way downstairs, underlining her new status as guest rather than prisoner. She walked to the panelling, found the hidden catch and silently opened the door into the *salone*.

Andrea was standing by the fireplace, staring down at the small heap of glowing logs.

Maddie took a deep breath. 'You see?' she announced. 'I actually managed the door.'

He turned abruptly, glass in hand, standing as if transfixed as Maddie walked towards him, a faint smile playing about her lips.

'My compliments.' He did not return the smile. 'You will be pleased to hear that your flight to London tomorrow has been booked, and that Camillo will drive you to Genoa. Perhaps you can be ready by noon.'

She was not deceived by the implied dismissal or the formal tone in which it was uttered. She had seen the swift flare in his eyes, and the involuntary movement of a muscle in his throat and knew that the significance of her attire—or lack of it—had not been lost on him.

She said with equal civility, 'That's very kind of you.'

'*Al contrario.* We shall both be relieved when our lives return to normal, and I was anxious that no more time should be wasted.' He paused. 'May I get you a drink?'

'Some white wine, please,' she said, slightly unnerved by what he had said. This, she thought, was not going to plan.

She took the glass he brought her and raised it in a toast. 'To the future—whatever it may bring.'

'For you there seems little doubt.' He raised his own glass. Drank. 'You will marry the man you love. Your faith in him has not wavered.'

'Apart from today,' she said in a low voice. 'When he didn't come to fetch me.'

'A small misunderstanding, soon forgiven I am sure.'

She stared at him. 'But you said in his place, you'd storm the place to get me back.'

'I said a good many things, none of which now matter.' He briskly finished his whisky and set down the empty glass on the dining table, at which, Maddie noticed with sudden disquiet, only one place had been set.

He added, 'And now you must excuse me, Maddalena. I am dining elsewhere tonight. I may not return before you go tomorrow, so please accept my best wishes for a safe journey and a happy arrival. What is it your Shakespeare says—that journeys end in lovers' meetings? I hope it will be true for you.'

He took her nerveless hand and bowed over it. '*Addio, mia bella.* Your *fidanzato* is a fortunate man.'

Stunned, she watched him walk to the door. She said in a voice she didn't recognise, 'I don't understand. You're leaving me to spend this evening—our last time together—alone?'

His voice seemed to reach her across a million light years of space. 'There is no "together", Maddalena. How could there be? And we can part without regret. One day you will thank me for that, believe me.'

'Will you at least tell me where are you going?'

He paused. Shrugged. 'To Viareggio, *carissima,* as I often do.' He added softly, 'But I think you already know that.'

And went.

CHAPTER FOURTEEN

'MY GOD, DARLING,' Jeremy said huskily. 'It's been absolute hell on bloody earth. I felt I was living through a nightmare.'

Maddie looked down at the glitter of the diamonds, now restored to her left hand. She said quietly, 'It wasn't exactly a walk in the park for me, either.'

But her nightmare, she thought, had begun forty-eight hours ago and was still continuing.

Jeremy shuddered. 'You must have been terrified.'

'At first,' she said. 'Then I got angry.'

'Although, as my father said, you were never in any real danger. It wasn't as if you'd been grabbed by the Mafia.' He lowered his voice confidentially. 'In fact, I gather it was all rather a storm in a teacup.'

'Really?' She kept her voice even. 'I didn't see it like that.'

'Perhaps not,' he said. 'Yet here you are, home, safe, and all in one piece.'

In one piece, Maddie echoed in silent incredulity. Are you blind? Can't you see that I've fallen apart? That I'm in bits?

Jeremy was speaking again, 'I suppose you've told your family—your boss—everyone—what happened to you.'

'No,' she said. 'My aunt and uncle, the girls, Todd—they all think I've been running round Northern Italy trying to track my lost soprano, and have now admitted defeat.' She gave him a steady look. 'I thought that was best.'

'Absolutely. It solves a lot of problems—awkward questions and stuff.' He shook his head. 'After all, the whole thing was utterly ludicrous. Completely OTT. All this panic and uproar just to get Dad to exonerate some long-dead former employee from a richly deserved charge of fraud. Well, who could believe that?'

'Who indeed?' Maddie agreed ironically. 'But if it was such a trivial matter, why did it take so long to fix it?'

He looked uncomfortable. 'Well, darling, it's the kind of situation that could easily be misconstrued. Dad had the bank's reputation to consider.'

'Yes, of course,' she said. 'Silly me.'

'And what's it to do with this Valieri guy anyway? He must be totally barking.'

'No.' Maddie considered for a moment. 'Just—single-minded and very determined.'

'Well, Trevor Simpson didn't see him like that. His report was very different.'

'I can imagine.'

He hesitated. 'For one thing, it mentions that when he arrived, you were out driving round the countryside in Valieri's company.'

Maddie turned her instinctive flinch into a shrug. 'What of it?'

'And then you refused to let Simpson bring you back.' He paused. 'You must see that it looks—odd.'

'Actually, I don't. I was offered a "get out of jail free" card for a few hours.' *Or free apart from the bitter cost in heartache, shame and regret.*

'I was going stir-crazy,' she went on. 'So I accepted.'

She added crisply, 'And I found your Mr Simpson quite loathsome. Is that sufficient explanation?'

'A bit of a rough diamond, perhaps,' Jeremy said stiffly. 'But Dad finds him useful and efficient.' He took her hand.

'I'm not trying to upset you, truly, but this is a difficult situation for me—and clearly I'm not handling it very well.

'But I have to say that meeting in a wine bar after work isn't the sort of romantic reunion I'd hoped for.' He put his lips close to her ear. 'Let's get out of here and go to the flat. Dad's promised we'll have it to ourselves.'

Maddie controlled a sudden shiver. She said, 'Jeremy, I can't. Not yet. I've been through an ordeal. I—I need time.'

He sat back, his mouth tightening in obvious disappointment. 'Which is something else we need to talk about. My father suggests that our wedding should be brought forward. That we have a quiet ceremony quite soon, and a big celebratory party as planned on the original date.'

'Bring the wedding forward?' she said slowly. 'But why?'

Jeremy looked uncomfortable again. 'He hopes it will make you feel more—settled. Besides, it's only what you once claimed you wanted,' he added defensively. 'Let's elope, you said. Special licence and a couple of witnesses.'

'Which you refused.'

'Surely I'm allowed to change my mind.'

'Yes,' Maddie said. 'But so am I. And I think the previous arrangements should stand.' She paused. 'Needing some recovery time doesn't make me a basket case.'

He took her hand again. 'Sweetheart, can't you understand that, after what happened, I don't want to wait any longer?'

She bit her lip. 'I think I've been subjected to enough pressure just recently. This is a major decision, Jeremy, and I won't be rushed.'

'Rushed?' he repeated as if the word was new to him. 'God, Maddie, we're engaged to be married. You've promised to be my wife. Does it really matter if it happens sooner rather than later?'

Logic suggested that it didn't. Gut instinct advised her to stick to her guns.

She said, 'Tell me something. Why didn't you bring that letter to Italy yourself?'

'I wanted to, darling, believe me. But it was—tricky. You must see that.'

'Tricky?' she repeated. 'What's tricky about a storm in a teacup? Be honest, Jeremy. Your father said no, and you wouldn't go against him. Not even if it meant being reunited with me a few days sooner.'

'It was natural for him to be concerned.'

'I wish he'd been equally concerned for me. I could have been free so much earlier.' She paused. 'Is that why he didn't want me to go to Italy—because he was afraid the past might come back to haunt him?'

'Of course not,' he said quickly. 'It was just some long-forgotten petty crime. He simply didn't wish to be forced into a number of untruthful and potentially damaging admissions about it.

'But, of course, your safety and well-being were paramount, so, in the end, he put his name to that tissue of lies. And that wasn't all either. He had to ask not to be put forward for a life peerage. This hit him hard, but he said no sacrifice was too great.'

Maddie thought of the Contessa collapsing into a flood of tears because the honour of the man she loved had been vindicated at last. Of Andrea dropping the letter into the flames as if it was coated in slime.

But she supposed Jeremy, the devoted only son, could hardly be blamed for believing anything his father told him.

Jeremy's voice became quiet, almost casual. 'Tell me, my sweet, did the Valieri man ever say what he planned to do with it? Dad's letter, I mean? He went to enough trouble to get hold of it, so he must have something in mind.'

He burnt it...

She almost spoke the words, but at the last moment something stopped her.

She said, 'He was hardly likely to confide in me.' And paused. 'Why do you ask?'

'For God's sake, darling, isn't it obvious? The bloody thing's out there like a time bomb waiting to go off.'

Maddie said carefully, 'Perhaps just having it is enough and he doesn't mean to use it.'

Jeremy's mouth hardened into an unpleasant line. 'Sure—and watch out for flying pigs. Do you really think a bastard like that can be trusted?'

'My experience of bastards,' Maddie said, 'is rather limited.'

He sighed. 'Darling, this is why I want us to get married as quickly as possible. Maybe the notion of a man wanting to cherish and protect his wife is an old-fashioned one. If so, I'm an old-fashioned man and proud of it. So why make me wait?'

Maddie took a deep breath. 'Maybe because of an inbuilt conviction that marriage is an equal partnership and that I'm quite able to take care of myself,' she retorted.

'Not,' Jeremy said, 'according to the evidence of the past few weeks.'

'But I wasn't the real target,' Maddie pointed out quietly. 'It was my association with your family that really exposed me to risk.'

'And is this why you're refusing to marry me?'

'I haven't refused,' she said. 'I just haven't made up my mind.'

'Well, we can discuss it at the weekend,' said Jeremy. 'Dad suggested we should go somewhere quiet and secluded together.'

Maddie wondered dispassionately how many times Nigel Sylvester had been mentioned since they'd first brought their drinks to this corner table.

She said quietly, 'I'm afraid that isn't possible. I've already arranged to stay with my aunt and uncle.'

He looked dismayed. 'Can't you see them another time?

Surely if you explained we need time together they'd understand.'

'Perhaps, but I owed them a visit before I went away,' Maddie returned. 'And anyway a few days at home will give me time to think. Then I promise you'll have your answer.'

She also refused more wine and dinner at her favourite restaurant. 'Can I take a rain check?' Sensing his annoyance, she gave him a placatory smile. 'I haven't been sleeping too well since I got back, and I need an early night.' *Alone*...

Outside the bar, Jeremy signalled to a taxi. As it drew up to the kerb, he took Maddie's face in his hands and looked into her eyes.

He said in a low voice, 'I hate myself for asking this, but I must. This Valieri—I need to know what happened while you were together. Oh God, Maddie did he use you—force himself on you?'

She met his gaze, telling herself she should be thankful that she could. Glad that she could be truthful about this at least.

'No,' she said quietly. 'He never did. On the contrary.' She swallowed. 'I was simply part of a business transaction. Does that reassure you?'

'I suppose it has to.' He bent his head and kissed her, and Maddie made herself respond to the pressure of his lips.

'We're together again,' he whispered, as he put her into the cab. 'Back where we belong. I know everything's going to be all right, and I'll be waiting for your answer.'

As the taxi drove off, Maddie glanced back and saw him still standing on the edge of the kerb, eyes narrowed, face frowning as he watched her go, and had the strangest impression she was looking at a stranger.

But then nothing in the past two days had seemed quite real.

Not from the moment she'd fled from the *salone* back to her room, ripping off the robe and nightgown and leaving them in a crumpled heap on the floor. Crawling into the bed like a small animal seeking its lair.

But not to sleep. Instead she'd lain, staring into the darkness, counting the hours. Twice she'd got up, stumbling over to the door to his room and standing there, her fingers clasping the handle but afraid to turn it.

Wondering which would be worse—to find the bed unoccupied or risk another rejection.

When he'd said it was over, she hadn't realised he also meant she had served her purpose. That at best she had been a challenge but now she had become an inconvenience to be dispensed with as soon as possible. A line had been drawn and her pathetic ill-judged attempt to cross it had simply ended in her own humiliation.

In the morning, all the other possessions she'd brought to Italy were waiting in the hall, as she came downstairs with her travel bag. Nothing had been overlooked.

Removing all trace of me, she thought, and the hurt of that was not assuaged by discovering at the airport that she'd been upgraded to first class.

Waiting for the flight to be called, she'd rung Aunt Fee, Todd and her flatmates warning them of her imminent return.

But not Jeremy. She wasn't ready to face him. Not immediately.

I've too much to hide, she'd told herself, and I need some leeway.

Because she was too muddled, too emotionally bruised to be making major decisions about her future. Her days at the House of the Wolf had thrown her entire life into chaos and somehow she needed to pick up the threads of her existence and weave them back into a pattern that made sense.

Because, with the only certainty in her reeling world, she knew that if Andrea Valieri had taken her when she offered herself, she would not have left.

That she would have given herself, body and soul, for good or ill, and for as long as he wanted.

And the knowledge terrified her.

But now she had a whole weekend of peace and quiet in which to pull herself together, close the door on the past, and rebuild her future. The real future she had so nearly betrayed.

'Back where we belong,' Jeremy had said, and he was right. Because that was surely what she had to aim for. To remember, to the exclusion of all else, why she'd fallen in love with him, and agreed to be his wife. Because nothing else mattered.

After all, it would be wrong to assign any real blame in the Marchetti affair to him. He wasn't responsible for something his father had done before he was born and lied about ever since.

Essentially, she needed to create a strong marriage which would act as a counterweight to Nigel Sylvester's influence. It wouldn't be easy, because she couldn't destroy Jeremy's illusions about his father, but it must happen if they were to have any chance of happiness.

And I'll make it happen, she vowed silently.

Sally and Trisha had gone to the cinema, so she had the flat to herself when she got back. There was quiche and salad waiting in the fridge, so she ate a quick supper and decided to look through some of the emails that had accumulated on her personal laptop while she'd been absent.

As she scrolled down, the name 'Janet Gladstone' leapt out at her. My wedding dress, she thought, faintly puzzled. I wasn't expecting to hear from her.

She clicked on the message, and sat, staring in disbelief. 'It was a rush,' it read. 'But I've managed to get it finished. Please let me know when you can come for a final fitting.'

For a moment, Maddie felt as if a cold hand had touched her skin. Did Mrs Gladstone practise clairvoyance in her spare time? she wondered. Because this was more than odd. In fact, it was seriously weird, and distinctly premature.

'What a surprise,' she wrote back, after some thought. 'I'll see you at the weekend.'

And I'll be asking some questions at the same time, she thought as she pressed Send.

'It's perfect,' Maddie said almost reverently, letting the wild silk shimmer round her as she turned slowly in front of the full-length mirror. 'Beautiful. And it needs no alterations at all.' She shook her head. 'Amazing. Thank you so much.'

Janet Gladstone beamed with satisfaction. 'Not completely finished. Just one last stitch needed in the hem before you leave for the church. I like the old superstitions.'

Before I leave for the church, thought Maddie, trying to imagine it. To see herself walking up the aisle on Uncle Patrick's arm to where Jeremy waited. To feel her heart lift as he turned to smile at her.

But this inner picture was strangely blurred, and, as she tried to focus, it wavered and vanished.

As the dress was wrapped in sheets of tissue then carefully encased in its plastic carrier, Maddie asked her question.

'Mrs Gladstone, why did you think this was a rush job? The date I gave you is still weeks away.'

'But Mrs Sylvester told me that date no longer applied. She said that she was calling on your behalf to warn me that the wedding would now be much earlier, and that the order would be cancelled if I couldn't finish the dress in the time available.'

She added, looking anxious, 'I hope I haven't got it wrong, but she seemed so definite.'

'Well, the mistake isn't yours,' Maddie said lightly. 'And what really matters is that I have a wonderful dress.'

She paid the bill and took the dress carrier back to the

parking area, placing it carefully across the rear seat of Aunt Fee's car.

She'd intended to go straight home, but when she reached the crossroads, she turned left, heading for Fallowdene.

The housekeeper who answered the door agreed that Mrs Sylvester was at home, and conducted her to the drawing room where Esme was lounging on a sofa reading 'Vogue', a tray of coffee on the table in front of her.

'Madeleine,' she said. 'To what do I owe this unexpected pleasure?' She put down her magazine and waved her to the opposite sofa. 'Mrs Ferguson, please bring another cup.'

'Thank you, but I don't want any coffee.' Maddie paused. 'I've just collected my wedding dress, and I'd like to know why you wanted it finished in such a tearing hurry—and in my absence.'

Esme Sylvester's elegant brows rose. 'The Gladstone woman's actually managed it? How unexpectedly efficient. But I was just the messenger. And a very surprised one, let me tell you.'

'What do you mean?'

She shrugged. 'I didn't think there was going to be a wedding. Neither my husband nor my stepson like having their express wishes ignored, and Jeremy wants a wife who'll do as she's told and fall into line when required. Your Italian trip was quite the last straw.

'But then you were kidnapped, and they had to think again.'

She paused. 'If it had been only about money, they'd never have paid, of course, whatever the kidnappers had threatened. Some statement would have been issued about it being morally reprehensible to yield to blackmail.

'But this, of course, was far worse. This was loss of face. Potential ruin.

'Which is why they had to get you home, and why Jeremy has to sweep you off your feet and into instant matrimony.

Because, my dear Madeleine, you now know far too much about the Tommaso Marchetti unpleasantness, and they need those particular facts kept safely in the family.'

Maddie's lips felt stiff. 'You—and Jeremy both know the truth?'

'Naturally.' Esme sounded almost bored. 'Jeremy and his father have no secrets from each other. And, unlike you, I never had any illusions about the man I was going to marry. But the rewards have more than compensated for any passing moral qualms. Will you be able to say the same?'

'I don't believe any of this,' Maddie said desperately. 'You're simply saying these things to make trouble, because you've never liked me.'

Esme smiled cynically. 'You mean Jeremy hasn't already questioned you about what the Valieri man intends to do with his information? Whether he can be trusted to keep his word about Nigel's confession?'

'How—how did you know that?'

'Because, my naïve child, I know the Sylvesters and you don't—or not yet, anyway. And until they get an answer, they won't stop asking.'

She paused. 'And I'm trying to do you a favour here, because you've no idea what you're getting into.'

She gave a short laugh. 'You always made it so transparently clear you were planning to prise Jeremy lovingly from his father's grasp. But that will never happen, because, whatever you may choose to believe, Jeremy is no longer the boy you fell in love with years ago, but his father's own son.'

She lowered her voice confidentially. 'In fact, I can see a time when Nigel will learn from him. And I'm not at all sure you'll be able to cope with that, however rich you become. You see, we're so very different, you and I.'

'Yes,' Maddie said quietly. 'Yes, we are.' She eased the diamond ring from her left hand and put it on the table. 'Thank you. It's been—illuminating. You see I'd almost convinced myself that Jeremy needed me.'

'Oh, no,' Esme said softly. 'Those two only need each other.'

Maddie was never sure how she got out of the house and back into the car. And of the journey home, she could only remember pulling over on to a verge somewhere and kneeling on the grass being violently sick.

And when the paroxysms were over, she sat up, knowing she was absolved from guilt and heart searching, and half-laughing, half-crying with the relief of it. Knowing too that being completely and utterly alone was so much better than settling for less than second best.

And that, somehow, she could learn to live with that.

CHAPTER FIFTEEN

WHAT TOOK MADDIE slightly aback was the general lack of surprise over the news of her broken engagement. Uncle Patrick murmured that they'd 'often wondered', while Aunt Fee merely whisked away the wedding dress, and produced one of her sumptuous roast duck dinners.

Trisha and Sally took her clubbing, and Todd, with his usual single-mindedness, said he welcomed the news if it meant she would not be leaving any time soon.

And no-one asked her if she was sure she was doing the right thing.

What did they see that I didn't? Maddie wondered, but decided not to enquire.

All the opposition came from Jeremy, who laid siege to her, with texts, emails, armfuls of flowers and visits to the office and the flat, with pleas to 'talk things over, my darling, before it's too late'.

To all of which, she replied quietly and firmly that there was nothing to discuss. Her decision had been made once and for all, and she intended to treat the past as a closed book.

The flowers she took to a local hospice. Her conversation with Esme she kept strictly to herself.

And if she seemed quiet, with a propensity for staring into space, lost in thoughts that were clearly not happy— well, that was surely natural after a broken engagement. So people drew the obvious conclusions, and tactfully forbore to ask questions that she would have found impossible to answer with any degree of truth, if at all.

Time passed slowly, turned into one week, then two, and if her days were easier than her nights, then that was something she admitted only to herself.

Work continued to be her salvation. She and a colleague were researching material for a programme on people whose newly discovered talents had changed their lives. They'd already talked to a roofing engineer who'd learned to play the clarinet and was now performing regularly with a jazz band, a security guard whose watercolours had found a market in a London gallery, while Maddie had just arranged to go to Oxford to interview a retired female academic who'd written an explosively bloodthirsty thriller, when Todd emerged from his office, his eyes popping with excitement.

He said, 'Remember your wild goose chase to Italy? Well, the goose has been found. Floria Bartrando has made contact, would you believe, and she's willing to talk to us.'

For a moment, Maddie felt as if she'd been turned to stone. When she could speak, she said, 'Well good luck to whoever does it.'

Todd stared at her. 'For heaven's sake, Maddie, it's you. She's asked for you by name.'

Maddie shook her head. 'I can't do it, Todd. I—I can't possibly go back to Italy. Please don't ask me to explain.'

'But she's not in Italy.' He slapped a triumphant hand on Maddie's desk. 'She's here in London, staying at the Mayfair Royal hotel, Suite Fourteen, and she'll see you this evening at half seven. How about that?'

She took a breath. 'I suggest you send Holly. I have plans for tonight.'

Todd gave her a level look. 'Then change them. I've told you—it's you she wants to see, and no-one else.' He looked at her pale mutinous face and sighed. 'God, I'll never understand women. You're gone for days on end looking for her, and now she's turned up you don't want to know. I thought you'd be turning cartwheels.

'Well, this is your project, honey, so—whatever the problem—deal with it.' And he went back into his office and banged the door.

She wanted to go after him—to scream, 'It's not a problem, it's a nightmare.' Except that would involve her in explanations she could not afford to make.

'I'm in the wrong job for secrets,' she muttered under her breath.

She achieved little for the rest of the day, and went home early, pleading a headache. 'Take some ibuprofen,' Todd called after her. 'Make sure you're on top form for seven-thirty.' And his tone made clear it was an order rather than a suggestion.

She dressed down deliberately for the interview—straight grey skirt, plain white blouse, low-heeled black shoes—and pulled her hair back from her face, fastening it severely at the nape of her neck with a black ribbon.

Making it clear to the Contessa that she was no longer the girl her son had brought to Portofino.

The Mayfair Royal was an old-fashioned hotel, with no canned music or loud voices in its hushed and spacious foyer, luxuriously decked out in mahogany and marble.

A polite receptionist confirmed to Maddie that she was expected, and directed her to the lift.

As Maddie emerged on the first floor, a thin grey-haired man was waiting for her.

'Signorina Lang.' He gave her a kind smile. 'My name is Guido Massimo. Will you come with me, please?'

She walked beside him, her feet sinking into the thick carpet, waiting as he produced the key card for Suite Four-teen and opened the door, standing back politely to allow her to precede him.

Maddie stepped into an elegant sitting room, furnished in shades of blue. Glancing round her, she supposed that the double doors to her left and right led to the bedrooms, while ahead of her, a pair of tall windows, giving access to a wrought iron balcony, admitted the fading sunlight of the early June evening.

Behind her, she heard the door close softly, and, turning, realised that Mr Massimo had not accompanied her into the room and that she was alone.

So who will be making the grand entrance? she wondered, mentally bracing herself. Floria Bartrando or the Contessa Valieri?

But when the left hand bedroom door opened, she stood transfixed, her eyes widening endlessly in disbelief as Andrea walked into the room, lean in a sombre dark suit, his shirt open at the throat, his silk tie pulled loose. He paused, hands on hips, tight-lipped, the golden eyes brooding as he looked at her.

He said, 'So you came. I was not sure that you would.'

'I am here,' she said, recovering her breath, 'to talk to your mother. No other reason.' She looked past him, proud of the chill steadiness of her voice. Thankful, too, for her sedate choice of clothing in such marked contrast to the little she'd been wearing at their last confrontation. A memory that made her want to die inside all over again.

'So,' she went on, 'where is she, please?'

'She is visiting friends outside London. She will return tomorrow.'

She swallowed. 'In that case, so shall I.'

'I cannot force you to stay,' he said. His fleeting smile was wry. 'Much as I might wish to do so. But before you go, answer me one question. Is it true that you are no longer engaged to Sylvester's son?'

She flushed. 'That is not your concern.'

'Then let us make it so,' he said. 'I have travelled a long way, Maddalena, to hear your reply.'

'Then you've wasted your time, *signore*.'

'Hope,' he said, 'is never wasted.'

On her way to the door, she turned. 'Hope?' she repeated incredulously. 'What can you possibly be hoping for?'

He said softly, 'Why, for you, *carissima*, if you are no longer promised to the man you left me for.' He took a step towards her. 'You by my side, in my arms, in my bed. Mine completely.'

Her outer tension had not relaxed, but she was trembling inside with shame and anger. And an irrational sense of disappointment.

'How very flattering,' she said savagely. 'So I'll be your girl in London as opposed to the ones in Genoa—Turin—Rome—or any bloody where. No doubt the list is endless. Is that what you're suggesting? Because the answer's no.'

'Do not insult yourself, or me, Maddalena. I do not pretend there have not been women in my life. I am not a eunuch.' His eyes met hers directly, compellingly. 'But, since I met you, no-one. I swear it.' He paused. 'It was—impossible.'

'You're conveniently forgetting your lady friend in Viareggio.' Maddie flung back her head.

He said quietly, 'I visited Giulia once, to say goodbye. She deserved that courtesy.'

'But you went back to her,' she said. 'The night before I left. You told me so.'

'No, *mia cara*. I used that as an excuse. *Infatti,* I drove to Trimontano and stayed alone at the hotel where you had your reservation, in the room where you would have slept.'

He shook his head. 'I wanted you so badly, my sweet one, that I did not dare spend another night under the same roof with you, or find you still there in the morning.'

'If that's true,' Maddie whispered, 'then why—why did you want to send me away?'

'In order to fulfil my bargain with the Sylvesters.' His voice was suddenly harsh. 'Because I had promised on my honour that I would do so, even though it was like tearing the heart out of my body.

'And I knew if I took you—enjoyed the sweetness you were offering—that I would break my word and never let you go.' He spread his hands almost helplessly. 'And I had no guarantee that you would want to stay, even if we'd become lovers. Persuading you to give yourself for one night is very different to asking you to be with me forever.'

He added more gently, 'And from the beginning, time after time, you told me all you wanted was to return to England and the man you were to marry. So, to have you and then lose you again if you realised that your heart truly belonged with him—that had all the makings of a special kind of hell.

'So I sent you back to him—my enemy that you loved—to find your real happiness—the happiness you believed in— and told myself I must learn to live without you. And that too was hell, especially when I learned you were once again wearing your ring, and preparing for your wedding.'

She said wonderingly, 'How did you know that?'

His mouth twisted ruefully. 'Because in spite of all my brave intentions, I could not release you. Could not say, "This, too, is over."

'You might be separated from me forever, but I still needed to know what you were doing—how you looked—if you were indeed happy. And I still had the means to find out.'

He saw the shock in her face and flung up a hand. 'Ah, *mia cara*, I am not proud of this. But I was desperate—desperate to prove that you, with your courage and your strength, could not commit your life to such a man.

'As before, I devoured every scrap of information that came to me about you, but this time for very different reasons. And I suffered.'

He shook his head, 'Holy Madonna, I did not know such

pain existed. That this was what love could do. I realised then that I had been insane to put my given word before what I felt for you, especially when I was dealing with a family themselves without honour,' he added grimly.

'I told myself that instead of sending you back to them, I should have gone on my knees to you and begged you to stay with me for the rest of our lives. To love me and be my wife.'

He paused, and she saw the naked vulnerability in his face. The fear and yearning in his eyes.

He said in a low voice, 'The good God knows I have given you no reason to care for me, Maddalena, but perhaps, if I am patient, you could learn. I ask only for that chance, my sweet one. The chance to hope.'

He took another step. 'Do I have that chance? Say something, even if it is again "no".'

A smile trembled on her lips. 'You haven't given me much opportunity to speak.' She took a deep breath. 'When you left as you did, I—I was devastated. I felt ashamed because I'd made a fool of myself, and guilty because, in doing so, I'd betrayed Jeremy. And I told myself he didn't deserve that because he wasn't responsible for what his father had done, and probably didn't even know about it.

'I wanted to make amends to him, to start over and recapture what we'd once had. But I couldn't. Because I wasn't the same person. But neither was he, and I realised that perhaps I'd never really known him. Just seen what I wanted to see. Believed what I wanted to believe.

'As I did when I first met you.'

'*Carissima...*'

'No,' she said softly. 'Let me finish, my darling. Since I came back, I haven't been living, I've been existing. And I also thought I had nothing to hope for. That all I would ever have was loneliness and regret. But here you are—like a miracle. And it makes no sense, because we hardly know each other, and maybe we'll both need patience, but if you truly want me, I'm yours.'

Andrea repeated, on a shaken laugh, 'If I want you? If...?' He took one long stride and she was wrapped in his arms, his mouth locked to hers in a deep and passionate kiss. She yielded rapturously, pressing closer against his body as if she wished to be absorbed into him, flesh, blood and bone.

He muttered hoarsely, 'So much for patience.' Then lifting her into his arms, he carried her into his bedroom.

She expected to be taken quickly, their mutual hunger swiftly appeased, and would have given herself without reserve to his urgency.

Only she was wrong. Because suddenly it seemed there was all the time in the world for them to savour every delicious, intimate minute. For her to discover that his hands were gentle and unhurried as he dealt with the fastenings of her clothing, smiling his delight into her eyes as he uncovered her completely. Whispering his encouragement as she began, shyly, to undress him in turn.

At last knowing the joy of his naked body against hers as she lay in his arms. The remembered pleasure of his fingers caressing her breasts, his tongue liquid fire as he teased her hardening nipples. The accompaniment of slow, sweet kisses as he stroked her belly and her slackening eager thighs. The flurried excitement of her breathing as his hand slid between her legs, pushing into her heated wetness while one fingertip played with her tiny engorged mound, making her entire body clench with aching desire.

And she was touching him too, running her hands along his shoulders, across his chest, and down over the flat abdomen to clasp the power and strength of his arousal, her fingers moving delicately, provocatively from the base of the rigid staff to its tip, until he groaned his pleasure aloud.

But when Andrea moved over her, lifting her towards him

to enter her, she tensed involuntarily and he paused, his eyes searching her face.

'What is wrong? You don't want this?'

'Yes—oh, yes.' She hesitated, then said in a rush, 'But I'm scared.'

'That I'll hurt you?' His surprise was evident. 'I promise I will not.'

'Not that. Scared of disappointing you. Of not giving you what you expect.'

'Ah,' he said softly, his eyes tender. 'And if I tell you that I am also nervous because for the first time I am making love to the girl I love and her happiness means everything to me —what then?'

Her mouth curved into a smile. 'Then maybe I should stop fussing—and be happy.'

'I think so,' he said, and eased his way slowly and gently into her body, filling her. And she took him, deeply and completely, all inhibitions flown, as if all her life she had been waiting for this moment. And for him.

She raised her legs, locking them round him, responding to every potent, fluid thrust, feeling with astonishment the sharp irresistible build of sensation from the innermost depths of her womanhood. Until all control slipped away, leaving her lost—consumed in a spiral of mindless agonising rapture.

Heard Andrea call out to her, his voice hoarse and almost desperate, as he shuddered into his own scalding release.

Afterwards, when the world had stopped reeling, they lay quietly together, their sweat-dampened bodies still joined, Andrea's head pillowed on her breasts.

And heard him whisper, 'You are mine and I am yours' against her skin.

Later, between slow, sweet kisses, they talked.

So,' he said. 'We get married at once. As soon as arrangements can be made.'

Maddie put her lips to the pulse in his throat. 'Are you sweeping me off my feet, *signore*?'

'I think I must, *signorina*.' There was faint ruefulness in his tone. 'I did not use protection when we loved, as I should have done.'

'Don't you want children?'

'Of course,' he said, dropping a kiss on her tangled hair. 'But maybe not quite so soon.'

'Well,' she said. 'Only time will tell.' She paused. 'Whatever is your mother going to say?'

His grin was lazy. 'If she arrives at this minute—a great deal.'

'But she told me about the prophesy—that a fair-haired foreigner would cause the end of the House of the Wolf.'

'But that has already happened, my sweet one. Now it is the House of Summer that awaits my summer bride.'

'Why, yes,' she said. 'So, it is. I—I'd forgotten that. But I still don't think your mother's going to be very happy about the situation. I knew she disapproved of me being with you at Portofino.'

'She was concerned,' he said. 'Because she knew I had fallen irrevocably in love with a girl who belonged to another man, and that if I could not have her as my wife, I would never marry, and there would be no heir to carry on the Valieri name. That grieved her for my stepfather's sake.'

He kissed her again. 'But what she will tell you when we all meet tomorrow, is that she intends to sing in public again—and the first time will be at our wedding.'

'Oh.' Maddie choked a little. 'Oh—that would be so wonderful.'

'And I have no doubt,' he added in a resigned tone, 'that she will wish to take you shopping.'

For a moment, she saw herself reflected again in a swirl of wild silk. Found she was visualising the aisle of a church, and seeing Andrea turning from the altar to watch her walk towards him, the passion in his gaze mingled with reverence. The man she loved, waiting with love.

'But not for a dress,' she said dreamily. 'Because I already have the perfect one. All it needs is one last stitch.'

And she raised her smiling mouth for his kiss.

* * * * *

THE HIGHEST
STAKES OF ALL

CHAPTER ONE

South of France, 1975

'PICKINGS,' Denys Vernon said with immense satisfaction. 'And very rich pickings by the look of it.'

Stifling a sigh, Joanna put down the *tartine* she was buttering, and followed her father's gaze to the new yacht that had appeared overnight in the bay below the Hotel St Gregoire.

It was certainly large and extremely opulent, effortlessly diminishing the lesser craft anchored nearby. A floating palace, she thought, of gleaming white paint and chrome. Very swish. And suddenly there. Out of nowhere.

'A wealthy sheikh, perhaps.' Denys continued his musings aloud. 'Or even foreign royalty.'

'Or merely someone sheltering from last night's storm,' Joanna suggested more practically. She paused. 'And, speaking of storms, the manager stopped me last night and asked when our bill would be settled. And he wasn't smiling.'

'Infernal bloody cheek,' Denys snorted. 'Gaston Levaux is becoming obsessive about cash. If he's not careful, the whole place will become insufferably bourgeois.'

'Just because he wants to be paid?' Joanna asked mildly. 'I thought making money was our sole reason for being here, too.' She gave him a level look. 'And the fact that we haven't been doing so well lately must have been reported back to the office.'

'I'm still ahead of the game,' Denys said sharply. 'All I need is one good night.' His eyes strayed back to the yacht. 'And one wealthy idiot who thinks he can play poker.'

'And maybe Monsieur Levaux is concerned about his job,' Joanna continued reflectively. 'People are saying openly that the entire BelCote chain is being sold off. He won't want any bad debts on his books when the new owners take over.'

'Well, I'm sure he doesn't need your concern.' Denys looked her over. 'I think you should visit the hotel boutique, my pet. Buy a new dress as a demonstration of good faith.' He nodded. 'Something short and not too sweet to show off your tan.'

'Dad, I have plenty of clothes.' Joanna spoke with a touch of weariness. 'Besides, we have no money to waste on empty gestures.'

'Not waste, darling. Investment. And please keep your voice down when you call me—that,' he added irritably. 'Someone might hear.'

'And draw the correct conclusion that I'm actually your daughter instead of your supposed niece?' She shook her head. 'How long can we keep this farce going?'

And, in particular, how long before you grow up? she wondered in unhappy silence as her father's mouth tightened petulantly. Before you acknowledge that you haven't been forty for some time. That your hair is only blond because it's tinted, and you're not wrinkled because you've had an expensive face-lift.

'It's working very well. For one thing, it explains the same surname on our passports,' Denys retorted. 'And, as I told you at the outset, it doesn't suit my image to have a daughter who's nearly nineteen.'

And it doesn't suit me at all, Joanna thought bitterly. How long will it be before I can have a real life—the life I once planned?

Teaching languages had been her aim. She'd been studying for her A levels prior to university when her mother had been taken suddenly ill, and diagnosed with inoperable cancer. Two months later she was dead, and Joanna's relatively stable existence up to that point ended, too.

Denys, summoned home from America as soon as his wife's condition became known, had been genuinely grief-stricken. It had been his inability to settle rather than any lack of caring that had kept them apart for so much of their married life. Gail Vernon wanted a permanent home for her only child. Denys needed to gamble much as he needed to draw breath.

However, he was a generous if erratic provider, and, to Joanna, he had seemed an almost god-like being, suntanned and handsome, whenever he returned to the UK. A dispenser of laughter and largesse, she thought, his cases stuffed with scent, jewellery and other exotic gifts as well as the elegant clothes he had made for him in the Far East.

'If he ever gets stopped at Customs, he'll end up in jail,' his older brother Martin had muttered.

Yet, somehow, it had never happened. And perhaps Uncle Martin had been right when he also said Denys had the devil's own luck. But lately that luck had not been much in evidence. He'd sustained some heavy losses, and his recoveries had not been as positive as they needed to be.

He was invariably cagey about the exact state of their finances, and Joanna's attempts to discover how they stood had never been successful.

'Everything's fine, my pet,' was his usual airy reply. 'Stop worrying your pretty head and smile.'

A response that had Joanna grinding her teeth. As so much did these days.

At the beginning, of course, it had all seemed like a great adventure. The last thing she'd expected was to be taken out of school and whisked off abroad to share her father's peripatetic lifestyle, travelling from one gambling centre to another as the mood took him.

Uncle Martin and Aunt Sylvie had protested vociferously, saying that she could make a home with them while she finished her education, but Denys had been adamant.

'She's all I have left,' he'd repeated over and over again. 'All that remains of her mother. Can't you understand that I need her with me?' he'd added. 'Besides, a change of scene will be good for her. Get her away from all these painful memories of my lovely Gail.'

With hindsight, Joanna wondered rather sadly if he'd have been so set on her company if she'd still been the quiet, shy child with braces on her teeth. Instead, she'd soared into slender, long-legged womanhood, her chestnut hair falling in a silken swathe to her waist, and green eyes that seemed to ask what the world had to offer.

Which, at first, seemed to be a great deal. The travelling, the hotel suites, the super-charged atmosphere of the casinos had been immensely exciting for an almost eighteen-year-old.

Even the shock when she learned that Denys wasn't prepared to acknowledge their real relationship hadn't detracted too much from the appeal of their nomadic existence. Or not immediately.

She'd realised quite soon that women of all ages found her father attractive, and tried, without much success, not to let it bother her. But while Denys was charming, flattering and grateful, he was determined to make it clear that it would go no further than that.

'I need you to be my shield—keeping my admirers at a distance,' he'd told her seriously. His tone had become wheedling. 'Treat it as part of the game, darling. Mummy always told me how good you were in your school plays. Now's your chance to show me how well you can really act.'

But why were you never there to see for yourself? Joanna wanted to ask, but didn't, because her father was continuing.

'All you have to do, my pet, is stick close to me, smile and say as little as possible.'

On the whole, Joanna thought she'd managed pretty well, even when the leering looks and muttered remarks from many of the men she encountered made her want to run away and hide.

The mother of Jackie, her best friend at school, had become involved in the women's movement, and held consciousness-raising sessions at her house. The iniquity of women being regarded as sex objects by men, had been among the favourite themes at those meetings, and while she and Jackie had giggled about it afterwards, Joanna now thought ruefully that Mrs Henderson might have had a point.

Eventually, it had all ceased to be a game, and she'd begun to see her new life for the tawdry sham it really was, and be troubled by it. Realising at the same time that there was no feasible way out. That, for the time being, she was trapped.

Denys was speaking again, his voice excited. 'I'm going to start making enquiries. Find out who the new arrival is, and if he's likely to visit the Casino.' He gave her a minatory nod. 'I'll see you back here after lunch.'

Here we go again, Joanna thought with a sigh as she heard the suite door close behind him. Looking for a non-existent pot of gold at the end of a dodgy rainbow.

'All I need is one big win.' She had lost count of how many times her father had said this over the past months.

And she sent up a silent prayer to the god of gamblers that the unknown owner would stay safely aboard his yacht for the duration. Although that, of course, would not help with the looming threat of the hotel bill.

She stayed on the balcony for a while, drinking another cup of coffee and enjoying the sunlit freshness of the morning after the unexpected heavy rain with thunder, lightning and squally winds of the previous night. But she was still unable to fully relax, not while the question of how long they could go on living like this continued to haunt her.

'You're my little mascot,' Denys had told her jubilantly in the early days, but she hadn't brought him much luck recently.

I shall have to start avoiding the front desk and use the staff entrance in the daytime, too, instead of just the evenings, she thought wryly as she pushed back her chair and went through the sliding glass doors into the sitting room.

The chambermaids were due soon, and she had to make sure that all signs of her nightly occupation of the sofa were removed from their eagle-eyed scrutiny.

It seemed a long time since their budget had been able to run to a suite with two bedrooms, and while she didn't begrudge her father his comfortable night's sleep, quite understanding that he needed to wake completely refreshed in order to keep his wits sharp, nevertheless she missed the peace and privacy which the sitting room could not provide.

When she was sure all was as it should be, she packed sun oil, her coin purse and a paperback book into her raffia bag, together with two leftover rolls from breakfast wrapped in tissues to provide her with a makeshift lunch.

She pinned her hair up into a loose knot, covering it with a wide-brimmed straw hat, then pulled a white cheesecloth tunic over her turquoise bikini, donned her sunglasses and picked up her towel. Thus camouflaged, she set off down to the swimming pool.

Few people, if any, recognised her in the daytime. Wearing espadrilles instead of the platform-soled high heels that Denys insisted on took at least a couple of inches from her height, and with her hair hidden, her face scrubbed clean of its evening make-up, and wearing a modestly cut bikini, she attracted little attention even from men who'd been sending her openly amorous looks the night before.

The St Gregoire charged a hefty number of francs for the hire of its loungers on the paved sun terraces, so Joanna invariably chose instead to spread her towel on one of the lawns encircling the pool, a practice not forbidden, but muttered at by the man who came to collect the money from the paying guests.

Ignore him, Joanna told herself, rubbing oil into her exposed skin already tanned a judicious golden brown. And try to pretend the grass isn't damp while you're about it.

She turned on to her stomach, and retrieved the book she'd
found in a second-hand store just before they'd left for France,
a former prize-winning detective story by a British author
called P. D. James, which had attracted Joanna because its
title, *An Unsuitable Job for a Woman,* seemed to sum up her
current situation.

Maybe I could become a private investigator, she mused,
finding her place in the story. Except I don't have someone
likely to die and leave me a detective agency.

A more likely scenario, if things went badly wrong this
time, was a swift return to the UK and a job for Denys in
Uncle Martin's light engineering works. It had been offered
before, prompted, Joanna suspected, by her uncle's very real
concern for her future. Although he'd had plenty of troubles of
his own in the past few years with the imposition of the three-
day week, strikes and constant power cuts to contend with.

But her father had replied, as always, that it would kill him
to be tied to a desk, and he had to be a free spirit, although
Joanna could see no freedom in having bills you were unable
to pay. One day, she thought, he might have to bite on the bullet
and accept Uncle Martin's offer.

And for me, a secretarial course, I suppose, she mused re-
signedly. But I'd settle for that, if it meant a normal life. And
not being lonely any more. I'm just not the adventurous type,
and I only wish I'd realised that much sooner.

It wasn't really possible to make friends when they were so
often on the move, but other girls tended to steer clear anyway.
And apart from one occasion in Australia, which she'd tried
hard to forget, she'd been left severely alone by young men,
too.

She stopped herself on the point of another sigh. Forget the
self-pity, she adjured herself, and find out how private investigator Cordelia Gray is going to solve her first solo case.

At that moment, she heard her name called, and turned to
see Julie Phillips approaching across the grass.

Joanna sat up smiling. 'Hi, there.' She looked around. 'What have you done with Matthew?'

'Chris has taken him down to the village.' Julie sat down beside her, shading her eyes from the sun. 'He wanted to buy something for his mother from that little pottery shop.' She sighed. 'I can hardly believe our week is up. And, would you believe, we're almost sorry to be going home. For which we have you to thank, of course.'

'That's nonsense,' Joanna said roundly. 'It was just lucky I happened to be at the desk that day, and was able to help.'

She'd been waiting to buy some stamps when she'd overheard the clearly distressed young couple protesting to an unsympathetic desk clerk about the hotel's policy of barring babies and young children from the restaurant after seven p.m.

As their French was clearly minimal, she'd helped translate for them, even though their objections were ultimately met with a shrug of complete indifference.

They'd adjourned to the terrace bar for coffee, where Joanna had learned they'd won their South of France holiday in a magazine competition, but their intended destination had been a three-star hotel in the BelCote chain.

A fire had resulted in a grudging upgrade to the St Gregoire.

'But we felt from the moment we got here yesterday that they didn't really want us.' Julie had said. 'They made a fuss about putting a cot in the bungalow, told us there was no babysitting service, then dropped the bombshell about the restaurant. If we wanted to eat there, we had to have the special children's supper at six.'

She'd sighed. 'We're just so disappointed with it all. It isn't a bit as we'd hoped. Now we feel we simply want to go home.'

Joanna could only sympathise but she was unsurprised. The hotel was a place where little children might be seen but not heard, and Matt had a good pair of lungs on him.

But the St Gregoire had accepted this family, however

reluctantly, and it was totally unfair to prevent them sampling the culinary delights on offer in the restaurant.

She took a deep breath. 'I've had an idea,' she said. 'We—I—never have dinner until at least nine. If you're prepared to eat early, I'll come to the bungalow each night as soon as the children's supper is over and look after Matt for you, so that you can dine together in the restaurant.'

There was a silence, then Julie said, 'No, we couldn't ask you. Couldn't impose like that.'

'I'd love to do it.' Joanna bent, and ran a finger down Matt's round pink cheek, receiving a toothless grin as a reward. 'I can't produce any references,' she added ruefully. 'But I used to babysit a lot for our neighbours in England. And I—I miss it.'

Husband and wife exchanged glances, then Chris leaned forward, his pleasant, freckled face serious.

'Well, if you really mean it, we'd be endlessly grateful. We were actually going to find out today how much it would cost to cut our losses and fly home.'

'Oh, you can't do that.' Joanna shook her head decisively. 'Because the food really is fantastic. You mustn't miss out on it.'

The final details of the arrangement were hammered out there and then. Julie assured her that Matt was a good sleeper who rarely woke in the evenings, but that she'd leave a bottle ready just in case. In return Joanna made it clear she would accept no payment whatsoever.

And on that they'd shaken hands on the deal.

Denys had received the news with far less amiability.

'What the hell are you thinking of?' he demanded incredulously. 'Who are these people?'

'A sweet couple with a nice baby they can't take into the restaurant for dinner,' Joanna informed him calmly.

'Then why don't they order room service, or switch from dinner to lunch?' he demanded irritably.

Joanna gave him a straight look. 'Because they'd be charged

a lot extra and they can't afford it. Not a pleasant position to be in,' she added with faint emphasis. 'And as long as I'm ready to eat with you later, why should you care?'

'Because you might be seen, and there could be talk. You're not here as some kind of domestic help, Joanna,' he added with a snap.

'No,' she said. 'But strangely I find I prefer it. And, whatever you say, I've promised. They're nice people, very different to those I usually have to mix with these days, and I have no intention of letting them down.'

It was a decision she hadn't regretted once, not even on the rare occasions when Matt had woken and grizzled. That brief hour or so in the lamp-lit peace of the bungalow's small terrace had become a welcome refuge.

A blissful break before she had to be on show, pretending to be someone else, she thought now with an inward sigh.

She said, 'I shall really miss my baby-watch.'

'Like an aching tooth,' Julie laughed. 'But surely you'll be leaving soon yourself, won't you?'

Joanna looked away. 'I—I'm not certain. It's not really up to me.'

'Well, think about us slaving away in the UK while you're still living in the lap of luxury.'

Joanna's smile held a touch of bitterness. 'There's more than one form of slavery,' she said quietly. 'And, believe me, I'd be out of here tomorrow, given the chance.'

Julie stared at her, her bright face suddenly troubled. 'Are you really so unhappy?' she asked gently.

'No, no, of course not.' Joanna shook her head. 'Just a touch of the blues, that's all. I—I have some big career choices looming.' *And that's only part of it.*

Julie got to her feet. 'Well, if you want my opinion, you should become a nanny,' she said, adding hastily, 'But not the stiff and starchy sort. I think you'd be magic, and then, when Chris and I get seriously rich, we can hire you.'

'I'll bear it in mind,' Joanna said with forced cheerfulness.

'And as for wanting to get out of here,' Julie went on, 'my gran always says, "Be careful what you wish for, because you might get it." So watch yourself, and please don't get whisked away before dinner tonight.'

Joanna laughed. 'I promise. But after dinner—all bets are off.'

Alone again, she returned to her book but found it difficult to concentrate. Julie's suggestion that she might become a professional nanny had set new ideas and career possibilities buzzing in her head, and she couldn't dismiss them, although she could foresee the problems of trying to free herself from the current situation.

She knew that Uncle Martin would get her back to the UK if she asked for his help.

But Dad needs me, she thought. He said so from the start. Things were going well for him then. So how can I desert him when the going's got tough?

She collected her things together, put on her tunic, and began to stroll back towards the hotel. She hadn't gone far when she spotted the hotel manager heading towards her, looking harassed and talking volubly, hands waving, to a plump middle-aged man with a swarthy skin and heavy moustache who was walking beside him, expensively dressed in a silk suit.

And Monsieur Levaux is the last person I need to run into right now, Joanna thought grimly. Plus I wouldn't fool him even if I was wearing a sack over my head.

She turned swiftly away, taking a narrower path to the right which circled the gardens and led out onto a small promontory beyond.

As usual, she had it to herself. Few of the guests ventured far from the pool, the beach or the various bars.

She lifted her face to meet the slight breeze from the sea as she walked across the tussocks of grass to the farthest point, and looked out over the rippling azure water.

The big yacht was still there, riding at anchor like a dignified swan, with small boats circling it like inquisitive ducklings.

On impulse, Joanna went over to the telescope that someone had helpfully erected on a small concrete platform, and fed the requisite number of centimes into the slot. She adjusted the focus and guided the tube into a slow sweep of the whole bay before returning to its current most prominent feature.

The first thing she looked for was the name, but the letters along the bow were in Greek, so she was none the wiser.

However, it couldn't belong to Onassis, because he'd died the previous year, nor, indeed, the rich sheikh her father had been hoping for.

And is that a good thing or a bad? Joanna wondered wryly.

In close-up, the yacht was even more spectacular, and Joanna found herself speculating how many crew members it took to preserve that stringently immaculate appearance. There certainly didn't seem to be many of them around at the moment, scrubbing and polishing.

In fact, she could see just one solitary individual leaning on the rail of the upper deck, and adjusted the telescope for a closer look. Her immediate thought was that he didn't belong in his pristine surroundings. On the contrary.

He wore no shirt, and she was treated to an uninterrupted view of deeply bronzed powerful shoulders and a muscular torso. With his tousled mane of black hair and the shadow of a beard masking his chin, he looked more like a pirate than a deckhand. In fact he made the place look distinctly untidy, she thought, deciding that he was probably someone from the engine room who'd come up for a breath of air.

She saw his hand move, and something glint in the sunshine. And with a sharp, startled catch of her breath, she suddenly realised that the tables had been turned.

That she herself was now under scrutiny—through a powerful pair of binoculars. And that he was grinning at her, displaying very white teeth, and lifting his hand in a casual, almost mocking salute.

How had he known she was looking at him? she asked herself as a wave of embarrassed heat swamped her from head to toe. And why on earth had she allowed herself to be caught in the act like some—some peeping Thomasina.

On the other hand, why wasn't he swabbing the decks or splicing the mainbrace—whatever that was? Doing something useful instead of—spying back?

Feeling intensely stupid, and wanting to scream in vexation at the same time, Joanna hurriedly abandoned the telescope and walked away with as much dignity as she could muster.

Which wasn't easy when every instinct she possessed and every nerve-ending in her body was telling her with total certainty that he was watching her go.

And knowing at the same time that it would be quite fatal to look back and check—even for a moment.

CHAPTER TWO

'So THERE you are.' Denys marched briskly into the sitting room, kicking the door shut behind him.

Joanna, curled up in the corner of the sofa, finishing off the remains of her breakfast rolls which had not improved with keeping, glanced up warily.

'It's where you told me to be,' she pointed out mildly, observing with faint disquiet the brightness in his eyes, and the tinge of excited red in his face. There was a bunched tension about him too that she remembered from other times. That, and the way he kept clenching and opening one fist.

She added, 'Has something happened?'

'It has indeed, my pet. We're about to hit the jackpot—big-time.' He paused for effect. 'Do you know the name of that yacht in the bay?'

Oh, God, she thought, cringing inwardly as she remembered that insolent, mocking grin. It would have to be that.

'I didn't learn Greek at school,' she said. 'Only Latin.'

He waved an impatient hand. 'Well, she's called *Persephone*. And she's owned by no less a person than Vassos Gordanis.'

Joanna frowned. 'Should I have heard of him?'

'You're hearing now.' Denys came to sit beside her. 'He's Atlas Airlines.' He counted on his fingers. 'He's the Andromeda tanker fleet. He's the Hellenica hotel chain—the outfit currently buying the building we're living in, along with all the other BelCote hotels.'

He smiled exultantly. 'He's one of the super-rich. Had the wit to stay out of harm's way on his boat and some island he owns in the Aegean, avoiding politics during these past years in Greece when the Colonels were in charge. But when the Junta was finally overthrown last year he began to operate freely again, and they say he's set to climb into the financial stratosphere.'

Joanna suddenly remembered the portly man in the silk suit she'd seen with Gaston Levaux. So that was what a Greek tycoon looked like, she thought, reflecting that the heavy-jowl-ed face had possessed undoubted shrewdness if nothing else to write home about.

'How did you discover all this?' she asked.

'Nora Van Dyne told me over bridge this morning.' His face clouded momentarily. 'She'll never make a card player. Talks too damned much. But she knows everything that's going on, and this time she told me something I wanted to hear.'

And don't I wish she hadn't? Joanna thought wanly. Why couldn't she go on chatting about the New York cultural scene, the cute things her grandchildren said last Thanksgiving, and what her late husband paid for all that wonderful jewellery she wears morning, noon and night?

Denys leaned forward. 'Do you know why he decided to buy the St Gregoire? Because he comes here each year to play poker with some of his cronies and business connections and has got to like the place. They have dinner in a private suite on the top floor, then they get down to the real business of the evening—by invitation only, of course.'

'I see.' Joanna managed to conceal her relief. 'Well, that settles that.'

'On the contrary, my pet. I had a quiet word with Levaux, asked him to pull a few strings. Get me into the game.' He smiled with satisfaction. 'And somehow he's done it. Probably thinks it's the only way he'll get paid.'

Joanna moved restively. 'Dad—are you quite sure about this?'

'Have a little faith, darling.' Denys spoke reproachfully. 'It's the answer to our prayers.'

Not for me, Joanna thought. Not for me.

'But I'll need you to pull all the stops out tonight,' he added, confirming her worst fears. 'So get down to the boutique. I've already spoken to Marie Claude, and she's picked out a dress for you.'

'But it's a private game,' Joanna protested desperately. 'You—you said so. I wouldn't be allowed in.'

'That's fixed, too. Levaux has explained I can't play without you—my talisman—my little lucky charm—and it appears that Mr Gordanis is prepared to stretch a point on this occasion.'

He paused. 'According to Nora, he's a widower with more than just an eye for the girls. In fact he's got one hell of a reputation. So you definitely have to be there.'

Joanna recoiled inwardly, knowing only too well what would be expected of her tonight and with a man whose sole attraction had to be his money. Because it would never be his looks.

She thought how she would have to smile and flutter her mascaraed lashes. Would have to toss back her hair and cross her legs as she perched artlessly on the arm of Denys's chair, distracting his opponent for that vital instant when he most needed to concentrate on the cards in his hand.

After all, she'd done it so often before, she thought bitterly. Had learned to move her young, slim body in deliberate, provocative enticement in order to make men stare at her, their fantasies going into overdrive, and their minds dangerously off the game.

She'd hoped, after the incident in Australia the previous year, that she'd be let off the hook, but her reprieve had only lasted a couple of months. Then it was business as usual, responding, when Denys signalled by brushing his forefinger across his lips, as if she was on auto-pilot.

She felt a knot of tension tighten in her chest. 'Dad—I'd really rather not be involved in this.'

'But you already are, my pet.' There was a harsh note in his voice. 'If we can't pay our hotel bill, you won't be spared. You know that. So be a good girl and collect your dress from Marie Claude. And I don't want you rushing to get ready this evening,' he added warningly. 'You need to take your time. Make sure you look dazzling. So tell those people they'll have to look after their own brat for once.'

Joanna sat up very straight. 'No,' she said. 'I can't. I won't. Or you'll be on your own in that suite tonight, looking down the barrel of this tycoon's gun.'

'You'll do as you're told, young lady—'

'No, Dad,' she interrupted quietly and firmly. 'Not this time. After all, you can hardly drag me in there by force, not if I'm to convince this Mr Gordanis that he's everything I've ever wanted in a man.'

She took a deep breath. 'But first I'm going to babysit for Chris and Julie, or the deal's off. And I have to tell you that this is going to be the last time I act as a diversion for you, because each time I do it I feel sick to my stomach.'

She paused again. 'You told me you wanted me with you because I was all you had left. Because I reminded you of my mother. So what do you think she'd say if she could see me—paraded around like this, like some—cheap tart?'

'My dear child.' Denys's tone was uneasy as well as placatory. 'I think you're taking our little deception much too seriously.'

'Am I?' Joanna asked bitterly. 'I wonder if the men whose wallets I've helped to empty would agree with you.'

'Well, you certainly don't have to worry about Mr Gordanis,' Denys said with faint surliness. 'His bank account will survive a quick raid.'

'I'm not worried about him,' she said quietly. 'It's you.' She hesitated. 'Dad—swear to me that if you start winning tonight you'll get out while you're ahead. Make enough to cover our expenses here and a couple of plane tickets to somewhere else, then stop.' She put a hand on his arm. 'Please—I'm begging you. Because I need a real life.'

He sighed impatiently. 'Oh, all right. If that's what you want. But I think you're being quite ridiculous, Joanna.'

'I can deal with that,' she said. 'It's feeling dirty that I can't handle.' She paused again, awkwardly. 'There won't be any other—problems, will there?'

His mouth tightened. 'That was a one-off,' he said. 'As I told you at the time.'

Yes, she thought unhappily. You told me. So I have to trust you. And I just pray that when tonight's over I'll feel able to do that again.

The dress from the boutique did nothing to reassure her, or lift the bleakness of her mood. It was a black crochet affair, with a deeply scooped neck and a skirt that just reached mid-thigh. The sleeves provided the most concealment, fitting closely to the elbow then flaring to the wrist, but that was little comfort when, underneath, the dress accommodated nothing more than a body stocking, giving the troubling impression that she could be naked.

She'd looked at herself in the mirror of the tiny changing room with something like despair. 'Surely there must be something else? Something not quite so—revealing?'

Marie Claude had shrugged, her eyes cynical. 'You have a good body. Use it while you are young.'

So Joanna took the dress back to the suite, and hung it in the *armoire*.

She spent the rest of the afternoon washing her hair and conditioning it until it shone with all the rich depth of a horse chestnut, then gave herself a pedicure, painting her toenails in the clear light red that matched her fingertips.

Lastly, she arranged the cosmetics she planned to use later on the dressing table, together with her precious bottle of Miss Dior, before changing into shorts and a tee shirt, and heading off to Chris and Julie's bungalow situated on the farthest edge of the hotel gardens.

Its remoteness didn't bother Joanna, who loved the sense of privacy imparted by the surrounding hedges of flowering shrubs.

'I expect we've been dumped here out of the way,' Julie had confided. 'But that's fine by us. Because if Matt decides to squall we don't have to worry about disturbing the neighbours.'

It had another advantage, too, thought Joanna. There was no direct sea view, so she was spared the sight of the *Persephone* together with her owner and any stray members of her crew who might still be hanging around, behaving like God's gift to women.

The sun was getting lower in the sky, but it was still warm, so she let herself in and took a bottle of chilled Coke from the refrigerator in the tiny kitchen, and the copy of *Watership Down* which Julie had promised to leave for her 'together with a box of tissues. It's all about rabbits'.

'And I'll give you *Jaws*,' Chris had teased. 'By way of contrast.'

She settled herself with a sigh into one of the cane chairs on the small verandah, relishing the peace, longing to start her new book, but unable to dismiss from her mind the horrors she knew were awaiting her later that night.

She had watched poker games in the past until her eyes glazed over, as they often did when a game continued through the small hours into dawn. But that was through boredom as much as tiredness. She had tried at first to establish some kind of interest in the game, but she still didn't follow its intricacies or understand its attraction.

In fact I wouldn't care, she told herself, if I never saw another pack of cards as long as I live.

But she wasn't likely to be bored this evening. Far too much depended on it, and the role of mindless dolly-bird would be even more difficult to sustain than usual.

It was a good ten minutes before Chris and Julie arrived with the baby, looking harassed.

'He's been really grumpy at supper,' Julie reported. 'Started crying and threw his food on the floor. I could feel waves of disapproval reaching me from the nannies all over the room.'

She unstrapped a red-faced Matt from his pushchair and lifted him out, whereupon he began to cry again, a steady, bad-tempered wail.

'Leave him to me,' said Joanna, sounding more reassuring than she actually felt. 'Go and have a smashing meal together, and I'll bath him and get him settled.'

Julie looked at her with a mixture of doubt and relief. 'Well, if you're quite sure…'

Half an hour later, Joanna wasn't certain of very much at all. Matt was standing up in his cot, roaring with discontent and shaking the bars, only desisting when Joanna picked him up and held him.

'You haven't got a temperature,' she told him. 'And I don't think you've got a pain anywhere. I suspect, my lad, you're just having a major strop.'

Any attempt to get him back in the cot, however, met with stern resistance, so in the end Joanna bowed to the inevitable, heated up his milk, and carried him out to the twilit verandah, settling his squirming red-faced person gently but firmly in the crook of her arm.

'This had better not become a habit,' she said, dropping a kiss on his silky head.

By the time he'd drunk nearly all the milk his eyelids were drooping, but he was still attempting to cry intermittently as he fought against sleep.

'Drastic measures called for, I think,' Joanna whispered to herself, and, cuddling him close, she began to sing, clearly and very sweetly, a song from her own early childhood, '"There were ten green bottles, hanging on the wall…"'

As the number of bottles gradually decreased, she allowed

her voice to sink lower and lower, until it was barely a murmur, and Matt, thumb in mouth, was finally fast asleep.

Joanna sat for a while, looking down, smiling, at the sleeping baby. A faint breeze had risen, bringing a delicious waft of the garden's evening scents. And also, she realised, something more alien. A faint but unmistakable aroma of cigar smoke.

But Chris, she thought, puzzled, was a non-smoker. Besides, it would be another half-hour or more before he and Julie returned.

Suddenly nervous, she wanted to call *Who's there?* but hesitated for fear of waking Matt. In the next instant she thought she could hear the sound of footsteps quietly receding, yet wasn't entirely sure.

She got carefully to her feet, listening hard, but there was nothing—only the distant sound of the sea.

I'm imagining things, she thought. Because I'm feeling jumpy about tonight. That's all it is.

Which was probably why the breeze seemed suddenly colder, too, she thought, shivering as she carried Matt inside and closed the door.

The crochet dress did not improve on acquaintance, Joanna thought, sighing, as she made a last check of her appearance. Worn with knee-length white boots that laced up the front, the outfit presented itself as the kind of sexy tease which needed a certain amount of sophistication to carry off, and she knew she was nowhere near that level.

However, she'd done her best. She'd used the heavier foundation she reserved for these occasions, transforming her face into a blank canvas, then smoothed shimmering silver on to her eyelids, accentuating it with softly smudged black liner, before adding two coats of mascara to her long lashes. The bronze blusher on her cheekbones had a touch of glitter, too, and she had applied a deeper shade of the same colour to her mouth.

Fancy dress and a mask, she told herself, as she applied

scent to her pulses, her temples, and the valley between her breasts. Think of it that way.

There was room for very little but the basics in her tiny evening purse, and as she searched in her shoulder bag for the compact of pressed translucent powder she always wore, she found the slip of paper Chris and Julie had given her, with their name, address and telephone number.

It was the nearest to a friendship she'd achieved since leaving Britain, and it was also a possible lifeline, she thought wryly as she tucked it carefully into her wallet.

Denys was pacing the sitting room, and he gave a nod of judicious satisfaction as she emerged from the bedroom.

'Once dinner is over,' he told her, 'someone will come to escort us up to the Gordanis suite.'

'Very formal.' Her tone was dry. 'As are you,' she added, removing a speck of fluff from the lapel of his dinner jacket. 'Is the black tie strictly necessary?'

He shrugged. 'It's a big night. And a very big game. Mr Gordanis can afford to impose his own rules.'

But can you afford to play by them? was the question she did not dare ask as they took the lift down to the dining room.

She ate sparingly at dinner, and drank even less, noting that her father was being equally abstemious. Afterwards they drank coffee on the terrace outside the dining room while the time ticked slowly past, building the tension inside her.

She said, 'Do you think it's not going to happen—that we've been forgotten?'

'No.' Denys shook his head. 'Apparently, he plays for amusement first with some of his friends. After they leave, the stakes rise and the game becomes serious. We'll be sent for soon.'

But it was well after midnight when Gaston Levaux appeared unsmilingly beside them. 'Monsieur Vernon. I am here on behalf of Monsieur Vassos Gordanis who invites you to join him.' He paused. 'I should warn you that you will be required to pay one thousand dollars simply to buy into the game.'

Oh, God, Joanna thought, suddenly weak with relief. We

haven't got a thousand cents. I never thought I'd be glad to be broke.

But her father was meeting Monsieur Levaux's questioning glance with an airy shrug. 'There's no problem about that. I was told he played in dollars and I have the money.'

Thanks, no doubt, to Mrs Van Dyne, Joanna whispered under her breath, silently cursing all rich American widows.

'I must also caution you that Monsieur Gordanis is a formidable opponent. It is not too late for you to make your excuses—or at least those of the *mademoiselle*,' he added.

'You really mustn't concern yourself.' There was a note of steel in Denys's voice. 'I'm looking forward to the game, and so is Joanna—aren't you, darling?'

Joanna saw the manager's mouth tighten. As they walked to the lift, he spoke to her quietly in French. 'Do you ever suffer from migraine, *mademoiselle?* If so, I suggest you develop one very quickly.'

If only, thought Joanna, aware that she was being warned and a little startled by it. Knowing, too, that she would probably have to develop a brain tumour in order to deflect Denys from his purpose.

When they reached the top floor, a small group of men were waiting in the corridor, laughing and talking. As Joanna emerged they fell silent, and she saw glances being exchanged, and even heard a murmur of, *'Oh, là là!'* from one of them.

You take no notice, she reminded herself stonily. You behave as if you were a dummy in a shop window. You don't see, hear, talk or think. And you just pray that Dad wins—and wins quickly.

The double doors at the end of the corridor swung open as they approached. The room ahead was hazy with tobacco smoke, and the smell of alcohol hung in the air. Half a dozen men were standing around, chatting as they waited for play to recommence, while a waiter in a white jacket was moving among them, refilling glasses and emptying ashtrays.

So many other rooms, she thought. So many other times, yet all the same.

Except, she realised, that tonight there were no other women present. It was then she saw Vassos Gordanis walking towards the door, smiling expansively and talking to a man in a dark blue tuxedo, who also seemed to be leaving.

As he saw Joanna, the smile faded from his pouched face, and she felt herself quail inwardly beneath his hard, opaque gaze.

A sudden hush had fallen on the room as everyone turned to look at her, too, and she knew an overwhelming impulse to turn and run, only Denys's hand was under her arm, urging her forward.

'Come along, my sweet,' he said. 'Come and meet our host.'

She thought, But we've just walked past him... And then the group in front of her fell back, revealing a circular table littered with chips and a scatter of playing cards.

But, more importantly, revealing also the man who was seated facing her across the green baize.

She knew him at once, of course. He was clean-shaven now, and the curling black hair was combed back, but the arrogant lines of his face with its high-bridged nose and strongly marked chin were quite unmistakable, as were the heavy-lidded dark eyes and that hard, frankly sensual mouth that she'd last seen smiling at her from the deck of *Persephone*.

Only he wasn't smiling now, and the hooded eyes studied her without any particular expression in their obsidian depths as he lounged back in his chair, his tie hanging loose and his frilled white shirt half-unbuttoned, providing her with an unwilling reminder of the bronze muscularity she'd seen only that morning.

He had a half-smoked cheroot in one hand, while the other held a short string of amber beads, which he was sliding constantly and restlessly through his long fingers.

He did not get to his feet at her approach, and instinct told her this was not prompted by any acceptance of male and female equality as preached by Jackie's mother, who saw any demonstration of masculine courtesy as a form of subjugation and therefore an implied insult.

No, this insult was quite intentional, she thought, designed to show her exactly where she stood in his personal scheme of things—which seemed to hover somewhere between contempt and indifference.

Why didn't you just bar me? she wanted to ask him. Tell my father that women were taboo? God knows I'd have been so grateful.

Instead, here she was, a total fish out of water, the cynosure of all eyes.

'Oh, Dad,' she whispered to herself, swallowing as Gaston Levaux began to perform the introductions. 'You really miscalculated here.'

However, on the plus side, Vassos Gordanis could not possibly recognise her. After all, she looked totally different from the girl in the straw hat whom he'd seen earlier that day. Her distinctive hair had been completely hidden then, while the heavy layer of make-up she was now wearing completed her disguise.

'And now,' Monsieur Levaux added with open reluctance, 'may I present to you Mademoiselle Joanna.'

'Ah, yes, I was informed she would be joining us.' His voice was low-pitched and husky, his English good in spite of his marked accent. The dark eyes swept her from head to foot in a glance that both assessed and dismissed. The firm mouth curled with faint insolence. 'So this is Kyrios Vernon's—lucky charm.'

She heard smothered laughter from the group behind her, and felt her skin warm.

'If she remains silent, then she may stay,' Vassos Gordanis went on. 'Tell me, *kyrie,* is she that miracle—a woman who knows her place and can keep her mouth shut? Or would it be better to send her back to her room before we begin?'

'Yes,' Joanna pleaded under breath. 'Oh, please—*yes*.'

But Denys was managing to mask his obvious discomfiture with a smile. 'She's indeed my mascot, Mr Gordanis. If she goes, she may take my luck with her. And she knows how to behave at these little gatherings. You have my word for it.'

'Yes,' Vassos Gordanis said softly, drawing on his cheroot and regarding its glowing end almost dispassionately. 'I am sure I can believe that.' He added silkily, 'And we should all enjoy such good fortune.'

Slipping the beads into the pocket of his dinner jacket, he gestured abruptly for a chair to be brought for Joanna and stationed exactly opposite to where he himself was sitting.

Which was the last thing she'd expected—or wanted, she thought, forcing a taut smile as she moved to the offered seat. Usually she kept her distance at the edge of the room until Denys made an excuse to summon her to his side. As she sat down, she tried unobtrusively to smooth her brief skirt over her thighs, and realised that Vassos Gordanis was watching the nervous movement, the corner of his mouth curling sardonically.

Remember what you told yourself earlier, she thought, taking a deep breath, and folding her hands carefully in her lap. You don't talk, you don't hear, you don't think. And now—above all—you don't look back at *him*.

'Gentlemen.' Their host acknowledged his other guests with a faint inclination of the head. 'Join me, if you please.'

He signalled again, and one of the dealers from the Casino came forward, gathering up the cards from the previous session before removing the cellophane cover from an unopened deck and beginning to shuffle it, swiftly and expertly. He dealt out six cards face upwards to decide the seating, and to her relief Denys was allotted the place beside her, with a tall blond American called Chuck on the other side.

Fresh decanters of whisky and brandy were placed on a side table, while around the table jackets were discarded and cigarettes and cigars were lit.

The stage is set, Joanna thought, and the serious business of the evening is about to commence.

And knew she had never felt so uneasy in her life.

CHAPTER THREE

THE game began quietly enough, the betting conservative, no very startling hands, and the atmosphere round the table relaxed.

Providing that I discount my own state of mind, Joanna thought wryly, trying to draw comfort from the air of calm confidence that her father was currently exuding. But it was still early in the proceedings, she knew, and the players would simply be testing each other's strengths and weaknesses.

At the same time, she was conscious that the pair of them were very much outsiders. That the rest—a couple of Frenchmen, a burly South African and her American neighbour—were all clearly long-standing friends and acquaintances of Vassos Gordanis, and each of them powerful and successful in his own right. Not the kind of company expected to welcome strangers into their exclusive and wealthy midst.

So, she wondered, what are we doing here? Why was it allowed?

The person who might have known, of course, was Gaston Levaux, but he'd left while the first hand was being dealt. He wasn't a friend by any stretch of the imagination, but for a moment she'd sensed he could be a reluctant ally.

And at least he'd never been openly hostile like the man she'd originally mistaken for Vassos Gordanis, who'd turned out to be one of several solidly built employees, stationed a deferential couple of feet behind their boss's chair.

Joanna was well aware that this man's overtly inimical gaze was focussed on her, and had been since the game began, and wondered if Denys had also noticed. And if so, would he take warning?

His decision to bring her tonight had been a big mistake, she thought, biting her lip, so the best she could do was keep still and try to be as unobtrusive as possible, keeping her eyes fixed on her clasped hands and registering no reaction to the run of play.

And her conviction that she was surplus to requirements was soon confirmed, when, after the first hour's play, Denys was winning quite comfortably without any dubious assistance from her.

It was true that the pots were only moderate, but that couldn't be allowed to matter. Not when they were building steadily towards their agreed purpose.

Just keep going in the same way, Daddy, please, she appealed silently, and we can be out of this room, this hotel, this place and on our way elsewhere by noon tomorrow.

At the same time, she couldn't avoid an odd feeling that the play so far had been almost deliberately restrained.

'Cigarette, honey?' The usual break had been called in the proceedings, and Chuck was offering her his pack of Chesterfields.

'No, thank you.' The room already felt like an oven, and her eyes were stinging from the smoke. She noticed thankfully that a member of the Gordanis entourage, in response to a murmured instruction, was sliding open one of the heavy glass doors which led out on to the balcony.

'Then how about a Scotch or some bourbon?' Her neighbour signalled to the waiter.

She shook her head. 'I—I don't drink spirits.'

'You don't smoke or drink? Then your vices must be the more interesting kind,' he drawled.

Think what you like, Joanna advised him silently. And then go to hell.

As the waiter came to her side she asked for Perrier water, and noticed his swift enquiring glance at Vassos Gordanis and saw the swift, barely perceptible nod in reply.

He's in control of everything, she thought with a sudden shiver. The air we breathe. Even what we have to drink.

She found herself suddenly wondering how old he was. He looked to be only in his early to mid-thirties, yet in spite of that he'd managed somehow to survive the dangers of the past few years in Greece under the Colonels, and prosper.

She recalled that Denys had mentioned he was a widower, and wondered how long he'd been married, and when his wife had died. Then paused, startled.

Now, why would I want to know that? she asked herself blankly. When there are other aspects of the situation that should concern me more?

Under the general buzz of conversation, she turned to Denys. She said very quietly, 'I'm being watched.'

'Of course you are, my pet.' He flashed a conspiratorial smile at her. 'You're a very beautiful girl, and I want you to be looked at.'

'But it's not in the right way or by the right person,' she protested, troubled. 'I really think it would be better if I found some reason to leave.'

'Don't be silly, darling.' His smile widened, became fixed. 'Everything's fine and I need you to stay exactly where you are. They're raising the ante and the stakes are about to become very interesting.' He took a satisfied breath. 'We're on our way, sweetheart. Trust me.'

'Then at least allow me to get some fresh air before you make our fortune.' She rose restlessly from her chair and walked towards the balcony door, taking care to look at no one, and to ignore the inevitable glances that came her way.

Once outside, she stood for a moment filling her lungs with a couple of deep, steadying breaths before advancing to the elaborate metal railing and leaning against it, moving her shoulders gently in an attempt to ease the tension in her muscles.

The darkness seemed to wrap her like a warm blanket, while below her the stillness of the hidden garden was disturbed only by the rasping of cicadas.

And beyond, in the bay, she could see the lights of the boats challenging the stars as they rode at anchor, dominated by the looming grandeur of *Persephone.*

No matter where I turn, she mused wryly, Vassos Gordanis seems to be dominating the picture.

But he'd chosen an odd name for his yacht, she thought, recalling the stories of the Greek myths she'd read at school. Persephone, if memory served, had no connection with the sea. She'd been a springtime goddess captured and carried off by Hades, the dark god of the Underworld, while she was picking flowers.

'A classic example,' her teacher Miss Gordon had said, 'of being in the wrong place at the wrong time.'

As a result of Persephone's abduction, so the story went, her mother Demeter was in such grief that she forbade the crops to grow until her daughter came back to her.

So Zeus, the supreme deity, decreed that Persephone should be returned to earth, as long as she had nothing to eat or drink while she was in Hades' power.

Only one day she'd found her favourite fruit—a pomegranate—in a dish on the table and eaten six of its seeds, enough to condemn her to spend half of each year in the Underworld. While the earth above stayed cold and barren, only coming back to life with her return for six months each spring.

'Which is,' Miss Gordon told them, 'a nice, convenient explanation for the annual change in the seasons.'

At the time, a much younger Joanna had mused wistfully that if Persephone had only managed to resist the temptation of the pomegranate altogether it would have been summer all the year round, with no frozen knees on the hockey pitch, chilblains, or horrible colds.

Now, with a swift wry smile at her own naïveté, she turned to go back into the suite, pausing with a gasp as she realised her way was blocked by a tall, lean and quite unmistakable figure lounging in the doorway.

Joanna took an instinctive step backwards. She said huskily, 'I—I didn't know anyone was there.'

The question *Why have you followed me?* was also hovering on her lips, but she bit it back. It was his suite, after all, and his balcony. And very soon it would be his hotel, too, so he could go where he pleased.

But it disturbed her that she'd been totally unaware of his presence, and especially that, while his face was shadowed, he could see her plainly in the light emanating from the room. And once again found herself cursing how little she was wearing.

Ridiculous, she thought with sudden breathlessness, to feel so exposed, so vulnerable, yet she did—even though Denys was within earshot.

He said softly, 'Forgive me for having startled you, *thespinis.*' He paused. 'It's a beautiful night, *ne?*'

She said, 'I—I just needed some air.'

He nodded. 'You find the atmosphere in the room tense, perhaps. It is understandable—when there is so much at stake.'

'Really?' She lifted her chin. 'I'd have said play has been quite moderate.'

'So far,' he said. 'But the evening has hardly begun. And, after all, so much depends on you, *thespinis.*'

'What do you mean?'

'You are Kyrios Vernon's lucky charm. He has said so.'

She bit her lip. 'Denys doesn't need a mascot. He's a very good player.'

'I think he will need to be.' Another pause. 'But I came to tell you that your drink is waiting.' He added softly, 'And that is a circumstance, perhaps, the only one, when the ice should not melt too soon.'

The words seemed to tingle over her skin in some strange way.

She swallowed. 'Is—is the game about to restart?'

'Yes,' he said, after a pause. 'It is getting late and I think we should waste no more time.'

He stood aside courteously to allow her to pass, but Joanna hesitated, reluctant to reduce the distance between them by so much as an inch.

Eventually she forced herself to move, edging past him, eyes on the ground, hoping her anxiety had not been recognised. Because it might amuse him, and she remembered his smile only too well, she told herself, renewed unease quivering in her senses.

No matter how many signals I may get from Dad, she thought as she went back into the suite, I cannot come on to Vassos Gordanis. He disturbs me in a way that has nothing to do with his being the richest man I've ever met.

And it doesn't involve him lusting after me, either, because he isn't the one who can't keep his eyes off me. He leaves that to the paid staff. Besides, I can usually recognise that response from men and I've learned to cope, if necessary.

Though not always with the greatest success, a small voice in her head reminded her, at least not in Australia.

I just know there's something else about him, she told herself restively, pushing the unbidden memory away. Something that I've never encountered before, and can't fathom. Some facet I don't even want to know about.

Please, she thought passionately, releasing her pent-up breath. Please let it all be over soon, so I never have to see him again.

All the players had changed seats during the break, her father included, but to her dismay Joanna found she was once again stationed directly opposite Vassos Gordanis.

She reached for her glass, and gulped down some of the

promised water, thankful for its refreshing chill against the dryness of her throat. And the ice was still intact, she thought, recalling his odd remark. It hadn't melted too soon at all.

Don't think about him, she told herself. Concentrate on the play.

She soon realised that her father's forecast that the stakes would be getting higher was fully justified.

The first pot, won by the South African Hansi Dorten with a straight, was worth over three thousand dollars, and she was relieved that Denys had decided to fold when the draw did not improve his original pair of tens.

But in the next hand his cards yielded a spade flush. There was a flurry of betting, then Chuck, Hansi and one of the Frenchmen all folded. But Vassos Gordanis, Henri de Morvan and Denys did not, each of them continuing to call and raise until there were over twenty thousand dollars' worth of chips in the middle of the table.

Joanna's hands curled into tense fists. This was it, she thought. The amount they needed to get them out of here, and some to spare. Make or break.

A second later it was all over. Vassos Gordanis shrugged ruefully, and tossed his cards towards the dealer, and Henri de Morvan followed suit.

Joanna watched Denys rake the chips towards him, her heart somersaulting. She had to bite the inside of her lip to stop a sheer grin of exultation spreading across her face. Because she didn't want any of these people, least of all the dark man sitting opposite, to know how much this mattered. How vital this was for her future. For everything.

She put her hand on her father's arm, pressing it warningly. Stop now, she urged silently. It's a big enough win, so make an excuse, cash in your chips and we'll get out of here.

But Denys was already selecting chips for the next game.

'Denys.' She lowered her voice to a whisper, her fingers tightening on his sleeve. 'Why don't we call it a night now—and celebrate?'

He glanced at her impatiently, ignoring the pleading in her eyes. 'Don't be silly, sweetheart. Your magic is working, and I'm on a winning streak, so we're going nowhere.'

But you promised, she wanted to cry aloud. You promised— you know you did....

And remembered too late that he'd sworn once before that she would never again have to use her eyes, her smile and her young body to divert another man's attention from the game, and how soon his word had been broken.

Or she would not be here, half-dressed, at this moment.

She sat, almost sick with fear, while the hand was played, but all the others folded after the draw this time, leaving Denys with another two thousand dollars to add to his winnings.

He sent her a triumphant wink as he prepared for the next game.

'Third time lucky, darling,' he muttered.

Then make this the last, Joanna implored silently. Please— please, Daddy. Quit while we're ahead.

I've never felt like this before, she thought. When he's been as confident as this, I've been right there with him. But maybe I've never been quite so disillusioned with my life before.

Yet in her heart she knew that wasn't it. That ever since *Persephone* had arrived in the bay and her father had announced his plans her every instinct had been screaming in warning.

And nothing that had happened since had done anything to reassure her.

She had learned to show no emotion, so her face was still, her eyes shuttered and her hands clasped loosely again in her lap as she saw Denys had been dealt a pair of kings and a pair of nines, with a small club as his fifth card. He discarded the club, asking for one, and received in return from the dealer the king of diamonds.

Three of a kind and a pair, Joanna thought, her heart beginning to pound. Full house. Good—but good enough? I just don't know.

The two Frenchmen folded quickly, but Hansi Dorten and Chuck briskly pushed up the betting, with Vassos Gordanis and Denys matching each call and raise.

Joanna reached for her glass and swallowed the remaining water as the pile of chips in front of her father began to diminish with startling speed.

'I'm out,' Chuck said wryly in answer to the South African's call and raise of five thousand.

'Fold,' Joanna whispered under her breath when it was Denys's turn to bet. 'Remember why you're here doing this, and leave us with something.'

Only to watch, helplessly, as her father pushed another pile of chips into the middle of the table and called.

'I also know when to stop,' Hansi Dorten said, tossing his hand on to the discard pile.

Vassos Gordanis counted out the requisite chips and added them to the pot. 'Call,' he said quietly. His hand moved again. 'And raise another ten thousand.'

Joanna was trembling inside. Showdown, she thought. The point of no return. Denys and Vassos Gordanis facing each other across the table, and between them—what? Thirty thousand dollars? Forty thousand? More?

Small change to a millionaire. The world to us. Or it could have been.

Because Dad hasn't enough left now for another call. Not at this kind of limit. He's been squeezed out. And we're wiped. We won't even be able to cover the bill for the suite.

Vassos Gordanis leaned back in his chair. 'What do you wish to do, *kyrie?*' It was a courteous, almost bland question.

Denys squared his shoulders. 'Naturally bet again, Mr Gordanis, if you are prepared to accept my IOU.'

The dark gaze looked past him with faint enquiry, and Joanna realised, startled, that Gaston Levaux had come back into the room, and was leaning against the wall, shaking his head in grim negation.

'I think our good Levaux doubts that you would have the ability to pay this debt if, of course, it falls due.' Vassos Gordanis reached pensively for another cheroot and lit it. 'However, there is a good deal of money at stake, and I wish to be fair. So I will give you the opportunity to back your hand once more—but only once. Therefore, you may call, and you may also raise me to whatever limit you wish and I will match it. Double the raise. Treble it, if you please. It is of no consequence.'

Denys stared at him, frowning. 'I don't take you for a philanthropist, Mr Gordanis, and I am not a charity case.'

'No,' the other returned softly. 'We are both gamblers, are we not? So, if you win, you take the money. All of it. There will be no dispute. I say it in front of witnesses.'

Joanna risked a swift glance round the table. The other men were very still, looking down unsmilingly at the table in front of them, but there was a tension in the air that was almost tangible.

'And if I lose?' Her father's voice was hoarse.

Vassos Gordanis shrugged. 'Then the money will be mine, naturally,' he returned levelly.

His eyes, brilliant as jet, and as cold, rested on Joanna, and she felt a tremor of awareness bordering on fear shiver through her body, as if cold fingers had trailed a path down her spine.

'But,' he added musingly, 'you would also owe me the amount you have wagered, and I would require that to be repaid.'

'And how could I possibly do that?' Denys flung at him.

'Not in cash, certainly.' He drew reflectively on his cheroot. 'But—in kind. That would be a different matter.'

'What the hell do you mean?' Denys demanded aggressively.

'I am wondering how much you are prepared to risk, Kyrios Vernon.' He nodded at Joanna. 'The beauty at your side, for instance. This girl—your charming talisman. How much do you consider she is worth to you?'

He leaned forward suddenly, and Joanna recoiled instinctively as she suddenly realised how right she was to have been afraid. And how much there still existed to terrify her.

'Because that is the pledge I require, my friend,' Vassos Gordanis went on, looking now at her father. 'In full and final settlement. If you play and lose, you give me the girl, and when she comes to me I take her for as long as I want her.' He paused. 'I also ask that you give me your word you will honour your debt as I have done, in front of witnesses,' he added almost casually.

As if, Joanna thought, a bubble of hysteria welling up inside her, he was attaching a postscript to a letter.

She wanted to protest. To scream at them all that she would never—never—submit to such a shameful bargain. That there was no amount of money on earth that could persuade her, either. That she would rather skivvy in the hotel, washing dishes or cleaning rooms, until their accommodation was paid for. Or starve in the gutter if she could get no work.

And, most of all, she wanted to tell them that Denys was not some kind of sugar daddy, as they apparently assumed, nor her pretended uncle—but her own real father, who would protect her with his life if need be.

Yet the ensuing silence was like a hand placed over her mouth. Her lips parted to speak but no sound emerged.

She would have given anything to get to her feet and storm out of the room in disgust, but all her energy seemed to have drained away, leaving her feeling as if she'd been nailed to the chair, unable to move so much as a hand in her own defence.

And if I tried to leave, she thought suddenly, would it be allowed?

Denys was speaking coldly, 'I presume, Mr Gordanis, that this is some crude and sordid joke.'

'And I have to tell you, Kyrios Vernon, that I am not joking,' Vassos Gordanis retorted. 'The money is there for the taking, by one of us. If you wish to fight for it, you must wager the girl. It is quite simple.' He shrugged again, his mouth twisting sardonically. 'But of course you do not have to accept my offer. You may prefer to fold and go on your way. Or you can be as serious as I am myself by naming your own figure and gambling on the cards you hold. Unless you have lost faith in the hand you have been defending?'

'No,' Denys denied thickly. 'I have not.'

Joanna felt as if she'd turned to ice. No? she thought almost blankly. Had she really heard him say no?

Because surely that had to be her response, as in—No, this cannot be happening.

Her father couldn't be contemplating playing on. It wasn't possible. He couldn't be staking her immediate future—her happiness—her innocence—on that kind of flimsy chance.

Even if he'd held a virtually unbeatable Royal Flush he shouldn't consider it. Not if he loved her...

Slowly she turned to stare at her father, willing him to look back, to meet the disbelief, the agony in her eyes, although instinct told her he would not.

Even my mother, she thought, anguished, always came second to this addiction—this monster eating away inside him. I think that in my secret heart I've always known that, so why did I ever imagine he'd be different with me?

She tried to say something. To beg for a reprieve—if not from Denys then from their adversary, who sat waiting, his face an expressionless bronze mask as the silence seemed to stretch into eternity.

Eventually, Denys spoke. 'I call,' he said hoarsely. 'And I raise—five hundred thousand.'

Vassos Gordanis looked at him, his brows lifted. 'Trying to scare me off, *kyrie?*' he enquired mockingly. 'I fear you will not do so. In fact, I am even more eager now to discover what could make her worth so high a price.'

He gestured imperatively, and the stout man approached and put a chequebook and pen on the table in front of him.

As if in a trance, Joanna watched him write the cheque and sign it, then place it with the pile of chips.

'I call,' he said, and sat back.

Denys put down his hand, face upwards. 'Full house,' he said. 'With kings.'

There was a pause, then Vassos Gordanis sighed, and lifted one shoulder in a philosophical shrug.

Bluffing, Joanna thought, a wild hope building inside her. He's been bluffing and Daddy's known it all along.

Hardly breathing, she watched their adversary turn his cards over. Saw the queen of diamonds go down, followed by the queen of clubs, to be joined next by the queen of spades.

He's got a full house too, she thought, her throat tightening in excitement and sheer relief as he put down his next card, the five of clubs. Queens and fives, which Dad's kings will beat. So I'm safe.

Only to see his long fingers place the last card on the table. A red card, depicting a woman holding a flower.

Joanna looked at it and the world stopped. Four of a kind, she thought numbly. Oh, God, he has four of a kind.

'The queen of hearts,' Vassos Gordanis said softly. 'So I win. Everything.'

And smiled at her.

CHAPTER FOUR

It was, she thought, like being enclosed in a glass case. A place where she could see what was happening but take no part in it, and where her voice could not be heard.

Aware, but isolated. But still able to think. To reason.

The queen of hearts...

At first she told herself that it must be a joke. That no one could possibly win another human being for a bet, however large.

Sooner or later, she thought painfully, this ghastly humiliation would come to an end, and she and her father would be allowed to leave, even if all they took with them was their freedom to do so. Because they were in worse trouble than they'd ever been in their lives, as Gaston Levaux's tight-lipped presence only confirmed.

We don't just owe the hotel, she realised. There's also Mrs Van Dyne, who may not be very happy when she finds out what a total mess we're in.

But I mustn't think like that. When we're out of here, we can work something out. Denys will bounce back somehow, as he always does. I'm sure of it. I'll really ask Monsieur Levaux to find me a job in the kitchens or as a chambermaid. Something. Anything. And we'll survive. We always have before.

She forced herself to lift her chin, trying to appear unconcerned as she focussed once again on the events taking place in front of her. Trying, also, to ignore a cold, sick feeling in the pit of her stomach as she saw Vassos Gordanis reach for his cheque and quite deliberately tear it into small pieces, before placing the fragments in his ashtray and setting fire to them.

As she observed him summon Gaston Levaux and issue low-voiced instructions which she could not hear, but which, some instinct warned, concerned Denys and herself.

As she watched the other players get to their feet, shaking hands with their host and each other, but avoiding even a sideways glance at her or at her father, who remained motionless in his chair, his head buried in his hands.

Behaving, she thought, in a way that suggests they're too embarrassed to acknowledge our continuing presence in the room.

And she began to realise, as fear stirred within her, that the outcome of the evening might not be as simple as she'd hoped, or tried to believe.

As Chuck passed her, she impulsively caught at his sleeve. 'Help me.' Her voice was a thread. 'Help me—please.'

'Nothing doing, honey.' He detached himself firmly from her clasp. 'I'm a married man, and I know what my wife would say if I turned up with a cute little number like you.' He paused. 'Besides, if you can't stand the heat, you should've stayed out of the kitchen.'

But I didn't choose to be in the kitchen, she thought as she watched him leave with the others and turned to her father, who was still sitting, slumped in defeat.

Do something, she cried out to him in silent desperation. Say something. Stop all this now. Because you can't let it happen to me. You can't…

She saw Gaston Levaux approach him, accompanied by one of the quiet men from the Gordanis entourage. Saw them help him to his feet, making him walk between them to the door. Away from her. Abandoning her to the mercy of this stranger on the other side of the table. Which could well be no mercy at all.

And, somehow, she managed at this moment of crisis to find her voice at last.

'Don't go.' It was almost a scream as she jumped to her feet, preparing to follow. 'Don't leave me. Please...'

She saw Denys turn and look back at her, his face grey, his eyes hopeless in a way she'd never known before.

He has to tell them, she thought wildly. He has to tell them the truth about me. Gaston Levaux isn't a bad man. When he knows I'm Denys's daughter, and not his niece or something worse, he'll talk to this Vassos Gordanis. Make him see reason. Make him understand that he has to let me go.

I'll go after them—talk to Monsieur Levaux myself. Persuade him to help...

She took two steps towards the door, only to be halted in her tracks by a bulky figure in front of her.

'Your time with the man Vernon is over, *thespinis*.' It was the stout man, his face unsmiling, who'd detained her. 'You must forget him and understand that you belong now to Kyrios Gordanis.'

'No.' She tried to dodge past him, intent on reaching the outside corridor and finding her father, refusing to be parted from him, but he was immovable. 'I don't belong to him or anyone else—and I never will,' she added, flinging the words at Vassos Gordanis, who was still lounging in his chair, his cheroot held in his long fingers.

He looked back at her, his face impassive. 'You speak as if the choice was ever yours to make,' he retorted coldly. 'Now, go quietly with Stavros. I have no wish to force you.'

The threat of it was enough to quell her, temporarily at least.

With a sob of pure fright, she allowed herself to be ushered away, conducted into an adjoining room, lavishly appointed with sofas, chairs and occasional tables. However, her escort led her across it without pause, and through another door into the bedroom beyond.

'You will wait here,' she was brusquely instructed. 'And

before he comes to you, Kyrios Gordanis requires that you go to his bathroom and wash the make-up from your face.'

Joanna wrenched herself free. 'Tell him I'll do nothing of the kind,' she said hoarsely. 'And that he can go to hell.'

He gave her a sour smile. 'Tell him that yourself, *thespinis*—if you are brave enough. But I do not advise it. You are here to obey his wishes, not defy them. It will be better for you to remember that.'

He turned and left, closing the door behind him.

She sank to her knees on the thick carpet, hugging her arms round her trembling body.

She'd never experienced this feeling before. Even during that terrible time in Australia she'd always known that her father would keep her safe. That nothing bad would happen to her.

Only the fragile cornerstone of her security had been removed, and her entire world was tottering on the edge of disaster.

As the minutes dragged past, she lifted her head slowly and looked around her, taking reluctant stock of her surroundings.

It was a large room, elegantly furnished in the Empire style, and dominated by the widest bed she had ever seen. The coverlet was deep blue quilted silk and had been turned down on both sides, revealing white linen sheets and plump, frilled pillows.

As she assimilated this, Joanna felt physically sick, realising all the chilling personal implications of what she saw. The dire consequences of that last reckless bet which had delivered her into the power of a man like Vassos Gordanis.

As she recognised, too, that no one was going to put a hand on her shoulder and say Wake up. You're having a bad dream.

Her worst nightmare was about to become reality, and there was nothing she could do, and no one she could turn to.

Because a man whose existence she hadn't been aware of

before today was going to walk into this room at any moment and claim the kind of intimacies she'd thought she would only share with someone she both knew and loved. Someone that in all probability she was going to marry.

Now, instead of tenderness, she would be subjected to a man's demands for raw passion. And nothing in her life so far had prepared her for this. On the contrary...

She drew a quivering breath. She knew, of course, the basics of what would be expected of her. She was neither ignorant, nor completely stupid, having sat through the embarrassment of sex education classes. But her actual experience had never proceeded beyond a few tentative kisses.

And there'd only been that one encounter that she'd found even remotely threatening, and even then Denys's approach down the moonlit garden, his voice calling to her, had provided her with instant protection from kisses that had suddenly become too rough and hands that had tried, with clumsy determination, to grope at her shrinking body.

And if those fairly trivial advances had repelled her, how could she possibly cope with the prospect of being possessed completely? Used by a man for his casual pleasure then discarded?

She could feel a knot of misery tightening in her chest. She was more alone than she had ever been in her life and tears were not far away.

But she would not allow herself to shed them, she thought, as she scrambled up from the floor.

She was damned if she was going to behave like a victim, she told herself with stormy resolution. When Vassos Gordanis eventually decided to put in an appearance, she'd be on her feet and facing him with the contempt and disgust he deserved.

Because, whatever happened with the other women who crossed his path, he would fail with her. He might have won her at cards, but that would be his only victory. He wouldn't even have the satisfaction of hearing her plead. Instead, she would confront him with her total indifference.

And when he realised he was wasting his time and let her go, she would approach Monsieur Levaux and ask him to ring her uncle and arrange for her father and herself to return to England.

Where she would pretend that nothing had happened to her. That the outcome of the game had merely been another kind of bluff.

Only it wasn't, of course, she thought slowly. Looking back, she had the odd conviction that the entire evening had been planned to end exactly in that way. As if Vassos Gordanis knew her father's weaknesses as a gambler and had deliberately exploited them.

But that's not possible, she told herself. Neither of us has ever set eyes on him before yesterday. I know that. My God, if we'd met before I'd have remembered—and made sure I avoided any second encounter.

At the same time, she found her mind being drawn unwillingly back to the scruffy pirate who'd sent her that laughing salute from his deck some lifetime ago, trying to equate him with the hard-mouthed man who'd looked at her in cold triumph as he put down the winning card, but failing totally.

If he was still the pirate, she thought, maybe I could talk to him. Because, however aggravating, he'd seemed—almost human.

And halted, her mouth twisting in self-derision.

Are you crazy? she asked herself. We're not talking about some nicer twin brother here. Vassos Gordanis is one person, not two. And if he had an atom of decency or humanity about him you wouldn't be in this situation.

The room suddenly felt airless and she went over to the French windows, pulling the blue drapes aside and opening one of the glazed doors.

The night was cooler now, she discovered as she leaned against the doorframe. She drew several deep breaths, trying to calm herself, but it wasn't easy with *Persephone* there, right bang in front of her.

She bit her lip. There seemed to be nowhere she could go to escape its owner, either mentally or physically, she thought bitterly.

And although the story of the girl being carried off to Hell was only a legend, invented thousands of years ago, in Joanna's own mind right now it was beginning to take on a kind of dreadful reality.

Like Persephone of ancient days, she was being taken from everything and everyone she knew and loved, by a man of whom she knew nothing except that he had the money and power to do pretty much as he chose.

I wanted my life to change, she thought, swallowing. Wanted to escape. But not like this. Never like this.

Then, in the stillness, she heard the rattle of the door handle and knew that her temporary reprieve had come to an end. That she was no longer alone.

Hands clenched into fists at her sides, she made herself turn slowly and look at him.

He came forward slowly, tossing his dinner jacket and black tie across the dressing stool, and halted to regard her in turn, hands on hips, his gaze almost dispassionate.

He said, 'You were told to wash your face, but I see that you have not done so.'

Joanna lifted her chin. 'I don't take orders from strangers.'

'But we are not destined to remain strangers, you and I.' He began without haste to unfasten the remaining buttons on his shirt. 'As you very well know. Therefore you would be wise to obey me, and do as you have been told.'

'Why should I?' she challenged.

'Because I require it,' he said flatly. 'I was told you were beautiful, but that is impossible to judge when you hide yourself beneath a layer of scented grease.'

Told? she thought dazedly. Who told you—and why?

'It is surprising, too,' he added drily, 'when your choice of clothing, by contrast, leaves so little to the imagination.'

'You disapprove of the way I dress?' she asked defiantly. 'Under the circumstances, isn't that a little hypocritical?'

'I am talking of how you present yourself to others,' he said. 'What you wear for my eyes alone will be an entirely different matter. So go and wash.' He paused. 'Unless you wish me to do it for you.'

She said swiftly, 'That's the last thing I want.'

'Truly?' he asked mockingly, sending his shirt to join his other clothes on the stool. 'I thought—under the circumstances—you would have other far more serious objections to my plans for you.'

Her resentment of his high-handedness was indeed the least of her worries, she thought, swallowing.

At close quarters, stripped to the waist, he looked even more formidable, the dark hair on his chest tapering into a deep vee which disappeared into the waistband of his pants.

Nor, she realised, dry-mouthed, had she overestimated the muscled strength of his shoulders and arms. It suddenly seemed far wiser, if she could make her legs obey her, to make the small placatory gesture of going to the bathroom to do as he asked.

There was no facial cleanser among the toiletries on offer, just soap and water which did little to remove her eye make-up and left her looking like a bush baby.

The mirror above the basin told her that he had followed her, and was leaning in the doorway, observing her efforts with cynically raised eyebrows.

She drained the water and turned defensively to face him. He walked across to her and took her chin in his hand, the dark eyes examining her for an endless minute. She saw his brows lift as if he was surprised at something. And not pleased.

But all he said was, 'A slight improvement,' then moved away from her, casually unzipping his pants and discarding them. He reached into the shower and turned it on, then, to her horror, stripped off the black briefs that were his only covering and stepped calmly into the cubicle, letting the flow of water cascade over his naked body.

For a second Joanna was motionless, caught between shock and sheer embarrassment, then she gave a panic-stricken gasp and flew back into the bedroom, bent on flight, in case he should decide to summon her back to join him.

But having reached the door she stopped. Because how far did she expect to get, when everyone in the suite beyond was in his pay?

It seemed that the only means of escape left to her was by way of the window. And as this suite was on the hotel's top floor, that would mean instant oblivion.

She shivered as she went out on to the balcony to check that there was no climbing shrub or convenient drainpipe that might at least give her access to a lower floor. But there was nothing.

A fate worse than death, she thought, looking over the rail into the darkness beneath. Wasn't that the famous—and totally ludicrous—cliché? Because flinging herself down into infinity would never be an option for her, however scared she might be.

But I'm going to survive, she told herself. And choose another very different cliché. Where there's life, there's hope.

I will get through this, she thought, no matter what he does. Because none of it will be happening to me, but to the stranger who wears sexy clothes and too much make-up. The girl I've always detested. And I'll keep the real Joanna Vernon, the girl with hopes and dreams of an independent future, somewhere safe where Vassos Gordanis will never find her.

But there was still bewilderment under the brave resolution. Because if all he required was the novelty of an unfamiliar female body for a few hours, he surely he didn't have to go to these lengths to get what he wanted.

Even without the lure of his millions, there were probably women in the world who might well be attracted by his particular brand of masculinity, even if she would never be one of them.

How could he do that? she wondered, pressing her hands to her burning cheeks. How could he just—strip off in front of her as if she didn't matter—as if she wasn't even there?

Was that really the way a man would behave with a girl he planned to seduce?

Or was it another deliberate insult? A succinct demonstration of how lowly a place she occupied in his scheme of things.

If so, why had he gone to all that trouble and risked all that money in order to acquire her? Because he certainly hadn't been carried away by some passionate and irresistible desire.

When he'd touched her for the first time just now his fingers had been firm rather than caressing.

In fact, I'm not convinced that he really fancies me at all, she told herself. In which case, why—*why* am I here?

I was told you were beautiful...

Was that really enough to attract the attention of a man who could afford to buy anything and cause him to track her down?

If so, he must be seriously disappointed now that he had seen her. Perhaps he was already regretting that he'd wasted his time on such unpromising material, and her approaching ordeal would not be prolonged.

You don't matter to him, she whispered silently. And he will never matter to you. Remember that, and you will one day be able to forget this and regain your own life.

She took a deep breath and, head bent, walked slowly back into the lamplit room.

'It is a long way down, *ne?*'

The sound of his voice made Joanna start and come to an abrupt halt. She looked apprehensively across to where he stood, framed in the bathroom doorway, his expression faintly ironic as he watched her. He was wearing one towel draped round his hips, and drying his tousled black hair with another.

Even though he was marginally more covered than before, he still had far too much bronze skin on display, she thought, focussing her gaze on to the floor as heated colour rose in her face again.

'Consider, too, the feelings of the unfortunate who would have to remove what was left of you from the pathway,' he added.

'Don't worry,' she returned curtly. 'I had no intention of jumping.'

'Or of looking at me directly, it seems.' He sounded faintly amused. 'But why run away so coyly, *thespinis* ? I am made no differently from any other man.'

I'll have to take your word for that, she told him silently, her flush deepening. Because you're the only one I've ever seen naked.

Aloud, she said, 'Perhaps I simply prefer—any other man.'

'That is, of course, a possibility,' he said musingly. 'Yet my lack of clothing did not seem to disturb you while you watched me through your telescope.' His smile mocked her. 'Or did you think I would not recognise you once your face was clean?'

'I was admiring the boat,' she said curtly, hating him. 'Your presence was—incidental.'

'You had no premonition, Joanna *mou,* that we would encounter each other again—and so soon?'

'If I had,' she flung back at him, 'I would have made sure I was long gone.'

'You would not have got far without money.' He tossed aside the towel he'd been using on his hair, and walked to the dressing table, picking up a comb. 'Besides, my friend Levaux would not have permitted you to leave.'

'Of course,' she said. 'He would have to obey the new owner's orders.'

'You are premature,' he said. 'The deal has yet to be finalised. That is the other reason I am here.'

At that, she did look at him. She said, her breath catching, 'So it's not my imagination. You did plan all this.'

'Why, yes,' he said softly. 'And my plan succeeded better than I could have hoped. I, too, like to gamble for high stakes, but I can afford to lose.' He paused. 'Unlike the man Vernon, who took the bait, as I was told he would, and is ruined as he deserves.' He added, 'He has the bitterness, also, of knowing that his woman now belongs to me, so he has lost everything.'

'How could you do such a thing?' Joanna asked, her voice shaking. 'What kind of barbarian are you?'

'A rich one,' he said flatly. 'And one whom it is unwise to cross—unless you are prepared to suffer the consequences. But perhaps, *thespinis*, you thought you were immune—you and your companion.'

'How could I possibly have crossed you?' she protested. 'Twenty-four hours ago I—I didn't know you existed.'

'Whereas I have been aware of you for the past year,' he said. 'And looked forward to our meeting. I do not think I shall be disappointed.'

The dark eyes went over her. Slowly and quite deliberately stripping her naked, she realised dazedly.

'Please me,' he went on, 'and you will find me generous.'

She said thickly, mind and body recoiling, 'And if I don't please you?'

He shrugged, and her throat tightened as she watched, as if mesmerised, the play of muscle under the smooth skin of his shoulder.

'Then you will learn to do so, and quickly,' he returned almost indifferently. 'You have no other option, as I am sure you will come to see when you have considered the matter further.' He paused. 'And you will have time to do so. Your clothes and other possessions have already been packed, and tonight you will be flown to Greece, where you will wait for me on my island of Pellas.'

His slow smile made her shiver.

'I find anticipation increases the appetite—don't you?'

For a moment, shock held her mute. She'd thought that being made to surrender her virginity to him there on that bed was the worst that could happen to her. Had steeled herself to endure it. She had never expected—this.

When she could speak she queried hoarsely, 'You're—taking me to Greece? But you can't.'

'And what is there to stop me?'

'The law. Because it's kidnap.' Joanna flung back her head. 'And that's a criminal offence in any country.'

'You have a short memory, Joanna *mou*.' Hands on hips he regarded her, the dark face forbidding. 'You are forgetting that I won you from the man Vernon in a poker game in front of witnesses. If you objected to your body being wagered in such a way, you should have said so at the time.' He paused. 'You may cheat others, my girl, but do not try to do the same to me. It is too late for that. And Pellas is where I keep all my prized possessions—until, of course, they no longer have the value of novelty and begin to bore me.'

'And what—what happens then?' The words almost choked from her.

'I sell them,' he said. 'To a new owner.' He added softly, 'I expect you to bring me a handsome profit, my lovely one, when I have finished with you at last.'

CHAPTER FIVE

His words seemed to echo and re-echo through the silence that followed.

Joanna stared at him, almost giddy with horror and disbelief, trying to tell herself that he didn't—he couldn't—mean what he was saying.

But if he was trying to frighten her then he'd succeeded beyond his wildest dreams.

She said in a voice she did not recognise, 'Why are you doing this?'

'You have brought this upon yourself, *thespinis*.' There was renewed harshness in his voice. 'You have chosen to use your body to turn men into fools. You would have attempted to do the same to me earlier tonight, if I had allowed it. Do not bother to deny it,' he added contemptuously as her lips parted in shock. 'Your guilt is known. But now things have changed for you, and it is your turn to be used. Used, then discarded.'

'Whatever I did, I did for my—for Denys.' She managed to keep her voice steady, although her mind was whirling frantically. I was right, she thought. But how did he know so much? How?

'And he needs me,' she went on. 'So, I—I can't leave France. Can't leave him behind. And I—won't.'

'Your loyalty is touching, but misplaced, Joanna *mou*,' he said coldly. 'Is it possible you can still care about him, after what he has done?'

'I do more than care.' She lifted her chin defiantly. 'I love him, and I always will—whatever he does.'

'Then I hope for your sake that the English saying is wrong—and that absence does not make the heart grow fonder.' His tone was cynical. 'Because you will never see him again.'

She caught her breath. 'What have you done to him?' she queried hoarsely. 'Oh, God, you haven't—hurt him?'

For a moment he looked almost startled, then his mouth hardened. 'I did not have to,' he told her brusquely. 'He has damaged himself quite enough, I think, and must live with the consequences.' He paused. 'I wonder, too, how much your loss will really matter to him when he has so many other problems pressing on him. After all, one woman is very like another.'

She flinched from the callousness of the remark. 'You think that he'll simply let me go? That he won't come to find me? You're wrong.'

'But there would be no point,' he said gently. 'He will never again be able to afford you.' He paused. 'If he ever could.'

'Then at least let me see him—to say goodbye.' She was pleading unashamedly now. For her father the initial shock would be wearing off now, and she knew he would be guilt-stricken and desperate. How he'd react if she simply vanished—if he had no idea where she'd been taken—didn't bear thinking about.

For a moment she was tempted to tell Vassos Gordanis the truth. To say, He's not what you think—he's my father. Knowing what he's condemned me to will be the end of him.

But something kept her silent. Because the evening's disasters had involved far more than just a card game, she thought. There was real animosity seething below the surface and until she discovered its cause it might be better to keep quiet about her relationship to Denys in case it simply added fuel to the flames, she decided, repressing a shiver.

'Your goodbyes were said, Joanna *mou,* when he decided

to bet against me.' His voice was inexorable. 'And I think you will find me an adequate substitute for a man three times your age.' His smile mocked her. 'Who knows? You may even discover that you enjoy sharing my bed.'

Oh, God, he was so sure of himself, she thought, her inner chill turning to fury. So arrogantly certain that any girl would succumb eventually and welcome him as her lover. That he probably wouldn't even have to try...

'Never,' she said, her voice shaking. 'Never in this world. Because you are totally vile. Vile and—disgusting. And I hate you. Just the thought of having you touch me makes me feel physically sick. So please don't wait to pass me on to the next man. Sell me now, because I'd rather be with anyone else on earth than with you.'

His brows lifted. 'I would not be so sure,' he told her sardonically. 'Nor do you have the power to be selective about your future, *thespinis*. Like it or not, at the moment you belong to me, and I alone shall decide when to let you go and on what conditions. As I thought I had made clear.'

She stared at him. 'Why are you doing this? Because it makes no sense.' She drew a small, harsh breath. 'I don't believe you even like me, let alone—want anything from me.'

He shrugged again. 'As I remarked just now, Joanna *mou*, you come to me highly recommended. And now this discussion has gone on long enough,' he added, yawning, as her hands clenched involuntarily into fists at her sides at his cold-blooded retort. 'I have negotiations to conduct tomorrow. A deal to make, therefore I need to get some sleep.'

Sleep? In spite of herself, Joanna found her gaze turning to the bed, a quiver of apprehension running through her.

He noticed and laughed. 'No, *pedhi mou*. I cannot spare the time or energy for your kind of distraction just now, when I have business to transact. But when we meet again on Pellas you will have no cause to feel neglected, I promise you. You will make a most interesting diversion for my leisure hours.'

He walked to the door and called, 'Stavros.'

The door opened so promptly that Joanna wondered if the Gordanis chief dogsbody had been standing with his ear pressed to the panels.

Vassos Gordanis spoke to him quietly in Greek, and he nodded impassively and came over to Joanna, holding out the trench coat he was carrying over his arm.

'You will wear this, *thespinis,* if you please.'

'Why should I?' She squared her shoulders mutinously, putting her hands behind her back.

'Because I wish it,' Vassos Gordanis interposed, his tone level. 'Let this be your first lesson in obedience to me, Joanna *mou.* From now on you will dress and behave with modesty. Do you understand?'

'Yes,' she said. 'I understand.'

But you don't. Do you imagine that these clothes were my choice? That I liked pretending to be something I'm not? Something I never will be, no matter what happens?

She took the coat, which clearly belonged to someone male and very much larger who could even be Vassos Gordanis himself, she thought, shuddering inside, and put it on, tying the belt round her waist with an angry jerk to keep it in place.

Then she walked to where he was standing.

'I understand completely,' she went on, biting out the words. 'You appalling bloody hypocrite.' And she swung back her arm and slapped him across the face with such force that her shoulder felt jarred. But it was like punching a marble statue. Even taken off-guard, he did not move an inch, or as much as put a hand to his cheek where her finger marks were immediately and clearly visible.

He said quietly, 'You will pay for that insult when we meet again, *thespinis,* and in coin of my choosing that you may not like. Because we already have another score to settle, you and I. The matter of Petros Manassou. Or did you think you had got away with it?'

She cradled her stinging hand in the palm of the other, staring at him in open bewilderment. 'I don't know what you're talking about.'

'No?' There was a jeering note in his voice. 'Then think back, Joanna *mou*. You will have plenty of time to do so while you are waiting for me to come to you on Pellas.'

He watched the angry colour drain from her face and nodded, his mouth twisting in a smile that did not reach his eyes.

'Now go,' he directed curtly. 'And have the wisdom to learn some manners—and perhaps a little remorse—before our next encounter.'

He turned away and walked towards the bed, casually loosening the concealing towel as he went, and Joanna hastily spun in the opposite direction, heading blindly for the door, her teeth sinking painfully into her lower lip before she could be subjected to another glimpse of her persecutor naked.

In the room beyond she paused momentarily, steadying herself with a hand on the back of the sofa. *Another score to settle...*

Revenge, she thought, horrified, her mind reeling away from the implications of the night's discoveries. I'm being taken away for some kind of revenge. Nothing else.

In his own words—'used, then discarded'.

But why? she asked herself, her heart thudding painfully against her ribcage. What can I possibly have done to deserve this treatment from someone I'd never even heard of yesterday? There—there has to be some mistake.

Stavros touched her arm, urging her onwards, and she shook him off almost savagely.

The hired help could keep his hands to himself. It was enough to know that some time soon she would have to endure Vassos Gordanis' touch, and worse.

And seeing him without his clothes on a daily or nightly basis was probably the least of it. She'd avoided it this time, but it was something she'd have to deal with—when she had to, and not before.

Or *if* she had to...

Because she wasn't beaten yet, she thought with sudden determination as she pulled herself upright and began to walk slowly forward. Not by a long chalk.

Because she wasn't about to have her life ruined over some imagined wrong by a man with too much power for his own good.

She hadn't yet reached his yacht, or his wretched private island. She was still in a large hotel with a foyer which, even at this time of night, would not be deserted. Quite apart from the staff, there would be people there who could hardly ignore the sight and sound of a screaming girl being dragged kicking and struggling off the premises, and would surely feel bound to intervene.

And the reception staff could hardly stay aloof either, not if she was claiming at the top of her voice that she was being kidnapped. They'd do anything to avoid that kind of scandal, she told herself.

Which meant that Stavros, still doggedly at her heels, would have to let her go. He'd have no choice. And, once free, she would immediately demand that the police be called, and insist on being reunited with her father. After which, it would be that emergency call to Uncle Martin and a speedy departure.

And let Vassos Gordanis see where his bet stood then.

She might not have to wait to reach the foyer, she thought hopefully. Not if she could outrun the man behind her and get to the lift first. She'd find a refuge somewhere. Even if she couldn't immediately locate Denys, she knew that Chris and Julie would help her without hesitation. And no one would look for her there at their secluded bungalow.

It wouldn't be easy in these ridiculous high-heeled boots, but it was worth a try, she thought, taking a deep breath as they approached the door to the corridor, bracing herself for the attempt.

Only to find the man she'd last seen taking her father away

stepping forward as she emerged, and placing a firm hand on her arm.

'Let go of me.' She tried to pull away, but he was unyielding.

He looked past her. He said with cold civility. 'I have my instructions, *thespinis*.'

Then it would have to be her original plan after all, Joanna thought as she was marched briskly to the lift. The hysterical scene in the foyer. And wondered how loudly it was possible to scream if she really put her mind to it. I'll give it my best shot, she promised herself, tension twisting in the pit of her stomach. Because the alternative is unthinkable. Unbearable.

She stood quietly, staring into space, as the lift descended. She needed to make them think that she'd accepted the fate imposed on her. That she'd been stunned into submission.

Well, they would soon think again. And so would their revolting bastard of a boss who, with any luck, would be attending his meeting with a bruised face.

She cast a swift glance at the indicator panel, noting with satisfaction that they were nearing the ground floor, and waiting for the lift to slow down. Except that it wasn't doing anything of the kind, she realised, her heart skipping an alarmed beat. Instead, it was continuing downwards to the hotel basement.

She said huskily, 'What's happening? Where are we going?'

'To the entrance used by the staff.' It was Stavros who answered, his smile grim. 'Kyrios Gordanis decided it would offer more privacy.'

'No.' Panicking as her plan began to come apart at the seams, Joanna began to struggle. 'No, I won't leave like this. I won't. I have to go to Reception—speak to someone. Let them know I'm going.'

'All the necessary arrangements have already been made. The car is waiting to take us to the airport.'

'I won't go.' She kicked the man who was holding her. He

winced but did not release his grip. 'Leave me alone, damn you. You can't do this.'

'Kyrios Gordanis' order were quite clear, *thespinis*. Fighting will not help you. I advise calm.'

She said between her teeth, 'To hell with calm.'

As the lift stopped and the doors opened, Joanna opened her mouth in the hope of attracting attention. But before she could make a sound...

'I regret this necessity.' Stavros sounded almost gloomy. 'But you have brought it upon yourself.'

The next instant he'd hoisted her over his shoulder as if she was a roll of carpet and was carrying her, squirming but helpless, down the passage towards the metal door at the end.

She was crying with rage and frustration, but suddenly, absurdly, she was thankful, too, that her indecently minimal attire was at least covered by the trench coat.

Her kidnapper had thought of everything, she stormed inwardly. Stayed one jump ahead of her all the time, as if they'd known each other for years and he could read her mind.

They were outside now, following some narrow path which, she guessed despairingly, must lead down to one of the side gates. So any remaining hope she might have had that their progress might be challenged was fading fast.

Being carried along like this with her head dangling was increasing her feeling of nausea, so it was a genuine relief to be set on her feet again.

Stavros walked to the rear passenger door of a dark saloon car and opened it. 'Conduct yourself quietly, *thespinis,* and all will be well. We have no wish to shame you.'

Was he being ironic? Joanna wondered wildly. Or did he have no idea of the real shame awaiting her on Pellas?

For a long moment she hesitated defiantly, then, with a reluctant nod, got into the car, shrinking into the corner as Stavros joined her.

As the vehicle moved off, she allowed herself a last, brief assessment of her chances if she were to jump out, but decided they were not worth considering. Even if the doors were un-locked, she would simply be retrieved and they would drive on.

No, she thought. Her best chance was to get away from Pellas itself before its master returned.

Not everyone in the world would be falling over themselves to do his bidding. Anyone as arrogant, autocratic and ruthless was bound to have enemies, even on his private island.

All she had to do was find one of those enemies and prom-ise a reward for her successful escape. Her father would not be able to pay, but Uncle Martin surely would, although the prospect of telling him and Aunt Sylvie about the turn her life had taken since leaving England made her shrink inside.

But it was still better than the alternative, she reminded herself grimly.

Anything was better than that.

She sat, her hands folded in her lap, staring out at the dark-ness, as she tried again to rationalise what had happened. To work out why Vassos Gordanis had singled her out from the rest of female humanity and was hell-bent on wrecking her life in this hideous way.

And it wasn't enough to tell herself that he'd simply made a terrible, disastrous mistake.

Another score to settle...

That was what he'd said.

Or did you think you had got away with it?

And he'd said something else—in Greek, although she'd only picked up on the word *petros* which, she remembered from her RE lessons, meant 'rock', as well as being a man's name. A play on words, she thought. That was it.

'Thou art Peter and on this rock...'

And she stopped right there, with a sudden painful lurch of the heart. For Petros, she thought, substitute Peter.

She closed her eyes, shivering. Because she'd only known one Peter. The boy she'd met so briefly and disastrously in Australia last year. Not all that tall, she thought, with hair verging on sandy and dark brown eyes. Quite good-looking, and much too aware of it. Full of himself in other ways as well, constantly boasting about contacts, deals, and all the money he was carrying to make them.

Apparently convinced that he was irresistible, when staying at the same hotel and seeking her out constantly, he'd been simply—unavoidable.

But he'd been Peter Mansell, not Petros whatever it was, she argued desperately. And not Greek, either. He was from California. He'd said so, and his accent had seemed to confirm it.

The boy that, ever since, she'd done her best to forget.

'You've ruined me. You've cheated me—all of you.'

She remembered the overturned chair falling to the floor, and his voice, hoarse with despair. And frank terror.

'You can't do this. You have to give me a chance to win some back. Or I'm a dead man—don't you understand?'

And she hadn't been able to look him in the face, knowing that the only cheat in the room had been herself.

Total betrayal, she thought bitterly, recoiling from the memory. Judas in hot pants.

She'd lived with the shame of it ever since. And now, it seemed, there was worse shame to come.

Because she could suddenly remember exactly what Vassos Gordanis had said. A name—Petros Manassou.

For which, she supposed, Peter Mansell was a fair translation, if you were young and silly and wanted to pretend for some reason that you weren't Greek but a rich American.

Another score to settle...

Or did you think you had got away with it?

Oh, God, she thought. Oh, dear God, if I did, then I know better now. Because it's all caught up with me at last, and I'm going to be made to pay. And this time there's no way out for me.

And as the car sped through the darkness Joanna drew a

slow shaking breath and made herself remember how it had begun...

'You're a pretty girl.' That had been Diamond Lenny, his eyes appraising her through a cloud of cigarette smoke. 'And he's a flash kid with a wad of money who fancies the pants off you. So get to work on him, babe. Give him the hots until he can't see straight, let alone think, then lead him to us.'

'No, I won't.' Her protest had been immediate and instinctive, and she'd turned to her father, her eyes imploring. 'Please, Denys.' She'd stumbled over the still unaccustomed name. 'You can't want me to do this. Tell him so.'

'No, Denys, mate, you tell her.' Impatiently, Diamond Lenny stubbed out his cigarette. 'Advise your little sweetie on the economic facts of life. That the hotel rooms, the fancy tucker and the sexy gear all cost money, and it's time she did a bit more than show off her legs and bat her eyelids at the punters. Made a definite contribution, in fact.'

He sent her a lascivious grin. 'You're female. You know how to get a bloke all worked up, then prim up and back off while he's trying to get his zip down. But if things should go a bit too far...' He shrugged. 'Old Denys will forgive you, won't you, mate? Just as long as you get the boyfriend and his cash to the back room at Wally's Bar tonight.'

'I know Lenny can sound a bit rough,' Denys had said uncomfortably when they were alone. 'But he doesn't mean half of it.'

'I think he does,' Joanna said flatly. She swallowed. 'You really expect me to lead Peter Mansell on over dinner? Let him think that I'll—give in to him later, so that you and those crooks at Wally's can take him for every cent he has?' She shook her head. 'I—I can't believe you really mean it.'

'He's been asking for it—bragging about being loaded all over town,' Denys said defensively. 'If it isn't us, then someone else will have him. And Lenny's right. We need the money.' He patted her arm. 'You can trust me, my pet. I won't let anything happen to you.'

She didn't look at him. She didn't think she could bear to, she thought desolately, and knew that she wanted to cry.

'Very well,' she said at last, her voice toneless. 'I'll try and do as you want, on condition that you don't ask me to do anything similar for as long as I live. And that afterwards we don't see Lenny or any of his revolting friends ever again—even if it means moving to another continent.' She added quietly, 'Daddy, I mean it.'

And he'd assured her that it would be a one-off. An emergency situation calling for desperate measures.

And over dinner, provocatively dressed, she'd endured Peter Mansell's hand on her bare knee, and his hot eyes devouring her. Had gone out into the night-scented garden with him, and stood feeling physically repelled while his mouth greedily explored her neck, and his hand fumbled with the front of her shirt.

While she'd made herself tell him that, yes, she wanted this, too, but she couldn't. That they must stop because Denys would be looking for her. That there was a card game that night and she was his lucky mascot.

Then whispering, 'But you could always come with us. And maybe, if Denys has too much to drink, we'll find some way to be together later—afterwards...'

She knew now with utter certainty that it was useless trying to blame her predicament on the Persephone myth. Simply being, as Miss Gordon had said, in the wrong place at the wrong time. Catching the eye of the Dark Lord of the Underworld and being carried off with him to Hell.

Because chance had never been involved.

And the Hell waiting for her was no myth, but all too terribly real.

CHAPTER SIX

JOANNA would never forget her first glimpse of Pellas, look-ing down from the window of the Lear Jet—Vassos Gordanis would, of course, have to have a Lear Jet, she'd told herself bitterly—on what seemed little more than a splash of dark emerald in a restless azure sea.

It looked so tranquil, she thought. As if nothing bad could ever happen there. Proving once again how deceptive appear-ances could be.

Nor was it her idea of a Greek island, she thought with vague bewilderment. She'd imagined bleached rock, studded with the occasional ruined temple. Not all that—verdancy.

Stavros was now her sole escort, his companion having pre-sumably gone back to the hotel to arrange another kidnapping, or whatever piece of criminality his boss had planned next. He'd informed her shortly after take-off that they would be landing on the neighbouring island of Thaliki, then complet-ing their journey by boat.

He had then gone to sleep, but she could not. She was too tense, her mind plodding in weary, hopeless circles.

We must have been so easy to track down, Dad and I, she thought sombrely, for someone who was rich enough—and angry enough.

And it was the anger that was preying on her mind. The anger and the contempt that Vassos Gordanis had displayed towards Denys and herself. The cold-blooded resolution which had driven him on.

And, worst of all, the desire for revenge which would use sex as a punishment, destroying her self-respect along with her innocence.

They must all have been in on it, she thought with a pang. All his friends helping him—believing the worst of me. Making quite sure the trap would close on his intended victim.

But was it loyalty Vassos Gordanis inspired or merely fear?

Because she kept thinking of that other victim—the boy, his white face damp with sweat. His mouth twitching, his eyes flicking from side to side as he said, 'I'm a dead man.'

Surely, she thought shivering, surely he couldn't have meant that. It had to be a figure of speech. Didn't it?

Or was it possible that being so rich and so powerful could set a man like that above the norms of human behaviour? Make him believe he could take ruthlessness to its ultimate point? And make others believe it, too?

And she wondered exactly what had happened to his wife.

But stopped short, knowing that she was being absurd, because Vassos Gordanis was not a mass murderer.

For a moment she was assailed once more by the unwilling and disturbing memory of the first time she'd seen him, watching her with lazy appreciation from his deck. Someone without an apparent care in the world, let alone dark thoughts of vengeance.

But that, of course, was before he'd discovered who she was. Since then he'd been ahead of her every step of the way...

Except now, when she was going to his island alone—to wait for him.

It occurred to her that she didn't even know where Pellas was. Greece had so many islands, so she had no idea which group it might belong to, or whether it would be in the Aegean or the Ionian Sea.

Not that it mattered that much, she reminded herself flatly. It was rather like pondering whether you'd rather be hanged or beheaded. Because wherever this place might be, the nightmare she was due to face remained exactly the same.

And, like a sentence of death, there was no way out.

The boat from Thaliki was another surprise. She'd expected something sleek and streamlined to complement *Persephone,* not an elderly fishing boat with peeling blue paint, chugging doggedly to its destination.

It would almost be a relief to get there, she thought, easing her shoulders wearily inside the trench coat. She was dazed with her lack of sleep, and although it was still early every stitch she had on was sticking to her. Walking across the Tarmac to the single-storey shack which served Thaliki as a terminal, she'd felt as if she'd collided with a wall of heat.

And these vile boots seemed to have become a size smaller, too. They'd probably have to be cut off her, and good luck to them. She never wanted to see them, or anything she was wearing, ever again.

'See, *thespinis.*' Stavros came to stand beside her in the bow, pointing. 'The Villa Kore.'

She looked in the direction indicated and saw a thickly wooded hill. Rising above the greenery at its crown was a large house, painted white with a terracotta tiled roof.

She swallowed. 'Kore?' she queried. 'Is that the name of some god?'

'The name of a goddess, *thespinis,*' he corrected. 'In your language Villa Kore means the House of the Maiden—she who was the daughter of the Great Mother.'

Who, Joanna recalled, Miss Gordon had also mentioned in those mythology lessons. The once supreme Earth Goddess in all her many manifestations—from Gaia, who'd preceded the Titans and the other male gods, to Astarte, Isis, Cybele and, in Greece, Demeter.

'The mysteries of Eleusis.' She spoke the thought aloud. 'So the maiden must be Persephone.'

'You know of these things?' He sounded genuinely surprised.

'I went to school,' she said. 'Like everyone else.' *Because I wasn't born behaving like a tart at poker games, whatever your boss may think.*

She looked back at the island. They were approaching a long curving strip of pale sand sloping gently into the sea. At one side, where a wooden landing stage thrust out into the water, a small group of men stood waiting, a couple of them with rifles slung over their shoulders.

'The firing squad?' she asked lightly, wondering if it was appropriate to joke about it.

'Security,' he said. 'A few years ago a photographer got ashore on Skorpios and took pictures of Madame Onassis sunbathing without clothing. Since then Kyrios Vassos has made sure no intruders land here.'

Joanna had a dim recollection of the fuss in the papers when the nude pictures of the former Jacqueline Kennedy had been published in Italy.

She shrugged. 'Well, he needn't worry about me,' she said. 'If I choose to sunbathe, I shall not be emulating the beautiful Madame Onassis.'

'I think you have forgotten you belong to Kyrios Vassos, and will therefore do whatever he requires, *thespinis*.' His tone was flat. 'But modesty is not his chief concern in the matter. The man on Skorpios could have had a gun, not a camera.'

'So presumably I'll be watched, and my movements will be restricted.' She stared rigidly in front of her.

'By no means. You are a guest on Pellas, *thespinis*.' He spoke with faint reproof. 'You are free to go wherever you wish.'

'Presumably because there's nowhere to hide and no way off, either,' she said with bitter accuracy. She paused, reluctant to ask the question that was burning in her brain, but recognising it must be done. 'When—when will Mr Gordanis be arriving?'

'When his business is completed—and when he chooses,' was the flat retort. 'Two days—three days. A week—two weeks. Who knows? What does it matter? After all, *thespinis,* as you have realised, you are going nowhere.'

And the faint triumph in his smile reminded her unerringly exactly who still held the winning hand.

She had braced herself for the inevitable curiosity when she stepped out on to the landing stage, but it did not transpire.

She could remember the previous autumn catching an episode of a new TV series starring David McCallum called *The Invisible Man.* Well, now, she thought ruefully, she knew what it was like to be the invisible woman.

Because no one even glanced in her direction as Stavros escorted her along the planking to the flight of steps at the end. And, though they seemed more concerned with unpacking various sacks and boxes from the boat, something told her that they were quite deliberately averting their gaze.

But it was probably nothing personal. Perhaps they were under orders not to ogle any of the women that Vassos Gordanis brought here for his amusement, she told herself. Anyway, she had far more to worry about than that.

'Is it far to the house?' she asked, breaking a silence that threatened to become oppressive as she stepped carefully on to the beach, cursing her boots under her breath.

'Not when you are accustomed.' He paused. 'But the path is uneven, and your heels are not suitable. You must take care not to fall.'

'Oh, dear,' she said, poisonously sweet. 'Are you supposed to hand me over to the great man undamaged?'

'To Kyrios Vassos you are already damaged goods, *thespinis.* But you would find a broken ankle painful.'

Damaged goods... The words stung, and she longed to fling them back in his face—and the face of the man who now owned her. Tell *him* that he was so wrong about her. Except she would not be believed.

Biting her lip, she sat down on the step behind her and began to unlace her boots.

She sat for a moment, flexing her bare toes, then rose leaving the boots lying in the sand.

'You do not wish to take them with you, *thespinis?*'

'I never want to see them again.' *Or anything else I'm wearing.*

It was cooler under the canopy of trees, and Joanna took a deep breath of pine-scented air.

The track was just as rough as Stavros had warned, with stones and tree roots half-buried in the sandy soil, and she picked her way carefully, Stavros walking beside her.

'The Villa Kore is a fine house,' he commented eventually. 'It is where Kyrios Vassos was born, and he comes here to relax and enjoy his privacy.'

'I can imagine how,' Joanna returned coldly.

'The *kyrie* likes also to live simply,' Stavros went on, as if she hadn't spoken. 'So while there is a generator for electricity, communication is by radio, and there is no telephone on the island.' He added, 'He desires you to know this so that you will not waste time searching.'

Joanna, who'd planned to do exactly that, felt her heart sink.

'He also wishes for you to have every comfort, *thespinis*. It is safe to swim from the beach, or there is a pool at the house, if you prefer. Whatever else you require, you have but to ask.'

'I want only one thing,' she said swiftly. 'To be as far away from your Kyrios Vassos as it's possible to get on this earth.'

'Ah,' he said. 'You are thinking of Australia, perhaps.'

Joanna, flushing, subsided. Of course Stavros would know the reason behind his master's pursuit of an insignificant girl, she thought. But instinct warned her it would be futile to ask him. That the information would come only from Vassos Gordanis—if at all.

They turned a corner and Joanna saw a dazzle of sunlight

ahead. Fifty yards later and she was taking her first good look at the Villa Kore.

It was larger than she'd realised—massive, even—but her first thought was, it looks cold. An impression reinforced by the blue shutters at all the windows like so many closed eyes.

The surrounding gardens were oddly formal, too, with their clipped lawns kept a vivid green by sprinklers, and the flowerbeds bright with blooms that appeared to have been planted by numbers.

After the unspoilt beach and the clustering trees, it was like crossing some barrier into a different world, Joanna thought, wondering if anyone had ever run on that grass or kicked a ball there.

Aware that she was being watched, she glanced back at the house and saw that a burly man, neat in dark trousers and a grey linen jacket, had emerged from the main entrance.

'Andonis Leftanou, *thespinis,*' Stavros informed her. 'He is major-domo for Kyrios Vassos and waits to welcome you. You should reply *efharisto,* which is Greek for thank you.'

'Except I don't feel very grateful.' Joanna gave him an icy look. 'Maybe I should tell him instead that, when I get out of here, I'm going to have your mutual employer charged with kidnapping, and the pair of you arrested as accessories and see how welcoming he is then.'

'Say what you wish, *thespinis.*' Stavros shrugged. 'It will change nothing. To him you remain the guest of Kyrios Vassos, to be received with courtesy.'

Andonis Leftanou's greeting was indeed polite, accompanied by a slight, dignified inclination of the head. But there was no warmth in his voice, or in his brief smile. And, once again, his eyes seemed to slide past her.

After the brilliance of the sun, the house seemed full of shadows, and as she looked round the wide hallway Joanna stiffened, aware of someone—a figure—standing in an alcove at one side, watching, motionless and in silence.

She caught her breath. 'Who is that?'

Stavros followed the direction of her gaze. 'It is Kore, *thespinis*.' He sounded almost amused. 'Nothing more. Come, look.'

It was the life-size statue of a girl, carved in white marble, the face remote and lovely, the mouth curved in a half-moon smile. She wore the classic Greek *chiton*, falling in folds to her bare feet, and one hand was extended, palm upwards, offering a piece of fruit.

For a moment Joanna thought she was holding an apple, then she looked more closely and saw that it was actually a pomegranate.

Persephone, she thought. The Maiden Goddess. Trapped here, too, at the pleasure of the Dark Lord, with the fruit of her own betrayal in her hand.

'It is beautiful, *ne?*' Stavros prompted.

Joanna shrugged as she turned away, feeling oddly disturbed. 'If you like that kind of thing.' She paused. 'Now, perhaps you'll show me where I'm to be kept until your master arrives.'

He nodded curtly. 'Hara will take you there.' He signalled to the far end of the hall and a grey-haired woman in a dark dress, and wearing a starched apron, came forward.

She was built on impressively generous lines, with a plump face that looked as if it should have been merry, yet her expression was set and dourly unfriendly as she indicated wordlessly that Joanna should follow her to the wide flight of marble stairs.

She led the way along the gallery to a door at the end and flung it wide, gesturing to Joanna to precede her into the room.

Lifting her chin, Joanna obeyed, and paused, her eyes widening as she surveyed her new surroundings.

As rooms went, this one was pretty breathtaking, she admitted reluctantly. The gleaming satin bedspread covering the wide divan was patterned in green and gold, and those colours were repeated in the luxuriously quilted headboard, and the curtains that hung at the long windows.

The floor was tiled in ivory, and the range of fitted wardrobes and drawers that occupied an entire wall had been constructed from wood the colour of warm honey.

Hara crossed the room, still unsmiling, and opened a door revealing a cream marble bathroom, with a shower as well as a deep tub. Joanna swallowed deeply as she absorbed its perfection, from the gold- framed mirrors above the twin washbasins to the array of expensive toiletries and piles of fluffy towels waiting in mute invitation.

She supposed now, if ever, was the moment to use the *efharisto* word, but when she turned to speak the older woman had silently vanished, and she was alone.

Her first act was to check the wardrobes for male clothing, but they were empty, indicating to her relief that Vassos Gordanis usually spent his nights elsewhere. Or had done so in the past.

She walked across to the bed and tested the mattress with an experimental hand. Was it only yesterday that she'd longed to sleep on something even half as comfortable as this promised to be?

Yet now she would have given anything she possessed to be back at the hotel, facing another night on that penance of a sofa.

And even the knowledge that for the time being she would be sleeping alone was no consolation.

Green and gold, she thought. Springtime colours. Yet every minute she'd be forced to spend in this house would be harshest winter. As cold and unforgiving as the man who would ultimately claim her in that bed. She sat down on the edge of the bed and began to unfasten the trench coat. She was too tired to think any more and too angry to cry.

She dropped the rest of her clothes to the floor, and slid naked under the covers.

Persephone didn't have to stay in the Underworld, she

thought drowsily. But she ruined her chance to leave and go
back to her old life when she succumbed to temptation and
ate those pomegranate seeds.

But nothing and no one will ever distract me, she vowed
grimly. Somehow, some day, I'm going to escape—and when
I do, it will be for ever.

After three days, Joanna was reluctantly familiar with her new
environment. She had begun by exploring the villa itself.

It was beautiful, with its wide marble floors and pale, un-
adorned walls, but everything she saw seemed to confirm her
initial impression that it was cold—even austere.

The main living room, or *saloni,* offered the most comfort, with a large fireplace, where logs were clearly burned
during the winter months, fronted by a fur rug, and flanked
by two massive cream leather sofas, deeply and luxuriously
cushioned. The presence of a hi-fi system and a television set
added a kind of normality, too, as did the glass-fronted bookcase crammed with titles in Greek, French and English.

Elsewhere, the furnishings, although elegant, had been kept
to a minimum, and there were few ornaments, bowls of flowers or any of the individual touches that might give a hint of
the owner's tastes. Yet this was his family home, so perhaps
he was accustomed to this impersonal grandeur. But it seemed
the last place where a man who sometimes looked like a pirate
would come to relax.

There seemed no trace of him anywhere, she thought with
faint bewilderment, nor, more tellingly, any mementoes of the
woman who had been his wife.

Joanna looked in vain for a portrait on one of the walls, or
even a photograph like the silver-framed picture of her mother
that Denys always kept on the table beside his bed.

But perhaps Vassos Gordanis confined the poignant souvenirs of his marriage to his bedroom—the one place she had
been careful to avoid.

And maybe, too, it wasn't the house, she thought, but the attitude of the staff which gave her such a sense of chill.

Because, she'd soon discovered, the men on the beach who'd ignored her had apparently established a precedent. There were, she'd learned from Stavros, over fifty people employed at the house, and in the olive groves and citrus orchards around it, most of whom lived on Thaliki and were ferried across on a daily basis.

But she rarely caught a glimpse of any of them, apart from Andonis, who served her meals with a kind of studied if mono-syllabic courtesy, and of course Hara, who had radiated un-gracious hostility from the first morning.

Although that did not prevent her from doing her job, Joanna admitted wryly. The hated mini-dress and other garments had been removed from the floor, never to return, while she slept. Her case had been unpacked, and its inadequate con-tents stowed in a mere fraction of the wardrobe space. And she was woken in grim silence each morning with coffee and the freshly laundered clothes from the day before.

Surely, she thought, if she had to be waited on, there must be someone younger and more cheerful among all these people.

But she soon discovered her mistake the first time she en-countered one of the young maids upstairs and smiled, only to find the girl looking away and spitting three times.

When Joanna went to Stavros to express her indignation, he'd only shrugged. 'She cannot be blamed, *thespinis*. She was warding off the evil eye.'

'But that's ridiculous,' Joanna said hotly. 'There's no such thing.'

'Not in your country, perhaps. Here—is different. It is a strong belief,' he added drily. 'Be glad you do not have blue eyes.'

'Is that what they all think?' she demanded. 'That I'm some kind of witch?'

'*Ne, thespinis*. Having learned from Hara a little of the harm you have done, that is indeed what they believe.'

'From Hara?' Joanna drew a furious breath. 'Well, that settles it. Please find her something else to do. Because I don't want her hanging round me any more, like some—geriatric Medusa.'

'Hara is the sister of Andonis Leftanou, and she has served the Gordanis family faithfully for many years.' His eyes snapped at her. 'I advise you do not speak of her again without respect.' He paused ominously. 'If you know what is good for you.'

'Good for me?' Joanna echoed in derision. 'What in this whole ghastly situation could possibly be described as good for me?'

'You are fortunate that things have not been very much worse.'

'Oh, sure,' she threw back at him bitterly. 'And no doubt it's also an honour for me to be forced to *belong,* as you put it, to your disgusting employer. Well, I hope he rots in hell— and you with him!'

Stavros looked at her with distaste. 'I suggest you keep such thoughts to yourself, *thespinis*. Or when Kyrios Gordanis arrives here he may teach you a much-needed lesson,' he added grimly, and walked away.

In an attempt to keep occupied and fight her sense of isolation, she swam each day in the pool, then lay on the cushioned lounger under its parasol provided daily for her use by unseen hands. She ate her solitary though delicious meals, provided by Andonis' wife Penelope, in a vine-covered arbour at one end of the terrace, rested in her room with the shutters closed for an hour or so each afternoon and spent her evenings alone in the *saloni*.

She didn't dare touch the state-of-the-art music system, in spite of the mouth-watering record collection in its well-filled racks, and there were few English language programmes to tempt her on television. There was also a video machine, with a number of pre-recorded cassettes, but these were labelled in Greek, and she wasn't sure how to operate the player anyway.

And all hell would freeze before she asked for help of any kind.

But if her days were difficult, the nights were far worse, when she woke with a start from disturbing restless dreams, convinced that a man's hand had stroked her face. Touched her body. And that he was there, lying beside her, his skin hot with desire.

Sometimes it was Peter Mansell who pressed his mouth suffocatingly on hers as she tried to fight him away. But invariably the dream would change at some point, when her oppressor would become Vassos Gordanis, his ruthless kisses stifling her pleas for help. Or for mercy.

It was all so terribly real. Too real. Because she awoke each morning drained and on edge, a feeling of dread never far from the pit of her stomach, wondering if this would be the day when she would be made to pay for the past.

Knowing that this brief respite could not last, and that, for her, time was running out.

CHAPTER SEVEN

JOANNA blew her nose vigorously, swallowing back the threatened tears. The last thing she wanted was someone to see her crying and misinterpret the reason, she thought, as she closed *Watership Down* and slipped the paperback into her bag together with her hankie.

During the past week, she'd devoured a Raymond Chandler and discovered Ernest Hemingway from the bookshelves in the *saloni,* but had hesitated to begin the book that Julie had given her, knowing that it would revive memories of the quiet evenings with baby Matthew—and a time when all she had to trouble her was shortage of money.

I didn't realise how lucky I was, she thought bitterly.

Suddenly restless, she got up from the lounger, putting on her hat and slinging her bag over her shoulder. Lunch would not be served for another hour or more, so she could fill in some time with a walk.

She'd explored most of the immediate vicinity, and all that remained was the unexciting prospect of the olive groves, where Stavros had assured her almost vehemently that there was nothing to see, and it would be better to go to the beach instead. He was probably right, she thought, but at least the trees would provide some shade, and less chance of running into an armed guard.

And it was pleasant to wander along, her espadrilles making no sound on the loose soil of the path winding between the trees, listening to the faint rustling of the silver leaves above her. There were nets spread on the ground beneath the branches, presumably to catch the fruit when it was harvested, in the way it had been done since the first olives were grown.

She recalled reading that the trees could live for hundreds of years, and, judging by the gnarled and twisted trunks she saw around her, some of these were very old indeed. Just being among them was an oddly peaceful experience.

And then she paused, frowning a little, as that peace was suddenly disturbed by the sound, not far away, of a child crying.

Except there were no children on the island. The only residents at the villa were Hara, who was a childless widow, and Andonis and Penelope, whose two sons were grown up and working on the mainland.

Puzzled, she followed the direction of the crying, and found herself on the edge of the grove, looking at a neat two-storey house fronted by its own fenced garden.

Yet Stavros had implied that the Villa Kore was the only house on the island.

And the house had occupants. A very small girl, incongruously clad in a pink taffeta dress, with a number of lace-edged underskirts, plus white shoes and socks, was standing at the gate, sobbing, her gaze fixed on a blue ball lying on the other side and well beyond her reach.

Joanna said gently, 'Oh, dear.' She picked up the ball and walked towards the gate, and saw the child retreat a couple of steps, her thumb in her mouth.

'Yours, I think.' Joanna pushed the ball carefully though the bars of the gate so that it bounced gently at the little girl's feet. 'And now you should say *efharisto*,' she prompted.

But the thumb stayed firmly and silently in place. Big dark eyes surveyed Joanna solemnly.

She was not, Joanna thought as she straightened, a very pretty child. But that was hardly her fault. Her black hair was pulled back into stiff braids, and the dress did nothing for her, either, being the wrong colour, and far too elaborate for playing in. What could her mother be thinking of?

She gave the little girl a swift, reassuring smile, then started back the way she'd come.

She heard a slight noise behind her and, turning, saw the ball was outside again, and the child back at the gate, watching hopefully. She said softly, 'So it's a game, is it?'

Retracing her steps, she returned the ball, but this time she only managed a couple of paces before she heard it bounce back again. She picked it up and walked to the gate, hunkering down so that she and the child were level.

Pointing to herself, she said, 'Joanna.'

But the child simply stared back unwinkingly and said nothing, her small face serious.

From inside the house, a female voice called sharply, 'Eleni,' and a young woman came out, shading her eyes from the sun. Olive-skinned and sloe-eyed, she had a full-lipped, sulky mouth, while a dark red dress made the most of a figure that bordered on the voluptuous.

As she caught sight of Joanna, her brows snapped together in a sharp frown and she marched down towards the gate, firing off a series of shrill questions in Greek.

'I'm sorry.' Joanna straightened awkwardly, passing the ball over the gate. 'I don't understand.'

The other halted, hands on hips, clearly taken aback. *'Anglitha?'*

Her voice sounded apprehensive, and when Joanna nodded, she crossed herself, seized the child's hand and began to tug her towards the house.

At the door, she turned. 'Go,' she said in halting, heavily accented English. 'You go. Not come here.'

More evil eye, I suppose, Joanna thought wearily as she retreated. But I only gave the poor little soul her ball back. I hardly turned her into a frog.

And you must have heard her crying, so why didn't you do something about it yourself?

Walking back to the villa, she kept picturing the small wistful face still looking back at her as she was being urged indoors by her mother. Besides the house being in the middle of nowhere, that garden was a very small playing space for a growing child, she thought, thinking of the expanse of unused lawn around the villa.

She recalled, too, one of her aunt's sayings—'all dressed up and nowhere to go.' Well, that was certainly true for little Eleni, she told herself with a pang.

As she emerged from the trees, a voice called, *'Thespinis,'* and she saw Stavros hurrying towards her, mopping his face with his handkerchief.

'I have been to the beach searching for you,' he told her snappishly. 'Where have you been?'

Joanna shrugged. 'Just for a walk,' she returned neutrally.

'You must come back to the house,' he said urgently. 'Come back quickly now. Because Kyrios Vassos is at Thaliki. Soon he will be here, and you must be waiting, *thespinis*. That is his order.'

All thoughts of quizzing him about her unexpected encounter vanished. Her heart was thudding unevenly.

She swallowed. 'He—he's on his way?'

'Have I not said so?' He gestured impatiently. 'Hara is waiting in your room. Make haste.'

The older woman swung round from the wardrobe as Joanna entered. She held up a dark green cotton skirt, ankle-length and patterned with daisies, and a scooped-neck blouse in broderie-anglaise.

'This,' she ordained brusquely. 'You wear this.' She paused. 'You wish bath or shower?'

Neither, with you around, Joanna thought. She said stonily, 'I can manage for myself—thank you.'

Hara gave her a beady look. 'You hurry. I return.'

Which was probably the longest verbal exchange they'd ever shared, Joanna thought.

Alone, she hung the skirt and top back in the wardrobe and

selected some white linen flared trousers and a matching shirt, covering her from throat to wrist.

The hall seemed full of people when she eventually descended the stairs, but they were all looking at the open door, where Andonis stood beaming, and not at her.

She sensed the excited stir, telling her the moment she'd dreaded had finally arrived. Then, as he walked in, clad only in ancient white shorts and a pair of canvas shoes, Joanna saw with a sudden lurch of the heart that the pirate had returned.

For an instant time spun away, and it was as if she was once more seeing him for the first time.

Except that she now realised what all those restless, troubled dreams had been telling her. That she knew exactly how that lean bronze body would feel against hers. How she would recognise the texture of his skin under her fingertips. And the taste of him beneath her lips.

He moved then, and she drew a hurried, horrified breath, her whole body taut as a bowstring, only to find him striding past her to where Hara was standing, and, in spite of her ample proportions, lifting her off her feet in a bear hug while she bridled in coy protest like a young girl, scolding fondly in Greek until he put her down.

Joanna thought helplessly that she had never seen such a change in anyone. Vinegar into honey. Never, surely, the same woman who, fifteen minutes ago, had thunderously condemned her choice of clothing as unsuitable attire in which to meet Kyrios Gordanis. And banged the door, muttering, when Joanna had refused point-blank to choose anything more feminine, or to loosen her hair, which she'd drawn severely back from her face and secured at the nape of her neck with a tortoiseshell clasp.

Hands clenched at her sides, she watched Vassos Gordanis greet Stavros, clapping him genially on the shoulder with a smiling word.

Then he turned to her, and all the laughter faded from his face, turning his mouth into a thin hard line.

For one absurd moment, she found herself thinking, no one will ever smile at me again...

Vassos Gordanis looked her over slowly, the harsh mockery in his eyes making her feel as if she'd been publicly stripped to the skin.

The clothes she had chosen covered her completely, just as she'd intended, but for one bewildered moment it was all she could do not to place protective hands in front of her body. Except that would amount to a victory for him, so she stood her ground, her own gaze defiant.

He said softly, 'Kyria Joanna—at last.' He paused. 'I trust you have not been too lonely without me.'

'Not at all,' she said. 'I hoped my solitude would never end.'

He shrugged. 'Who knows? You may find my company even more to your taste.'

She lifted her chin. 'Not in your lifetime, Mr Gordanis.'

'You sound very certain.' She heard the note of faint derision in his tone. 'But you may be persuaded to change your mind.' He paused, letting her know he'd absorbed her swift, angry intake of breath, then added flatly, 'Now, come and have lunch with me.'

'You do not seem very hungry.'

Joanna looked up from the grilled fish she was pushing round her plate. 'Are you surprised? When I'm being treated in this monstrous way?' She put down her fork. 'Please—why are you so determined to do this?'

'To make you pay in kind for what you did. But also...' he paused reflectively '...also for my private enjoyment. And I am no longer sure which is the more important consideration.'

She said rather breathlessly, 'Stick to your revenge, Mr Gordanis. You'll get nothing else from me.'

'There is a saying, I believe, that revenge is sweet.' His mouth curved cynically. 'Maybe you will demonstrate its truth.'

'You have no conscience, do you?' she said quietly, after a pause. 'No conscience at all.'

'And what of your own moral code, Joanna *mou?*' He poured himself some more wine. 'Which belongs, no doubt, to your country's much vaunted "permissive society".' He pronounced the phrase with scorn. 'Does that bear scrutiny, I wonder?'

Yes, she thought. *Yes!* Except in one instance that I have always regretted and that you have somehow discovered. And I never found Britain particularly permissive. Not with my aunt and uncle around.

'But this is a pointless discussion,' he went on. 'You are here with me because that is what I have decided, and you will remain also for as long as I decide. So accustom yourself, and quickly, because your protests do not impress me.'

His gaze flicked dismissively over her. 'Nor does this belated attempt at modesty,' he went on. 'You are for sale in a buyers' market, Joanna, and your charming body is your main asset,. I suggest you make the most of it later, when you are in bed with me.'

He added softly, 'When your only concealment, *agapi mou,* will be your beautiful hair.'

Joanna pressed her hands to her burning face. 'Don't.' She choked on the word. 'Oh, please—don't talk like that.'

'And you once dared to call me a hypocrite.' He sounded almost amused. 'So what would you prefer us to discuss?' He paused. 'Do you have a topic of interest? Or shall we speak instead of Petros Manassou?'

'I never knew anyone called that.' She didn't look at him, but knew her flush had deepened.

'Peter Mansell, then,' he said with a shrug. 'And do not pretend you have failed to make the connection. Honesty will serve you better now.'

She bit her lip. 'Perhaps—but I don't understand what he has to do with you.'

He said flatly, 'He is the only son of my cousin Maria. Does that make the situation clearer for you?'

Her heart sank like a stone. *Oh, God—oh, God...*

'Yes—I suppose,' she said at last. 'But why was he using a different name?'

'He went to Australia to carry out a business transaction, for the first time unsupervised. He wished, it seems, to prove himself.' His mouth tightened. 'To demonstrate he could succeed in this without reference to his family connections.'

By bragging everywhere about his money? Crowing over his commercial acumen? All the deals he'd achieved single-handed?

She kept her head bent. 'You thought he was old enough—experienced enough—to be trusted?'

'I knew nothing of it until it was too late,' he answered coldly. 'He was sent by his future father-in-law, apparently to test his ambition and his reliability. Without your intervention he might possibly have done so. Fortunately the money your dubious friends took from him formed only the first tranche in a complicated series of payments. But it was enough to ruin him and the future he'd hoped for.'

'You said his future father-in-law.' Joanna swallowed. 'He was—going to be—married?'

Peter had never even hinted at that, she thought. On the contrary, he'd boasted openly about his bachelor status. Given the impression that all the girls in California were at his feet.

And all of it complete and utter fantasy.

'Once,' he said. 'No longer, however. Maybe never—until his criminal folly can be forgotten. I arranged for the money to be repaid, of course, but after such a betrayal of trust the bride's family broke off the engagement, and made no secret of their reasons. It has caused a breach between friends that may never heal.' He paused. 'Yet, fortunately for his ex-fiancée, who is a pious, modest girl and Maria's goddaughter, they only know half the story. Your part in it Petros confessed to me alone. Not even his mother knows of his shame in that respect.

She has experienced enough heartbreak over this whole affair, so she was told only that I would pursue and punish the gamblers who cheated him.'

He added softly, 'And I have done so. You, Joanna *mou*, are the last. And in your case I decided, as they say, that your punishment should fit your crime. Exactly.'

She touched her tongue to her dry lips. 'And everyone knows this—of course? Even—Hara?'

'Especially Hara,' he said harshly. 'She was my nanny when I was a baby, then went to my cousin when Petros was born.' The dark gaze was scornful. 'It is as if you had harmed her own child.'

A perfect child who naturally could not be blamed for his youthful mistakes. And who had, anyway, found his own scapegoat.

'Please,' she said huskily. 'Please—you must let me explain...'

'No explanation is necessary,' he denied brusquely. 'Petros is young and still naïve about women, which must have made it pitifully easy for you to become his pillow friend—show him what he thought was Paradise—then lead him to your associates like an Easter lamb to the butcher's knife.'

Joanna said hoarsely. 'He said that? That I'd— That we'd...' She was nearly choking. 'But he can't have done. Because it isn't true—I swear it. Oh, God, you—you have to believe me.'

'No,' he said. 'I do not. Or do you think I share the naïveté of my fool of a cousin? You forget, Joanna *mou*, I watched you that night in France, and so did every other man present, wondering what it would be like to have you under him—to touch you and kiss—to possess you. Just as you intended. And as you did to that boy.'

He lit a cheroot and drew on it, watching her through the smoke. 'Petros assures me your performance in private is an even greater thrill than the public display,' he added almost casually. 'That, in bed, you are inventive and inexhaustible as well as beautiful. Let us hope his judgement does not err—in this at least.'

How could he have said that? Joanna wondered dazedly, cringing from the memory of Peter Mansell's hoarse breathing, the unavailing attempts to push his tongue into her mouth. The hands pawing clumsily at her breasts while she fought to hide her revulsion.

But the fact that he'd lied about her so hideously—gone to such appalling lengths to justify his conduct—did not make her guiltless, although she would have given anything in the world to be able to throw the entire accusation back in Vassos Gordanis' mocking face.

To tell him passionately that she'd done nothing—*nothing*. That Peter/Petros was a coward and an idiot, totally and stupidly responsible for the troubles his own conceit had brought on him.

Except, of course, she couldn't say that. Because she had indeed let him suppose that she might belong to him—eventually. And she could also have stopped him going to the poker game. Could have warned him off somehow, then made up some story to account for his absence, braving the wrath of Diamond Lenny.

But she had not. Leaving her, she realised wretchedly, with no real defence. And facing instead the wrath of Vassos Gordanis.

'Your silence is revealing, *pedhi mou*,' he commented. He got to his feet and walked round the table, pulling her up from her chair and holding her against him, creating a moment when she was aware of the warmth of his bare chest penetrating the thin fabric of her shirt and felt her nipples harden suddenly against the lacy confinement of her bra.

She smothered a gasp of pure shock and lifted her hands, pushing him away and taking a swift instinctive step backwards.

His mouth twisted cynically. 'However, it seems our time apart has not yet endeared me to you, Joanna *mou*,' he remarked. 'But be warned. I find your attitude a challenge, not a deterrent. If you fight me you will lose, and the manner of my victory may not be to your taste. Do you understand me?'

It would be truthful to say no. To explain that nothing in her life had prepared her for this. For him. But knew that he would not believe her.

'Yes.' Her voice was barely a whisper. 'I—understand...'

Vassos Gordanis nodded abruptly. 'And now there are matters that demand my attention so I must tear myself away from you.' He took her hand and raised it, brushing her clenched knuckles with his lips. It was the briefest caress but it seemed to shiver through her entire being, increasing this whole new dimension of physical awareness that had come so shockingly into being when she'd found herself in his arms.

Leaving her mute and trembling when he released her.

'But only, I promise, for a little while,' he added mockingly, and went.

I can't stay here just—waiting, Joanna thought desperately, watching his tall figure walk back into the villa. *I can't...*

She looked down at her fingers as if expecting to see them branded by the touch of his mouth.

Because she deserved to be marked, she told herself with bitterness. She should carry a lasting scar for that instant of supreme folly—supreme weakness.

How could such fleeting contact evoke a physical response she had never dreamed could exist—or imagined she would ever be capable of? Especially with him.

She felt almost sick with self-betrayal.

But at least he doesn't know, she thought desperately. And I must make certain that he never finds out.

So she couldn't go on standing there in the sunlight as if she'd been turned to stone like the statue of Persephone. She had to try and hide her inner turmoil, and behave as if this was any other day. And that Vassos Gordanis' arrival had prompted nothing but her indifference.

Act like the girl he thinks I am, she told herself. Uncaring and unprincipled.

Tension was building in her, like a knotted cord twisted round her forehead. She lifted a hand to release the clip fastening her hair, then paused as she remembered his words—*your only concealment...*

And shivered at the thought of what awaited her that night.

Although there was nothing she could do. This was his house. His island. If she ran away and hid somewhere, she'd simply be found and brought back to face his displeasure.

And in some strange way the thought of his anger was almost worse than the prospect of the other kind of passion she could expect from him.

There was only one place for her to go. The room that had been almost a refuge since she arrived. That might still provide her with sanctuary if only for a few hours. Until Vassos Gordanis had completed his work and remembered her again.

Slowly, head bent, she walked into the house and went upstairs.

As she walked into the bedroom she halted, thinking she'd come to the wrong place. Because it was like a warehouse, the floor and bed strewn with flat beribboned boxes and crumpled tissue paper. And in the middle of it all Hara, directing two of the maids who were hanging things in the wardrobe and placing them in the drawers.

Dresses, Joanna saw with disbelief, and skirts in silk and lawn. Soft floating things. Filmy nightgowns and negligees. Lace underwear.

She said, 'What is this?'

'Clothes, *thespinis,* for you to wear.' Hara didn't add, For the pleasure of Kyrios Gordanis, because she didn't have to. As the furtive exchange of glances between the maids made more than clear.

A rich man was indulging his mistress, who would be

expected to show him proper gratitude for his generosity when they were alone. Or not...

Joanna lifted her chin. 'Then you can just take them away,' she said crisply. 'Because I don't want them.'

'This is the order of the *kyrie*.' Hara's tone was firm. 'He is not to be disobeyed.'

Joanna picked up the two nearest boxes, walked to the open window and out on to the little balcony, and threw them over its rail.

'And unless you obey *me*, the rest will go the same way,' she informed her gaping audience. 'I have clothes and I require nothing from Kyrios Gordanis. So get it all out of here and then go, please. I have a headache.'

There was a horrified silence, then Hara said something curt in her own language and the two girls began removing the garments and carrying them away in armfuls, whispering together as they did so.

When it was finished, and the maids had gone, Hara said quietly, 'This is not wise, *thespinis*.'

'Really?' Joanna met her gaze defiantly. 'Well, I don't think I care any more.'

Hara went on looking at her, but an odd bewilderment had replaced her usual hostility, and something that was almost pity.

Although that was nonsense. Hara might not wholly approve of the way her master was conducting his revenge, but at the same time she was a Greek woman who probably believed in Nemesis, the goddess of retribution. She would no doubt think that Joanna had asked for all the trouble that was coming her way and then some. There was no sisterhood here.

She said, 'You wish I get you something—for the headache?'

'No,' Joanna returned. 'I just want to be alone—please.'

There was another silence, then Hara shrugged and left, closing the door quietly behind her.

Joanna sat down on the edge of the bed, running a weary

hand round the nape of her neck. She felt hot and sticky, and the thought of a cool shower had a definite appeal.

Collecting her elderly white cotton dressing gown, she trailed into the bathroom and set the water running, before discarding her clothes and pinning her hair on top of her head.

The gentle cascade was like balm against her heated skin as she soaped her body, then rinsed and rinsed again.

As she patted herself dry she gave a small sigh of satisfaction, then reached for her robe, tying the sash loosely round her slender waist.

She unfastened her hair and shook it loose as she walked back into the bedroom.

And stopped dead in her tracks, her eyes dilating.

'You have been a long time, *matia mou,*' said Vassos Gordanis. He too was wearing a robe, but in crimson silk, as he lounged on the bed. 'I began to think I would have to fetch you.'

He smiled at her. 'But here you are—so my waiting is over at last. Now, come to me.'

CHAPTER EIGHT

FOR a moment Joanna stood staring at him, unable to move or speak. Those last few precious hours of freedom she'd counted were gone, she realised dazedly. Time had finally run out.

Eventually, she said hoarsely, 'I—I don't understand. I thought—you—you said you had work to do.'

He shrugged, the robe slipping away from one tanned, muscular shoulder. 'I found concentration difficult, *agapi mou*. During our separation I found that I desired you more than I had planned to do. So I decided that while work could wait, you could not. And I could not.' He held out his hand. '*Ela etho,*' he commanded softly. 'Come here.'

She said, dry-mouthed, 'It's the middle of the afternoon!'

'The time of siesta,' he said. 'A habit I understand you have acquired since your arrival. Today you will spend it with me instead of alone.'

'But I have a headache.' She despised herself for the note of pleading she could hear in her voice.

'I also ache,' he said with faint amusement. 'But in a different way. Perhaps we will heal each other.' He added more crisply, 'And now, Joanna *mou,* please do not weary me with any further excuses. You know why you are here.'

She made herself move then. Made herself walk to the bed, knowing with certainty that there was nothing else she could do, and also that there was a part of her—a part she tried desperately to banish—that flared with sparks of excitement.

He took her hand, drawing her down beside him not un-gently. She saw that he was no longer smiling. Instead his ex-pression was serious—even intense—as he reached for the sash of her robe and untied it slowly, almost carefully, push-ing apart its concealing folds.

She knew that this was only the beginning, but all the same she turned her head away, closing her eyes so she would not have to see his dark gaze burning over her naked body.

If I don't look at him, she thought, maybe I can pretend this isn't really happening. But that won't work, either, because he's been there in my dreams every night since we first met. Which is something I need to forget.

The silence that followed was broken only by his sigh of pleasure, hardly more than a breath.

She lay still as he removed her robe completely, her hands clenched at her sides to hide the fact that her body was, against her will, responding to his touch.

He said softly, 'You are very lovely. But worth the ruin of a man's whole future life? I truly wonder.'

She had not, of course, realised that shutting off the sight of him would simply heighten all her other senses, making her vividly aware of the slight dip in the mattress as he moved even closer. So close that she thought she could feel the strong heavy beat of his heart echo in her own bloodstream. Could absorb the clean, soap-enhanced scent of his warm skin. Hear the sharp rustle of silk as he discarded his own robe.

He began to touch her, his hand skimming lightly from the curve of her cheek down her throat to her shoulder, then moulding the slender outline of her body in one long, sweep-ing movement that, in spite of her inexperience, Joanna recog-nised as more a declaration of intent than a caress. A gesture that promised total possession.

In her self-imposed darkness, she was conscious of other things, too. The strange sensation of a man lying next to her, his heated nakedness grazing her own skin. The powerful and potent reality of his male arousal.

She felt his fingers cup her chin, turning her face towards him, and then experienced the first brush of his lips on hers, lingering, searing, and oddly, unexpectedly gentle. He kissed her again, his mouth persuasive—insistent. Seeking, some instinct told her, the beginnings of a surrender she dared not risk. Because once she had yielded she knew with utter certainty that there would be no way back—and, more shockingly, nor did she want there to be.

His hand found her small breast, taking its rounded softness in his palm, his thumb teasing her nipple and bringing it to aching, hardening life with an ease that amazed her. And warned her, too, that her lips were beginning to soften under the subtle pressure of his kiss. Even—parting…

With a gasp, she jerked her mouth from his, at the same time seizing his wrist and dragging it away from her.

She felt him pause, and waited, her pulses pounding unevenly. Wondering.

He said quietly, 'Look at me.'

She obeyed unwillingly, her gaze uncertain as it met his.

'So what are you telling me, *matia mou?*' Propped on an elbow, he studied her, his expression enigmatic. 'That any further attempt to arouse you for our mutual pleasure would be wasted?'

No, she thought. That I'm out of my depth and liable to drown in a sea of longing. Because you make me feel—make me want impossible things. And I can't let that happen. I can't let *you* happen.

'Think what you please.' She found a voice from somewhere, as she stared rigidly past him. 'It makes no odds to me. I hate and despise you, Vassos Gordanis, and nothing you say or do to me will change that. Not now. Not ever.'

There was a tingling silence, then Vassos said softly, 'If you imagine I shall appreciate such frankness you are wrong. My own wishes are very different.' His hand cupped her chin as he stared down at her, his dark eyes brooding. 'But I am not unrealistic. I expect you to give no more than you have offered in the past to any other man.'

She swallowed. 'I offer nothing, Kyrios Gordanis. So—take what you want, then leave me alone.'

'And if I had met you under other circumstances, is that still what you would have said to me?' He moved, drawing her closer. 'If I had come ashore from *Persephone* that afternoon and found you, asked you to come with me—be with me— would you have fought me then?'

'Yes,' she said, aware that her heart was suddenly thudding against her ribcage. 'Because once you'd discovered who I was you'd have remembered your revenge, and everything would have been just the same.'

'Perhaps,' he said. 'But—I wonder. About that—and also other things.' He bent his head, brushing her mouth once more with his, surprising her with his sudden gentleness. 'For example,' he went on softly, 'how can lips that speak such hard words taste so sweet?'

The erratic behaviour of her heartbeat held her mute as, once more, his fingertips stroked her breast, luring the delicate nipple to pucker in response before taking it between his lips in an arousal as delicious as it was irresistible.

Only she had to resist it, she thought, stifling a gasp. That— and the slow, beguiling glide of his hand down her flushed and restless body to the curve of her hip. Had to, or she would never be able to live with the shame of it.

Vassos raised his head and looked down at her. He said quietly, 'I warned you that I would not be cheated of my satisfaction, and I meant it. But it is a pleasure I find that I wish you to share, Joanna *mou*. So—I ask you to put your arms around me and give me your lovely mouth.'

She said huskily, 'You ask for too much.'

A bronzed shoulder lifted in a shrug. 'Then remember, *matia mou,* that the choice was yours.'

He lifted himself over her, almost negligently parting her

thighs with his knee, before sliding his hands under her flanks and lifting her towards him.

Joanna felt the rigid hardness of him pressing against her, demanding entry to the secret place of her womanhood, and gave in to the sudden scald of excitement deep within her.

Hastily, she shut her eyes again, telling herself it was so that she would not have to see his smile of triumph as he achieved his ultimate revenge. Knowing that she had to hide that unwelcome, impossible stir of desire in case he recognised it. Determined to deny him any kind of response, whatever the cost.

Vassos moved with commanding purpose, penetrating her with one powerful thrust of his loins, and in that same instant her world blurred into a pain she'd never dreamed could exist as her virgin flesh impeded his invasion.

Spikes of coloured light danced behind her closed lids, her resolution to remain silent and passive forgotten with her first shocked cry.

Then, it was over. She heard him say, *'Theos,'* his voice raw and shaken, then pull away from her. Out of her.

Vassos flung himself on his back beside her, his breathing hoarse and ragged, and she lay motionless, slow tears squeezing from beneath her lids and scalding a path down her face. The flash of pain had subsided, and his withdrawal had left her hating herself for aching for his continued touch.

He moved again, and Joanna flinched involuntarily. But he was only reaching for his robe and dragging it on, fastening the belt as he left the bed and walked to the door. He threw it wide and shouted an imperative summons.

A moment later Hara appeared, and he bent his head, talking softly and rapidly in his own language. Joanna saw the older woman's hand go to her cheek in a kind of horror as she listened. She began to speak, but he silenced her, patting her shoulder and turning her towards the bed before he left, closing the door quietly behind him.

Which, in some strange way, seemed to make things a

hundred times worse, Joanna thought numbly. Simply watching him walk away, without a word except a muttered blasphemy.

A sob rose in her throat, and then another, and she found she was crying in earnest, her body shaking as she turned to bury her wet face in the pillow.

And then she felt herself lifted with astonishing gentleness and held against Hara's generous bosom, while her hair was stroked and words were murmured that she could not comprehend but which sounded oddly comforting just the same.

She didn't understand this *volte face,* but somehow it didn't seem to matter.

It was a while before she felt sufficiently in command of herself to draw back, wiping her wet face with her fingers.

She saw Hara looking down at the bed, and, following her gaze, saw with desperate embarrassment that there was blood on her thighs and on the sheet.

She said shakily, 'Oh, God—I—I'm so sorry.'

'No need for sorrow.' Hara's tone was kind but firm. 'Sometimes, for a girl, the first time is easy. For others, like you, not good. It is how it is.' She touched Joanna's hot cheek. 'And now that Kyrios Vassos knows that you are a girl of purity—of honour—he will be kind to you in bed. Make sure there is no more pain, only pleasure.' She smiled. 'Now I fill bath for you.'

'No,' Joanna said. 'That's the last thing I want.'

'Not bath?' Hara was bewildered.

'Mr Gordanis being—kind.' She sat up. 'He'll never come near me—never touch me again.'

'*Po, po, po.* Such foolishness,' Hara chided. 'How could he know? If he had been husband on wedding night, same pain, same blood.' She gave Joanna a look that was almost roguish. 'There will be more loving. You are beautiful girl, Kyria Joanna. You need beautiful man to give you joy in bed. Make…' She stopped suddenly, an awkward expression flitting across her face. 'Make much happiness.'

And she bustled off to the bathroom, leaving Joanna to wonder what she'd intended to say.

But, she discovered, she was glad of the bath. Thankful to sink down into warm scented water and reclaim her body.

If only, she thought, it was as easy to erase from her mind the way her body had reacted to his touch at the beginning—how her lips had bloomed under his kiss and her breast had seemed to swell under the provocative stroke of his fingers.

The way her body had seemed prepared to welcome him.

And, to her eternal shame, she felt her nipples again tauten into rosebuds at the memory.

There was more humiliation waiting for her in the bedroom. The maids who'd been there earlier were just leaving, having changed the bedlinen at Hara's direction.

Now everyone in the house would know what had happened, she thought, and wanted to howl all over again.

Hara sat her on the dressing stool and began to brush her hair.

'You rest now,' she ordained. 'Later, I bring the new dresses,' she added guilelessly. 'Make you look beautiful for Kyrios Vassos.'

'No,' Joanna said, swiftly and definitely. 'I meant what I said. I won't accept anything he's bought me. And I don't want to look beautiful for anyone—least of all him. Because if I'd been ugly I wouldn't be here, and none of this would have happened.'

Argue with that, she thought, but Hara didn't even try. She simply closed the shutters, drew the curtains, and put Joanna to bed as if she was a child, covering her with a sheet.

'Now sleep, *pedhi mou*,' she said quietly, and went.

But oblivion, so much desired, was a long time coming. Joanna was too tense, too alert, every distant quiet noise of an occupied house assailing her ears in stereophonic sound, and her eyes constantly returning to the door, scared that it would open to admit him.

Because how could she ever bear to face him again—even if he didn't want—want…?

But there was no question of that, she assured herself. He would let her go now. He had to. She'd surely paid for what she'd done, so there was no reason for him to keep her any longer. Not when she would never provide him with the kind of entertainment he required.

She burrowed deeper into the mattress, shivering. How could she have allowed herself to be used like that? She would make sure that no man ever got close enough again to treat her in the same way. She would rather remain celibate for the rest of her life.

She slept at last, deeply and dreamlessly, and woke to find vivid sunset light falling in slats across the floor.

For a moment she wanted to stay where she was. To ask for her dinner to be served up here in this room. Except he might join her, and she could not risk that.

Behave as this was any other evening, she thought, gritting her teeth as she pushed the sheet back. As if nothing had happened between you. Or nothing that mattered anyway.

She washed and cleaned her teeth, then swept back her hair and plaited it into one long braid before dressing in the daisy skirt and cotton top she'd rejected only that morning, and not the lifetime ago that it seemed.

As she descended the wide sweep of marble stair, she looked across at the statue of Persephone.

You should never have eaten those pomegranate seeds, she thought. But I won't make the same mistake, because I'll accept nothing from Vassos Gordanis. Not one stitch of clothing, not one stone of jewellery. And none of this so-called 'kindness,' because I know what that really means.

And I'll give nothing, either. Not a kiss, a touch nor a smile of my own free will—no matter what he does. I'll make him desperate to be rid of me.

'Thespinis.' She realised with a start that Stavros had appeared, and was waiting for her at the foot of the stairs. 'Kyrios Vassos wishes to speak with you in his study.'

How totally incongruous that sounded, she thought, as she nodded briefly and followed him. As if she was being summoned to the school principal's office for a reprimand.

She was taken to a room at the rear of the house, overlooking the swimming pool.

Vassos was sitting at a massive desk, checking a sheaf of papers in front of him. As Joanna entered he put down his pen and rose to his feet. He was wearing white jeans that hugged his lean hips, topped by a dark red shirt, open nearly to the waist.

It was almost the same colour as the robe he'd worn earlier, and for a moment she paused, her memories holding her captive.

Don't let him see, she repeated silently. Don't let him see...

'*Kalispera.*' His voice was coolly courteous, as if, for him, those brief tumultuous moments in her bedroom had never happened. 'Please have a chair.'

Not a rebuke after all, she told herself, a bubble of hysteria building inside her as she seated herself opposite him. But something that seemed more like a job interview.

He opened a drawer in the desk and extracted the UK passport which had been taken from her by Stavros before she left France. He flicked it open, studied her photograph, then skimmed through the other pages. He put it down and looked at her.

He said quietly, 'Joanna Vernon. So you are related to him, and never his mistress as you appeared to be.' He paused. 'Levaux told me there was a story that you were his niece, which no one believed. Is it perhaps true?'

Joanna hesitated, then shook her head, realising that there was little point in persisting with the fabrication. She said, 'Not his niece. His—his daughter.'

'Daughter?' The word was almost explosive. He leaned

forward, resting clenched fists on the desk, the dark eyes blazing. 'You say you are his *daughter?* Is he quite mad? What kind of father is he to treat his own child in such a way—expose her to such dangers? Such shame?'

She smoothed a non-existent crease from her skirt. 'Perhaps a desperate one.'

'That is an excuse?'

'No,' she said. 'A reason, but not one that a man with your money could ever understand.'

'You are wrong,' he bit back at her. 'Wealth does not make one immune from desperation or any other condition of the human spirit.' He shook his head. 'And your mother permitted him to do this? How is it possible?'

'No.' There were tears thick in her throat, and she swallowed them back. 'I started travelling with Daddy after my mother died. He said he—needed me.'

He muttered something harsh and ugly under his breath, then sat down, glancing at the passport again. 'You are—eighteen?'

'Almost nineteen.'

'A child still.'

'Hardly that,' she said. 'Any longer.'

His mouth tightened. Then, 'A child,' he repeated coldly. 'Whose innocence he chose to barter. It is beyond belief. Beyond decency. How could he do such a thing?'

'He is a gambler,' Joanna said slowly. 'He was on a winning streak, and facing the opportunity of a lifetime. It probably didn't occur to him that he could lose. It rarely did, even when he could afford to do so.' She paused. 'And of course he didn't know how heavily the odds were stacked against him.'

He said softly, 'That final hand. You think perhaps I cheated? I did not.'

'What does it matter—now? What does anything matter?' She lifted her head and looked at him. 'And who are you to dare talk of decency? If you'd had even a streak of humanity you wouldn't have enforced that bet. No one could possibly sink that low.'

He said slowly, 'Petros lied when he said you had given him your body, but did he lie about the rest? Did you lure him to be cheated at that card game?'

'Yes.' She bit her lip. 'He—he told you the truth about that.'

'And was it your own idea or the suggestion of your father that you should do this?'

Joanna swallowed. 'Not—just him.'

'Then your answer is yes, and he deserved to be punished in the way I had chosen,' he said flatly. 'Even though I thought I was taking his pillow friend, not his daughter.'

'And if you'd known?' she said. 'If he'd told you—appealed to you—would it have made any difference?'

There was a silence, then he said, 'No, Joanna *mou*, on re-flection—it would not. On the contrary, it would have taken my revenge on him to another dimension—to watch him real-ise exactly what he had lost and suffer.'

She said breathlessly, 'You think he isn't suffering now—knowing the hell he's condemned me to and unable to help me?'

'If so, he is being tortured in comfort, Joanna *mou*, as you are yourself.' His mouth curled. 'It seems your father left France in the company of a Mrs Van Dyne. I am told she is a rich New York socialite.'

She stared at him.

'I don't believe you,' she said at last, her voice uneven. 'If it was true—if he's all right—why hasn't he come to find me?'

Vassos shrugged. 'Perhaps because he would have to reveal your true relationship to his new companion, and it is not con-venient for him to do so at this time.' His glance was measur-ing. 'Would you have told me of it if you were still a virgin? I think not.'

She stared down at her hands, tightly clasped in her lap.

'Well, now you've punished us both, and your revenge is complete. So you don't need to keep me any longer.'

'Our views of necessity differ, Joanna *mou*. And I have no intention of allowing you to leave,' he added softly. 'At least not until I have had everything I want from you. And how long that will take, only you can decide.'

She said huskily, 'I—I don't know what you mean.'

'Begin thinking like a woman,' he said, 'and it will soon become clear. Which brings me to something I must ask you. May I assume that your total lack of experience extends also to the use of birth control? You do not have to speak,' he added as embarrassed colour stormed into her face. 'Just nod or shake your head.'

He watched the tiny movement of confirmation, and sighed. 'As I thought,' he commented, half to himself. 'And does it also follow that you have no wish to bear me a child?'

She looked up quickly, her eyes blank with horror as she met his frankly sardonic gaze.

'Again I have my answer,' he murmured. 'So I shall take the responsibility for your protection. When, of course, your body has had time to recover from its recent ordeal,' he added courteously.

She said hoarsely, 'Am I expected to thank you?'

He shrugged. 'Perhaps, one day, you may be grateful.' He got to his feet. 'And now I must return to the tasks I neglected earlier. We will meet again at dinner, Joanna *mou*.' He paused. 'When you will choose something to wear from the clothes I have brought you. They have all been returned to your room— even those you threw in the garden.'

She rose, too, and faced him, lifting her chin. 'I would prefer not to.'

'But it is not your preference that is under consideration,' he said. 'And if you continue to defy me I shall dress you with my own hands.' His smile grazed her. 'It will be no hardship, believe me. The reality of you naked exceeded anything I had imagined.'

He watched the heated colour swamp her face, his smile widening.

'And to know that I will be the first to enjoy you completely is an undreamed of pleasure also,' he told her softly. 'I look forward to the moment.'

He sat down, reaching for the papers he'd been reading earlier.

'Until later, then,' he added, as Joanna turned and headed blindly for the door

CHAPTER NINE

JOANNA felt drained when she reached her bedroom that night. She had it to herself, to her relief, although Hara had clearly been there at some point, to turn the bed down on one side only.

She changed into one of her own cotton nightshirts, hanging the slender shift in leaf-green silk that she'd worn for dinner back in the wardrobe with the rest of the clothing Vassos Gordanis had provided, then sat down to brush her hair.

This must rank, she thought, as the worst evening she'd ever spent—in the company of a man who had deliberately outraged her both physically and emotionally, and announced his intention of continuing to do so at some future point.

An abnormal, even impossible situation by any standard, which he, somehow, had made seem almost normal and even—feasible.

Because when he eventually joined her in the *saloni* he had turned into the perfect host, politely attentive and, she thought, grinding her teeth in chagrin, undeniably charming.

He had acknowledged the new dress with a slight inclination of the head, but there'd been none of the edged remarks she'd expected.

He'd offered her ouzo, which she'd refused, and white wine which, against her better judgement, he'd persuaded her to accept.

And then, over a lamplit dinner on the terrace, he'd chatted to her, lightly and without any hint of flirtation, let alone sexual innuendo, on neutral topics, and in a way that demanded a response from her that could not be as exclusively monosyllabic as she'd planned.

Someone had clearly told him she was a reader, because he enquired as to her favourite authors. Whether she preferred Dickens to Thomas Hardy, or *Jane Eyre* to *Wuthering Heights*. Asked if she'd enjoyed *The Day of the Jackal* and if she thought *The Dogs of War* was as good.

'You must tell me if there are any books you would like to read, and I will get them for you,' he went on, and Joanna looked away.

More pomegranate seeds, she thought, but she was not going to be tempted.

However, it was a novelty for her to have this kind of conversation again. Denys had no interest in books, and had often told her she was wasting time reading when she could have been acquiring skills as a poker player which would stand her in good stead for the future.

It occurred to her, reluctantly, that if Vassos Gordanis had been anyone else she might almost have begun to enjoy herself. And realised just how dangerous that was.

'But it seems you do not care for music,' he said, over the coffee that had been served indoors in the *saloni*.

'That's not true,' Joanna said defensively. 'I'm just not used to that kind of system.'

'Ah,' he said. 'You wish me to demonstrate its use, perhaps?'

'No, thank you. It—it's not important.' She put down her empty cup and drew a breath. 'May I go to my room, please?'

He glanced in surprise at his watch. 'So early? Why?'

'Because I—I can't do this,' she said raggedly. 'Can't sit here and chat as if—as if…'

'As if we were friends?' he supplied with a touch of mockery. 'You don't think in time we may become so?'

'I know we won't.'

'You disappoint me,' he said softly. 'However, run away, if that is what you wish.'

She was on her way to the door but she halted, swinging round to confront him.

'Wish?' she repeated. 'Do you know what I really wish, Mr Gordanis?'

'Of course, Joanna *mou*,' he drawled. 'You would like never to set eyes on me again, unless I am lying dead at your feet. Is that a summary of your feelings?'

'Yes,' she said defiantly.

'But sadly your wish will not be gratified, unlike my own.' He paused. 'And my name is Vassos,' he added. 'In future you will use it, if you please.'

'I take it,' she said, 'that is an order, not an option?'

'Bravo, *pedhi mou*.' His smile mocked her. 'You are beginning to learn.'

And today's lesson would seem to be don't challenge him, Joanna thought, as she put down her hairbrush and rose. Just put up and shut up.

It was a hot still night, and she opened her balcony doors to catch any stray breath of wind before fastening the shutters.

She turned back the coverlet, folding it neatly at the foot of the bed, then slipped under the sheet. As she turned to switch off the bedside lamp she heard the rattle of a door handle, and Vassos sauntered into the room.

He was barefoot, wearing black silk pyjama pants that sat low on his lean hips.

Joanna involuntarily pulled the sheet tighter, her eyes dilating as he walked towards the bed.

He halted, brows lifting as he regarded her. 'You have nothing to fear tonight, *pedhi mou,* I give you my word. But I did not bring you to this house in order to sleep alone. Although I have decided for once to spare your blushes,' he added, indicating his attire, his tone almost rueful. 'In truth I had forgotten I possessed such things.'

He turned off the light and slid into bed beside her, reaching for her and drawing her quivering body against his in one easy movement.

'Relax,' he told her softly as she tried to pull away, bracing a hand against his shoulder. 'I ask only that you lie quietly in my arms. Accustom yourself to being in bed with me.'

She said hoarsely, her heart hammering as she experienced the warmth of him against her, penetrating the thin cotton of her nightshirt, 'Never. Never in this world.'

'But this is a different world, Joanna *mou*.' He took her hand from his shoulder, placing it instead on his hair-roughened chest, so that the heavy beat of his heart resonated through her palm. His other arm went round her, holding her, his fingers resting lightly on her hip. 'A world where your life is mine,' he added quietly. 'So try to accept that. And me.'

She felt the fleeting pressure of his lips on her hair. 'Now, let us sleep.'

Sleep? her mind screamed silently. No matter how tired she was, did he really think she could simply curl up against him and close her eyes? Was he mad?

She lay, staring up at the ceiling, silently counting the minutes, listening—waiting on tenterhooks for his breathing to deepen—to become rhythmic. For his clasp to slacken.

Eventually, when she thought enough time had passed and it seemed safe, she began to move, trying to edge slowly and carefully away from him. But, to her exasperation, her progress was minimal, hampered by the soft mattress and the cling of the sheet.

While reclaiming her hand from his chest was yet another problem. As she tried to slide her fingers out from beneath his, she found herself encountering far too much warm, bare skin.

Frustrated, she made a final determined attempt to lift herself away, only to feel her knee graze his silk-clad thigh.

As she froze, his voice came to her in the darkness, his tone even, almost conversational. 'Continue to wriggle like that if you wish, *pedhi mou,* but I should warn you my self-control is not limitless.' He paused. 'However, you might be more comfortable like this.'

He turned on to his side and pulled her back against him, wrapping his arms round her, and shaping her to the curve of his body.

He whispered, 'Now, close your eyes.'

Burning with helpless resentment, she obeyed, although she knew she still wouldn't be able to sleep. Not—close to him like this.

For one thing, she couldn't empty her mind of images from the past twenty-four hours. And not just the memory of what had happened in this bed a few hours earlier.

It was the other aspects of him that were teasing at her brain, from the laughing pirate who'd come striding in to recapture his domain, to the cold-eyed interrogator who'd faced her across his desk, demanding truths that had come too late to save her, who'd then in some extraordinary way become a pleasant companion at dinner.

And, strangest of all, the man who was holding her at this moment, quietly and without threat, his steady breath warm on her neck. A situation she didn't really wish to contemplate.

Yet Vassos Gordanis was not the only enigma that Pellas had to offer, she thought. And it was much safer to think about the other one.

To contemplate the house in the olive grove, and remember a small child dressed up for a non-existent party who'd briefly enjoyed a simple, silly game, as well as the shrill voice of the mother who'd warned her to stay away.

But why? she wondered. What harm had it done to befriend a little girl who'd seemed to share her own sense of isolation?

Besides, what was that kind of sultry beauty doing in the back of beyond? Unless, like a good wife, she lived where her husband's work took her.

Except, of course, the Gordanis workforce lived on Thaliki, so why was this little family an apparent exception?

But I can't think about that now, Joanna decided drowsily. I'll mention it to Hara. I'll do that tomorrow after I've had my swim. The one good thing about being here.

She imagined herself in the pool, floating lazily on its surface in the sunlight, sighing her contentment as the softest of warm breezes began to drift dreamily and enticingly across her body, making the tips of her breasts harden into rosy peaks under its slow caress and her soft thighs tremble.

And, as her entire body shivered with this new and astonishing pleasure, she thought—I want this never to end.

Yet end it did, and she turned languidly to swim for the side of the pool, but instead of the tiled edge she'd expected found her fingers clutching a pillow.

Her eyes snapped open. My God, she thought as she sat up, pushing her hair back from her face. I've been dreaming. How extraordinary.

Stranger still was the discovery that she was alone in the bed. But worst of all was the shocked realisation that she was naked, the nightshirt she'd been wearing lying in a crumpled heap on the floor.

She snatched it up with a gasp, holding it against her in a protective gesture that even she could see was totally useless.

He took it off, she thought, hot with embarrassment. Took it off when I was too deeply asleep to know what he was doing. And then he...

She swallowed. Well—at least it hadn't been *that*. She'd have to have been in a coma to sleep through a repeat of what he'd done to her the previous afternoon.

But that was small consolation when more details of that sweet and frankly sensuous dream were crowding back into her mind, and she couldn't be sure what was dream and what reality. Because something had created that delicate whisper

of sensation across her body, which reason told her could only
have been his hands—or even more disturbingly his mouth.

At least he wasn't here, she thought feverishly, so she didn't
have to face him—wondering—knowing she could never
ask.

She heard a chink of china from the corridor, signalling
Hara's approach with her coffee, and tugged the shirt back on.
It was far too late for her to worry about appearances, but, for
reasons she couldn't explain even to herself, she knew she'd
rather give the impression that Vassos had spent the night in
his own room.

But Hara's attitude was briskly incurious as she poured the
coffee. And she had some news of her own to impart.

'Kyrios Vassos go to Athens,' she announced. 'Go very
early.'

'Oh.' Joanna was aware of an odd *frisson* which she told
herself was relief not disappointment.

'Back tonight,' Hara added, as if offering consolation.
'Today you rest. Make yourself beautiful for him.' She went
to the wardrobe and took a turquoise bikini from the selection
in a drawer, producing a filmy thigh-length jacket in turquoise
and gold to go over it. She gave Joanna a beguiling smile. 'You
stay by pool, *ne?*'

Joanna sipped her coffee and decided to distract herself
from the notion of making herself attractive for Vassos by introducing another topic.

'Perhaps,' she returned. 'I haven't decided.' She paused.
'Hara—who lives at the house in the olive grove?'

The jacket slipped off its hanger to the floor and the older
woman bent to retrieve it. She straightened, looking flushed.
'Is not important, Kyria Joanna. Not a problem for you. Best
to keep away.'

So I've been told, Joanna thought.

Aloud, she said, 'But it must be lonely there—especially
for a small child. I might stroll over there later—play a game

with her, or take her for a walk. Maybe bring her back to play in the pool.'

'*Ochi!*' Hara's vehemence was startling. 'No, *thespinis*. Not possible. The child belongs in other house, not here. Better you go to beach for walking.'

'Then perhaps I'll talk to—to Kyrios Vassos about it,' Joanna said, stumbling slightly over the unfamiliar name.

Hara's face assumed its former stony expression. 'No, *thespinis*. You must not speak of this. It is not permitted. There are things you do not understand.'

She placed the clothes she was holding on the dressing stool and hurried to the door.

Joanna watched it close after her, her initial bewilderment giving way to anger.

Not permitted? she echoed silently. No prizes for guessing who'd issued that edict. Hadn't the Greeks invented the word tyrant—a description clearly tailor-made for the owner of Pellas?

She could see now why Stavros had been so anxious to steer her away from the olive groves without actually forbidding her to go there.

Nothing to see indeed, she thought indignantly. Only human beings.

From what Hara had said, it seemed obvious that the girl and her baby had been put into virtual exile.

Another form of Gordanis revenge? she wondered bitterly. But what on earth could they have done to deserve it?

Things you do not understand...

She clattered her cup back on to its saucer.

'No, Hara,' she whispered under her breath. 'You're the one who doesn't understand. That little girl is scarcely more than a baby, so, whatever's happened, she's the innocent party in all this—and she's unhappy. Also lonely. I saw it in her eyes. And I knew she didn't want me to go.'

Although the mother wasn't neglectful in material ways. The

tot was clearly well-nourished, and her clothes were expensive if unsuitable.

But how much time did she actually spend with her, teaching her all the skills a growing child needed. Or simply talking—laughing with her? Making her feel loved and secure?

That's what really matters, Joanna told herself passionately. And while I'm around I'll make sure that's what she gets. And it will help me, too. Give me some kind of purpose in this life that's been forced on me.

She showered, dressed in a pair of white shorts and a jade-green tee shirt and went down to have breakfast. It seemed a more protracted meal than usual with Andonis hovering to ask if she would like a fresh pot of coffee—more hot rolls—grapes instead of nectarines.

Afterwards, he asked her if she'd enjoyed the honey that had come with the bowl of thick, creamy yoghurt, and, when she said in perfect truth that it was delicious, began telling her in detail how it had come from the bees his older sister Josefina kept on Thaliki.

After which Hara arrived, apparently to supervise the maids who were sweeping the other end of the terrace, and Joanna realised, lips tightening, that she was being watched.

Accordingly, she crammed on her hat, picked up her bag and set off ostentatiously in the direction of the cove. Once out of sight of the villa, she sat down on a convenient boulder, allowing some fifteen minutes to elapse before doubling back.

I feel like a character out of a thriller, she reflected, wrinkling her nose as she skirted the gardens and reached the olive trees without the alarm being raised.

She found her way to the house without difficulty, but there was no Eleni to be seen, playing in the garden or standing at the gate. In fact the whole place looked oddly deserted. She stood at the fence for a moment or two, listening to the silence, then tried the gate, only to find it locked. So that, she thought, would seem to be that.

Yet where could they possibly have gone—and so quickly? Had she been deliberately delayed over breakfast so that they could be moved on?

Ah, well, she thought with a soundless sigh. So much for my good intentions. She turned to go and paused as something seemed to flicker in the corner of her eye.

Was it her imagination or had a shutter moved at an upstairs window? She waited for a moment, gazing upwards, but all was still again, and with a small, defeated shrug Joanna went back the way she had come.

She spent the day quietly, reading in the shade of the terrace, trying not to think about Vassos' return, and what it would mean.

He did not return in time for dinner, and as she ate her solitary meal Joanna began to hope that he would remain in Athens overnight.

When she went to her bedroom, one of the new nightgowns was waiting for her on the bed. It was the most beautiful thing she'd ever seen, she thought numbly, gazing in the mirror at the simple column of cream satin, slashed to the thigh and falling from a wide band of lace which veiled her breasts without totally concealing them.

Even she could appreciate that, although Vassos had clearly bought it for his own delectation rather than hers.

Only he was not here to see it, she reminded herself thankfully, as she climbed into bed.

She was woken by a hand on her shoulder, and Hara's voice saying her name.

She sat up. 'What's wrong?'

'All is well, *thespinis*. Kyrios Vassos has returned and is asking for you.'

She almost said, But it's the middle of the night, remembering just in time that was probably exactly the point.

'Not good to make him wait,' Hara warned as Joanna slid reluctantly out of bed. She was holding a large shawl, fine and light as gossamer, which she wrapped briskly round the girl's shoulders before ushering her out of the room and down the corridor.

She paused before a pair of double doors, knocked, then turned the elaborate iron handle, indicating that Joanna should enter.

He was standing by the open window, looking out into the darkness, glass in hand. He was not wearing the crimson dressing gown, she saw with relief, but a simple white towelling robe. His hair was damp, and there was a faint hint of soap and some expensive cologne in the air.

He turned slowly and looked at her. *'Kalispera.'*

She held the shawl closer. 'Isn't it a little late for good evening?'

'I was delayed in Athens.' He drank some ouzo. 'Hara said you were sleeping. Were your dreams very sweet, *matia mou?*'

'I—I don't remember.' But an unwanted memory of what had invaded her rest the previous night brought swift colour to her face.

'Then I shall feel less guilty about waking you.'

'I doubt you even know what guilt is.'

He shrugged a shoulder. 'Perhaps I discovered it today when I listened to Petros trying to make excuses for all the lies he told about you, Joanna *mou.*' He added grimly, 'And about other matters.'

She looked down at the floor. 'I feel almost sorry for him.'

'After what he has done?'

'Yes,' she said in a stifled voice. 'Because it doesn't even compare with the misery you seem determined to inflict on me.'

'You were brought here to make amends, Joanna *mou,*' he said, after a slight pause. 'Perhaps I now wish to do the same.'

'Then let me go.' She stared at him in open appeal. 'I swear

I'll say nothing about what's happened. And if—anyone asks, I'll pretend you only ever meant to frighten me.'

'But I think I have indeed frightened you, *pedhi mou*. And hurt you also. I cannot let you go thinking that is how it must be between a man and his woman.'

'I am not your woman!'

'Not yet,' he corrected softly. 'But that is about to change.' He looked her over again, his mouth curving in sensuous appreciation, then drank the rest of his ouzo and put the tumbler down before he walked to her, parting the folds of the shawl and pushing it from her shoulders.

She heard him catch his breath sharply, then she was lifted into his arms and carried across to the vast bed which dominated the room, and which she had been trying so very hard to ignore.

He settled her against the mounded pillows and lay beside her. He pushed her hair back from her face, his thumb gently stroking her cheek, then slid one narrow satin strap from her shoulder, kissing the faint mark it had left on her skin.

The band of lace had slipped, too, baring one rounded breast, and he sighed against its scented flesh as he bent to take her nipple between his lips and caress it softly to unwilling but involuntary excitement.

This time it would be different, she thought. He expected to get pleasure from her and—unbelievably—to bestow it, too.

But she could not allow that to happen. She had to somehow keep her resolve to give nothing—and ask for nothing.

He raised his head, said her name softly, then kissed her, his mouth moving on hers with delicate, deliberate restraint. Reviving memories of the delicate dream-like caresses of the previous night.

It was she thought almost like a warning—signalling his determination to lead her slowly to a submission that she would be ultimately unable to resist.

Her task was to convince him all over again that he was wrong. That he could not arouse her to yield to him.

Having first convinced herself…

His fingers found the long slit in her gown and slipped inside, skimming over the smooth skin of her thigh before moving persuasively, subtly, up to her hip where they lingered.

His kiss deepened, coaxing her lips to part for him, reminding her that she could not afford the slightest intimacy. But how could she go on resisting when his hand was beginning to trace the slender planes and angles of her pelvis? Eliciting a quiver of response deep inside her that shocked her by its intensity. And scared her, too, because it threatened to weaken her resolve.

And then, quite suddenly, the kiss was ended, the hand removed.

'You are still fighting me?' Lying on his side, he watched her, his expression quizzical. Against the white robe, his skin looked darker than ever. Barbaric. 'Why?'

From somewhere she found the defence she so desperately needed. Forced the words from her throat. 'Because I hate you.'

'But I do not ask for love, *matia mou*,' he said softly. 'Just to teach you to need my body as much as I want yours.'

'That will never happen,' she said huskily, after a pause.

'No?' His smile was slow. 'You seem very sure.' He hooked a finger under the other strap of her nightgown, pulling it down and baring her breasts completely.

'And yet you do not seem completely immune,' he added, teasing each nipple in turn with a fingertip, watching them lift and harden at his touch, and sending a tremor of that same sharp sensation lancing through her entire body. 'Let me show you a little delight, my lovely one,' he whispered.

He pushed up the satin skirt, his hand stroking her slim thighs, then parting them without haste to discover the molten sweetness they sheltered.

Joanna stifled a gasp as she felt the sensual glide of his fingers exploring her secret woman's flesh, her first experience of such a seductive caress—and its devastating effect.

His fingertip found one moist silken place and teased the tiny bud it hid, making it swell and bloom under his touch to aching tumescence and her inner muscles contract in a scalding spasm of longing she'd never known could exist.

She was lost suddenly, breathless and drowning, then fighting her way back to the surface of her control with the last drop of will-power she possessed.

She heard him whisper, 'I want you so much, *agapi mou*. Don't make me take, when I wish so badly to give.'

His lips were gentle at the side of her neck, his hands sliding down to fondle her breasts with equal tenderness, touching them as if they were flowers.

She was aware of the throbbing heat of his erection, and her pulses were going crazy, desire clenching inside her like a fist.

How it must be...

He released her, turning away, and for a moment she thought he was leaving the bed, but one glance over her shoulder revealed that he was only removing his robe, then reaching for a drawer in the night table and making use of the contents of a small packet he'd extracted from it.

As he had told her, he still intended to make her completely his. And for one brief, desolate instant she remembered the beguiling sensuous web he'd begun to weave for her, before Vassos moved over her—into her—in urgent and breathtaking possession.

Making her realise that when his passion was spent, desolation was all that was left for her. And, what was worse, reminding her that she'd brought it entirely on herself.

CHAPTER TEN

IT SEEMED almost as if her body had been ready—even waiting—to be united with his. As if it was only the driving rhythm of his possession that could appease the throbbing ache now building slowly and insidiously far within her.

Tempting her to put her arms round him and offer her parted lips to the kisses she'd once denied him. To arch her body towards him, taking him ever more deeply into her in the ultimate surrender.

Above all to pursue and capture those incomprehensible but exquisite sensations that seemed to be hovering, tantalising her, just beyond her reach, and so discover for the first time the reality of passion's physical conclusion.

And then, just as Joanna realised, stunned, that this might be an actual possibility, it was suddenly over. She heard him cry out hoarsely and felt his body shudder into hers. For a moment he lay still, his face buried in her breasts, his slackened weight pressing her into the mattress, and Joanna conquered an impulse to lift a hand and stroke his sweat-dampened black hair.

How can I even think of something like that? she asked herself incredulously. When I hate him? And when I've told him so?

Yet was that really what she felt? Or did she only hate the senses that had so nearly betrayed her?

Before I met him I never knew, she thought. Never imagined—*how it must be*...

After a while Vassos moved, lifting himself silently away from her. He got up from the bed, picked up his discarded robe and walked across to a door she guessed must lead to his bathroom.

As soon as she was alone, Joanna hastily adjusted her nightgown, pulling up the straps of the bodice and tugging the skirt over her legs so that she was reasonably covered again. Then, heart racing, she waited.

He was not gone for long. When he emerged, she saw thankfully that his robe was now wrapped round him. He came back to the bed, not hurrying, and lay down beside her on his back, his arms folded behind his head as he stared up at the ceiling.

He turned his head slowly and looked at her. 'I hope this time you experienced less discomfort, and that you did not find my demands too excessive?'

She touched the tip of her tongue to her dry lips. 'No, I—I didn't.'

'Then that is a beginning at least,' he said. 'Even if not the one I hoped for.'

She took a deep breath, trying desperately to pull herself together. To regain control of her thoughts as well as her emotions. 'May I go now, please? Or do you—want…?'

'No,' he said harshly. 'You may leave.'

She slid off the bed, retrieving the shawl on her way to the door, enfolding herself in its softness, even keeping it round her as she climbed back into bed in her own room. It was far too warm a night for it to be necessary but she found it oddly comforting just the same.

But why should she need comfort? After all, she knew now the worst to expect and it was—endurable, wasn't it? Or even dangerously more than endurable, she thought, remembering the seductive caress of his hands and lips as they'd gentled her body, coaxing her towards the threshold of delight. And if she had refused to cross it with him, she had only herself to blame. Or thank.

At any rate, it would not last for much longer. She was sure of that.

He'd made it clear that he had not found tonight particularly rewarding, she thought. So he would soon be looking for a more amenable girl to be—what had he called it?—a pillow friend.

She turned over restlessly, looking for a cooler place on her own pillow, which didn't seem friendly at all, remembering, as she did so, the previous night and how he'd held her, lulling her to sleep in spite of herself.

The way, too, that he'd caressed and fondled her gently while she slept. The touch of his hands and mouth on her skin tonight had totally convinced her of that, she thought, her body warming. Denial might be convenient but it was also pointless.

She was suddenly stifling in the shawl—and in the nightdress, too, she decided, stripping herself of them both. Even the sheet across her body was more than she could stand.

She was not just hot, either—she was on fire, every pulse beating a tattoo that echoed the throbbing hunger filling her innermost being, and that even her comparative innocence could recognise was unsatisfied longing. A renewed awakening of her flesh that had been ignited the first time he had lain with her.

I can't let myself want him, she told herself with a kind of desperation as her body twisted on the mattress. Not after the way he's treated me—after every terrible, vile thing that he's done. I must be going crazy even to contemplate it.

She sat bolt upright, trying to control the flurry of her breathing, to quell the tumult of her senses.

Sleep, she thought. Oh, God, I really need to get some sleep. Then, tomorrow, I can forget this madness and begin again.

But she soon found that was not going to be as easy as she'd hoped. Half an hour later she was still wide awake, staring into the darkness, the sheet beneath her damp with perspiration.

She put her hands flat on her breasts, touching them softly, tentatively. Feeling her nipples diamond-hard against her palms.

Is this how it's going to be—this agony of need each time? This longing for him to make me in some way—complete?

The questions beat at her brain, or at the brain of the stranger she had suddenly become. This creature of sensations and yearnings she did not even recognise.

Yet the alternative was to go to him—offer herself—and that was unthinkable. Wasn't it? Because what could she possibly say to him? What excuse could she give?

She gave a little shaken sigh. Maybe words would be unnecessary, and her presence, returning to lie beside him in the night, would be enough.

Moving like an automaton, she climbed off the bed, reaching down for the shawl, letting its soft folds settle round her nakedness.

She went to the door, but as she began to open it she heard not far away the quiet sound of another door closing and froze.

She peeped cautiously through the narrow opening and saw Vassos, clad in jeans and polo shirt, coming down the passage towards her. He strode past without even a glance in the direction of her room, and Joanna stood in the darkness, waiting until the sound of his rapid footsteps faded.

She went back to the bed and lay down, trembling, telling herself she should be thankful that she'd been spared the humiliation of arriving in his room to find it empty or—even worse—of bumping into him on his way out.

At the same time she found herself wondering where he could possibly be going at this time of night. And why...

But that, she thought, is not my concern. It simply means I've been saved at the last minute from making another terrible mistake. Persephone must have been watching out for me.

She pulled up the covering sheet and turned over, but it was more than two hours before she finally fell asleep, exhausted from the solitary vigil of lying in the darkness, listening for the sound of his return.

While some instinct she'd not known she possessed warned her that she waited in vain.

Joanna walked along the edge of the sea, small warm waves lapping round her feet. To a casual observer, if there'd been one about, she probably looked like a carefree girl in shorts and a sun top, happily enjoying a paddle in the sunshine.

Only she could know she was a seething mass of nerves.

It was a week since Vassos had walked past her and out into the night. Seven days and seven nights during which she'd been taught unequivocally just what it was to be the object of a man's passionate desire. And the exquisite agony of forcing herself to seem indifferent to his lovemaking.

He sent for her each night—that went without saying. But he also came to her room in the drowsy afternoon siesta hours. Their encounters were prolonged and almost magically sensuous, with Vassos, at times, almost fiercely intent on wringing some kind of erotic response from her trembling, fevered flesh, and at others enticing her with a tender yearning that almost stopped her heart, as if his whole body had been created as an instrument for her pleasure.

And Joanna lay beneath him, refusing to show any sign of emotion, even in the extremity of surrender when her desperate senses screamed for satisfaction.

He wanted to win, she reminded herself when she was once again alone. He'd won her at cards, and now he wished to complete his victory. His touch, his kisses, had one purpose—to prove that she was indeed a woman like any other in his experience. And if she thought he meant more, then she was fooling herself.

In one matter he was utterly scrupulous, however. He always used a sheath which, she supposed ruefully, was a kind of caring, if not the kind she had secretly begun to crave from him.

She was not proud of such blatant weakness, but she could not deny it, either. Whenever he was around she found she was watching him almost obsessively from behind the screen of her sunglasses, drinking in every inch of the lean body she'd once shrunk from.

But it was just sex—that was all, she assured herself almost feverishly. Nothing more. So there were no deeper feelings involved. How could there be when he would always be the man who'd kidnapped her in order to take her for revenge?

Yet he had somehow, against all the odds, made her want him in return so much that her mind seemed to ache as well as her body.

Sometimes, in the night, when she was back in her own room, she heard again the approach of his footsteps in the passage and sat up, lips parted breathlessly, staring at the door. Willing it to open. And, by some miracle, for everything to change.

But it never did. Instead Vassos simply walked on, leaving her still wondering. And sometimes crying inside.

Although she could admit now, in the brilliant sunshine, there were other matters apart from the strictly personal also preying on her mind.

For one thing, it had occurred to her that since her arrival no one, least of all Vassos himself, had mentioned his wife in any way.

And her visits to his bedroom had revealed at a glance that he wasn't treasuring as much as one solitary souvenir of the woman who'd once shared it with him.

It was almost, she'd decided, puzzled, as if the late Mrs Gordanis had never existed.

Perhaps, she thought, aware of a swift pang, he had loved her so much that he could not bear to be reminded, even marginally, of the happiness they'd enjoyed together.

In addition, there was also the matter of the mysterious

house in the olive grove, and its occupants, although Vassos' continuing presence had offered her no opportunity to return there and see if Eleni and her mother had returned—if, of course, they had ever been away.

But he'd left that morning to fly to Athens on business, so she would be alone for ten days or more, as he'd sardonically informed her. And she was going to need something to distract her in his absence—if only to protect her against missing him too much.

She folded her arms round her body, shivering a little in spite of the heat. It was still a shock that she could even admit to such feelings—or confess inwardly that she'd hoped against hope that he would invite her to accompany him on his trip.

As it was, she'd made sure she was awake especially early that morning, going out on to her balcony to listen for the sound of the high-speed launch that would take him across to Thaliki.

And she'd remained standing there long after the engine noise was no longer audible, staring at the azure glimmer of the sea in the distance over the top of the pines. Stared until her eyes blurred, and pressed a finger against her trembling mouth in case she called 'Don't leave me. Don't go,' into the empty air.

Just as a few hours before, when he lay against her in the aftermath of his climax, she had almost begged him, Don't send me away tonight. Let me stay with you. Make love to me again. Share with me what you feel. Teach me to be your woman at last.

But she had bitten back the words, because she still couldn't acknowledge, even to herself, that withholding her body had been useless. That from the very beginning, when he'd been no more than a pirate smiling at her from the deck of a yacht, it had been her heart that was really in danger.

And each time she lay in his arms, listening to the soft Greek words he whispered to her as his hands roamed her flesh with sensual expertise, she became more deeply lost in a longing that was so much more than physical.

Terrified that one night she might even whisper the words that must forever be taboo between them. *I love you...*

'I didn't want this,' she whispered in wretchedness. '*I don't want this.* Because I've no idea how to deal with it. Or with him. Or what I shall do when he decides to end it.'

But at least she no longer feared that he would pass her on to another man, as he'd originally threatened to do. That, she supposed, was something she had to be thankful for.

And another positive move would be to stop tormenting herself like this over a situation that she could not change and instead try to assuage her own loneliness and heartache with another attempt to help a solitary child who needed a friend.

She walked out of the water, wincing a little as her feet encountered the hot sand, balancing quickly on one leg and then the other in order to resume the espadrilles she was carrying.

As she did so, she realised she was not alone. That one of the security guards was stationed in the shade of the trees, watching her. As she walked up the beach towards the track he straightened, throwing away the cigarette he'd been smoking.

Now, where had he sprung from? she asked herself, annoyed.

His name was Yanni, and he was the only one of Vassos' watchdogs that she'd come to dislike. The others faded away politely at her approach, but Yanni always grinned insolently when he saw her, and she seemed to encounter him in all kinds of unlikely places.

Joanna was conscious of his gaze following her now as she started up the track. But he never spoke to her, so there was no real complaint she could make about him. She just knew she was glad when the bend in the path took her out of his line of vision.

She wandered casually through the gardens, in case her

progress was being marked from the house, but all seemed quiet, and she was soon in the welcome concealment of the olive trees.

As their peace closed round her again, it occurred to her that there were times when her life with Vassos assumed a kind of normality. When they actually talked together. Had real conversations. Although these generally occurred over the meals they shared on the terrace.

She recalled he'd spoken one evening of all the miles his work caused him to travel, and how he always waited with impatience to return home.

'But why here?' she'd asked, greatly daring.

'Look around you,' he said. 'It is very beautiful, although you, of course, cannot be expected to find it so.'

Yet I could, she thought, if things were different. Then caught herself guiltily, knowing she was straying into forbidden territory.

She'd shrugged. 'It's certainly very secluded. Why is that?'

'It was my grandfather's decision.' Vassos played with the stem of his wine glass. 'He was first a businessman, but also a scholar. His chief study was the ancient mythology of our country, and for that he required privacy. So when he found Pellas and bought it, he made sure it was his alone.'

She almost said, But what about the house in the olive grove? but stopped herself just in time.

'When the Germans came during the war, they considered it too small to be of strategic importance,' he went on. 'So my mother was able to take refuge here when my father joined the partisans. And I was born here.'

'And you've always lived here?' Once more she thought about his wife.

'Here,' he said. 'Or on the *Persephone*.' His mouth twisted. 'There have been times in my life when it was safer to keep moving.'

'I wish,' she said, 'that my father had felt the same way.'

'Do you, *pedhi mou?*' He sent her a meditative look across the candles. 'Well, perhaps you cannot be blamed.' He paused. 'You are shivering a little. Let us go into the *saloni* and listen to some music.'

Usually it was classical music, drawn from a range of composers from Mozart to Stravinsky. Sometimes he chose the insistent beat of Greek bouzouki. But that night he'd slotted a very different tape into the deck, and Joanna recognised with astonishment some of the tracks she'd danced to at the last school disco, in an emerald mini-skirt and the platform shoes that Jackie had loaned her because Gail had refused point-blank to let her have a pair, maintaining she'd sprain her ankle or worse.

She gave a swift sigh and Vassos looked at her, brows lifting. 'You don't like this tune?'

'No, I love it.' She shook her head. 'It just brought back—a memory, that's all.'

The tape moved into the soft insidious rhythm of Donna Summers' 'Love to Love You, Baby', and Vassos rose and came across to her. 'And this also?' he queried.

'Well—no.'

He switched off the central light, leaving the room lit by a single lamp, before taking her hand and pulling her to her feet. 'Then let us create a new one.'

For a moment she hesitated, self-conscious, because it was a long time since she'd danced and her male partners had been few anyway.

Then the music took her and she began to move in shy enticement, matching the lithe grace of the man dancing a couple of feet away from her. The man who reached for her and sent her spinning away from him, then brought her back, close to him, his hands clasping her hips, her fingers splayed across the warmth of his shoulders through the fine linen of his shirt. The man she longed to kiss her as the music ended. To kiss her and carry her to his bed as the song seemed to promise.

But he had not done so, Joanna thought as she looked up at

the rustling silvery leaves of the olive trees and felt her throat tighten. And, for the first time, that night she had spent entirely alone.

When she arrived at the house, she saw Eleni in the garden, listlessly pushing a little pram with a doll in it up and down the path. This time she was wearing a yellow lace dress which struck Joanna as even less suitable or becoming than the last one.

She walked to the gate, smiling. '*Kalimera,* Eleni.'

The child paused warily, and her thumb stole to her mouth.

Joanna went down on her haunches, her smile widening in warm encouragement. 'Do you remember me? From the other day?' She pointed at herself. 'Joanna.'

There was a silence, then Eleni made a first hesitant attempt at the name.

'Well done.' Joanna laughed and clapped her hands. She was rewarded with a smile from the little girl, fugitive at first, then more confident, lighting up the small face in a way that seemed curiously familiar. And which tugged all too potently at her heartstrings.

'You again.' The voice came sharply from behind her, and Joanna rose and turned to confront the child's mother, who'd apparently emerged from another part of the grove and was standing, hands on hips, her sloe eyes snapping.

She was wearing a blue dress today, its bodice buttoned awry over her full breasts and the skirt creased. Her hair looked dishevelled and she was holding a lighted cigarette.

Looking a mess was one thing, Joanna thought, her mouth tightening. Going off on some errand, leaving Eleni to play alone, was quite another.

She took a deep breath, keeping her smile resolutely in place. '*Kalimera, kyria,*' she returned politely.

'Why you here, Gordanis' woman?' The demand was sulky. 'He send you? Why he not come?'

Joanna bit her lip. 'Kyrios Gordanis is away—on business in Athens.'

'Athens, *po, po, po*. Maybe he has woman there. Real woman,' she added scornfully. 'No pale—no skinny like you.'

Joanna felt her colour rise. 'Maybe,' she agreed evenly. 'But I came to visit Eleni, not discuss Kyrios Gordanis' affairs.'

'Why you visit?' The woman came nearer, tossing away her cigarette end. 'You think you make friend of daughter her papa like you better, *ne?*' The full mouth curled. 'I don't think so.'

Joanna was very still. 'Her—papa?' she repeated slowly.

'You not know?' There was real malice now. 'You make baby with Gordanis, *anglitha,* be sure you give him son, or he build house for you, hide you and girl baby, too. Forget her.'

Joanna wanted to cry out, I don't believe you. You're lying.

Instead, she turned and looked at Eleni, and saw the solemn mouth curve once more into that slow, entrancing smile. And knew, with a sinking heart, why it had seemed so familiar.

Realised, too, why she had been warned to keep away. Because she'd been intended to remain in total ignorance about Vassos' discarded mistress and her forgotten illegitimate child. His unwanted daughter.

She said quietly, 'I understand. I—I'm sorry I intruded.'

The girl came nearer. Her voice became ingratiating. 'You tell Gordanis that Soula say come see his girl. Each day I dress her—make fine for her papa. Each day he stay away—see his friends—his women. Not her. Never her. She cry. He not hear. Not care.' She paused. 'You come, *thespinis*. Talk—play with Eleni—so you can say to him how good, how pretty. Maybe in bed he listen to you.'

Words of instant negation rose to Joanna's lips, but when she looked back at Eleni she knew they would never be uttered. That she could not simply walk away and not return—no matter now much hurt this unbearable truth might be causing her.

Because there was a small, vulnerable girl who was being hurt far more. Who needed the companionship and care that neither her father nor her mother seemed prepared to offer.

And for that reason she could not turn her back.

She said abruptly, 'I'll come back tomorrow, *kyria*. Teach her to play a game with her ball. But not those clothes, please. Shorts and a tee shirt.'

To the child, watching hopefully through the gate, she said more gently, searching for the Greek words, '*Avro*, Eleni. *Endaxi?*' Then turned swiftly and went before she could be tormented by another glimpse of that smile.

She walked fast, head bent, staring down at the ground with eyes that saw nothing.

Vassos, she thought, pain twisting inside her. How could you do this—you with your sense of family? Your own child—your little girl—how can you keep her here and ignore her even if you no longer want her mother?

Nothing you've done to me is anywhere near as cruel as this.

She thought of Eleni waiting each day. Hoping…

All dressed up and nowhere to go.

She shook herself, forcing back her tears.

Well, that child was not going to end up emotionally damaged if she had anything to do with it.

When Vassos returned she would confront him. Brave his undoubted anger and remind him of his paternal responsibilities. Tell him that, for one thing, his daughter was sometimes left completely alone in that deserted spot.

If her mother's not prepared to look after her properly, he should employ a nanny, she told herself.

For a moment she was haunted by an image of Vassos and his former mistress together, passionately entwined, and bit her lip hard as she wondered how they had met and become involved.

Soula might have grown blowsy since that time, but she was still good-looking in a blatantly sensual way, and Joanna could see why he would have been attracted.

Although that did not necessarily mean he'd intended their association to result in a child or welcomed the birth when it came.

But it does explain why he's so careful to use contraceptives when we're together, she told herself forlornly. *It's not to protect me, but to ensure that he doesn't repeat his mistake.*

'And does it also follow that you have no wish to bear me a child?'

His words—making it seem as if the decision was hers.

She found herself wondering why this total estrangement from Soula had come about. Had he become ashamed of the liaison, aware that he'd let his body rule his brain? Or had it ended with some tumultuous quarrel which had turned him implacably against his former lover?

Whatever the cause, it's hardly likely he'll ever discuss it with me, Joanna thought, sighing. *Because Vassos didn't account for his actions. He just—decided, and that was it. I'm the living proof of that.*

She stopped for a moment, leaning against the trunk of an olive tree, aware of the scrape of its gnarled bark through her thin clothing.

But she'll still know as much about him as I do, she thought wretchedly. *Will be aware of every intimate detail. The birthmark like a tiny dark rose on his shoulderblade. The heat, the strength of him as he moves to his climax and the huskiness in his voice when he comes.*

Each time I see her I'll have to remember that, and learn somehow to endure it. But I also have to think of Eleni shut behind that gate on her own. It's her well-being that has to matter now, not my jealousy of her mother or her resentment of me.

And if I can somehow persuade Vassos that his daughter needs him, and doesn't deserve to be hidden away like this, then perhaps my time here won't be such a complete disaster after all.

And if I keep telling myself that, I may even come to believe it.

CHAPTER ELEVEN

'KYRIOS VASSOS sent another radio message this morning, *thespinis*.' There was reproof in Stavros' voice. 'He wished to speak to you. Asked that you be fetched.' He paused. 'I had to tell him once again that you could not be found.'

'I went for a walk,' Joanna returned evenly, replacing her empty coffee cup on its saucer. 'He can hardly expect me to hang around the house all day in case he makes contact.'

The expression on Stavros' face indicated that was probably exactly what his employer required.

He said heavily, 'If you were at the pool or on the beach, *thespinis,* there would not be a problem.' He paused again. 'But, as we all know, you are not. And when Kyrios Vassos returns he will ask questions.'

'Which I shall answer, and then ask a few of my own,' Joanna said crisply.

Stavros looked anguished. 'You must not—cannot do such things. You concern yourself in matters you do not understand, and you risk much anger.'

'On the contrary, I know exactly what I'm doing, and why. Besides, your boss is not the only one with a temper,' she added recklessly.

And my being in love with him does not make him right all the time, she thought, watching Stavros trudge despondently away.

142   THE HIGHEST STAKES OF ALL

She poured herself more coffee and sat back, looking out across the moonlit garden.

She'd known from the start, of course, that her prolonged daily absences would be noted and conclusions drawn, and she'd already run the gauntlet of reproachful looks and muttered remarks from Hara and Andonis.

But this was the first time she'd been openly challenged about where she spent her time and its possible consequences.

Although it's not all unalloyed delight for me, either, she thought with a faint sigh.

She had not anticipated that Soula would make her welcome, but she hadn't foreseen quite the level of sneering contempt that would greet her every time she appeared at the house. And she knew that, if it hadn't been for Eleni's growing delight in her company, she might well have given up.

Soula was no great housekeeper, either, and to judge by the amount of cigarette butts in the saucer on the living room table each day, she smoked like two factory chimneys.

Her cooking was marginally better, however, and there was usually a pot of reasonably palatable stew on the stove, and a batch of fresh bread.

The real bonus, however, was her habit of absenting herself, sometimes for a couple of hours or more, as soon as Joanna and Eleni had settled into their routine. She never offered any explanation for her disappearances and Joanna didn't ask for one, either, especially as Eleni seemed far more relaxed while her mother was away.

The language barrier was less of a problem than she'd envisaged. Eleni, once she was less shy, proved to be a bright child, with an enquiring mind and a reasonable vocabulary. By using picture books or simply pointing to things Joanna was able to expand her own knowledge of Greek and teach the little girl the English equivalent. Eleni's physical co-ordination was improving rapidly, too, now that she was allowed to run about without any frilly frocks to dirty or damage.

There was a pile of colouring books and drawing pads and

a box of crayons all unused and gathering dust on a shelf in the living room, plus a tub of Play-Doh, and Joanna used those to keep Eleni entertained indoors in the heat of the day. She also made sure that the child had a short rest after her lunch, overcoming her initial resistance by singing her softly to sleep, usually with 'Ten Green Bottles'.

At other times they were outside, either with the ball, or playing hilarious games of hide and seek and tag among the olive trees. In a large shed at the rear of the house, home to an elderly and disused olive press, Joanna also discovered a small tricycle, still in its original wrappings, and under her guidance Eleni soon learned to master it.

Best of all, the little face peering through the gate each morning was no longer wistful but bright-eyed and eager.

At the same time, the imminence of Vassos' return from Athens was never far from Joanna's mind, together with the inevitable row that would follow once he discovered how she'd been using her time. If, of course, he didn't already know.

The possibility that he might be angry enough to send her away had occurred to her, too. Especially as she'd offered him no incentive to keep her around, she reminded herself wryly.

Sighing, she pushed her chair back and rose. She'd finished yet another book, this time James Clavell's *Shogun,* and needed something new to read in bed. Something sufficiently absorbing, she reflected, to see her through yet another restless, miserable night.

She walked into the *saloni* and stood for a moment, listening to the silence all around her.

The Villa Kore seemed so terribly empty without Vassos' vigorous presence. She had become so swiftly accustomed to the sound of his quick stride, his voice calling to someone. The occasional burst of impatience when an order had not been carried out to his satisfaction. All of it so much a part of him.

I miss him so much, she thought. Want him so dearly. And I always shall, no matter what he is or what he has done.

I never dreamed how I would ache for his lips. Hunger for the touch of his hands on my skin. Long for him to caress me as he did that first night when I lay in his arms.

Nor did I ever realise—how could I?—how precious those brief moments of actual possession would become—especially as they are all I may ever have of him. All he will permit.

Oh, God, she thought with a pang of sadness, it was so much easier to hate him. And made so much more sense.

Vassos Gordanis. Absolute ruler of his domain, and the man she had chosen to defy—not just in his bedroom but by openly ignoring his explicit instructions.

But I won't think about it now, she told herself. There'll be time enough for that when he returns.

Won't there?

She chose a book almost at random, and went out to the stairs. She paused at their foot, looking at the statue of Persephone.

Was that why you ate the pomegranate seeds? she asked silently. To give you an excuse to stay with your own Dark Lord—because you, too, had learned to love him? Because you knew your life would always be winter without him?

And she shivered as she went up to her room for yet another night alone.

It was late the following afternoon when Joanna eventually made her way back through the olive grove.

Almost as soon as she'd arrived at the house Soula had disappeared, staying away this time until Joanna had begun to glance uneasily at her watch.

'Where have you been?' she'd asked sharply when, at last, the Greek girl came sauntering back through the trees, smoking the inevitable cigarette. 'I thought you were never coming.'

Soula shrugged, unperturbed. She looked, Joanna thought, relaxed and almost cheerful for once. 'Is a problem? Then why you not go? Leave Eleni in garden.'

'Because I would never do that,' Joanna returned icily. 'And nor should you.'

'Is safe,' the other retorted. 'What harm to Gordanis' child on Gordanis' island?' She paused, giving Joanna a speculative glance. 'You come back tomorrow, *anglitha?*'

Joanna swallowed her anger at Soula's cavalier attitude to childcare. 'Yes,' she said shortly. 'I'll be here. And then I think we need to have a talk, *kyria.*'

Eleni's small fingers caught a fold on her skirt and held it while she whispered something.

'She asks you promise,' Soula translated.

Joanna ran a hand over the child's springing dark hair. 'Tomorrow,' she said softly. 'I promise.'

There was a reception committee consisting of Stavros, Hara and Andonis drawn up on the terrace at the villa, and as soon as Joanna saw them she knew.

She halted. 'Kyrios Vassos?' she asked, looking from one grave face to another, aware of the unsteady thud of her heart against her ribcage.

Stavros gave the sideways tilt of his head that signified assent.

'He is waiting for you, *thespinis.*'

He did not add, 'And has been doing so for some time,' because he didn't have to. It was implicit in the way they were all looking at her. In their obvious apprehension.

And Joanna didn't have to ask where to find him, either. She just walked into the villa and went straight to his study.

Not a job interview this time, she thought, smoothing her damp palms down her skirt as she reached his door, which was standing ajar. Probably dismissal without notice or a reference.

She pushed the door open, and went into the room.

Vassos was standing at the window, his tall figure like a statue carved from obsidian against the deep afternoon sun. He did not move as she entered, and, after a moment, she said his name softly and tentatively.

He turned then, his gaze sweeping her, his mouth a hard line. She could feel the anger in him reaching out across the room to her like a clenched fist.

Fear dried her mouth as it had on the night of the poker game, but it was important not to let him see that. Because in that way he would gain the upper hand, and make it impossible for her to say all the things that she knew must be said.

'So,' he said. 'You have returned.'

'You—asked for me?' She kept her tone level.

'I sent for you,' he corrected harshly. 'I am told that you have been meddling, *thespinis*. Interfering in matters that are not your business, and doing so against my expressed wish. But that ends now. You will not go to the house of the olive press again. Let that be clearly understood.'

Joanna lifted her chin. 'My understanding is rather different. I believe that a child who is lonely and possibly neglected should be everyone's business, Kyrios Gordanis.'

'Enough!' His tone was molten. 'It is not a subject for discussion. I have given you an order, Joanna. You would be wise to obey it.'

'In this case I think I prefer compassion to wisdom,' she flung back at him. 'You once had some very hard words to say, here in this room, about my father, and how he'd allowed me to be treated. The dangers I'd been subjected to. Well, let me tell you that your own ideas on fatherhood win no prizes either, Kyrios Vassos. In fact, you're far worse, for you've chosen to ignore your child's existence completely, presumably because you no longer want her mother.'

Vassos came round the desk towards her, his dark eyes blazing, but Joanna stood her ground defiantly.

'And if Denys was rarely around,' she went on, 'I had a mother who loved and took care of me all the time I was growing up. Soula can't even be bothered to play with your daughter or teach her basic things. What's more, she vanishes for whole chunks of the day, leaving Eleni alone in the middle of nowhere. You may not think that matters, but I do.'

She swallowed. 'As parents, the two of you are a total disaster, and it's that lovely little girl who's suffering. I'm not going to abandon her to suit some—tyrannical whim of yours.'

Vassos had halted and was staring at her as she reached the end of her breathless tirade, his eyes narrowing in disbelief.

'Soula?' he grated. 'You think that Soula is Eleni's mother? That she was my mistress? Are you insane?'

Joanna felt as if she'd been winded. 'Not Soula's child?' she managed. 'Then—whose?'

There was a silence, then Vassos said with cold reluctance, 'The child was born to my late wife, Ariadne Philipou, several months after our marriage. The identity of the man who fathered her is still unknown to me.'

'But Soula says it's you,' Joanna protested. 'And that's what she tells Eleni, too. Lets her think that you're her papa and one day you'll come to see her.'

'Then she lies cruelly—on both counts,' he returned implacably. 'She is making a fool of you, Joanna, for some purpose of her own. A situation that will be dealt with,' he added ominously.

He turned away, walking back to the window. 'My wife died of a brain haemorrhage shortly after the birth of her daughter,' he went on, his words staccato. 'And because I could not bring myself either to acknowledge her lover's bastard as mine or admit the shameful truth, I let it be thought that the baby, too, had not survived. That I had suffered a double loss. *Theos!*' His brief laugh jarred bitterly. 'What a joke. What an eternal nightmare of a joke.'

Stricken, Joanna tried to say his name, but her lips could not frame the word.

'I had the baby brought quietly to Pellas,' Vassos continued after a pause. 'And established her at the house belonging to the old olive press, with the woman who had been my wife's maid and probable accomplice in her affair. So Soula knows the truth, whatever story she may spin now.'

He swung back and looked at Joanna, his face a bronze, unyielding mask.

'Now do you wonder, *thespinis,* why I do not visit the child? I feed, clothe and provide for her, but that is all. She is too potent a reminder of my life's worst mistake and the woman who betrayed me.'

'But that can't be right.' Joanna's voice was barely a whisper. 'Vassos, Eleni must be your child. She—she's just like you. She even looks at me with your smile.'

There was a silence. She saw his mouth tighten, then he said quietly, 'Can you be so sure? The good God knows there have been few enough smiles between us, Joanna *mou.*'

She said haltingly, 'But I think enough for me to remember—and recognise.'

He raised his eyebrows, clicking his tongue in negation. 'Maybe the resemblance you see is of your own imagining, because you wish it to be so. I know it is not possible.'

'If you'd just go to the house,' she begged. 'See for yourself.'

'There is no point.' His tone hardened. 'My bride taunted me with the news of her pregnancy on our wedding night, just after the consummation of our marriage had revealed that she was by no means the innocent virgin her father had claimed.'

'She told you—that?' Chilled with bewilderment, Joanna wrapped her arms round her body. 'Oh, how could she?'

He shrugged. 'We were not marrying for love, Joanna *mou,*' he said cynically. 'It was not a romance. Our union had been arranged as part of a much wider business arrangement with the Philipou organisation. My father told me bluntly it was time my bachelor existence, however enjoyable, came to an end, and I accepted that. Therefore Ariadne and I were acquainted, but no more. However, you must believe that I intended to treat her gently and with the respect her purity deserved once she became my wife. She, on the other hand, made it clear that she wished to punish me because I was not the man she wanted.

'Her confession had the desired result. I left her bedroom and never returned, while the amount of time we spent in each other's company afterwards can be counted in hours and minutes rather than days. But neither of us knew that she had a serious health problem, although it seems she complained of headaches from time to time.' He spread his hands. 'Now you know it all. But it changes nothing,' he added warningly. 'You should not have involved yourself with the child Eleni, and you will not do so again.'

Joanna looked down at the floor. She said with difficulty, 'I know I spoke harshly to you just now. I realise you don't deserve it, and I—I'm sorry for the things I said. I—didn't understand.'

'No,' he said bitterly. 'In truth, Joanna, you understand very little.' He paused. 'However, I will instruct Stavros to deal with the matters you have brought to my attention. It may be that the child would be better in the care of a respectable family on Thaliki, although they will need to be well paid for their discretion.'

'But whatever her mother did, Eleni isn't to blame.' Joanna looked at him pleadingly. 'She's an innocent party in all this. And what she needs more than anything is some real family life.' She hesitated. 'What about her grandfather? Mr Philipou? Wouldn't he take her?'

'He died six weeks after the wedding, in bed with his mistress,' Vassos said curtly. 'My own father died two years ago, believing I was a childless widower, and that is how it remains. I have taken financial responsibility for Ariadne's child. I shall do no more. And nor will you, so there is nothing further to discuss.' He walked to his desk and sat down. 'I will see you at dinner.'

'But I promised Eleni I would go back tomorrow,' Joanna said desperately. 'So, please may I do so—even if it's only to say goodbye? I—I can't break my word. Not to a child.'

Vassos looked at her with hauteur, his dark brows drawing together. 'You had no right to give such a promise,' he said coldly. 'And my decision is made. Perhaps you will think of the consequences in future before you interfere in affairs that do not concern you.' And he drew a file towards him and opened it, signalling the end of the interview.

She said very quietly, 'Vassos—I beg you. Have a little mercy. I—I'm all she's got.'

'That is hardly an argument to use with me, *matia mou*.' He did not look at her. 'Saying you can be generous with a child who is a stranger to you when you have given me less than nothing. Perhaps you have not considered that mercy can work both ways.'

He added politely, 'And now, if you will excuse me, I have work to do.'

She said numbly, 'Yes—yes, of course.' And left him, the dismissive words 'less than nothing' still burning in her brain.

And they were still there, tormenting her, hours later as she lay in bed, watching the moonlight make patterns on her tiled floor through the slatted shutters and waiting for the summons to his room that she knew now was not going to come.

The evening, as a whole, had not gone well, starting with her realisation that the table on the terrace was set for three and Stavros would be joining them for dinner.

It was not the first time it had happened, of course, but she'd thought that, after this time apart, Vassos would wish to be alone with her.

Instead she had sat, toying with her food, while the two men spoke softly to each other in their own language, their faces serious and purposeful. When the meal ended, Stavros rose, bade her a punctilious goodnight, and went. And almost at once Vassos excused himself quietly, saying he had work to finish, and left, too.

Leaving her without the chance she'd hoped for to begin to put right all the things that had gone wrong between them earlier. The assumptions she'd made—the accusations she'd levelled—had given him every right to be angry with her. She accepted that.

Soula duped me, she thought, and as a result I simply fooled myself into seeing a resemblance that didn't exist. Maybe—as Vassos said—I wanted it to be so, and it became so.

That must be how it happened.

And yet—and yet...

She stopped there. It was no good wishing that things were different. That she could wave a magic wand and make everything right. She had to deal with her life here as it was.

But at the same time she knew that she needed to try to find a chink in the wall of bitterness he'd built around himself after the appalling events of his marriage.

To repair the damage, somehow, and in doing so perhaps find again the man who'd held and caressed her with such astonishing tenderness.

The man she'd deliberately rejected to protect herself from the truth of her own feelings. A truth she could not admit in words.

He'd spoken of mercy, she thought. But instead she would offer him warmth, desire and passion, letting him see in this long-delayed surrender how deeply she'd yearned for him.

She slid out of bed, shrugging off her nightgown and letting it fall to the floor. She wrapped herself in the shawl, and walked in barefoot silence the length of the passage to Vassos' room.

She'd thought he would be asleep, but he was sitting propped up by pillows, reading more documents by the light of his bedside lamp.

As she hesitated just inside the door, he looked at her, brows lifting.

He said quietly, 'I did not invite you to join me.'

'Nevertheless I'm here.' She paused, aware this was not what she'd expected, adding uncertainly, 'Do you want me to leave?'

The dark eyes surveyed her, lingering on the lines of her

slender body which the cobweb veiling of the shawl did little to conceal.

'No,' he said, a faint smile playing about his mouth as he put his papers on the night table. 'Perhaps, after all, I do not.'

In obedience to his brief, imperative gesture, Joanna dropped the shawl and walked naked to the bed. She was blushing as she did so, but her gaze did not waver from his.

She lifted the cover of the single sheet and slid on to the mattress beside him.

He turned on to his side, propping himself on an elbow. His voice was even. 'What are you doing here, Joanna?'

She played with the embroidered hem of the sheet. 'Maybe I don't like sleeping by myself.'

'Yet when I have been here you have done so every night except one.' He sounded almost matter-of-fact.

Her flush deepened. 'Yes, I know that. But we've been apart for over a week. I thought you might have—missed me.'

'You assume then that I also spent my nights alone during my time in Athens?' He sounded amused.

For a moment Joanna felt winded, as if she'd been abruptly rammed in the stomach by a fist.

She swallowed, controlling the sudden anguished flurry of her breathing. Fighting the flare of pain his casual remark had ignited.

She said in a low voice, 'You indicated this afternoon that I should learn to mind my own business. Therefore, I have no right to know what you do when you're—away from me. Or even to ask.'

And, hardest of all, no right to care...

'My congratulations,' he gibed. 'It seems you have mastered one lesson at least. Now, why are you really here?'

She was silent for a long moment, then she said, her voice quivering a little, 'Perhaps to acquire a—different kind of knowledge.'

She touched his bare shoulder with fingers that trembled, letting them trace an uneven trail down his chest.

Vassos drew a sharp breath, then took the edge of the concealing sheet and tossed it away, down to the foot of the bed, leaving them naked together in the lamplight.

She was assailed by the thought of the sophisticated and experienced women who had been his lovers in the past. Maybe, she thought unhappily, in the very recent past, as he'd hinted. And what did she have to offer? she asked herself as nervousness mingled with a sense of her own gaucherie almost overwhelmed her.

When she spoke, her voice shook. 'I thought that you...'

'Oh, no, *pedhi mou.* If, at last, you truly wish to know how the joining of a man and a woman can touch the edge of Paradise, then you must discover this for yourself. Seduce me as at first I tried to seduce you.'

She said wretchedly, 'But I don't know how. I—I don't know anything...'

'It is not so difficult.' His voice gentled. 'Unlike a woman, Joanna *mou,* I cannot hide the fact that I want you. So you can only win. And, as a beginning, you could kiss me.'

He reached for her, drawing her close and winding his fingers in her hair as he brought her mouth slowly to his.

Her lips were shy as they touched him, but she had the remembered gentleness of his own first kisses—the offered tenderness to guide her as her mouth moved softly, persuasively on his, caressing the firm contours of his lips until finally she coaxed them to part for her, her body melting at the honeyed sweetness of his tongue gliding against hers.

As their kiss deepened, became more urgent, Joanna slid her arms round his neck, arching her body against him so that the already sensitive peaks of her breasts grazed his chest in aching tumescence, and, in turn, she felt the steel hardness of his erection surge against her in unspoken demand.

She was drowning in her longing for him, scalding in the liquid heat of her own desire. Desperate to take him inside her and surrender to the promised consummation of her need.

But some instinct told her not yet. Wait a little. And, in

obedience to its compulsion, she began to press tiny, fleeting kisses to the strong column of his throat. Swift, teasing contacts that would arouse but not satisfy, she thought from some warm, dazed corner of her mind, wondering how she could possibly know this.

At the same time she allowed her hands to slide across the width of his shoulders, then move with lingering emphasis down the lean strong body, following the dark shadowing of hair from his chest to his stomach and beyond. And where her hands touched, her mouth followed.

Vassos lay back, his eyes closed, his body taut under the silken passage of her fingers and lips. He did not speak, but the sharp indrawn breath he could not control told her better than words of the effect her untutored caresses were having.

And when she reached the proud male shaft, encircling its heated, jutting power in the clasp of her hand and stroking it gently, she heard him give a hoarse groan of pleasure.

He turned to her, his mouth seeking hers, invading it in passionate demand, while his hands cupped her breasts, fondling their delicate curves, stirring her to a delight that was almost pain as his fingers teased her engorged nipples.

Her arms went round him, her hands exploring the long, graceful back and flat, muscular buttocks, and he smiled into her eyes as his hand slid down between her parted thighs to discover the burning moisture of her surrender and to explore it with heart-stopping eroticism.

Joanna gasped against his lips as his questing fingertip penetrated the satin folds of her secret woman's flesh to find her tiny hidden bud and caress it to a pinnacle of aching, soaring arousal.

Every nerve-ending in her skin seemed to be coming searingly alive under the rhythmic certainty of his touch—every sense, every atom of feeling in the core of her being gloriously coalescing into some unimagined and unimaginable culmination.

She felt herself poised on an unknown brink, and from some

distant space she heard her own husky whisper—'Please—oh, please...'

Heard his own hoarse response, *'Agapi mou.'*

And in the next instant found herself overtaken and overwhelmed by the piercing, shuddering wonder of her first climax.

As the pulsations reached their peak, Vassos' hands closed on her slender waist, lifting her over him, then lowering her on to him with infinite care until his hard, virile strength was totally sheathed inside her, forcing a small sob of delight from her quivering lips.

And Joanna, obeying the same instinct that had guided her before, began to move on him, with him, her inner muscles still clenching powerfully and sweetly around him, and her sensitised skin responding rapturously to the warm drift of his hands on her breasts, her belly, her hips and down to the shadowed cleft of her thighs.

Aware of the intensity of his half-closed eyes as they watched the sway of her slim body above her, and the harsh sigh of his breathing.

She heard it quicken almost hectically, then Vassos flung back his head, his skin dewed with sweat, the veins standing out on his neck, and a sound that might have been her name was torn from his throat as she felt him spasm fiercely inside her.

She slumped forward, burying her face in his damp shoulder as she yielded to the delicious languor enveloping her.

They lay wrapped together for a while, until the wild spinning of the world returned to normality and their breathing steadied, then Vassos moved slowly, detaching himself from her.

There was a long silence, then he said quietly and coolly, 'So, Joanna *mou,* having pleasured me so exquisitely, have you nothing to ask from me in return? Some favour, perhaps?'

Only—how soon can we do this again? Joanna reflected,

blushing a little. Then paused, wondering, because surely he must know the pleasure had been completely mutual.

She said aloud, 'I—I don't understand what you mean.'

'No? Yet it is surely quite simple. You want my permission to visit the child Eleni, as you requested this afternoon. And you are determined to have your way. After all, what else could have prompted the ardour of such a performance?'

He added silkily, 'I do not complain, you understand. But I must also be realistic. You wished to buy my acquiescence by offering me the only coin you thought I would accept. But you should be more subtle in your trading, *pedhi mou*. Because, in spite of this delightful and astonishing interlude, my answer to your request still remains—no. And as I shall not change my mind, no matter what further enticements you offer, you may prefer now to return to your own room. But please believe I shall always be—grateful.'

CHAPTER TWELVE

JOANNA stared at him, stunned. For a moment her mind ran riot as she told herself he could not be serious—could not possibly mean those unkind, cynical remarks that he'd almost negligently tossed at her.

Not after what had just happened between them—surely? All that passion and glory reduced to the level of a—trade-off? It couldn't be true.

But there was none of the former tenderness in the level dark gaze, and no hint of amusement to soften the hard lines of the mouth that had set her ablaze with kisses such a short while before.

She found her voice at last. 'You really think that is why—'

'Of course,' Vassos interrupted coldly. 'What other reason could there be for such a transformation? Or did you think I would share your naïveté and assume your surrender was genuine and without strings?' He shook his head almost grimly. 'You misjudge me, *pedhi mou*.'

And you, she thought, misjudge me. Completely. Because I gave you my heart as well as my body just now. God knows, I didn't expect love in return, but if you'd spoken just one word of kindness my soul would have followed and I'd have been yours for ever.

There were tears, thick and painful in her chest and burning her throat, but she would not weep in front of him in case he thought it was just another ploy. Another trick to have her way over Eleni.

She said, her voice shaking a little, 'Yes, *kyrie*. It seems that I have made a mistake. But it will never happen again.'

It was torture having to leave the bed, naked under his sardonic gaze, in order to retrieve her shawl, but she did it, wrapping herself closely in its folds with hands that trembled, then walking to the door without looking back.

She managed to regain her room before she began to cry, throwing herself across the bed, and stifling her sobs in her pillow.

And when the first storm had subsided she got up stiffly and went to the bathroom, standing under the warm torrent of the shower, letting it wash away all trace of anything and everything that had happened that night.

Wishing at the same time that it was possible to remove the memories and the regrets as easily as the tearstains.

I should have known, she thought wearily as she dried herself. Should have realised what Vassos would think when I just—turned up in his bedroom like that. Except, of course, I wasn't thinking, because I totally forgot to use any reason and let myself be carried away by the force of my emotions. By my need for him.

I was stupid—*stupid*—and now that it's all gone wrong I have no one to blame but myself.

But, dear God, I wanted him so badly. Wanted to know at last what it was to be a woman. His woman. And to give him everything.

Instead, she now had to come to terms with the inescapable fact that becoming his sexual partner for a brief while did not make her into any kind of woman, she thought bitterly, and it never would.

She'd proved nothing except that she was still a child—a pathetic child, like poor little Eleni, hoping each day for a love that would never be offered. And having to wake each morning to the sombre reality of disappointment.

She chose a clean nightdress, straightened the disordered bed, and crept under the covering sheet to lie wakeful and wretched, her awakened body restless. And it was not until dawn streaked the sky that she finally fell into an uneasy sleep.

It was late when she awoke, and as she sat up pushing her hair out of her eyes, she saw the bedroom door open and Hara appear almost as if she'd received some signal.

'Kyrios Vassos says to let you sleep,' she announced. 'He has important visitors from mainland, talking business this morning. I bring you breakfast here.'

Presumably because he doesn't want my presence known, Joanna thought bleakly. Though I'm sure the fact he has a mistress will come as no surprise to any of his guests.

'And am I to stay here in my room until the business is concluded?' she asked tautly, as she drank her orange juice and spread apricot jam on a warm roll.

Hara looked shocked. 'By no means, *thespinis*. Kyrios Vassos suggests you spend the day by the pool. He will join you later when other men leave.'

Joanna poured some coffee. She said woodenly, 'Just as he wishes,' and saw the fleeting look of relief on the older woman's face.

But while he's safely occupied with his talks, she thought, I have some business of my own to conduct. Because I refuse to just vanish from Eleni's life, no matter whose child she may be. It would be too cruel. So, whatever he says, I will see her again, even if it is only to say goodbye.

And if I'm simply justifying everything he said to me last night—so be it. He would expect no better.

Her breakfast finished, she dressed in brief candy-striped shorts and a matching halter-top in blue and white, and set off with her book, sunglasses and tanning oil for the pool, where a lounger had already been placed for her under the shade of a parasol.

Making sure I obey orders and keep out of harm's way, she

thought wryly. And for the first hour she did exactly that, although it would be unwise to wait too long before she departed on her mission, she decided, getting up from her lounger.

She deliberately uncapped her sun oil, and left her book lying casually open on the lounger, as if she only expected to be gone for a few moments, then made her way to the far side of the pool area and through a gap in the hibiscus hedge.

There was no one about, the air hot and still, apart from the drone of insects. None of the security men was visible, not even the obnoxious Yanni, so presumably everyone's attention was firmly focussed on the meeting inside the villa.

Besides, she thought, Vassos would no doubt consider that his word was law, and she would not dare to flout it.

Well, he was wrong about me last night, she told herself defiantly, fighting down the hurt that the memory of his words engendered. And he's wrong again today, although he'll never know that.

All the same, she found herself hurrying, trying to figure out what she would say when she arrived at the house—whether or not she would challenge Soula over her assertions. And why she'd made them.

But it's probably better not to ask, she thought. Instead keep it short and simple. Explain that I may be leaving Pellas quite soon, and won't have time for more visits. Because it could even be the truth.

Sighing, she rounded the final bend in the track and halted, staring with disbelief and sudden fear at the small crumpled pile of pink lying on the sandy ground straight ahead of her, with an overturned tricycle beside it.

For a second Joanna remained motionless, then she broke into a run, dropping on her knees beside Eleni.

The little girl's eyes were closed, she was breathing rapidly and her skin looked sallow. There was a bruise on her forehead, and even Joanna's untrained eyes could see that one small wrist looked an odd shape.

Her heart sank. Her first-aid experience was non-existent,

but she seemed to remember that fractures should be supported.

She threw her head back and yelled Soula's name as loudly as she could. There was no answer, and after a moment she shouted for her again, adding, '*Ela etho!* Come quickly.'

But there was still no reply.

Shut up in the house, no doubt, Joanna thought bitterly. Smoking and reading those picture magazines of hers. So God knows how long Eleni's been lying here.

But what on earth was the woman doing, allowing her to come out unsupervised? Because she could see what had happened. The tricycle's front wheel had hit a hidden root and Eleni had been thrown off.

Well, I'm not leaving her, she told herself with grim resolve. I won't let her come round and find she's alone and in pain. I can carry her to the house, where I shall a few things to say to Madam Soula. But first I have to do something about her wrist.

After a brief hesitation she stripped off her halter-neck, and managed to fashion it into a makeshift sling. As she gently moved Eleni's arm into position, the child moaned faintly and opened bewildered eyes.

'It's all right, Eleni *mou*,' Joanna said quietly, and stroked the tumbled dark hair as the little girl began to cry. 'I'll try not to hurt you, but we need to find help.'

She got to her feet, lifting the child carefully in her arms. It was only about fifty yards to the house, but when they reached it the gate was standing wide open, and the door was also ajar.

Soula must have realised Eleni was missing and gone to search, she told herself, as she deposited the whimpering child on a couch covered by a crocheted blanket, at the side of the room, and surrounded her with cushions.

Her first task was to find a teatowel or something similar and make a proper sling, so that she could retrieve her top. Even in front of Eleni she felt thoroughly self-conscious without it, and she had no wish for Soula to return and find her bared to the waist, as she could well imagine the kind of sniggering contempt she'd have to endure.

As she crossed to the small dresser to look for a towel she noticed that the votive light which burned in front of the icon had been allowed to go out—only to realise in the next instant that the icon itself wasn't there.

For a moment she hesitated, then made for the flight of steep wooden stairs in the corner. Eleni's room was tidy enough, but the larger room with the double bed was in complete disarray, its sheets rumpled and one pillow lying on the floor, with yet another overflowing ashtray on the night table.

As Joanna looked around her, wrinkling her nose at the stale atmosphere, she saw that the clothes cupboard was standing open and empty, as were the drawers in the adjoining chest.

My God, Joanna thought, drawing an appalled breath. She's not out searching at all. She's—gone. She knew I was coming, so she's abandoned Eleni and skipped.

And if I hadn't disobeyed Vassos the child might have been left to lie on the path, alone and injured, with potentially disastrous consequences.

Her nails curled into the palms of her hands. 'The witch,' she said aloud, her voice shaking. 'The evil, disgusting, *bloody* witch!'

She heard a little wail from the room below, and ran for the stairs.

'It's all right, darling,' she called. 'I'm coming.'

'So I see,' said Vassos.

He stood in the open doorway, dark against the brightness of the sun, his hands on his hips, his face a mask of anger carved from granite. He was wearing dark pants and a white shirt, and his wide silk tie was pulled loose.

Joanna halted at the foot of the stairs, her hands lifting to cover her bare breasts in an instinctive gesture of modesty. As if, she thought with a pang, there was any part of her he had not seen—or touched—or kissed.

She said, 'Oh, Vassos, I'm so thankful that you're here.'

'Are you?' His mouth curled into a smile that was grim and derisive at the same time. He looked past her at the stairway. 'Who is up there?' His tone was politely enquiring.

She stared at him. 'Are you mad? What are you talking about? There's no one.'

'I am expected to believe that?' He took a step forward. 'Just as you tried to persuade me you came here each day to visit a child who is nothing to you?' He shook his head slowly, his eyes going over her. 'I think not. So, I ask you again, Joanna, who have you just left in the bedroom?'

'Not a soul. The house is empty. See for yourself, if you want.' Her voice shook a little. 'Soula's left, and taken all her things. I only discovered it when I came back here with Eleni. She was in the grove, you see, and I found her. She's had an accident and broken her arm, so I had to use my top to make a sling for her,' she added, glancing down at herself and biting her lip.

'I saw the icon was missing, and went to check upstairs. I found that Soula had—gone—vanished—and if I hadn't come today Eleni would have been totally alone, because no one else ever comes here. God knows what might have happened to her. She's only a baby,' she went on, her voice cracking. 'A baby who desperately needs to see a doctor, while you stand there making—ludicrous accusations.'

She saw him turn, as if aware for the first time of the child in her nest of pillows.

He walked over to the couch and bent to look at the small arm in its makeshift support, and Joanna heard him say something quiet and savage under his breath.

'How did this happen?' he demanded.

'She fell off her tricycle. She bumped her head, too.'

'Yes.' He straightened, discarding his tie, then stripping off his shirt. He tossed it to Joanna. 'Cover yourself,' he directed brusquely.

'Oh, what does it matter?'

'It matters to me,' he said. 'We have to return to the villa, and I do not choose that any man but myself should see you even half-naked.'

The crisp fabric was still warm from his body, and she was aware of the scent of the cologne he used as she slipped her arms into the sleeves and fumbled the buttons into their holes.

'What's going to happen?' she asked, as Vassos bent and lifted the child into his arms with infinite care.

'She shall be taken to Thaliki. There is a hospital there. It is small but efficient, and she will receive excellent treatment.'

'And—afterwards?' Joanna watched him carry Eleni to the door. Look at her, she begged silently. Oh, my darling, look at her and see what I saw—please.

'Decisions will have to be made,' he returned curtly. 'Also Soula must be found. Wherever she is hiding,' he added ominously. 'She may have abandoned her charge, but there is no way that she can have left the island.'

She had to trot to keep up with his long stride. 'Why did you come here? I thought you were in a meeting.'

'It ended much sooner than I expected,' he responded bleakly. 'And in agreement, which I also did not anticipate. Once my colleagues had departed, I looked for you. When you could not be found, I guessed where you must be.'

'I had to do it,' she said in a low voice. 'You must understand that. And Soula must have known that, too.'

'It was a risk she had no right to take,' he said harshly.

After that there was silence between them until they reached the villa, where Andonis met them with an appalled look at the small crying burden in his employer's arms, then burst into a flood of agitated Greek.

Vassos listened, his head bent, his mouth hardening.

He turned to Joanna. 'Soula may have left Pellas after all,' he said harshly. 'The *caique* I use for night fishing has also disappeared, and so, it seems, has Yanni, one of the security men.' He paused. 'Did you ever see them together?'

Joanna bit her lip. 'No, but she was often missing in the afternoons.'

He said something under his breath. 'Then Hara will tend the child until Stavros returns with the launch and she can be taken to hospital.' His tone was brusque. 'There is nothing more for you to do.'

Joanna faced him, chin lifted defiantly. 'On the contrary, *kyrie*,' she said crisply. 'I shall go to the hospital with her. She's frightened and in pain, and she needs one familiar face around. Someone who actually cares about her.' She paused. 'And—in case you've forgotten—her name is Eleni.'

'This is not your concern—' he began, but she interrupted him fiercely.

'So you've told me, but I've just made it so. I'm going to my room to put on some proper clothes, so bring her there to me, please.'

She walked past Andonis, who looked as if he'd been poleaxed, and made for the stairs, aware that Vassos was staring after her.

In her room, she dragged off his shirt, wrenching open the buttons with such force that she sent several of them skittering across the floor.

'To hell with it,' she muttered, sending the shirt to join them. 'He'll have a thousand others to take its place.'

She removed her shorts, replacing them with a green dress, full-skirted and short-sleeved, grabbed at random from the wardrobe.

She was dragging a comb through her hair when Vassos knocked abruptly and entered with Eleni, crying loudly and fretfully now in his arms, and an anxious Hara close behind.

'Stavros has been contacted by radio,' he said. 'He will be here very soon.' He paused. 'The *caique* has been seen drifting, perhaps with engine trouble, by some fishermen.'

She said stonily, 'I wouldn't care if it had blown up.' She

sat down on the chair by the window. 'Give Eleni to me, please.'

He said more gently, 'Let Hara take her, Joanna *mou*.'

'No.' She shook her head. 'I began this. So I'll look after her while she's here. After all, you can't pretend that anyone here wants her, not when you all did your best to keep us apart.' She took the sobbing child gently on her lap, looking down at the creased and dirty pink dress.

'And, whatever you decide for her, *kyrie,* she'll need new clothes,' she added. 'Normal things, too. Not more of these awful party frocks that Soula picked for her. Because her life's going to be no party.'

'Joanna.' His voice was quiet. 'Let us talk about this.'

'And say what? That I shouldn't have interfered? I think it's already been said.'

She bent her head. 'And I suppose I have to agree with you. If I hadn't—intervened as I did, Soula would never have dared to go off like this and Eleni wouldn't have been put in danger.' She paused. 'Also you wouldn't have been forced to remember your—your marriage and its unhappiness. Is that what you want to hear?'

'No,' he said. 'But why should you believe me?' He turned and left the room, signalling to Hara to accompany him.

Joanna leaned back, careful not to jolt Eleni's injured arm. She felt very tired suddenly, with the beginnings of a headache. But that was nothing compared with the desolation inside her.

I wanted to help, she thought wretchedly, but instead I've simply made everything much worse. Because this accident will have to be explained somehow, and that will trigger all the problems that Vassos most wants to avoid.

And now, she realised, to add to her feelings of guilt, the child's warm body was curling trustingly into hers, and her sobs were beginning to subside a little.

'Try and sleep, darling,' Joanna said softly as Eleni's thumb stole to her mouth and her eyelids drooped. 'The doctor will stop your poor arm aching very soon.' And quietly she began to sing, '"There were ten green bottles, hanging on the wall…"'

She was over halfway through the song, deliberately allowing her voice to sink lower, watching Eleni's small face relax and her breathing steady and deepen, when she felt her own skin begin to tingle as if she was being watched. Knowing that there was only one person in the world who could trigger that particular reaction.

But when, at last, she ventured to glance towards the doorway it was empty. I must have been imagining things, she told herself with an inward sigh. Or just indulging in some wishful thinking.

And her song was finished, and she was sitting cradling the sleeping child, prey to her unhappy thoughts, well before Hara came to tell her that Stavros and the launch had returned and it was time to go.

The hospital on Thaliki might not be large, but Joanna saw at once that it was scrupulously clean and efficiently run, as Vassos had said.

Dr Deroulos, who came to take charge of Eleni, was a short man, his hair and beard grizzled, his eyes calm and kind, as Joanna haltingly explained there had been an accident with a tricycle.

'These things happen with small children,' was his comment. He gave Joanna a thoughtful look. 'And you, *thespinis?* Who are you?'

She said quietly, 'I'm Eleni's temporary nanny,' and did not look at Vassos, standing beside her like a statue.

Eleni was borne away to have her arm set and plastered, and to be checked for any signs of concussion after the bump on her head.

Joanna and Vassos retired to a small, square waiting room, silently taking chairs on its opposite sides. After a while, Joanna ventured to steal a look at him from under her lashes,

and saw that his face was set like stone, and that he was staring into space with eyes that seemed to see nothing.

After half an hour had passed, with nothing being said on
either side, they were joined by Stavros. Vassos listened to his
murmured words, then rose, looking across at Joanna.

'The police have boarded the *caique* and arrested Yanni
and Soula,' he said brusquely. 'I am required to help deal with
this matter, and I must also arrange for Kostas, who goes fishing with me at night to collect the boat. There will be state-
ments. Maybe a question of charges.' He paused. 'Will you be
all right—alone here?'

'Yes,' she said. 'Of course.'

And being alone is something I shall have to get used to.

She paused. 'Did you say you go fishing at night?'

He paused at the door, brows lifting. 'Sometimes,' he said.
'If I find I cannot sleep. Why do you ask?'

'It just seems—an odd thing to do,' Joanna returned, thinking of all the times his footsteps had passed her door in the
darkness.

'But then,' he said softly. 'So many other strange things
seem to be happening in my life. *Herete andio,* Joanna.' And
he went.

Over an hour had passed before Dr Deroulos returned with
the news that the fracture had been reduced, the bump on
Eleni's head was just what it seemed and nothing more serious, and the little girl would soon recover from the anaesthetic
she'd been given while her arm received attention.

'Oh, thank heavens.' Joanna sank back on her chair. 'I've
been so worried.'

'You must not blame yourself, *thespinis,*' he told her kindly.
'And nor, I am sure, does Kyrios Gordanis. A healthy child
must be allowed to run and play. And little Eleni, in spite of
her unpromising beginning, is now fit and well. Her father
must rejoice to see it.' He glanced round. 'He has gone somewhere?'

'To the police station, I think,' Joanna said awkwardly. 'There's been a—problem with the previous nanny.'

'*Po, po, po,* he should marry again,' the doctor said. 'Provide his daughter with a mother's care. After all a young, virile man cannot be expected to grieve for ever.' He frowned a little. 'I think it haunts him still that he was not present at the birth or at his wife's side when she so sadly died. But with a premature child like Eleni these things are not always possible to arrange. I just thank the good God that, after a struggle, we were able to save her for him, so he did not have a double tragedy to bear.'

Joanna stared at him. 'You say Eleni was—premature?' She shook her head. 'I—I didn't know that.' She hesitated. 'How early was she?'

'Barely seven months.' He sighed. 'And so tiny—so fragile. For days she hovered between life and death.'

Joanna said urgently, 'Did Vassos—Kyrios Gordanis, I mean—know this? How delicate Eleni was—and why?'

'He was in shock after the death of Kyria Ariadne, *thespinis*. Like a man living through a nightmare. My colleague Dr Christaphis decided it would be wrong to burden him with the possibility of further sadness.'

He smiled suddenly. 'And it did not happen. The Holy Virgin had the child in her protection and she was spared, to become healthy and happy.' He spread his hands. 'So what was said or not said at the time surely cannot matter. Not now. Not any more.'

'On the contrary,' Joanna said softly, her heart lifting. 'I think it could matter very much, Dr Deroulos. Very much indeed.'

CHAPTER THIRTEEN

IT WAS another hour before Vassos returned.

Joanna had spent the time on tenterhooks, mentally rehearsing what she wanted to say. What he so desperately needed to know.

But when he finally appeared in the waiting room doorway, she took one look at his exhausted eyes, and the greyish tinge to his skin as he halted, putting out a hand as if to steady himself against the doorframe, then jumped to her feet, spilling the remains of the coffee they'd brought her down her skirt.

All the careful words were forgotten. She said, 'Vassos—about Eleni. There's something I must tell you.'

He lifted a silencing finger. 'I already know what you are going to say, Joanna. I have heard the whole story from Soula Karadis, no doubt in the vain hope that the truth would make me grateful enough to spare her.'

His voice was almost toneless. 'It would seem that my late wife hated me even more than I thought possible. She did have a lover before our marriage—but her pregnancy by him was just a figment of her imagination, invented to drive me away. Which means that Eleni is indeed my daughter, born from the one moment of intimacy in our marriage. But brought into the world much too soon, when her mother decided to throw herself down a flight of steps to rob me of the son she believed she was carrying. Something else I did not know until now.'

He added harshly, 'It is almost beyond belief. Yet, having known Ariadne, even briefly, I find I can—and do—believe it.'

He looked at her. 'And you have heard—what?'

'Nothing like that,' she denied huskily. 'Just that Eleni was born at least two months premature, and they were afraid she wouldn't survive.' She ran the tip of her tongue round her dry lips. 'But no one told you at the time because it was felt you had enough to bear with your—grief for your wife.'

'Ironic, is it not?' His smile was a slash of pain. 'And yet I think I did experience an element of grief, if only for a young life cut off so suddenly and so harshly. Guilt, too,' he added bitterly, 'that I did not realise just how much she resented our proposed marriage and stop it for both our sakes while I had the chance. Although it is doubtful if that would have kept her alive.

'But she had her revenge.' His voice thickened. 'She died leaving me with the hideous belief that my daughter was another man's child. Someone I could not even bear to look at. And by doing so Ariadne robbed me of the right to love her—to enjoy her babyhood and watch her grow.' His voice sank to a whisper. 'And I might never have known. Never...'

'But you do know now,' Joanna said fiercely. 'So everything can change. That's what really matters.' She looked away from him, her throat tightening, longing to go to him and feel his arms close around her. But instead forcing herself to remain where she was. 'It—it's all that can matter.'

'Except,' he said, 'that I owe this knowledge to you. If you had not gone to the house today...' He closed his eyes. 'I do not want to think what might have happened.'

'Then think of something else,' she said. 'Like being beside Eleni's bedside when she wakes up next time.' She paused, trying to smile. 'I hope she'll be more welcoming for you. She was cross and a little nauseous when she came round from the anaesthetic, and demanded to be sung to.'

'Ah,' Vassos said quietly. 'That same song I first heard in the gardens at the St Gregoire?'

She stared at him. 'You—heard me?'

'I heard a baby crying,' he said. 'And a girl singing a lullaby. So, I stood and listened for a while, and wondered if the singer was as lovely as her voice. I did not know, of course— how could I?—that she was the beauty I had seen earlier from the deck of *Persephone,* or the girl I planned to meet later that night across a poker table.'

He drew a deep breath. 'And today I heard you comforting a sick child with the same melody. And for a moment I could not believe it.' He paused. 'Why were you there in the garden that night?'

She looked down at the floor. 'I was just babysitting for a couple I'd met.' She found a resolute smile from somewhere. 'And I really liked taking care of Matthew, so I've decided I shall train to look after children professionally one day.'

One day when I'm back in England, and need to find a life for myself—a life that you are no longer a part of. When other people's children may be all I can hope for...

He was frowning. 'Is that why you told Deroulos that you were Eleni's nanny?'

'I had to think of some reason for being here.' She flushed a little. 'After all, I could hardly say I was your mistress.'

'No,' he said, his mouth twisting. 'Perhaps, for the time being, the fiction that you are Eleni's nursemaid will serve us better, *pedhi mou.*'

And maybe, she whispered silently, for the sake of my aching heart, it might be better—easier—if fiction becomes fact. If I become your employee instead of your pillow friend from now on—until you send me away.

As they walked along the passage towards the small private room where Eleni was installed, Dr Deroulos was coming to meet them.

'Your daughter is awake, Kyrios Gordanis.' He turned a

kindly smile on Joanna. 'And once again demanding you, *thespinis*.'

Joanna halted. She said quietly, 'I think she should spend some time alone with her father now.' She indicated her coffee-stained skirt. 'Maybe I could go somewhere and clean my dress?'

'But of course. It will be a pleasure.' He signalled to a female orderly, and Joanna was whisked off to a gleaming washroom and supplied with a sponge and towels for a strictly rudimentary rescue job.

But what did a ruined dress matter? she asked herself bleakly, surveying her reflection in the mirror, when it was her life that was about to fall apart?

Yes, Vassos was grateful to her, but she did not want him to turn to her in gratitude, because her intervention had restored his child to him. She needed far more from him than that.

Now, when it was too late, she wanted the tender, passionate lover whom she'd so signally rejected so many times. Wanted to offer him again all the warmth and the ardent, generous desire he'd kindled in her. And to prove to him, beyond all doubt, that her gift to him came from the heart, and without strings.

I love him, she thought painfully, and I always will, but I can't stay with him, longing all the time for something he can never give. Knowing I have nothing to hope for except his transient desire. And even that will end.

He took me for all the wrong reasons, at a time when his bed and his life were both empty and he needed entertainment. Distraction.

But now the circumstances have changed. He has a daughter to love, who will adore him in return. And one day he'll remarry, this time to a girl who will love him and give Eleni brothers and sisters. And then that barren house will come alive again at last.

At which time, please God, I shall be far away.

When she finally emerged from the washroom, she turned

initially to go back to the waiting room, then after a moment's hesitation made her way quietly along the passage to
the ward.

The door was open and she could see Vassos kneeling
beside the bed, Eleni's small hand clasped in his, and his head
was bent as if he was crying—or praying.

Whichever it was, Joanna thought, her heart twisting as
tears stung her eyes, her presence would only be an intrusion.
And she stole silently away.

She had herself strictly under control when he eventually
returned to the waiting room.

'How is she?' she asked brightly.

'Well, and asking for almond biscuits.' He paused. 'However,
the doctor suggests that she remain here overnight so that he
can make sure there are no after-effects from all the shocks
she has suffered today.' His smile was wry. 'I suspect I am not
the least of them.'

Joanna bit her lip. 'Ever since she's been able to understand
what was being said to her, she's been told, "Papa will come."
And now you have done.'

'And now Papa will stay,' he said softly. 'And we will take
her home in the morning.'

Joanna glanced uncertainly at the waiting room chairs. 'You
mean—spend the night here?'

'No.' His tone was faintly brusque. 'Thaliki has a hotel—
the Poseidon. They will have a room for us.'

'But we'll need two,' she said. 'One for you—and another
for Eleni's nanny.'

There was an odd silence, then he said, 'Is that truly what
you wish? To spend this night apart from me?'

'Yes, or I wouldn't have said it.' She lifted her chin, fighting her inner misery. 'You should know that by now.'

'At times like this I feel as if I know nothing about you,
Joanna *mou*,' he said harshly. 'Nothing at all.' He paused.
'And now Eleni is waiting to say goodnight to you. I warn

you, she may ask for another song. I hope she will not also
be disappointed.'

And he walked out into the corridor, leaving her to
follow.

It had been, Joanna thought, as she lay in bed, staring at the
ceiling, the longest two weeks of her life. And here she was,
faced with yet another sunlit morning. Which, somehow, she
would have to survive.

At least in the daytime she could keep busy, looking after
Eleni who'd adapted with astonishing speed to her new circumstances, even with a plaster on her arm. Proving, Joanna
mused, just how resilient children could be.

And for this, admittedly, Vassos deserved much of the
credit, approaching his new role as a father with patience,
humour and an element of firmness. Above all spending un-
stinted time with her, overcoming her initial shyness and, in
return, receiving his daughter's unquestioning adoration.

But, rather to Joanna's concern, Eleni was inclined to treat
her in much the same way, which she feared might lead to
problems when a real nanny was eventually appointed in her
place.

Vassos had made several flying visits to Athens over the
past fortnight, presumably to interview potential candidates,
but seemed to have made no final choice.

In fact, Joanna had started to wonder if he might choose a
British nanny, as he also appeared to be teaching Eleni to use
English as well as Greek names for the things she saw around
her, but when she'd ventured to ask him, on one of the few
occasions when they'd been briefly alone, he'd retorted that
English was the international language of commerce throughout the world and Eleni, as an adult, might well need to speak
it fluently.

Which did not sound, she thought unhappily, as if he ever
expected to have a son to succeed him.

Apart from that, relations between them were studiedly

formal. And when Eleni was not around he seemed quiet and preoccupied, as if in another less sunlit world.

She'd become a member of his staff, she thought painfully. Just as she'd asked. Except that she'd never dreamed how difficult it would be to make such a transition. To share a roof with him, but nothing else.

In the daytime she could cope. Just. But the nights were a very different matter.

She was no longer occupying her former room but, at her own suggestion, had moved to one adjoining Eleni's new nursery, in case the little girl needed anything in the night.

Hara had indicated, clearly bewildered at this turn of events, that a couple of the maids could take over Eleni's night-time supervision, the entire household having become her devoted slaves from the moment the child entered the villa, but Joanna had refused with determination, saying that the little girl would prefer to see a familiar face if she woke.

In fact Eleni was a sound sleeper, so Joanna was rarely disturbed in this way, but that made little difference to the wreckage of her own sleep patterns. Heartache and loneliness were her regular companions during long and restless vigils.

And when she did sleep her dreams were erotic fantasies that woke her, gasping, her body on fire, her hands reaching for him and finding emptiness.

She was losing weight, and the shadows beneath her eyes were deepening into violet pools.

I'm fretting, she told herself wryly. And, heaven help me, it shows. So, perhaps it's a good thing that Vassos rarely looks at me these days.

She flung back the sheet and left the bed, taking a quick shower before dressing in a midi-skirt, in shades of rust and gold, topped with a sleeveless cream shirt. Her hair she brushed back and secured at the nape of her neck with an elastic band.

Then she went next door to rouse Eleni, wash and dress her, then take her down to breakfast on the terrace.

Vassos rose from the table at their approach. *'Kalimera,'* he said softly, inclining his head to Joanna before going down on his haunches to greet Eleni with a kiss as she ran to him.

Joanna sat down, busying herself with buttering a slice of bread, adding honey, and pouring a glass of milk for Eleni. She applauded, smiling, as the little girl, prompted by Vassos, pointed to each item in turn and said its English name, before collapsing in giggles.

As Joanna poured her own coffee, and set down the pot, Vassos said abruptly, 'Joanna, I must tell you that Stavros has gone to Thaliki to bring back Eleni's new nursemaid. My cousin Maria has found a girl who has worked with English families in Athens, so can speak your language well. Her name is Mitsa, which is short for Artemis, and she comes highly recommended.'

He paused. 'I have also made immediate arrangements for your departure, which I hope will please you. When breakfast is over, I suggest that you pack.'

Joanna stared at him, her whole being suddenly numb. She said in a voice she didn't recognise, 'So soon?' *And just that brief dismissal as if there had been nothing between us? Nothing...*

'I feel it would be best,' he said. 'Before Eleni becomes too dependent on you.'

Her mouth was dry. 'Yes,' she said. 'I suppose that is—a danger. And I—I wouldn't want to do anything to hurt her.'

His faint smile did not reach his eyes. 'No,' he said. 'That is one thing I can be sure of. And in that she has been fortunate indeed.'

She forced herself to drink her coffee and eat a roll with black cherry jam, in spite of the desperate churning of her stomach.

I'm going, she thought. I'll never see him again, and I don't know how I can bear it. Especially when he clearly can't wait to be rid of me.

She supposed she should ask about her travel plans—or at

least what UK airport she was destined for. She'd find Chris and Julie's address—ask them if they could put her up for a night or two while she tried to make some kind of rational decision about her future.

She pushed her chair back and rose. 'If you'll excuse me, I'll get ready. I'll only take the things I brought here with me, so it won't take long.'

He took a table napkin and wiped Eleni's sticky fingers. 'As you wish,' he said, after a long pause, adding, without looking up, 'Eleni will stay with me while you make your final preparations.'

When she reached her room, Hara had already brought the small case which had arrived on Pellas with her. It was open on the bed, displaying its meagre contents, the black crochet dress and the white boots on top of the other things.

'This is a day of much sadness, *thespinis*. Why do you go when you are needed here?'

'Someone called Mitsa will be looking after Eleni,' Joanna returned over-brightly. 'She'll be fine.'

'I do not speak of the child, Kyria Joanna, but her father. Who is to care for Kyrios Vassos if you do not?'

Joanna retrieved the black dress and its body stocking and began to change into them. Leaving, she thought, the way she'd arrived.

She said haltingly, 'Well, there's you—and Andonis. And Eleni herself, of course. And there are plenty of other women in the world—especially his world.' She tried to smile. 'He once told me that one girl is very like another.'

'*Po, po, po,*' Hara dismissed with a snort. 'That is when he knew nothing. Now he knows everything—and he suffers. You should stay,' she added coaxingly. 'Make him happy in bed. Give him more babies.'

Joanna shook her head. 'That isn't possible.' *Because it's the last thing he wants. He's made that clear.* 'I have another life in England,' she hurried on. 'And I need to get back to it.' *And somehow begin to heal...*

Hara snorted again and went off, muttering under her breath.

She was fastening her case when Stavros knocked at the door. 'Kyrios Gordanis requests you join him in the *saloni, thespinis.*'

He took the case from her hand, and followed her to the stairs. Joanna went down them, the heels of the white boots clicking, her head held high, feeling the thud of her heart against her ribcage.

'Please don't let him offer me money,' she whispered under her breath. 'Just my ticket home and no more. I need to get through this with my pride left, if nothing else.'

And knew just how deep, how painful and how endless 'nothing else' might well be.

Andonis was waiting to open the door of the *saloni* for her, and, taking a deep breath, Joanna walked into the room beyond and paused, looking across at Vassos, his face pale under its tan and strangely haggard, the dark eyes fixed on her with an aching intensity that struck her like a blow—because she recognised it. Shared it.

Joanna took one quick, involuntary step towards him, then stopped as another voice said her name, and she realised for the first time that they were not alone.

Incredulously, she whirled round in the direction of the speaker.

'Daddy?' Her voice cracked on the word. 'What are you doing here?'

'I've come to take you back where you belong, Joanna.' Denys Vernon crossed to where she was standing and kissed her awkwardly on the forehead. He was wearing a light-coloured suit with wide lapels and a flowered shirt open at the neck, all clearly expensive. His hair had been cut short on top, growing down into sideburns.

He looked sleek and prosperous, Joanna thought, but his eyes were restless and did not meet hers.

He added, tight-lipped, 'Mr Gordanis has finally decided he has no more use for you, and has summoned us to fetch you.'

Vassos said nothing, but turned away, walking over to the windows, his body taut, his hands clenching into fists at his sides.

'Us?' Joanna repeated without comprehension. She looked past her father at the sofa behind him, and her eyes widened as she recognised his companion. 'My God,' she said shakily. 'Mrs Van Dyne.'

'Mrs Vernon, if you don't mind, honey.' The older woman was her usual immaculate self in ice blue silk. 'Which is a surprise for you, I can see.' She shrugged. 'But you were news to me, too, especially as I knew back in France Denys had been passing you off as some kind of niece.'

Her eyes went disparagingly over Joanna's outfit. 'Well, your millionaire seems to have got you cheap, my dear, unless you have some serious jewellery packed away in that little hold-all. After all, he should pay for his pleasures, if that's what they were, of course. You're hardly the sophisticated type, but I presume he's still going to be generous with the severance cheque.'

She paused. 'Besides, there's always the additional question of compensation. Poor Denys, suffering the trauma of being robbed of his own child and in such a way. He may be scarred for life. Plus, it's cost us an arm and a leg getting here from the States, not to mention the inconvenience.' She rolled her eyes. 'That crazy little plane from Athens to that other island, then a boat trip, of all things.'

She glanced round her, lips pursed. 'But at least, having snatched you, Mr Gordanis has kept you here in this hide-away, instead of flaunting you round the world as his floozie. Maybe we can keep the whole thing under wraps and get you decently married off, after all.'

'Married?' Joanna repeated in bewilderment, her mind whirling under the torrent of words.

The elegant shoulders were shrugged. 'Well, you aren't

trained for anything, so Denys informs me. And you're short on qualifications, so you can't expect me to support you as well as him.' She sniffed. 'We daren't risk the top drawer, of course, but there are plenty of young lawyers and executives at the country club. It shouldn't be too much of a problem, especially when it's known you're my stepdaughter. Just as long as the newspapers don't get hold of what's been going on, which none of us want, I'm quite sure.'

She gave Joanna another disparaging look. 'A few trips to the beauty parlour and some better clothes will help, of course. We certainly don't wish to advertise that you're second-hand goods.'

She nodded briskly. 'So, when your father and Mr Gordanis have had their little chat about money, we can be getting back to civilisation, thank the Lord. And I want to make it quite clear that this—incident—is now permanently over, and we don't refer to it again. As far as the world's concerned, honey, you've been vacationing with friends.'

Joanna looked at the dark, unmoving figure by the window. The profile hewn out of stone. The rigid curl of his fists.

'Yes,' Denys joined in, his tone blustering, yet uneasy at the same time. 'My wife is quite right. You're going to pay for what you've done to my innocent girl. So don't think you can simply hand her back and get away with it.'

'No.' Vassos' voice was quiet and husky, with a note in it Joanna had never heard before. 'I have never thought that. And believe me, Kyrios Vernon, I will pay. Pay whatever you ask, and far more besides.'

Now he knows everything—and he suffers...

Hara's words were suddenly beating in Joanna's brain. And, as if a new sun had arisen above the eastern horizon, illumining her entire world, she realised what she had to do.

Lifting her chin, she said, coolly and clearly, 'I'm sorry to spoil all these careful arrangements, but I'm afraid it's not quite as simple as that. Because I have no intention of leaving. You see, I realised this morning that I'm going to have Mr Gordanis' baby, and that changes everything.'

There was a moment of stunned silence. Joanna was aware of Vassos swinging round from the window, his dark face incredulous.

'Are you crazy?' her stepmother demanded derisively. 'My God, I'll bet he has the known world littered with his bastards. One more won't make any difference, you little fool. He'll still dump you.'

She allowed her voice to become more coaxing. 'Look, honey, you can't be that far on. Nothing that a good gynaecologist can't sort out for you. Cut your losses and come away before the press finds out and goes to town on you. Look what poor Maria Callas went through.'

'Wait.' Vassos' voice cut across any further arguments she was about to marshal. He walked across to Joanna and took both her hands in his. He said gravely, 'You told me once, Joanna *mou,* that you had no wish to bear me a child. Something I have never forgotten. If you have now changed your mind, tell me why.'

She looked up at him, her heart twisting at the searching, agonised tenderness in his eyes. She said softly, 'I think you already know.'

'Yet I need to hear you say it.' His voice deepened. Became urgent. 'Or shall I speak first? Tell you what is in my heart too? *S'agapo, matia mou.* I love you.'

He lifted her hands almost reverently to his lips, kissing the soft palms. '*M'agapas,* Joanna? Can you love me, in spite of all the wrong I have done you? And will you stay with me and become my wife, and let us make each other happy for the rest of our lives?'

Her lips trembled into a smile. '*S'agapo,* Vassos *mou.* I love you so very much. And I'd marry you today if it was possible.'

For the first time in weeks his face relaxed into something approaching the familiar grin. 'I think it will take a little longer than that, *agapi mou*. But I also have no wish to wait. Nor any intention of doing so,' he added softly, his lips brushing her ear, making her whole body thrill to his touch, and its promise.

'Just hold it right there.' Nora Vernon was on her feet. 'I've heard of this before—girls falling in love with their kidnappers. So what's your thinking, Mr Greek Almighty? That it will be cheaper to fool her into believing you want her rather than paying us to take her off your hands? Well, forget it. A few sessions with a good therapist will stop that nonsense, and you can pay for those, too.'

She turned on her husband. 'Don't just stand there, Denys. She's your daughter! She's not thinking straight. You've got to do something.'

'Yes, Kyrios Vernon,' Vassos said harshly. 'Do something, indeed. For the first time in your life behave like a father and give my Joanna your blessing and your consent to our marriage. Because whatever you or this—woman of yours may say or do, I shall take your daughter as my wife to cherish always.

'And why did I have to send for you?' he added contemptuously. 'Why did you not seek me out long ago and force me to give her up, at gunpoint if necessary, after what I had done? I traced you without difficulty. Why could you not find me? What excuse do you have?'

He drew a deep unsteady breath. 'Because I, too, have a daughter, *kyrie,* and I know now that if a man ever took her from me in such a way, I would find him and kill him. It has made me realise exactly the wrong I have done. Therefore I decided I must let Joanna go from me, even though I would be tearing the heart out of my body, because it might be my only hope of putting things right between us. But you—you never lifted a finger to rescue her,' he went on, eyes blazing remorselessly at the man who stood, head bent, in front of him. 'You left her to endure whatever treatment I chose to inflict on her while you saved yourself.

'I am not sure you would be here now if your wife had not believed you could make "a fast buck", as I believe the saying is. Cash in on your child's supposed disgrace at my hands.' He shook his head. 'Even so, I told myself if I restored her to you it would be a step towards forgiveness, and a new beginning for us both, even if I did not deserve such happiness.'

He drew Joanna close, his arm strong around her slender waist, his voice quiet and sure. 'Because—unlike you—I would have come to the other ends of the earth to find her again, and, if God was good, to teach her to love me. To persuade her that my life was hers.'

His clasp tightened a little. 'Our need for each other did not flower slowly and gently from trust and liking, as it should have done—I wish with all my soul it had happened that way—but it is no less real. And, no matter how it began, it is ending well. She is my woman, I am her man, and nothing can change that.'

He added curtly, 'You will be notified when the arrangements for our wedding have been made, so that you may attend if you wish to do so. And, in time, you will be free to visit your grandchildren.'

'Denys?' His wife's face was cold with fury as she got to her feet. 'Are you going to stand that kind of talk from this— barbarian? Let him dictate to you?'

There was a silence, then Denys Vernon said tiredly, 'What has he said that isn't the truth? Of course I should have come to fetch her. I wanted to, Nora, as you well know. Asked for your help. But you wouldn't allow it. Not until now—when you thought there might be money to be made. He's right about that, too, heaven help us.'

He straightened sagging shoulders. 'But I shall come to the wedding, and this time give my daughter away in the true and proper sense. That is if she can forgive me for the part I've played in all this.' He added heavily, 'You, Nora, will please yourself, as you always do.'

As she parted her lips to speak, her skin mottled with anger, he raised a silencing hand. 'And before you tell me again that you took me from the gutter, I know it. I only wish I could feel more grateful.' He took her arm. 'Now, let's leave while there's still a way back for us.'

Joanna detached herself gently from Vassos' embrace and went to him.

'Daddy.' She put a hand on his sleeve. 'There'll always be a way back. I discovered that a little while ago in this room, just when I thought I'd lost everything.' She added more strongly, 'And the past is exactly that. It's over. So I'd love you to give me away.'

He said unsteadily, 'Bless you for that, my darling. I've been so terribly ashamed—about everything.' He paused. 'I'll be waiting to hear from you. From both of you.' He took her in his arms and held her for a long moment while his wife, stony-faced, walked to the door.

Then he followed her, as Joanna watched, tears stinging her eyes.

Vassos said gently, *'Agapi mou,'* and, gulping, she flew back to his arms. He lifted her and carried her to a sofa, set-tling her on his lap, before taking the elastic band from her hair and combing the shining strands loose with fingers that shook a little.

She said in a whisper, 'Were you really going to send me away?'

'Only so that I could come and find you, my precious one. As I should have done that day when we first looked at each other. As I almost did,' he added in a low voice. 'Until I told myself I was there for revenge, not to fall in love. Then, that night, when I realised who you were, I cursed the Fates for playing me such a trick. For making you a girl I could never have as my own. Only to find, when I took you, that I had been wrong—about you—about everything—and that somehow I must atone for what I had done. I thought—I hoped—that when we were truly lovers things might change. That I could per-suade you to enjoy being in my arms. Make you want to stay for ever. But it did not happen, and I knew I had only myself to blame. That I had hurt you, repelled you.'

'You think I didn't want you?' Joanna played with one of the buttons on his shirt. 'Oh, Vassos, I did. Almost from the beginning, even though I wouldn't admit it.' She swallowed. 'After I'd left you that first night, I couldn't sleep for thinking of you, so I decided to go back to your room.'

He turned her face up to his. 'Then why did you not do so, my sweet one?'

'Because you decided to go fishing.' Her mouth trembled into a smile. 'I watched you leave. And after that—you were so different. I didn't know how to get near you.'

'One smile, *agapi mou,* one touch of your hand would have been enough,' he said unsteadily. 'I was dying for you. Desperate to love you as you deserved. But scared to show you in case you turned away for ever.'

He paused. 'I went to Athens to think. I feared you would always regard Pellas—and this house—as a prison, and that if there was to be any hope for us it would have to begin elsewhere. Even when you gave yourself to me at last, I could not believe that you really wanted me. I thought you were simply using my need for you for your own purpose, and I was bitter. Then, when I heard the truth about Eleni, I knew I had to begin my atonement by returning you to your father. That there could be no other way.'

He gave a faint groan. 'I was trying so hard to behave well, but when they came and I heard his wife—how she spoke to you—what she was planning—I knew I could not let you go. I would beg you on my knees to stay with me.'

She kissed him softly. 'Except I didn't give you the chance.'

'No, *agapi mou.* Instead you gave me the whole world.' He paused. 'Is there really to be a baby? I ask because it has occurred to me that when you came to me at last I forgot to be careful.'

Joanna smiled into his eyes, her hand stroking his cheek

'No, darling, I'm not pregnant. Not yet. What I said just now was a promise for the future, not a statement of fact. Although I think Eleni would like to have a little brother or sister, don't you?'

'Yes, my dearest one.' Vassos drew her closer. 'But first, and more importantly, I want to have a wife.'

'But until you're married,' she whispered, 'won't you still need a pillow friend?'

'A pillow friend.' He kissed her. 'A companion.' He kissed her again.

'And a sweetheart for the whole of my life. And do you know something, *agapi mou?*' he murmured against her lips. 'By some miracle they are all called—Joanna.'